OATHS & CONQUESTS

WARHAMMER
AGE OF SIGMAR

Collections

Novels

• KHARADRON OVERLORDS •
C L Werner
BOOK ONE: Overlords of the Iron Dragon
BOOK TWO: Profit's Ruin

• WARCRY •
Various authors
An anthology of short stories

Warcry Catacombs: Blood of the Everchosen
Richard Strachan

Soul Wars
Josh Reynolds

Callis & Toll: The Silver Shard
Nick Horth

The Tainted Heart
C L Werner

Shadespire: The Mirrored City
Josh Reynolds

Beastgrave
C L Werner

Blacktalon: First Mark
Andy Clark

Hamilcar: Champion of the Gods
David Guymer

Scourge of Fate
Robbie MacNiven

The Red Feast
Gav Thorpe

Gloomspite
Andy Clark

Ghoulslayer
Darius Hinks

Neferata: The Dominion of Bones
David Annandale

The Court of the Blind King
David Guymer

Realm-Lords
Dale Lucas

Novellas

City of Secrets
Nick Horth

Audio Dramas

• REALMSLAYER: A GOTREK GURNISSON SERIES •
David Guymer
BOXED SET ONE: Realmslayer
BOXED SET TWO: Blood of the Old World

The Beasts of Cartha
David Guymer

Fist of Mork, Fist of Gork
David Guymer

Great Red
David Guymer

Only the Faithful
David Guymer

The Prisoner of the Black Sun
Josh Reynolds

Sands of Blood
Josh Reynolds

The Lords of Helstone
Josh Reynolds

The Bridge of Seven Sorrows
Josh Reynolds

War-Claw
Josh Reynolds

Shadespire: The Darkness in the Glass
Various authors

The Imprecations of Daemons
Nick Kyme

The Palace of Memory and Other Stories
Various authors

Also available

Realmslayer: The Script Book
David Guymer

WARHAMMER
AGE OF SIGMAR

OATHS &
CONQUESTS

WILLIAM KING • ROBERT RATH • EVAN DICKEN
JAMIE CRISALLI • MICHAEL R FLETCHER • GRAEME LYON
DAVID GUYMER • ANNA STEPHENS • MILES A DRAKE
ERIC GREGORY • MICHAEL J HOLLOWS
DALE LUCAS • RICHARD STRACHAN

BLACK LIBRARY

A BLACK LIBRARY PUBLICATION

First published in 2020.
This edition published in Great Britain in 2020 by
Black Library,
Games Workshop Ltd.,
Willow Road,
Nottingham,
NG7 2WS, UK.

10 9 8 7 6 5 4 3 2 1

Produced by Games Workshop in Nottingham.
Cover illustration by Alexander Mokhov.

See Black Library on the internet at

blacklibrary.com

Find out more about Games Workshop
and the worlds of Warhammer at

games-workshop.com

Printed and bound by CPI Group (UK) Ltd, Croydon, CR0 4YY

From the maelstrom of a sundered world, the
Eight Realms were born. The formless and the divine
exploded into life.

Strange, new worlds appeared in the firmament, each one
gilded with spirits, gods and men. Noblest of the gods was
Sigmar. For years beyond reckoning he illuminated the realms,
wreathed in light and majesty as he carved out his reign. His
strength was the power of thunder. His wisdom was infinite.
Mortal and immortal alike kneeled before his lofty throne.
Great empires rose and, for a while, treachery was banished.
Sigmar claimed the land and sky as his own and ruled over a
glorious age of myth.

But cruelty is tenacious. As had been foreseen, the great
alliance of gods and men tore itself apart. Myth and legend
crumbled into Chaos. Darkness flooded the realms. Torture,
slavery and fear replaced the glory that came before. Sigmar
turned his back on the mortal kingdoms, disgusted by their
fate. He fixed his gaze instead on the remains of the world he
had lost long ago, brooding over its charred core, searching
endlessly for a sign of hope. And then, in the dark heat of
his rage, he caught a glimpse of something magnificent. He
pictured a weapon born of the heavens. A beacon powerful
enough to pierce the endless night. An army hewn from
everything he had lost.

Sigmar set his artisans to work and for long ages they toiled,
striving to harness the power of the stars. As Sigmar's great
work neared completion, he turned back to the realms and saw
that the dominion of Chaos was almost complete. The hour
for vengeance had come. Finally, with lightning blazing across
his brow, he stepped forth to unleash his creations.

The Age of Sigmar had begun.

CONTENTS

THE FIST OF
AN ANGRY GOD

William King

All around, the buildings pulsed. Tall crystal towers flickered from pink to orange to lime, then for an eye-deceiving moment looked like ordinary stone before beginning their kaleidoscopic shimmering once more. Their ever-changing radiance transformed the underbelly of the red storm clouds of Aqshy into something far more sinister.

Balthus had a moment to notice this after he dispatched the blue horror with his blade. The thing burst asunder in a shower of magical sparks, the last of its foul kind to fall in this skirmish. A sense of relief filled him. No matter how many times he faced these creatures of Chaos, he always feared the things might go on splitting and replicating forever.

He wondered whether the city's unnatural light served any purpose other than to confuse the eye and make the mind wander, then realised that as far as the worshippers of Tzeentch were concerned that was probably enough.

Thunder boomed. Lightning slashed the sky then struck the

nearest tower. At the point of impact, the shimmering lights went out, their colours frozen at the instant when Sigmar's wrath descended. On the rooftops and battlements, the lightning coalesced into the massive armoured forms of Balthus' fellow Stormcast Eternals. A Judicator unit seemed born of the storm, crackling missiles pouring from their shockbolt bows, raking the oncoming wave of acolytes from above and to the flank, smiting them with the chained lightning of Sigmar.

The Chaos worshippers fell, only to be replaced by tzaangors – horned and beaked beastmen who howled and shrieked as they advanced, brandishing their massive blades in challenge. Still, fewer of them were sallying forth to face the wrath of the Stormcasts. Was it possible that their reserves were finally running out?

Balthus gestured for his men to follow, sweeping his sword downwards and pointing with its lightning-lit tip to where the strongest enemy loomed. Just for a moment, he felt a sense of deja vu. He had made the gesture a score of times since his reforging, but it always felt like the thousandth time, as if he were repeating something from a previous life.

He raced forward, broken shards of crystal turning to powder beneath his armoured feet, releasing the smell of incense, lovely at first but with a sickly aftertaint – a smell he had come to associate with the cultists of the Changer of Ways and their sorcerous rituals.

'Onwards, brothers! We're almost there. Just one last push!'

The Liberators responded to their Prime's shout, their war cries torn from their throats: 'For Sigmar! For the storm eternal!' They raced towards the daemonic horde, determined to take revenge for the enslavement of their realms and the killing of their kin.

It would be soon now. This was the last of the nine great fortresses of Azumbard. Over the past eight months, the others had fallen one by one to the fury of Sigmar's faithful, their sorcerous defences cracked, their fanatical occupants slain, and their souls sent tumbling to eternal damnation. Now the last citadel loomed. It had held out longest, its approaches trapped, its walls seemingly insuperable, protected by the mighty magics bound into every stone.

There had been times when Balthus had almost despaired. Almost. They had fought for every stride of their advance. Slowly, pace by pace, they had taken the surrounding territory. It seemed at last that victory was within their grasp. This area would be cleansed, purified and freed from the taint of Chaos.

He lengthened his stride, determined not to let any warrior of his chamber plunge into the melee before him. He leapt a low crystal wall and aimed a blow at the twisted, bird-beaked features of a tzaangor, his blade arcing down, splitting its skull and splattering brain stuff in the faces of the surrounding cultists.

He stormed through the ranks of the Arcanites, killing a score, their weapons bouncing off his armour, each blade making the heavy sigmarite ring.

He fought his way into an open square, flanked by defensive towers. Once again, he was struck by the resemblance of the place to somewhere he had once known. There was a sense of having been here before, but he could not say why.

Perhaps it was the resonance of the incomprehensible sorcery of the Tzeentchians. They often worked strange spells, the purpose of which no sane mind could understand. Over the long months of fighting, there had been moments when Balthus had *seen* the shouts of his foes and *felt* the sounds of their battle cries in his bones. Of course, Sigmar protected him, and such lapses were soon overcome. Perhaps this was just another effect like those.

His Liberators smashed their way to Balthus' side, moving into tight formation around him.

'We have them on the run now, Liberator-Prime!' Tulius' bellow carried across the din of battle. Balthus heard the confidence in his voice and the sense of inevitable victory. Today, they would win! Today this accursed place would finally fall!

Balthus pushed the thought to one side. Victory was never certain until the last foe had fallen or fled the field. Nothing could be taken for granted, particularly not here and now. The warlord who held the tower had proven the most cunning of foes, the most tenacious of defenders. Too often in the past month, they had lost comrades when victory seemed assured. Traps had sprung. Ambushes had enveloped them. Destructive spells had torn defeat from the jaws of victory.

'Perhaps they have finally run out of reinforcements,' Pindar said, descending from above on golden wings to join his friends in the eye of this storm of sigmarite. The Prosecutor sounded cool and calm, as if he had spent the past hour soaring above quiet farmlands instead of the killing grounds outside a citadel of humanity's greatest foes. The stormcall javelin in his hand showed his readiness for combat.

'I would not count on that,' Balthus said. 'They always seem to be able to summon more.'

'No sorcerer possesses inexhaustible reserves of energy, no citadel holds an infinite number of guardians,' said Tulius.

'It feels like this one does,' said Balthus, wondering at the despondency he felt. Perhaps there was sorcery in the air, subtle and demoralising. He should not feel this way when the light of victory glowed in his comrades' faces.

'Look, the Towerbreaker comes. Its day has finally arrived,' Tulius proclaimed. Balthus glanced back and saw the great battering ram carried forward by a hundred Stormcasts. Lightning glittered around its tip. 'Let's clear the way. No Hallowed Knight is going to beat the Knights Excelsior through the Final Gate of Azumbard!'

They charged forward before the arcane siege engine, hewing through the last of the beastmen and clearing a red road of ruin to the pulsing gate of the citadel. A one-eyed symbol of Tzeentch blazed like the sun on its crystal frame. The heavy, regular tread of the ram bearers announced their arrival. Balthus looked up, fearing hot oil or crystal lava or noxious spells, but he saw only a scant few defenders, lobbing missiles desperately.

'Heave,' shouted Sacristan Engineer Sextus, positioned at the head of the ram. The Towerbreaker swung forward and hit the gate. The lightning stroke of impact blinded Balthus. When his vision cleared, he saw that the gate still stood. The air stank of ozone and incense.

'Heave,' shouted Sextus. Once more the Towerbreaker crashed into the portal. The lightning was so bright this time that Balthus feared more than temporary blindness. It took longer for his sight to return, but when it did he saw that the gate had buckled, the crystal had fractured, lines of fire spreading through a web of cracks.

'Heave, brothers!' The thunder was so loud it was deafening, the lightning so intense it felt like the end of the world. The earth trembled and the towers shook. There was a shattering sound, and the echo of a thousand tinkling bells. When Balthus opened his eyes, the gateway was gone as if it had never been.

'I told you it would be so,' said Tulius.

Pindar was already soaring forward into the tunnel. Balthus raced after him, eyes scanning left and right, looking for murder holes, or trap runes, or arches through which their foes might pour. They encountered no resistance and emerged into a vast courtyard, and an eerie silence.

Ahead, another archway pierced a great gatehouse, but this one had no door. It yawned before them like the gateway to Death's realm. Balthus liked the feel of this less and less.

He strode forward and the warriors of his chamber surged around him, racing towards the gaping entrance. Behind, he heard the feet of the Towerbreaker's bearers as they advanced in unison, even though there seemed no gateway ahead for them to shatter.

He wanted to shout at his companions to wait. The hairs on the back of his neck prickled, but they all seemed caught up in the exaltation of victory, of achieving their long-awaited goal of invading the final citadel. They rushed forward headlong, seeking foes to slay.

Were they right to? Had the cultist attack been merely a last, suicidal sally – an attempt to drag their foes down to death with them? Balthus thought it unlikely. Their foes had shown nothing but cool cunning and determination previously. He could not believe that they had transformed into mindless berserkers in their final hours.

Why not? part of his brain whispered. *Tzeentch is the master of change.* He wondered whether that thought was his, or if it had entered his brain wafted by the perfumed breeze and the sparkling air.

Perfumed breeze? Sparkling air? His troops glanced around bewildered. Were they also victims of subtle sorcery? He clutched the amulet on his chest and the confusion receded from his mind, as the cool, clean power of Sigmar flowed into him.

Behind him he heard the tinkling of bells, and something else, something that sounded like a portcullis dropping. He saw that the doorway, so recently shattered by the Towerbreaker, had reformed. The way out was blocked. Thin horns sounded. Colours swirled, forming mandalas in the air from which capering daemons spewed. From the towers around the courtyard, hordes of acolytes emerged.

'Form up on me,' Balthus shouted, rallying his men into a shield wall against which the Chaos horde would break. He knew that it would not be enough. There were too many foes and they were cut off from their own allies. For every cultist who fell, another charged forward. When a Stormcast died, they discorporated in a flash of lightning, returning to Sigmar and the storm.

Balthus fought on till he stood atop a pile of cultist corpses. In the distance, he heard a woman's voice cry, 'Do not kill them all. I want one alive, for my experiments.'

Something slammed into his head. Sparks flickered across Balthus' field of vision. He twisted to strike at his attacker and another blow crashed into the back of his skull. He tumbled forward into darkness.

Consciousness returned slowly. As always, fragments of dark dreams drifted up with it. He fought against a pack of daemons inside an oddly familiar palace. A shrine was defiled by the hordes of Chaos. Friends and family fell, and finally he died in a blaze of lightning. The nightmare was always the same, and he knew it was significant. He shook it off and tried to rise.

Something restrained him. Looking down he saw he was shackled by chains that bore the sign of Tzeentch. They glowed with magical energy. The bars of the cage that surrounded him did the same. Overhead, trapped lightning crackled in a gigantic crystal sphere. On all sides mirrors echoed his motion endlessly. A look of horror flashed across his thousand faces for a moment, to be replaced by a mask of stoic calm.

Rage rose within him, banishing the last fragment of nightmare. He remembered the trap and the strange sorcery that sprang it. He remembered his fallen comrades, returned to the storm, borne by the lightning. He threw himself forward, tugging against the chains with all his superhuman strength. They grew tight, resisted, and he tugged harder.

'By all means strain against the shackles,' said the female voice he had heard before. Its tone was cool and amused. 'Show me how strong you really are.'

Balthus glared around, seeking the source of the mockery. He found it below him. She looked little more than a teenager. A mass of black curls covered her head, the hair so lush and thick that it almost concealed the tips of the small horns that peeked through. Her diaphanous gown barely concealed her slim figure. A silk slipper covered one foot. Her other leg ended in a hoof that was shod in silver and marked with runes.

She was inspecting a device of brass and gold, marked by massive gauges. As he threw himself forward, needles moved across their faces, and when he ceased to strain, they dropped back to their resting position. The woman looked at them, marked something on a wax tablet and gave her attention back to him.

She laughed as if delighted. 'Far stronger than a mortal man, less strong than some daemons.'

'Go back to the hells that spawned you,' Balthus cursed, his rage turning his voice to a growl. She smiled up at him winningly. He saw that her canine teeth were long and sharp. Her cheekbones were high, and her violet eyes very large.

'I am not what you think I am,' she said. 'And I suspect you are not what you think you are either.'

Her words did not make much sense. Perhaps she was trying to confuse him. Yet so far she had not attacked him, and she had made no effort to ensorcel him that he could detect.

Be careful, he told himself, *just because you cannot see it, does not mean it is not happening.* This was the lair of the spawn of Tzeentch. It would be filled with cunning traps, not all of them physical.

'I am Aesha,' she said, and paused as if she expected him to recognise the name. He did not give her the satisfaction. 'And you are Balthus.'

She smiled when she saw his frown. Clearly, she understood the thoughts passing through his mind. 'Your companions shouted your name in battle.'

'How do you know that?'

'I would not be much of a sorceress if I could not watch my troops in the field. Not much of a commander either.'

'A sorceress?' Balthus glanced at the amulets and sigils spangling the chains on her neck. 'In the service of the Lord of Lies by the looks of you.'

'That too,' she agreed. She studied the machinery again as he strained against the chains.

'Keep it up,' she said. 'I would like to test your endurance over the long term as well.'

There was a thundercrack, and the lights guttered and died for a moment. The sorceress looked up and said, 'The lightning eats away at my wards. Soon, they will collapse.'

She did not sound too troubled by the prospect. She seemed rather to be amused by it.

Balthus said, 'You might have captured me but Sigmar will prevail. Your tower will fall.'

'Most likely. In the meantime, you will continue to help me with my experiments.'

'I will never help you,' he replied, although he felt certain he knew what her response was going to be before she even spoke.

'You already have.' She uttered a word of power and a glowing disc flickered into being beneath her. Slowly it raised her into the air, until she was level with him. She was a small woman, even by the standards of mortal men. Compared to his massive altered form, she looked tiny. Despite that, she did not seem intimidated. 'It's quite fascinating really.'

She gestured around her, and he saw his reflection spring into being in many sorcerous mirrors. They did not all show his heavily armoured body. One showed his skeleton with its reinforced bones so different from a normal man's. Another showed his form as it would be stripped of skin, just muscle and vein and sinew. A third showed an outline that seemed to be made of light, and he knew without having to be told that this was his soul, and the flows of energy within revealed the magic bound in his body.

'So like a normal man and yet so unlike. So much alteration to tissue. So much magic compressed so effortlessly into one form. Spells of amazing complexity and power. Nothing less than I would expect from a god.'

She sounded sincerely impressed as well as curious. He studied her again. Her face was guileless and fair, and in that moment he felt certain he was being deceived. The wiles of the followers of Tzeentch were famous, and this one ranked high among the Changer of Ways' servants. He knew he must be wary, and that he must escape soon lest he be ensnared.

She looked directly into his eyes. 'It has taken me a long time to begin to understand what was done to you and your brethren. There is something beautiful about it. Something awful too.'

'It will take more than a few parlour tricks done with mirrors to impress me.'

She shrugged. 'These mirrors took years of work and countless souls. Many had to make sacrifices to complete them. They are works of art in their way. They will reveal all there is to know about your physical form, your spirit and the magic that was used to create you. Or perhaps I should say recreate you.'

'What would you know of such things? Of the work of a true god?'

'More than you might think. I have studied your Sigmar and all his works for an age. I have interrogated daemons and the spirits of the dead. I have learned all I can from the lore that survived the wreck of the World Before Time. Centuries turned to millennia while I did my research, and you, my friend, you represent another piece of the puzzle I have been trying to solve.'

'What do you mean?'

'How do you become a god?'

'What?'

'You heard me.'

'How would I know?'

'Your Sigmar started off as a mortal. Many of the gods did – Tyrion, Teclis, Alarielle, even Nagash. In the World Before Time, they were mere mortals. Somehow, they were transformed, or they transformed themselves.'

Understanding struck him. 'You seek the key to how they did it – so that you might become one yourself.'

'Yes.'

'You are insane.'

'I am ancient, and I am a sorcerer. These things give you a different perspective on what most call sanity.'

'And you really think that by studying his magic you can learn to do what Sigmar can?'

'He did. He must have. No mortal is born with such knowledge.'

His lips twisted into a sneer. 'Your master will object.'

'Perhaps. If he finds out. That is why we are alone in this warded place. Neither he nor my rivals can see us here.' Her smile was peculiar.

He threw himself forward against the chains once more, drawing them tight. As he brought his strength to bear, they pulled back against him. She watched, fascinated, the glowing disc carrying her in a circle around the hanging cage so she could view him from every angle. No matter where she moved, her reflection did not appear in the mirrors.

'The more you struggle, the more you are bound. It is part of the spell on your shackles. Whatever force you apply they absorb. They feed on it.'

Something told him that in this at least she spoke the truth. The chains did grow tighter when he pulled on them. He wondered if this was some form of subtle torture, and whether if he kept pulling, they would become so tight they would lop off his hands and his feet, and turn his limbs to bloody stumps. Even the sigmarite of his armour was starting to groan under the pressure.

It came to him that there was a way out of this trap. One that she seemed not to have realised. It would mean his death, but it would not matter. His spirit would be freed on the passing of this body, and he would be reforged to fight another day in a new one. He smiled and threw all his strength at the chains. They tightened and the sigmarite halter creaked with the force. He spoke a curse upon her.

She looked at him for a moment, saw what he was doing. Her violet eyes widened, and she raised a hand and incanted a spell. A wave of pain and power flowed through the chains, and he tumbled forward into what he hoped was oblivion.

'Now, let us see what is revealed by this one's dreams,' were the last words he heard her utter.

All around him the palace burned. The halls echoed with the screams of the dying and the shouts of triumph of the cultists who charged through the corridors, their hands stained red with noble blood.

As he raced through the Via Sacra, clutching his blade, Lightning, tighter in his fist, he came face-to-face with a massive beak-faced beastman. It capered along the corridor drunk on victory, an ancient tapestry wrapped round its shoulders like a cloak and the severed head of an old man dangling by the hair from its left hand.

The beastman raised the head high and drank the blood dripping from its severed neck. The gore formed a red froth around its mouth. The creature of Chaos saw him and tossed the head at him, sending it tumbling through the air, crimson drops splattering the walls. It bounced off his breastplate and rolled away across the floor. To his horror, he recognised it as belonging to Theobald, his father's chancellor.

Interesting, said a female voice he knew he should recognise. He did not dare risk seeking its source with the monster thundering towards him. *There's something wrong here*, he thought, but he could not tell what. It was probably the horror of having the hordes of Chaos swarm over the city walls and pass through the gates the traitors had thrown open. Now they were here in the palace, and the trail of dead bodies led him to believe that treachery had opened his father's stronghold to them as well.

He raised his sword on high. It shimmered with the chained lightning from which it took its name. He smote the beastman with it. Electricity crackled as he struck the monster. Its muscles spasmed and dung sprayed as the thunderbolt ripped through its body. It was dead before it hit the floor.

'Theobald, you are avenged,' he shouted, not caring who heard or what it might summon. The time for stealth was over. The city had fallen, his home burned, and the forces of evil strode victorious through the rubble.

Somewhere in the distance, he heard a voice shouting, 'For Asqualon and King Aldred!'

A response came, 'For Sigmar! Fall back and regroup in the Temple of the Storm!'

He recognised the voice of his father. He would have known it anywhere.

Aldred! There's a name I have not heard in a long age, said the female voice. *I had thought him long forgotten.*

He glanced around and saw no one. Was he going mad? Was this some spell? He had vague memories of it from some other place, where a city burned, and war raged through its streets. *This is a dream,* part of his mind whispered.

But such a powerful one, said the woman's mocking voice. *And surprising too.*

He had no time for this madness. He must get to the Temple of the Storm and guard his father. As the son and heir, it was his duty. He had sworn an oath he could not break. He charged through the palace, slaying beastmen as he went, leaving bloody footprints on the glorious tilework, racing past the corpses of friends and companions and servants.

So many dead. Even if by some miracle they threw back the cultists, life would never be the same. And he knew that today, there would be no miracles. Their foes had proven too strong and too treacherous. They had taken advantage of the civil war and the insurrection to overthrow the old order and raise the banners of their daemon gods.

He heard fighting close by. The symbols carved above the doorway let him know he was nearing the king's entrance to the temple, the private archway through which only the royal family and their most trusted retainers could pass. Beside it two soldiers lay in pools of their own blood. One sprawled on his back, his chest still rising and falling faintly. He had no time to help the dying man. Ahead, his father fought and might even now be dying. Why had he allowed Lady Dalia to distract him, this night of all nights? She had sought one last evening of love before the end. They had both known it, although neither spoke of it.

Beyond the archway a horde of savage cultists bellowed and screamed. The king stood near the altar of Sigmar, surrounded by his bodyguards. He met his father's gaze.

'Son,' the king said, and stretched out his arm imploringly. Even as he did so his eyes widened, and a glittering shard smashed into his chest, driving through the robes right into his heart. A pulse of magic flickered through the king. He writhed in torment as his skin transformed into a layer of translucent crystal through which muscle and bone could be seen.

A sorcerer, he thought, and glanced up at the gallery above. A woman stood there, the cowl of her cloak thrown back, a strange polychromatic aura glistening around her left hand. She had a narrow, high-cheekboned face, and her lustrous black curls formed a dark halo around her head. Somehow, he knew her eyes would be violet. He had seen that face before.

Yes, I was there, said the woman's voice, though her lips did not move, and the sound seemed to be inside his head. *And it appears you were too. How strange.*

There was no way to reach her and no time. Something massive was pushing its way through the cultists. Awful energies flowed around it. Huge wings rose from its back. Twin avian heads perched atop long serpentine necks that writhed horribly as their eyes sought prey.

Halgar, the captain of his father's guard, knelt before him. 'King Leoric,' he said. 'Command us.'

No, not his father's guard – his. He was the king of Asqualon now, for however many heartbeats he had left.

'Rise, man, and fight!' he shouted, and then there was time for nothing more. The daemon tore through the elite guards as if they were children with wooden swords. Its monstrous claws shredded armour like it was paper. The swirling energy surrounding it transformed its attackers into puddles of boiling protoplasm. It loomed over him, looking down with glowing eyes that held only mockery, then emitted a long screech that somehow suggested terrible laughter. He smelled its scented breath, driven towards him by the faint movements of its wings.

One of the heads glared at him. As he met the daemon's gaze a voice sounded within his head, so loud it almost drowned out all thought. *Abase yourself before me, boy! Put down that pitiful little blade and I will let you live so that in time you will come to worship me.*

'Never,' he said. 'I will die first.'

There was nothing else to do but attack. His guards were all fallen. He was surrounded by cultists. The most sacred shrine of Sigmar in all the land would be corrupted. He lashed out with his blade and it bit into the daemon's flesh. The lightning sparked and was absorbed.

The daemon reached out with one claw and grabbed him by the throat. He felt the unholy strength of the thing and knew it had only to close its fist and its dagger-long talons would end his life. He stabbed at it again and the blade pierced its flesh. The daemon flinched but ignored his stroke. The booming voice filled his mind.

You will be a fitting sacrifice when I consecrate this altar to myself. I will tear out your heart, devour it and spit the pulp on Sigmar's most holy shrine. Your god's time is over, boy. The Age of Chaos is here.

The daemon dragged him, blood dripping from his neck, towards the altar of Sigmar. The cultists howled their adoration and chanted its praises. He saw one face, watching him from the balcony. A mocking smile hovered on her lips, her violet eyes expressed satisfaction and anticipation.

Yes. That is how it was.

Somehow, despite the pain, he managed to maintain his grip on his sword. He knew he was going to die, but he was going to do so with defiance on his lips and his blade in his hand. 'Sigmar!' he shouted. 'Give me strength and give me vengeance!'

Something answered. Overhead, thunder boomed. A lightning bolt smashed down, crashing through the temple roof and striking the point of his upraised blade. The weapon seethed with colossal godlike energies, far too much for any mortal frame to wield. He knew he had only a moment to do what needed to be done.

Both daemon heads turned to look at him, the thing's posture expressing something like surprise. *What... is this?* The thought echoed through his mind like thunder rolling through a cavern.

He drove the lightning-engorged blade right through the daemon's armour, pinning it to the altar. The daemon screamed and discorporated, leaving only its hell-metal shell.

It was the last thing he saw before oblivion took him.

Balthus' eyes opened. He was still in the cage. Still bound by chains. The sorceress sat cross-legged on her floating disc, a grimoire open on her lap before her. Her expression was strange.

'What did you do?' he asked. The confusion he always felt on waking was there, but it was mingled with rage and something else he barely understood.

'I showed you that which was hidden. I looked into your dreams.' Her tone was odd. If he had not known better, he would have said there was sadness in it, and regret and bitter knowledge. 'It's always the same, isn't it?'

He surprised himself by saying, 'Yes. I always dream of that place.'

'I meant all you Stormcasts are the same. This is always what you remember. If I killed you and you were reforged, you would lose another piece of yourself, but some part of your final moments would always remain. That battle will be the last thing you remember even if you remember nothing else. Even if another age passed.'

Balthus clamped his mouth shut, not willing to give away more to the enemy.

'There's no need to look so sullenly determined,' she said. 'I have already performed the divinations.'

'On me?'

'No. Your companions. You are not the first Stormcast Eternal to be a guest in this fortress.' She gestured at the mirror and an image appeared. He saw a different Stormcast in the armour of a Hallowed Knight, trapped in this cage and slain with a spell. He saw the body discorporate into lightning and the lightning trapped in the great crystal sphere overhead.

'Murderer,' he said.

'This is war. You would not hesitate to kill me. Why would I not do the same?'

'That's the question, isn't it,' he snarled, 'why have you not killed me?'

'Because I am learning from you, and now, I suppose, because we have something in common.'

'We have nothing in common.'

'We both remember Asqualon as it was,' she said.

'Asqualon?' he said.

'The city in your dream. I was born there. As were you, it seems. Prince Leoric was your name. I saw you ride past during your celebration parade for the victory at the Fields of Sarel. You had Lightning scabbarded at your side. The air smelled of ozone and storm winds as you passed.'

All this sounded familiar, suggested memories just out of reach. 'You lie,' he said desperately, but his curiosity was piqued.

'I can assure you, I do not. My master has far more accomplished deceivers than I. My chosen weapon is the truth. It will set us free. Eventually.'

'You expect me to believe that?'

'Believe it or not as you choose, but we both know that you were once Prince Leoric of Asqualon.'

'You could have picked that up from my dream.'

'I could and did, but that in no way alters the strangeness of the fact I already knew. I suspect my master is playing games with me once again.'

'With you?'

'Why else would the last two survivors of Asqualon meet after long millennia have passed? One can never discount coincidence, of course, but I mistrust it. The schemes of gods often bear a strange resemblance to coincidence. Fates can be woven by those who know how.'

'You expect me to believe you were there when Asqualon fell?' He forced doubt into his voice, but he remembered the figure on the balcony in his dream.

'Why not? You were, albeit in a different body.'

'I doubt you were the same either,' he said, looking at her hoof.

'One gift of the Changer of Ways. Another is a great extension of the years available to me.'

'He is the Prince of Lies.'

'Few know it better than I, but that does not change the truth of some things.'

'If you were really there, then you know the destruction he wrought.'

'I welcomed it.' Even knowing what she was, the pure malice of her smile was still shocking.

'Then you are every bit as evil as your master.'

'No doubt. But why do you think I helped summon his daemons that night?'

'Because you sought power.'

'No, because I sought justice, and he gave it to me.'

'Justice? You call murder and destruction, justice?'

She laughed at him. 'Your father killed my father and thousands like him. My father's crime was to steal to feed his starving daughters. Was that justice?'

'Your father was a criminal.'

She spat her words out contemptuously. 'My father was poor. Like tens of thousands of others in Asqualon. He dwelled in a hovel and ate dry bread when he could steal it, while your family lived in a palace and dined on luxuries. Your father fought wars that beggared the kingdom. Kill a starving peasant for stealing a loaf and you call it justice. Kill a nobleman who has stolen the lives of a thousand others, and you call it insurrection.'

Balthus looked down at the floor of the cage. 'I don't remember.'

'I do.' He heard the utter certainty in her voice, and the controlled anger.

'And so you helped the Changer of Ways overthrow all that was good.'

'It was good for you. Not for me. And there were a lot more like me than you. You believed your world was paradise. I believed your world was hell.'

'And now our roles are reversed.'

'No. Now you believe this world is hell and I do too. The difference is that I have always lived here.'

'Sigmar will change the world. Order will be restored. The Dark Gods will be overthrown. The realms will be made whole again.'

'Perhaps. For a time. And then what? Sigmar lost it all once. Even if he wins, he will lose it again. For a time, there will be peace but then the injustices will start, and the proud nobles will find reasons to scheme against their rivals and covet their lands. And the people will plot…'

'You are deluded.'

'Perhaps we both are, but it's too late for that knowledge to do either of us much good.'

'I fight for right and the vengeance of those enslaved by your masters.'

Her laughter was like the tinkling of temple bells. 'What do you think you are? A hero? A champion of all that is righteous?

You are the mailed fist of an angry god, one driven by petty spite over what he has lost. That is what he has made you. That is why you remember only what he wishes you to remember. Your reason to hate and to fight his foes.'

'You lie!'

She shook her head. 'Believe me, I know far more than you about the scheming of gods. I have had millennia to contemplate it. You think it's an accident that all you remember is the thing that motivates you to kill in Sigmar's name. If I were to slay you now, and you were to be reforged, do you think you would remember this conversation or anything else that would give you reason to doubt? No. You would be a slate wiped clean, knowing only your desire for vengeance and your hatred of the foe. You would never remember your doubts. It is beautiful in its ruthless simplicity. The greatest servants of Order have rebelled in other places and other times. It seems unlikely that you Stormcasts ever will.'

He studied her for a moment and looked at the crystal sphere overhead, and he remembered her words and his dream. 'Were you really there in the Temple of the Storm? Did you really kill my father?'

She considered this for a moment. 'Yes, I was and, yes, I did. And I saw you drive your blade into Arkatryx's chest and pin him to the altar. You drove it so deep that no one could draw it out afterwards. With it I began my study of your god and his magic.'

'You wanted its power!'

'I wanted to change the world. I thought I could make Asqualon a paradise for the people.'

It was his turn to laugh. 'You thought you could create paradise by summoning daemons.'

'I almost did once. I would have succeeded, had it not been for the treachery of my rivals. I might yet do so again. If I can learn the secrets of your god.'

The tower shook and the lights guttered. The trapped lightning in the crystal sphere above provided the only illumination. Balthus felt his chains go slack and he threw himself forward, only to feel them stiffen as the sorcerous spells came back.

'It seems your comrades are getting closer to breaking into my tower. I will have to prepare a proper reception for them,' Aesha said.

Thunder boomed again. All went dark once more. The chained lightning in the globe flared fitfully and Balthus remembered his dream. He remembered who had killed his father. 'You said the schemes of gods often bear a resemblance to coincidence – did it occur to you that this coincidence might have been engineered by my god and not yours?'

Understanding passed across her face, then he shouted, 'Sigmar! Give me strength and give me vengeance!'

The lightning in the crystal sphere leapt from its prison, smashing down on the cage. Its power would have fried anyone but a Stormcast; it gave Balthus strength. The bolt shattered the chain and sent the cage plunging to the floor, cracking the tiles as it split open. Balthus came upright, grabbed a piece of shattered stonework and threw it at Aesha with all his strength. It clipped her side and sent her reeling. The sorcerous disc flickered out and she too tumbled to the floor, landing poorly.

She picked herself up and gestured. Power gathered round her fingers and leapt towards him. He dived behind one of the strange measuring machines as the ravening bolt of energy tore up the ground where he had stood.

He grasped one of the heavy gauges protruding from the spell engine and tore it free from its mounting. Sparks fizzled around him and the scent of lilac and sorcery filled his nostrils. He lifted the gauge like a spear but saw that Aesha was already gone, hobbling towards the great arch of the doorway. He raced after her, closing the distance, wondering why she had not summoned her flying disc or stood to face him. Perhaps she was hurt worse than it had first looked. Perhaps she had gone to find help. It did not matter.

The thunder rumbled once more. The spell-powered lighting dimmed, but the flash of the levin bolts themselves provided fitful illumination. He sensed Sigmar's power flowing around him. Each of those thunderbolts represented the arrival of Sigmar's chosen. It seemed the wards around the citadel had finally broken. If he could hold out long enough, he might yet survive this.

Even as that hope flared in his heart, he heard beastmen approaching. Aesha's guards were here at last, a mass of mutated monsters swarming towards him. He wielded the brass instrument like a hammer, smashing through the flesh of the Tzeentchians. He remembered the sorceress' mocking words. Now she would see the fist of an angry god.

Charged with Sigmar's holy lightning, driven by his fury for vengeance, he ploughed through the beastmen, leaving a wake of broken and bloody bodies behind him. From ahead he heard the sorceress chanting and saw a polychromatic glow. She was once again summoning magic. Who knew what daemons would soon arrive or what new trap she might spring? He smashed his way forward, determined not to allow another of his brethren to fall because of her.

He entered a vast, high-ceilinged, cathedral-like space, breaking the bones of a massive tzaangor and plunging the brass spike of the broken gauge into its chest. It was dark save for the glow of the sorceress' spell. Behind her a massive object loomed, a huge shadow in the gloom.

He raced towards her, wondering what new devilry she planned, and saw that she was already starting to shimmer.

Her chanting continued, and the glow intensified, seemingly

drawing all the light from the chamber. He towered over her and raised his improvised weapon high.

'Vengeance!' he roared.

She smiled up at him. Sadly, he thought. 'You don't even recognise this place, do you?'

The lightning flickered and he saw. He stood within what once had been the Temple of the Storm. The plinth of the strange statue was what remained of an altar, a massive suit of misshapen armour pinned to it by an ancient rune-marked blade. He recognised the hammer sigil on the hilt.

He remembered her words about how his final blow had driven Lightning into the stone so deep it could not be pulled out. He looked up, searching for the gallery where the sorceress had stood in his dream, and saw it was there. 'This is Asqualon,' he said.

'Yes,' Aesha replied, 'Enjoy your birthright while you can remember it. I doubt you will when we meet again.'

She was already starting to fade, as whatever spell of translocation she had cast took hold. Cultists and tzaangors poured in through every doorway. He needed a better weapon than the bent gauge. He sprang onto the altar and gripped the hilt of the sword that only the royal blood of Asqualon could draw. It slid free from the stonework easily. Lightning blazed along its length, coils of power encircling the blade.

He raised it above his head, and lightning danced all around him. The power of the storm filled him. He charged to meet his enemies. 'For Sigmar and vengeance!'

In the aftermath of the battle, as the Stormcasts scoured the ruins for the enemy leader, who had eluded Sigmar's vengeance, they found Balthus surrounded by a mountain of dead beastmen. The corpses of his foes looked as if they had been scorched by lightning. His armour was dented and broken in a thousand places.

He lay like one dead, and they wondered if somehow the power of Sigmar had failed and he had not returned to the storm. Then his eyes opened and he struggled to speak.

'What is it, brother?' the Stormcasts around him asked.

Balthus raised the sword aloft and studied the way small lightning bolts danced along the length of the blade. 'I still remember Asqualon,' he said. 'And I will the next time we meet.'

They could get no more from him than that, even as they bore him aloft on their shoulders and carried him in triumph through the wreckage of the strange machinery destroyed by Sigmar's wrath.

THE GARDEN OF
MORTAL DELIGHTS

Robert Rath

Arise, all ye spirits, arise in the soul glade,
O children of the Everqueen, what dost thou see?
A foe-host has come bearing ember and axe-blade,
To poison the water and butcher the tree.

Armour of ore they have pillaged from mountains,
And pelts of thick fur torn from unwilling beasts.
They come hence with daemons, both fair and befouled,
And ecstatic moans on the lips of their priests.

Grant them bitter welcome with stone-sword and claw-root,
With borrowed earth-arms do we strike the first blow.
And soon we shall lay these gifts back in the soil,
All slick with the nourishing blood of the foe.

Hold fast, forest children, the Mirrored One cometh!
He cuts down our kinfolk, blades thick with sap-gore.

I weep at the sound of your pain-song and fear-dirge,
And reap lamentiri to sow you once more.

Hold fast, he comes!
He comes! Hold fast!
Do not break the song.

Wilde Kurdwen removed her claw from the dryad's root, unable to bear the dream-song. A season's cycle later, her last battle-chant still echoed in the souls of those she had failed.

They still sung, still striving to answer the war cry of their branchwych.

Indeed, the dryads twitched as they dreamed. Finger-branches clenched and released. Gnarled roots, planted deep in rich earth, twisted like running ankles. The flowers that bloomed from their chests, arms and legs shivered. From afar, it looked as though a flock of purple butterflies had alighted on their bodies, their petal wings opening and closing like eyelashes.

But there were no butterflies here. Nothing so delicate could live on this island.

Crouched, she could even imagine these sisters back in a Neos glade, their disquiet merely the natural, traumatic cycle of growth and regrowth. And indeed, many ripe fruits hung from these elegant spirits. Berries clustered around their throats like jewels on the neck of a high-born bride. Dark spices burst up through the cracked bark of their roots. And the feathery pollen stems inside the purple flowers would, after being pounded, dry into the finest sapphrin. They were blossoming, verdant.

Yet these dryads dreamed of battle. Of trespassers. Of blades stained amber by torchlight, of men with nets and kin cut down.

And they dreamed of axe blades chopping deep into their own flesh.

For these twitching, still-living dryads had no heads. Each one was decapitated, planted, a vehicle only for growth. New shoots emerged from the stumps of their necks – for dryads are resilient spirits – but soon the menial gardeners would come to trim them back.

They were not allowed to grow, for dryads themselves did not produce the fruit, spices or fine edible flowers. These delicacies came from the plants grafted on to their bodies – their shoots inserted into the living bark and wood-flesh with sharp knives and sealing wax – parasites that supped from the dryads' life force to make their branches heavy with culinary delights.

And no matter how much Wilde Kurdwen tried to fool herself in the quiet hours of night, there was no forest glade beyond this copse of headless spirits, only an obsidian wall that blocked the spirit-song.

High above, the branchwych saw the torches of warriors patrolling the battlements.

It was not a prison – it was a pleasure garden.

Red juice ran from the corner of his mouth, past his sharp chin and down a throat elegant as a swan's. A concubine dabbed at it with a war banner he'd pried from the hands of a dead witch aelf.

It was a petty pleasure, wiping his mouth with their sacred colours. But Revish the Epicurean lived for pleasure, petty or not, and he was old enough to know that the smallest experiences often brought the greatest joy.

He raised another tangberry and bit, rolling it in his mouth, tasting it with a tongue that split like a snake's. Days ago, he'd felt the stub of a third tip sprouting below the others, and had sacrificed six prisoners to thank Slaanesh for his newly expanded palate.

He had been force-feeding one prisoner spiced crème for weeks, and it was his liver that had preceded this delectable tart.

Revish staffed the fortress kitchen with chefs – human trophies of his conquests – and it was always good to have more than one on hand. After all, they tended to go mad fulfilling his culinary desires.

For Revish the Epicurean coveted taste above all else. In past centuries he had held other fascinations, it was true. The pounding blood-song of his body as he pursued the enemy. Carnal delights of flesh. Exotic intoxicants. Yet for centuries, he'd found no battle glee as savoury as the first bite of a buttered eel, no pleasure of the flesh greater than a gryph-hound grilled with expert precision. Nothing so intoxicating as wine from a good vin-grape, made plump by rich soil and warm sun.

So he'd put aside the shallow, adolescent pleasures of violence, sensuality and athleticism. The tongue was his altar now, and upon it he sacrificed all manner of animals, plants, sweets and men.

And it was well known that the master was not to be disturbed at his meal – which was why his warrior-consort Sybbolith waited patiently, her boot on the neck of the prostrate man.

'Speak,' said Revish, as the concubine dabbed his face with rose water.

'A menial from the pleasure gardens,' Sybbolith said. Her eyes, golden and whiteless like those of a jungle cat, stared at her lord. Her thumb slid tenderly over the hellstrider whip coiled at her belt. 'He broke the rule.'

The menial quaked, bones showing through his translucent skin. Hands filthy with dirt. It was impossible to tell whether he was twenty or sixty – like the cooks, the garden menials did not last long.

'Is this true, filth?' asked Revish.

The question was rhetorical, since as a garden menial, the man's mouth was padlocked shut. But he tried to answer nonetheless, and as he gibbered Revish saw that the muzzle was ill-sized, leaving just enough room to slip a mashed berry through.

'Is it true?' he repeated, but this time, he addressed his question to the figure who stood in the shadows of the audience chamber. 'Did he eat from the pleasure garden?'

The branchwych limped into the light, body creaking like a great oak in a windstorm. A rusting metal collar encircled her neck, its sigils glowing pink. Stone amulets rattled in her wooden antlers.

Her voice, high and melodic, filled the chamber with birdsong.

'I have witnessed this truth, my lord. But he is a good gardener–'

Revish held up a hand and stood, reluctantly leaving the upholstered embrace of his human-leather chair.

'My dear seedling,' Revish said. 'You know I do not like killing. I have as much natural inclination to kill a man as I have to cook my own meals. The fruits of violence, like the act of feasting, I am happy to enjoy. But the labour of death is not to my taste. I am no Khornate barbarian, glorying in slaughter.' Light danced on his mirrored armour as he approached the cowering menial. 'But whether to kill or spare is not my choice. Our gods have laid out their ways of justice. Is that not so, darling Sybbolith?'

'It is so,' responded the Seeker.

'And though those ways are cruel and capricious, mortals can do naught but follow them. You, who have your own goddess-queen, no doubt understand this.'

The branchwych hesitated, nodded.

From the floor, the hollow-cheeked menial stared at Revish's breastplate, entranced by the sight of his own horrid reflection. He tried to speak, and the lord hushed him, placing a long finger close to his lips.

Then he opened his arms, as if accepting the divine burden. 'My Prince Slaanesh, the god of my house, says that there can be no mercy for the disobedient. As a natural insubordinate myself, that is not to my liking, but my Prince says rule breakers must be punished. And we have one rule here.'

It happened so fast even Sybbolith flinched, a cry of ecstatic surprise escaping her shark-toothed mouth.

Revish's hands dropped beneath his cape and the axes came spinning out.

No clumsy woodsman's tools these – they were sharp sickles, like the pickaxes used for scaling ice floes in frozen lands. So sharp were they that even as the whirling blades punched into the menial, the blood did not come immediately. Instead, it seeped slow and languid as if from a razor cut.

There was no sense wasting it, after all. Blood was a valuable ingredient.

So when his precision butchery concluded and the menial ceased to wail, Revish lost no time in asking:

'Can we use this man, seedling? As fertiliser?'

The branchwych shook her head, staring at the slaughtered gardener. 'He will make the fruits bitter, the spices plain.'

'The hog trough, then,' said Revish. 'And I will go to the garden and count the cost.'

The concubine had already brought rose water, and he dipped his hands in the bowl to clear the blood. Aware that the meal and audience had concluded, attendants began to shift and move about their business.

Sybbolith slid up beside him, voice low. 'My lord, a word.'

'Not unless the words are new ones, my little horror.'

She leaned in, tiptoed so that when she whispered, her lips brushed his ear. 'My ships have been probing the Gushing Rapids. The summer rains have made them navigable. If we provision the fleet...'

'We'll speak later,' he said.

'But lord, we agreed that this summer we would return to the search. Our foothold is secure, we can...'

'Can't you see I'm dealing with something, Syb?' He pushed past her. 'Whichever watchman spotted the menial eating my berries, give him a day in the harem.'

He drew up alongside the wych and offered his arm. She ignored it, and he guessed that she did not understand the human gesture.

Indeed, she was so much more than human. Even the issue of her name was aloof and exotic – she insisted that her people did not use forms of individual address, and after a year he still simply called her 'seedling' or 'wych'.

She had fascinated him ever since he had sighted her during a raid on Neos. He could still hear her keening a war song, and picture the grass of the scorched battlefield sprouting anew beneath her bare feet.

And it was then that he knew he must possess her.

In movement and aspect she reminded him of a daemonette – she had the same otherworldly motion, a vaguely human form animated by a non-human spirit – but she exuded a vitality the handmaids of Slaanesh lacked. Daemonettes were hungry. They took you to great heights but left you lessened. This exquisite creature, on the other hand, projected youth and vitality.

Revish had lost control. Cut his way to her, axes gouging deep into the dryads separating them. He still remembered how the blood-sap made his axe hafts sticky and his tabard stiff. How the strange-toothed wyrm living in her shoulder had lunged for him and blunted its teeth on his greave before he knocked it to the ground and pulped it with a stomp. How he'd tackled her, the strange rough bark feeling so odd under his hands as he pinned her down.

He had also taken twenty of her dryads. It had been easy enough corralling them once Sybbolith had torn their branchwraith's head from its body. His warriors had brought nets for the purpose.

He wanted them for his garden. To let him explore all the culinary pleasures of this Realm of Life.

He escorted the wych in silence through the tower's entrance hall, past tapestries that, if one looked at them too long, brought hallucinogenic glimpses of other realms. Her injured leg creaked. Ecstatic moans drifted up the corridor.

'Sounds of the harem,' chuckled Revish. 'My man gets his reward. Everyone will want to catch a thieving menial now.'

'Dost thou visit the harem?' she asked.

'Regularly, yes. It is my harem. And it is expected.'

'Then thou hast many progeny.' She nodded approval. 'Life blesses.'

'I have no children.'

She stopped, turned. As her head cocked, stone trinkets clattered in her branch-horns. 'I am sorry, but I understood that the purpose of a harem was...'

'It is.'

'Then art thou sterile?'

'No,' he said quickly, then laughed. 'The point of the act is not to produce children. It is to become lost in waves of rapture. To briefly feel the euphoric ravishment of our lord Slaanesh.'

'It seems a lot of work for little result,' said the branchwych.

'Children would... distract from the pursuit of pleasure.'

'Aye,' she agreed. 'As they should. Pleasure is not the point of life, my lord. The point of life is to create more life. A being without progeny hath no legacy.'

'Perhaps that is why we do not have children,' replied Revish, climbing the stairs of the north tower. 'To keep us rooted in the now. We are in pursuit of the infinite present. An unending ecstasy beyond time and the Mortal Realms.'

'I see,' said the wych. 'Thou hast strange beliefs, Revish... and thou dost fight hard for a man without a future.'

He laughed as they stepped out on the parapet, following the fortress wall to the pleasure garden. He could see the wych breathe deeper as they stepped outside into the wind. The orchids that spilled down her wood-scalp raised, turning their faces towards the sun. Her amber eyes, dark and flat inside the fortress, lit like lanterns. He knew that here, above the walls, she could hear the songs of nature.

It thrilled him. Seeing its power work upon her. He had never met a thing, even daemons in the Realm of Chaos, that were so *of* a place.

Ghyran and the wych, the wych and Ghyran – indivisible and inseparable.

Below them, docks radiated off the island's shore, jetties pushing into the glass-green sea in a circular pattern, like the spokes of a broken wagon wheel. An enormous star of Chaos, cluttered with the sleek, black hulls of warships.

'Raiding season,' said Revish.

'Berry season,' said the wych, and took his hand. It was warm, like a polished stone in the sun. 'Let's see what we have grown.'

He let her pull him towards the garden.

'I wish I'd stripped the flesh from his bones,' growled Revish. 'Given him to Sybbolith, told her to take her time about it.'

'I was away,' said the branchwych. Even her inhuman sing-song held a tone of apology. 'I cannot be here when they prune the dryads. Even wearing this.' She gingerly touched the iron collar with its sigils. 'It cannot block the loudest screams of the spirit-song. Not this close.'

A bloodcurrant shrub speared its way out of a dryad's chest. Berries hung in bunches, crimson-black amid the whorls of serrated leaves.

'How many did he eat?'

'Twice the seasons,' she replied, then recalculated. 'Eight, as thou and thine say. Seven more in his pockets. They were served at dinner.'

He nodded. 'This was a terrible violation.'

'Indeed, the garden must always have balance. Clumsy harvesting, overeating, these things destroy the cycle. The garden can sustain one man eating from it, but no more.'

Revish looked at his beautiful cultivation. Twenty dryads, their humanoid forms thrust into the earth and sprouting every kind of summer fruit. Tangberries hung like dewdrops from one, while another's arm-branches had grown long and flowered pink – crimson stonefruit now nested in the leaves. Three others, planted hand-and-foot and woven together, formed a trellis that hung heavy with vin-grapes.

'When will they be ready?'

'Another month more,' said the wych. 'Two, if thou wishest the wine extra sweet.'

He nodded. In this long year, he had learned patience. That the pleasure of *now* was often worth sacrificing for greater delight later. He had forced the wych to plant the dryads in berry season, last year. He'd been pigheaded and eaten the fruit too early.

That had angered her. Indeed, she'd even tried to poison him. A silly thing to do. He went through food tasters almost as fast as chefs, and each morning, he had his chamber pot examined before it was dumped over the fortress wall. He'd given her the limp for that – broken the leg, let it regrow crooked through an iron corkscrew – but they had quickly come to an understanding.

He allowed her to keep her dryads alive, headless and immobile, laced with foreign plants, but still experiencing the yearly cycle so important to the sylvaneth. The garden was her domain, provided that she keep the peace and provide him with the greatest produce that had ever touched his three-lobed tongue.

Sweet cob in autumn, along with crisp apples the size of babies' skulls. Winter spices and pom-clusters that stained his chin purple when the snows came. Hot crisproot and coiling ferns in spring, cooked savoury alongside venison. And now, the berries he had been too impatient for last summer.

Revish removed his mirrored gauntlet and reached out, feeling a leaf between his fingers. Closed them around a womb berry big as a human eyeball, feeling the tender flesh, yielding as that of a lover.

'May I?' he asked.

The wych nodded.

It left a residue on his fingers, this berry. So tangy that he could not help licking them clean after relishing the juices that burst on his tongue. It was all he could do to keep from plucking another, and he contented himself with sucking the seeds from his teeth.

'Thank you for killing the man,' said the wych.

'You seemed hesitant.'

The wych stroked a dryad, picked a beetle off a leaf. 'My kin do not make decisions in haste,' she said, letting the insect scuttle over her fingers. It was greying, blighted. One of the tainted insects that occasionally rode in on the wind, carried from Nurgle's territory. 'But though thy speed distressed me, thy calculus was correct. All life is precious…'

She trapped the beetle between two twig-like fingers, crushing it, rolling the broken body so it shredded.

'…but pests must not be tolerated in the glade,' she continued, regarding the smear left on her bark. 'My kin and queen understand that. And so does my Lord Revish.'

'So we are starting this absurdity again,' he breathed.

'It is not an absurdity,' she pressed. 'Thy god is not like the Great Blight. Unlike Nurgle, thy god wishes to cultivate. Cultivate pleasure, true, but now my lord sees how pleasure and nature intertwine.'

'This,' he gestured around them, 'is an experiment.'

'A successful one.' She stepped close.

He caught the scent of the wild orchid from the blossoms that spilled down her shoulders.

'But the pleasure garden is not thine only experiment,' said the wych. 'This whole island is a walled garden. On the mainland, Nurgle rules. His rot permeates soil and stream. Nothing grows. But my Lord Revish knows how to be a steward.'

He stepped back, light-headed. It was clumsy, this flirtation, by the standards of a Slaaneshi court. Yet he found it so enticing. Her eagerness and youth. The wholesome exuberance. Revish had spent long years in the company of those dead, those soon to be dead, and daemons who had never truly lived.

'Your Everqueen would not agree to an alliance.'

'Perhaps not the queen, no. But we in the Harvestboon Glade are young and practical. Not so tied down with grudges. If thou wert to expand – take sword against Nurgle in Invidia, cultivate it as you have this island – Harvestboon might approve. Trade peace and the exquisites of our branches in exchange for wild places left alone. And my lord… wild fruits are sweeter than those grown within walls.'

'And if they didn't agree?'

She smiled, an expression that looked both strange and frightening on the moist bark of her lips. 'Then we two could do it alone.'

The wych turned, beckoned towards the small half-cellar that he'd dug so she could grow mushrooms during the wet season. Nothing special, a few planks over a hole in the ground. They had to stoop to get inside, and Revish was shocked to see great, heart-shaped leaves covering the earth floor.

'Dost thou know what this is, my lord?' she said, brushing back the foliage.

His breath caught. Bioluminescent glow radiated from an orb's emerald surface. It was large, the size of a great melon or a newborn child.

'A soulpod,' he breathed. It must be.

'The start of new growth,' she said. 'The first sowing that will bring life back to Invidia. Under thy hand, my lord. Thou said that thou had no children, but it is not true. This can be our progeny.'

Revish knelt and stroked the glassy surface, saw a coil of life move inside at the warmth of his touch. She laid her hand over his.

He could see his own face, reflected in the surface.

Sybbolith brushed past the Chosen guarding Revish's private chamber. She did not ask to enter and they did not try to stop her. Everyone in the fortress knew what had happened to the last man who'd done that – she still wore his skin as a stocking.

She closed the door behind her.

'I've told the fleet to prepare,' she told Revish.

'Excellent,' he said. He tied his silk robe closed and offered a plate. 'Candied lips? Freshly severed.'

'I'm glad we agree,' she said, ignoring the confections. 'If we sail in two weeks, the rivers will still be full. We could hit the Dreamloss Realmgate, or if opportunity presents, take another run at the Gates of D–'

'I have an alternative plan.' He dropped into a chair and rapped a nautical map with his knuckles. 'We sail north, to the Nothing-well Peninsula. Garrison it, prepare to cut off the southern half of Invidia and take it in the name of Slaanesh.'

Sybbolith dropped her chin, studied him with her cat eyes. 'Turn on Nurgle. Stab the Father of Plagues in the back. Why?'

'How better to honour the Prince of Pleasure than by giving him a place in this realm?'

'By finding him and freeing him from his prison,' she hissed. 'This place has twisted you up, Revish. Ever since we came here, you've been eating too much, drinking too much.'

'Pleasure is our god's blessing, my little horror.'

'Pleasure with purpose. Ecstasy that binds us to Slaanesh, and elevates us into his experience.'

'I don't feel our Prince the way I used to,' admitted Revish. 'Centuries ago I loved the flesh, but it no longer thrills me. Then, those tapestries – the sacred art – but I scarce look at them now. Violence holds no interest... but a *legacy*. Syb, if I could create something–'

She raised a hand for silence, sat down across from him. 'Revish, I have seen this before. You have served our Prince for a long while. The same things, the same sensations, do not stimulate us forever. It will come back. You will rediscover forgotten raptures. The important thing is to keep moving, to keep searching. This realm was never meant to be more than a transit to the next–'

'The branchwych has suggested an alliance. Slaanesh and sylvaneth, giving us a continent if we turn back Nurgle's desolation.'

She paused. 'The plant cannot convince the Everqueen to ally with Chaos.'

'If not, then we need no alliance. She has a soulpod,' smiled Revish. 'We can start our own glade. Reforest the Nothingwell. Raise our own race of Slaaneshi dryads. The land would garrison itself. It is a good plan.'

Sybbolith ran her tongue across the inside of her saw teeth. 'Are you my lord, or not?'

'What?'

'Lord Revish is a conqueror. A reveller. He's no farmer who reaps barley.'

'We don't grow barley–'

'Do you remember last year? We burned everything from the coast to the Jadewound. Made a play for the Gate of Dawn. Took slaves, razed cities. Soldiers screamed your name while in the grip of nightmare. Then that wych came, and you haven't left this island since. She's made herself your gaoler. Removed a Slaaneshi lord from the battlefield for an entire year. She's manipulating you.'

Revish looked at her, really looked at her, for the first time in ages. Sybbolith had changed since she'd walked the path of mutation. It was not the confidence, she had always had that; it was the divine certainty. The fact that Slaanesh had bestowed more gifts on this hellstrider than even her consort-warlord possessed.

'The wych has offered me a future,' said Revish. 'Not an endless search across realms and gateways. She's offered something of herself rather than taking.'

Silence hung between them. Sybbolith dropped a hand under the table, the hooked, retractable claws of her left hand sliding out in case it came to a fight.

'Very well,' she said. 'If you think she's so wholly devoted to you.'

'She is.'

'Then ask something of her. Something important and painful. Tell her you want to eat the soulpod.'

'What?'

'Come now, Revish. Don't claim it hasn't occurred to you. What would it feel like to eat a soul?' She preened. 'Having done it, I can tell you it was... invigorating.'

'It would be a waste.'

'If she's in your power, if she is so *enraptured* of you, she'll give it. And you won't have to take a single bite. But if she resists, you'll know that she has her own agenda. Unless, of course, you don't dare ask something of your own prisoner.'

Silence again.

'I'll give you the night, Revish. But if you don't ask her at dawn, I'm leaving. My riders and I, we move fast. And if we move, you'll never catch up.'

* * *

Revish came to the garden via the parapet, down the tower that connected the garden to the fortress' battlements. It was wider than his private entrance, with enough room for the retinue that came with him.

Sybbolith stood at his shoulder, and four Chosen at his back. The great curved horns on their helmets scraped the ceiling of the tower's spiral staircase.

The dryads rustled as they passed, the tread of armoured feet calling up unpleasant notes of nightmare in their death-dream.

'What is this?' asked the wych. 'We made a pact. No warriors in this place, it disturbs–'

'The soulpod,' said Revish, eyes red from sleeplessness. 'I want it.'

'I need the correct ground to plant it,' said the wych. Her amber eyes darted from the hellstrider to the warriors and their great axes.

'I wish to eat it.'

'Thou wish…'

'To eat. Devour. Consume. I have decided to see how it tastes.'

The wych's keen eyes darted towards Sybbolith. 'This is her doing. She's turned you against–'

'Give it to me.'

'I will not sacrifice the future for today's pleasure.'

Revish nodded and one of the Chosen raised his double-handed axe and turned to the nearest dryad.

'No, please–'

The dryad shrieked as the axe blade crashed into it. It warbled, screamed like an injured raptor with each blow. Even the Chosen, hardened to the death-wails of men, stepped back from the sheer emotion of it. Dark sap flecked the grass. Bunches of bloodcurrant burst, staining the pale interior flesh-wood imperial purple. The screams continued longer than anyone expected.

The wych was on her knees, hands on her face, wailing with

grief and sympathetic pain. She reached a hand out to the dryad, now nothing but twitching roots that whined like a dying hound.

Revish reached behind his cloak and drew his pointed razor-axe. 'The next I do myself.'

The wych brought the pod, cradling it to her chest, singing softly to it as if to calm its spirit. Then she handed it to Revish two-handed, giving the surface a last brush of her fingertips before stepping back.

Revish looked at the soulpod, seeing his reflection in it. Inside, something moved.

She had given it to him, true. But she had resisted. If he handed it back, said it was all a test, his weakness would be exposed.

'Well?' said Sybbolith.

He bit into the rubbery surface, feeling the gooey interior flood his mouth as the internal waters broke. It tasted of loam and dirt. It was bitter.

So bitter.

And then it bit him back.

Bone-hard mandibles pierced his face. Chitinous coils wrapped his throat. Whatever had emerged from the pod, it was strangling him.

A Chosen stepped forward and grasped the wriggling, segmented body and the creature snapped away from Revish, launching itself at the new attacker, burrowing itself between the warrior's pauldron and helmet, into his throat. Blood fountained high, spraying a headless dryad as he collapsed among the roots. Other Chosen dashed forward, stomping and slashing at the fat, hard body as it slithered into the dryad grove.

It was a grub. One of those damn worms the wych had launched at him when they'd fought a year ago. She'd *tricked* him.

He looked into the mirror of his vambrace. From ear to chin, his face was gory ruin. Ivory teeth showed through the ripped flesh of his cheek. One eye, plump and purple with venom, had nearly swollen shut. His three-lobed tongue probed through the ragged flesh, tasting the iron wine of his blood.

Revish snarled at his ruined beauty, gripped his axe haft and looked for the wych.

She was already gone, darting through the grove.

Leaving a trail of laughter behind her.

Kurdwen cackled as she ran. It was no longer the youthful, songbird laugh she had affected for the past year, but the mad, crow-like bark of a wych crone old as the forest.

It had been so tiring to be young, to wear the ebullient mask of spring that Revish found so alluring. That was not who she was. Kurdwen was an autumn hag through and through, with a heart full of dry leaves and chill winds.

Indeed, even as she fled her youthful trappings fell away. The orchids on her scalp browned, shedding petals so they pinwheeled to the ground in her wake. Bark hardened and roughened. The twisted wood of her leg that was trapped inside the corkscrew – the portion she had let go dry and brittle – cracked and fell away, letting the bent limb spring supple to its full length. Her lithe, ancient form thrilled at the cast-off artifice.

And she sang, a full-throated spirit-song that roused the mutilated dryads. They were not alive, or not sentient, at least. Echoes of their former selves, raw nerves responding to their environment much like the revivified skeletons of Nagash's horde. And for a year, she had been filling them with memories of their last battle – the echoes of her war song.

Now, they heard the cry again.

Dryads reached out like sea anemones, swiping at the Chaos warriors behind her. One snatched a Chosen and held him wriggling, crushed against her chest, while her neighbour punched her root claws through his breastplate over and over. Blood fell on the rich earth.

Behind her, Revish and his retinue hacked towards her, battling through the grove like men cutting a trail through jungle.

She was far ahead, nearing the entrance tower with its guards.

And as she saw their look of hesitation, she tore the lock off her nullifying collar.

Humans, even Chaos-corrupted ones, had such foolish faith in the strength of iron. After all, iron rusts. Particularly this close to the sea. Especially when a wych squeezes drops of salt water into its workings patiently, day by day, for an entire year.

The clasp came free, and she flung the circlet at one of the warriors guarding the tower steps, winging it end-over-end. He raised his shield to deflect it.

He never saw her leap at full run, never saw her coming with her whole body and whole spirit, never saw how she had broken off a tip of her own wood-antler and held it like a dagger.

Gnarled root-feet hammered the shield with the force of a club and he went over backwards. She plunged the antler through his visor slit and he choked on blood and broken teeth.

The other warrior struck at her with a mace as she crouched on the struggling man. She ducked the first blow, got in under his guard and grabbed at his throat, but he struck out with his shield boss and slammed his mace down, crushing her left arm.

She retreated.

Through the visor slit, the man's eyes betrayed fear. But this wych was unarmed and unarmoured. She'd struck at him and missed. She was wounded, sap clotting on her useless left arm. He brought up his shield and advanced on her with deadly steadiness.

But Kurdwen had not missed, and instead of a weapon, she held out something better – a bone totem, snatched from the warrior's throat.

Cold words ran through her smile. Syllables that tasted like bare branches and myrrh resin. Her wooden hand felt the amulet, but her spirit-hand felt the labyrinth of meat within him. Her fingers slithered through the warm, subterranean rivers of his organs, following the pulsing streams of blood until she caressed his greasy heart.

Then she snapped the amulet in two.

The mace dropped from nerveless fingers and she was past him, up the stairs.

She did not need to look behind her to know that Revish and his men were pursuing. Her bittergrub still lived, and through his segmented eyes she saw Revish and his Chosen surrounded, wading through a forest of scathing branches and entangling roots.

And she saw the purple streak of Sybbolith, twisting and sliding between reaching talons.

Kurdwen slammed the tower door and threw down the bar. She leapt up the spiral stairs throwing braziers and torches behind her.

Then she was in the wind, the salt kiss of free air whipping her vine braids wild. Above the walls, able to hear the songs of life, the songs of power and war these obsidian walls made dead.

And she joined the chorus.

> *Arise, all ye spirits, arise from your slumber,*
> *O children of the Everqueen, come to my call.*
> *From ditch-moat and hog-pen come make thee a war-host,*
> *To burn their black sea-steeds and crumble their wall.*

At the base of Lord Revish's private tower, the ground began to churn and sink. Keening, like the squeal of enormous predators or screeched violin notes, emanated from the sinkhole. Roots speared up, hooked the earth, and dryads pulled themselves free. Dozens of them.

They dug their talons into the curtain wall's black stonework, finger-shoots sprouting to give them purchase between the blocks, climbing upwards like a swarm of beetles fleeing a rising stream. As the wave of them approached, she could feel her reserves increasing – four seasons of magical drought, and now the spring bubbled anew.

'Welcome, sisters,' she whispered.

One looked up at her and shrieked in alarm.

Kurdwen leapt high and away like a stag, the hellstrider's six-tailed whip cracking by as it missed her by a twig's breadth. She landed in a crouch, sprang backwards and vaulted off her hands to avoid the disembowelling follow-up lash.

If she'd had her greenwood scythe, she could have defended herself – but it was hanging up in the audience hall, among Revish's trophies. And while she could spare enough glamour to stop a weak heart, combatting a mighty champion of Chaos was another matter entirely. Especially when she needed the magic for something greater.

So she fled, bolting along the parapet with all the energy of a hare. Got distance. Poured all of herself into her song.

> *The Mirrored One lives, claim revenge for thy sisters,*
> *Cut down in defence of our twice-hallowed glade.*
> *The foe-men sit idle, in unguarded chambers,*
> *So bring them the talon, and bring them the blade.*

Sybbolith followed, ducking and leaping the dryad limbs that reached for her over the battlements. She decapitated one with her clawed hand. Lashed another by the neck and tossed it into space. Grabbed a third that got too close and punched through its oaken forehead with a tongue sharp as an awl.

And when they grew too thick on the parapet, she jumped onto the sawtooth battlements themselves, leaping from promontory to promontory without slowing her gait.

Kurdwen reached the end of the parapet. She yanked at the door to Revish's private tower and found it locked.

She could turn and meet the hellstrider, or jump into the courtyard.

'Run, little wych,' howled the oncoming champion.

Kurdwen jumped, aiming for the soft manure of the hog pen, singing still.

And as she fell, the whole world rocked.

The earth below her erupted, its displacement buckling the wall's flagstones upwards. An upheaval of soil and moss rose to meet her.

She hit hard, rolled, scrambled for a handhold. Felt a sharp spear pierce her thigh-branch. Still, that was purchase enough and she held on, grabbing the great wooden antler as the rest of the earth and stones fell away.

Kurdwen had not known the seed would sprout into a treelord, but she'd done everything she could to tip the chances. She'd hidden the biggest soulpod inside the menial along with every treelord lamentiri she'd hung from her antlers like meaningless trinkets. Tricked the poor man into eating the bloodcurrants. Declined using his body as fertiliser so Revish would send it to the nutrient-rich soil of the hog pen.

Even then, she couldn't be sure it would have the desired effect. Soulpods didn't work that way. But the Queen of the Radiant Wood had smiled, and now she stood on the shoulder of a new-born champion of the forest.

And she whispered what he must do.

The treelord reared his great arms back and speared the defensive wall with his root talons, green shoots unspooling, working their way in between the stonework.

Kurdwen stroked the antler, eye to eye with the champion on the parapet. Sybbolith staggered, thrown from her footing as the growing tentacles of green shifted the wall's stability. Dryads crawled away like lizards, leaving the hellstrider alone on the rocking structure.

In those jungle-cat eyes, Kurdwen saw something that looked a great deal like fear.

'Thou wert right,' she said. 'I was trouble.'

Then the treelord ripped his arms backwards and the wall collapsed in on itself, stones clattering against each other with a sound not unlike the felling of great trees.

Dryads surged through the breach, scrambling over the obsidian blocks – but the hellstrider was gone. Crushed perhaps, her body pinned to the earth under immovable stones.

But Kurdwen was not so sure. Because for a fleeting moment, she thought she'd seen an impossible thing – a figure dancing on air amidst the falling stones. Leaping from block to block with feline precision, tumbling like an acrobat through the debris and towards the dry moat.

Towards the fleet.

Later they would search for Sybbolith among the burned wreckage of the docks, picking through the shattered hulls of ships that the treelord had hoisted clear of the water and hurled onto the rocky shore.

There was no trace, except for a host of dismembered dryads – and the stories.

Stories of coastal ravagers who pillaged and vanished. Riders whose serpentine mounts leapt from the deck of low-hulled ships and plunged ashore through the roiling surf.

Tales of a woman with golden cat eyes, sailing west towards the Gates of Dawn.

Revish the Epicurean strode into his audience chamber feeling *alive*.

He alone had cut his way out. Twenty dryads in the garden, more on the walls. Claw-marks scored his mirror-crystal armour. One axe had been lost, lodged in a dryad who'd taken it with her as she toppled off the wall and into the dry moat. He'd left behind the corpses of his Chosen – they had sacrificed themselves for their lord, as was their purpose. The wall had been breached, but walls could be repaired.

The important thing was he'd lost himself in the exuberance of it. He'd never been so close to death for so long, and in that liminal space he found a new passion – the thrill of survival against the odds. Adrenaline, battle-fear, would be his new addiction. His consort would be pleased.

Face bloodied, hands sticky with sap, he called out to the lithe, inhuman silhouette sitting in his throne.

'Syb! You were right. The battle-lust has returned. I feel…'

The figure leaned into the light, grinning. Stone trinkets rattled in wooden antlers.

'Thou wert saying? How dost thou feel?'

He stopped short. 'Deceiver.'

'Harsh judgement from a man who tried to devour our dear child,' said Kurdwen. She stroked the bittergrub that lay around her neck like a fox fur. It cooed softly. 'Not very pleasant of dear father, was it, my lovely? Trying to eat thine egg sac.'

She scratched it under the mandibles.

When Revish took a step forward, it turned its pincers towards him and hissed.

'You bewitched me,' said Revish. 'Fed me sweets to keep me docile. Promised me children.'

'And I have delivered.' She swept a thorny hand around the chamber. Polished wood whispered on stone, and the forest folk emerged from behind hallucinogenic tapestries, baroque screens and captured war banners. 'These are, in a way, our daughters.'

'Absurd.'

'All the things I taught thee, Revish, and thou still dost not understand.' She stood, pushing herself to her feet with her reclaimed scythe. 'Dost thou even know the purpose of fruit?'

His brow furrowed.

'A plant must spread its seeds. So it grows a tasty morsel to attract dumb beasts to eat them. Beasts… like birds, or wild asses, or Chaos lords.'

Revish growled, raised his axe. The dryads drew closer.

'Think of it, Revish. All those fruits that passed your table. Apples in autumn, berries in summer… all impregnated with soulpods. After all, they come in many forms. And every morning, a servant would take thy chamber pot, examine the night soil and throw it into the dry moat outside the window. An army grown under your nose.'

He sputtered.

'I'm Kurdwen, by the by. Wilde Kurdwen. We do use names, I just don't make a habit of giving mine to men that consort with daemons.'

He flung himself at her, wild, furious, screaming at the edge of exhaustion.

She turned his blow and dipped the sickle into his mouth, hooking him through his torn cheek like a landed fish. Dragged him staggering across the audience chamber and threw him into his throne. Vines tightened around his wrists and ankles. His face went white.

'Please, no, please,' he begged. 'I… I can be a partner. Keep clear of your woods. I'm a good steward.'

'A good steward,' the wych cackled. 'This *good steward* deforested this island to build his docks. This *good steward* diverted a river to build his fortress of pleasure. This *good steward* looked at us as nothing but foodstuffs.'

'I can be of use, I promise.'

'Oh yes,' she smiled. 'And I know just the role.'

It is known on maps as Hermit Island, but for as long as folk can remember, the people of the Jade Kingdoms have called it Wych Isle.

Deep forests cover it, gnarled roots extending to the rocky shore. Yet despite this abundance, it is tradition that it is unwise to cut timber there, or spend the night ashore.

Those who beach on the isle by day have seen strange sights. The broken ribs of great ships tangled in the underbrush. Black foundation stones, long dismantled by root and vine.

But the talented trail master, or unluckily lost, may find another structure. Four walls still standing, closed with a rusted iron gate set with sculpted ivy leaves. Trees choke the interior, soaring above the old walls.

At its centre, in the oldest oak of all, can be found a suit of crystalline armour halfway swallowed in the bark, as if melting into the wood. Long ago, it's said, a warrior died leaning back against the trunk, and over the long centuries the tree grew around him. Devouring and digesting him over slow ages.

And atop the armour rests a skull, sunken back into the bark.

Its jaw hangs open, they say, as if in a centuries-long scream.

SHRIEKSTONE

Evan Dicken

'Grimnir will avenge me.' The fyreslayer died laughing, wheezing through a grin gone wet and crimson as Ratgob worked his moonslicer deeper into the stunty's miserable guts.

The loonboss scowled down at the red-bearded corpse. In his reign as High Creeper of Shriekstone he'd gutted plenty of duardin – heard everything from screams to death oaths.

Never laughter, though.

With a grunt, Ratgob tugged his moonslicer free and scuttled over to watch the slaughter.

His lads were doing the Bad Moon's work. Mobs of black-robed grots surrounded the surviving fyreslayers, poking with rusty blades as the stunties bellowed in their ugly, hard-edged tongue. Ratgob had spied the nasty brutes earlier in the evening, climbing the switchback that led to Shriekstone's corroded gates. The fyre-slayers had been careful, but the mountain had eyes. Ratgob caught the fools in a double ambush, letting them slaughter a mob of malingerers while he crept from one of the many secret passages that honeycombed Shriekstone.

The thought made the loonboss smile – no one out-creeped the High Creeper.

'Spook! Spook!' The call went up, and Ratgob's glee curdled as the shaman was borne forward by staggering slaves. Festooned with bells and clacking bones, Vishuz Spookfinger perched precar-iously upon the skull of a giant cave squig, jabbering and howling. The lads parted before him, shrieking as they crawled over one another in their hurry to escape the shaman's ire.

Unarmed and bloodied, the last stunty struggled to its feet to glare up at Spookfinger.

'Stab 'im!' The shaman crooked a knobby hand at the fyreslayer. 'Saw off his filthy beard!'

One of Spookfinger's loons charged from the mob, mouth foam-ing with madcap as he raised his notched spear.

Ratgob's moonslicer took the lad's head clean off.

'You ain't the Creeper.' Ratgob stepped from the gloom. 'I say who gets shanked and who don't.'

For a moment, Ratgob thought the shaman would leap from the skull and rip him apart. The air between them hung thick as the spore fields in the lower vaults of Shriekstone.

At last, the shaman gave a mocking bow. 'You're da boss.'

Ratgob regarded him through narrowed eyes. Give a git a big skull and he starts getting big ideas. Wouldn't be long, now. When the time came, Ratgob only hoped Spookfinger tried something more original than a knife in the back.

The loonboss turned back to the surviving stunty. 'Why you creeping 'round my mountain?'

'You speak our tongue?' The fyreslayer's face twisted into a look of disgust.

Ratgob shrugged. 'How else am I gonna boss my slaves 'round?'

The stunty looked like it was about to get surly, so Ratgob set it straight with a good poke. Once the worst of the bleeding had stopped, the loonboss asked his question again.

'*Grobi* filth, we shall stomp your miserable bones to powder.' The fyreslayer gave a wracking cough, spattering his beard with dark blood. 'By Grimnir's fist, the ur-gold of Lachad shall be ours again!'

'Lachad?' Ratgob ran his tongue across his jagged teeth. 'Never 'eard of it.'

'We stand in the Magmahold's very shadow.' The stunty gestured at Shriekstone's summit. 'Foolish *skaz*, flee back to your wretched holes. Runefather Thunas-Grimnir the Unflinching has summoned the Lachad Lodge. Our Lofnir brothers stand with us. A dozen fyrds have sworn vengeance before the Oathflame.'

Ratgob scratched his ear. 'Y'wot?'

'A host the likes of which Ghur has not seen in an age!' The runes embedded in the stunty's miserable hide shone as it jabbered at the surrounding mob. 'We will come in our thousands, our tens of thousands. There will be no place to hide, no hole safe from our axes. Flee! Before the Lachad Lodge crushes–'

'Enough of dat.' Ratgob dragged his moonslicer across the stunty's throat. Grinning, the loonboss spun on his heel, arms spread wide. 'All right, lads, let's get this lot dressed for dinner.'

Although the gits set to with a will, Ratgob could not help but notice the mutters and sideways glances. It was a safe bet none of them understood the stunty's words, but all the shouting had them spooked.

To be fair, it had spooked Ratgob, too.

He glanced at the sky, empty but for a few racing clouds. Stars moved against the flat black as the beastly constellations of Ghur fought their endless, nightly battles. Still, he could feel it out there, like an itch at the base of his skull, a jabbering buzz so faint Ratgob couldn't be sure if he had imagined it.

Some bosses claimed to feel the touch of the Clammy Hand, the buzz rising to a scream as the Bad Moon spoke to them. *Surely* it would have something to say about the stunty warhost stumping towards Shriekstone.

Ratgob cocked his head. Nothing.

'Yer done for.'

'Wuzzat?' Ratgob spun, moonslicer coming up. Spookfinger had hopped down from his squig skull to creep closer while the loonboss was thinking.

'Nuffin', boss.' Spookfinger raised his hands. Face-to-face, the shaman was just a weedy git, all bony and squint-eyed. 'Just wonderin' what yer gonna do 'bout that horde of stunties?'

'Never you mind that.' Ratgob should have known the shaman spoke duardin. A glance at the mob showed the lads had almost finished stripping the dead stunties. Ratgob headed for the scuffle, wanting to get stuck in before they nicked all the best shinies and choicest chewy bits.

'Seems important s'all.' Spookfinger trailed behind. 'Our bones gettin' stomped to dust.'

'Only nutters believe stunty gab,' Ratgob snarled back. 'They *always* lie.'

'Shank me, dey must've brought every bearded nutter in Ghur.' Ratgob squinted into the scryeball and gave a low whistle. There had been other stunties – small raiding parties filled with fools bound for Shriekstone's slave pits and stewpots – but this was different.

The bristling Bruteplains beyond Shriekstone crawled with redcrested fyreslayers, formations of half-naked stunties marching in a column that seemed to stretch to the horizon. At the fore roamed packs of frenzied, jabbering brutes, their spiked hair more garish than the glittering golden runes beaten into their flesh. Worse, Lachad Lodge did not march alone. Their stunty allies had brought teams of huge, shaggy crag sloths to drag cannons and organ guns, and massive airships floated overhead like corpses bobbing in a well.

'Wuzzat, boss?' Krudgit shifted with a jingle of glass bottles, trying to peer over Ratgob's shoulder. Ratgob's chief poisoner was tall for a grot, long-limbed and knobby kneed, almost spider-like in his proportions, with a head like a bloated egg sac and small, dark eyes the colour of rotten meat.

'Nuffin.' Ratgob sat back from the scryeball, wiping off the accumulation of mould that filmed the greasy lens. Shriekstone once had dozens like it – the mountain covered with blinking eyes – but, over centuries, the High Creepers had plucked them out until only one remained.

Couldn't have the lads spying on each other, that was for bosses only.

'Stunties comin', ain't dey?'

'Nevva you mind.' Ratgob flapped a hand at the poisoner's bag. 'What you got fer me?'

'Distilled troggoth bile, viledust, ground splintermoss, and I got a new one.' Glass shattered as Krudgit dropped his sack and began to root amidst the vials. 'My own special blend of double-strengf loonmist. One sniff an' those stunties won't know you from Gorkamorka.'

'Good lad.' Ratgob moved to pat Krudgit on the shoulder, but thought better of it. 'Best get back to work, den.'

'An' the stunties, boss?'

'Just leave 'em to me.' Ratgob narrowed one eye. 'An' keep your gob shut. I need time to fink.'

'Yes, boss. Course, boss.' Krudgit gathered up his dripping sack and scuttled for the door.

Ratgob watched him go. No chance of things staying quiet, but it would take time for the news to filter through Shriekstone – time the loonboss needed to grab his dosh and run.

Filling a sack with his shiniest, most portable loot, Ratgob hurried along the mildewed galleries overlooking the great halls of Shriekstone. Once, the channels had flowed with nasty, glowing magma, but the fire had long ceased to burn, every fleck of gold scraped from the walls, every scowling stunty statue smashed to rubble. Now, the canals were home to spiders and other lovely oozing, crawling things.

Shriekstone wheezed like a stunty with lungrot, the old ventilation system choked with delightful fungal growths. Ratgob had never figured out whether the mountain was one great sedentary beast or thousands of little ones, but the rocky flesh did make quite a satisfying squeal when you cut into it.

The loonboss ran his fingers along a balustrade gone soft with moss. It seemed a shame to leave all this. A Creeper with no Shriekstone was no Creeper at all.

The mountain spread before Ratgob like an algal bloom. Gits scuttled through the gloom carrying picks, sacks and shovels; others prodded coffles of gaunt stunty slaves or led huge segmapedes loaded down with baskets of meat to toss to the squigs in the pits gouged into the floor of the central hall. As long as a troggoth was tall, the great insects trundled along on scores of legs, mandibles snapping at the occasional grot who ventured too close.

Great stone pillars supported the cavern roof, rickety scaffolds and rope bridges hanging between them like the web of a mad arachnarok. Once, the pillars had borne the faces of long-dead stunties, but, over many years, the gits had hacked the stone into more pleasing visages –Blisterblade Grothammer, Shkrug

Neverchosen, Morg Six-Knives and dozens of High Creepers Ratgob couldn't recognise. Only the cruellest, most tricksy gits ruled
long enough to see their faces completed.

Inevitably, the loonboss' gaze was drawn to his own monu-
ment – barely a shadow on stone, the beginnings of a chin and
handsomely hooked nose hacked into the scowl of some ugly
stunty king. There would be no time to finish, now.

With a snarl, Ratgob scuttled deeper. Beyond the columned halls
lay miles of tunnels, straight passages criss-crossed by hundreds of
pleasantly twisted snickelways. Fungal beds filled the old vaults.
Ratgob's lungs tingled at the heady mix of spores that hung over
the vaults, but he drew no pleasure from it. The invaders would
probably burn the groves of gourmet mushrooms and scour the
intricate lichen murals from the walls.

'Stunties got no appreciation fer art,' the loonboss muttered to
himself as he crept along the gallery that ringed The Pit, careful not to dislodge any loose rocks. In the old days it had been
where the stunties emptied their rotten guts after too much brew,
but generations of slime and accumulated filth had blocked off
the sluiceways, The Pit itself now home to a horde of slumber-
ing troggoths.

Ratgob paused, squinting into The Pit. The troggoths might
have something to say about fyreslayers smashing up the place.
Unfortunately, the trogghorde was just as likely to munch on
grots as stunties.

From the darkness below came a low rumble, a tremble in the
stone that was either a troggoth shifting in its sleep or the slow
flow of magma deep down below the mountain. An uncomfortable
reminder that, while Shriekstone had been dormant for generations, it had once roared with burning, bubbling fire.

With a shiver, Ratgob hurried away. As he moved through the
deeper caves, he noticed a change in the hold – a skulking silence

that seemed to press around him like a damp blanket. Shouts and titters gave way to furtive scampering, and Ratgob spied more than one pack of gits darting into the darkness, bulging sacks slung over their shoulders.

Word of the stunties had got out. The lads were abandoning Shriekstone.

Still, Ratgob hesitated. The sight conjured a strange tightness in the loonboss' throat. He had been runted here, scrapped his way up through the mobs, and shanked more grots than he could remember. The thought of his mountain filled with nasty, bearded brutes set the loonboss' fangs aching.

With surprise, Ratgob realised he was not going to run – not yet, at least.

He shook his head. 'A Creeper without Shriekstone is no Creeper at all.'

With a sigh, the loonboss hefted his moonslicer and went to rally the lads.

Ratgob leaned against the rear wall of the vault, partly to have something solid at his back in case things took a bad turn, but mostly because it concealed a secret escape tunnel.

It was proof of the lads' unease that only a few tussles had broken out among the mess of bosses, foregits, nutters, loonchiefs, spikers, eviscerators and fraudmarshals that crowded the mossy treasure vault deep within the bowels of Shriekstone. They clustered in a tight knot near the entrance, well out of reach of the giant cave squigs chained to the walls.

Dirty gold winked in the torchlight, piles and piles of the stuff scraped from every wall, statue and cranny over generations – all the dosh in Shriekstone, or at least all the dosh the High Creepers had managed to nab. Ratgob enjoyed dragging stunty slaves down to the vault, letting them see all the gold so he could watch the mad hunger in their eyes become terror as he fed them, one by one, to the guard squigs.

Ratgob took a deep breath. This was it – he either convinced the bosses to stay and fight or they ate him. Simple, really.

'I'm High Creeper!' Ratgob pushed from the wall, spreading his arms as if to gather the treasure close. 'You fink I'm just gonna scamper and let the stunties nab all dis?'

There were some mutters from the crowd. Grot eyes glittered in the darkness, gazes sharp as knives.

'Krudgit.' Ratgob gestured at the poisoner. 'You gonna just leave your venomenagerie? Pull up your deff garden and take it wiv you?'

All eyes went to the poisoner, who shuffled from foot to foot, nervous at the attention. 'No, boss.'

'An' you, Rankfish.' Ratgob nodded at a scarred foregit standing near the front of the pack. 'Spent yer life cuttin' tunnels into this mountain. What you fink the stunties gonna do wiv all that?'

Rankfish scowled, knuckles whitening on the haft of his sharpened shovel.

'Dey gonna knock 'em in.' Ratgob clanged his moonslicer against the wall, and the mountain gave a delightful screech. 'Ruin everyfing!'

'No stunty is settin' one greasy boot in my 'oles!' Rankfish shouted back, the other foregits shaking picks and cracking their whips.

'Magrot, Filthmiser, Throttle!' Ratgob shouted over the noise, picking the three nastiest bosses from among the mob. 'You scrapped hard for everyfing you got – big names, bigger knives.'

The bosses grinned as laughter rippled through the crowd of grots.

'Fancy skulking back down to the tunnels?' Ratgob asked. 'Tusslin' wiv other mobs for scraps? Gettin' kicked around by ratsneaks and orruks?'

That earned snarls from the bosses, many spitting at the mention of orruks.

'We gots it good 'ere, *real* good. Dis mountain is ours.' Ratgob scraped the blade of his moonslicer along the wall, and the stone gave a low, pained moan. 'It's *ours*. An' no zoggin' stunty is gonna take it away!'

Ratgob slapped his chest for emphasis, but instead of cheers a hush fell over the crowd. He glanced over to see Spookfinger standing atop his squig skull.

'Lot of stunties out there, boss.' The shaman cocked his head. 'Lot of axes, lot of guns, lot of beards. Maybe too many, I fink.'

Ratgob considered giving Spookfinger a good poke. Instead, he smiled. 'I've got a plan to sort those stunties.'

'Mind sharing it, boss?'

'So youz can steal it? I fink not.' The loonboss gave a nasty grin as a stroke of genius hit. 'Bad Moon told me just what to do.'

'The Moon…' Spookfinger's eyes narrowed, '*spoke* to you?'

''Course it did.' Ratgob lifted his moonslicer to point at the ceiling. 'It told me what to do – wiv the stunties, wiv *you*.'

The shaman crossed his arms. 'You 'spect us to believe you'z been touched by the Clammy Hand?'

Ratgob tried not to snicker as he gave a solemn nod. 'It also told me it was sending us a treasure trove! Erry one of dose stunties is a walkin' pile of shiny bits. You lot will be up to your necks in dosh!'

'We gets to keep it all?' Krudgit glanced at the other bosses, yellowed fangs bared in a half-snarl.

Ratgob shrugged. 'Dat's what it said.'

'You 'eard the Creeper!' Rankfish raised his pick. 'Get out dere and nab every git still skulking 'round Shriekstone.'

Krudgit started the cheer, but it was not long until the others joined in, grinning as they looked at the treasure, short-sighted as stunty slaves. Shouting and jostling, the bosses charged from the chamber.

'Clammy Hand?' Shaking his head, Spookfinger watched them go. 'Pack of nutters, all of 'em.'

'Go on, run.' Ratgob let his grin turn ugly. 'See how far you get.'

'I'm stayin'.' Spookfinger gestured at his slaves to heft the squig skull, then shook a bony finger at Ratgob. 'But only cuz I hate stunties more'n I hate you.'

Scowling, the shaman was carried from the vault. It was only when the flap of running feet had faded that Ratgob allowed himself to sag against the wall. He had won over the lads, but what he really needed now was a cunnin' plan – more than one, actually.

There were *a lot* of stunties outside.

Shriekstone's clammy gates shook from the impact of skycannon and volley gun shot, raining bits of scrap on the unfortunate gits who had been 'volunteered' to defend the entrance. The rock lobbers and bolt flingers the lads had managed to drag over had been unable to do more than keep the small fleet of airships that bombarded the gate from drawing too close. Ratgob's best archers sat farther back in the cavern, ready to feather any grot who tried to run.

The loonboss would have preferred to fling open the gates, but then the stunties would *know* it was a trap.

'Why 'aven't dey trotted out big guns?' Krudgit scratched behind one floppy ear, nodding at the huge, silent siege cannons silhouetted in the twilight – far larger than the airship guns.

'S'like I said.' Ratgob glanced back at the mob of sneaks crouched in the darkness of the secret tunnel. 'Shriekstone used to be a nasty, burny place – one good blast might get the magma flowin', melt all dat gold the stunties are afta. Dey gots to be *real* careful.'

'If you say so.' Spookfinger took a sip from a questionable-looking bottle, smacking his lips loudly.

Ratgob hissed the shaman to silence. It was unlikely anyone would hear them over the gunfire, but fyreslayers had a way with stone, a sensitivity to tips and taps echoing through the rock. It was only a matter of time until the invaders found the secret tunnels; best to use them first. Leading to the lower plateau, the tunnels would let Ratgob's lads slip behind the stunty camp. All they needed to do was stay quiet until nightfall.

As if to mock Ratgob, Ghur's hateful sun dawdled on the horizon. Even at dusk, the brightness was almost too much to bear, but Ratgob made himself look. The fyreslayer camp was a riot of activity. The stunties were digging in for a siege, throwing up walls with contemptuous ease. Teams of red-bearded brutes levered great boulders into place, while others filled the gaps with unmortared stone. Great tents stood near where Ratgob's tunnel let out, a seemingly endless train of wagons unloaded barrels and crates.

After an eternity, the light faded. And still Ratgob waited.

The scheme was to strike before the stunties had fully dug in, the lads charging while Ratgob's sneaks spiked the fyreslayers' supplies. Ratgob figured on good odds something would go wrong, but was pleasantly surprised when loons burst from dozens of holes around the mountain, desperately clinging to the backs of bouncing, jabbering squigs.

The fyreslayers reacted quickly, but there was only so much they could do to halt the hoppers' mad charge. Ratgob clapped a hand over his mouth to stifle a laugh as he watched a squig snap the head from a bellowing stunty, its rider hurling a lit torch at a nearby powder keg. The barrel ignited with a muffled whomp, consuming the squig, its rider and a dozen stunties in a ball of red-orange flame. Caught off guard, fyreslayers fought with axe and pick, rune-etched blades flickering as they carved squig flesh.

'C'mon, lads, while they're proper muddled.' Ratgob levered open the concealed door and slipped into the gloom, his sneaks close behind. Faces masked, their weapons blackened with soot, they crept along the shadow of the half-built wall, breaking into smaller groups as they approached the provision tents.

A pair of axe-armed stunties stood outside the nearest tent, weapons drawn, their pained gazes focused on distant fires.

Spookfinger leapt from the gloom, jabbering and hooting, and a plume of greasy smoke billowed from his outstretched hand to wreathe the stunties and set them coughing and retching.

Ratgob's moonslicer caught the first fyreslayer in the neck, and sheared through flesh before getting stuck in the stunty's thick neck bone. The other guard turned, axe slicing down as Ratgob struggled to free his weapon.

The axe cut Ratgob's billowing sleeve. The stunty pulled back for another slice, but a glass vial tumbled from the dark to shatter on its bare chest. A cloud of inky fog billowed around the guard's face. The fyreslayer took a surprised breath, pupils going wide as it glanced around, mouth hanging open.

'Raiders!' Krudgit shouted at the stunty, then gestured at the distant battle. 'In the camp!'

The guard blinked at him for a moment and gave a quick nod. 'For Lachad!'

Ratgob watched, open-mouthed, as the stunty charged off into the darkness.

'Toldja, boss.' Krudgit flashed him a jagged grin. 'Double-strength.'

Ratgob sucked air through his fangs, the beginnings of a scheme tickling his thoughts. 'You gots more of dat loonmist?'

'I could make more.' The poisoner winked. 'A lot more.'

Ratgob nodded. 'Good to know.'

They slipped into the tent. The interior was filled with barrels, each stamped with the symbol of a flaming bearded skull with 'XXXX' etched upon its forehead.

Spookfinger paused, frowning. 'Dis isn't food.'

'Stunties'll fight wivout food, dey'll fight wivout water, dey'll even fight wivout weapons.' Ratgob gestured for the other sneaks to spread out, then scuttled over to pry the top off a barrel and tip a vial of fizzing liquid into the contents. 'But wivout ale?'

For once, Spookfinger's nasty grin was not pointed at Ratgob.

They moved among the barrels, the tent silent but for the sounds of creaking wood and the occasional soft giggle. By the time the sounds of distant fighting had begun to fade, they had tainted most of the beer.

With a snarl, Ratgob gestured the sneaks out of the tent, and they skulked quickly back to the cave.

The loonboss gnawed at his cracked lips, smiling as he closed the secret door behind them. His sneaks hadn't killed many stunties, not directly, but, like a fine patch of fungus, a good plan needed to be cultivated.

Ratgob had spread the spores. Now it was time to watch them grow.

Even from the far end of Shriekstone's great entrance hall, Ratgob could see tears of fury glitter in the runefather's eyes. It seemed impossible, but the loonboss thought he heard a shift in the mountain's ululating cries, a strange warbling note that sounded almost hopeful.

'By Grimnir, what have those monsters done to you?' Runefather Thunas-Grimnir kicked the twitching git from his grandaxe as he reined in his snorting magmadroth to gaze around the vast cavern.

Led by more stunty lords on hateful, spitting magmadroths, ranks of fyreslayers poured through the shattered gates, their war chants drowning the shrieks of the fleeing gits. Many of the stunties looked unsteady on their feet, skin sheened in sickly sweat, wracked by coughs that produced small puffs of yellow spores. More than a few of the brutes seemed to be kept upright by fury alone. Even if the fyreslayers were too stubborn to die, Ratgob's poisoned brew had done its work.

A few of the loonier lads stopped to fire at the approaching wall of blazing steel, only to have their arrows swept aside by the raging stunties.

'Now, boss?' Spookfinger asked from the darkness behind Ratgob.

The loonboss could almost feel the heat of the oncoming magmadroths. He squinted at the floor, judging distance as the fyreslayers charged across the hall. By the Bad Moon, there hardly seemed to be an end to them.

Still, the lads had done a good job spreading bits of moss and loose gravel across the floor of the hall. Hopefully it would be enough to conceal the shoddy carpentry.

As if to echo Ratgob's thought, there came a deep crack from under the claws of the advancing magmadroths. The slats covering the squig pits might be stout enough to support the weight of fleeing gits, but a mess of charging war-beasts was *much* different.

Ratgob cackled as the floor gave way, tipping Thunas-Grimnir and the other foolhardy magmadroth riders into the seething mass below. The squigs fell upon the fallen magmadroths like creatures possessed, gnawing and chomping at the flailing beasts. Caught in their charge, the front ranks of the fyreslayer host tumbled into the pit, there to disappear amidst the churning scrum of squigs.

'Beware the pits!' Thunas-Grimnir's voice rose above the din. He hacked at the mass of maddened squigs, unable to stem the toothy tide that swept over his magmadroth, dragging the great beast down. At last, roaring like a burning troggoth, he was forced to leap from the magmadroth's back or be enveloped by the gnashing horde.

'Hearthguard to the fore!' The runefather leapt to catch the edge of the pit, where he was quickly dragged up by the other stunties. With delight, Ratgob noted the other magmadroth riders had not been so lucky.

A knot of pike-bearing fyreslayers adorned with tall helmets and necklaces of animal claws pushed to the front. They took aim down into the pits, but before they could fire more than a few blasts the squigs boiled up from below, the howling, gnashing horde hopping up the scaffolds Ratgob's lads had thrown down earlier.

'By the Oathflame,' Thunas-Grimnir bellowed as the pike-wielding stunties disappeared beneath the wave of teeth and claws. 'Pull back, form ranks!'

Runes flashed and axes bit into rubbery flesh as the fyreslayers fought to stem the tide. Here and there the flare of a magmapike cast crimson shadows across the gloom, but the fury of the stunties' charge had spread them out across the hall, their endurance sapped by the poisoned ale.

Ratgob saw a fur-cloaked fyreslayer with an enormous double-bladed axe rear from the carnage, a squig clamped onto his drooping crest. With a roar, he carved a circle of ruin, runes flashing gold amidst the sprays of crimson. Squigs piled about his feet, still biting and snapping through reflex alone. One sunk its fangs into the fyreslayer's bare calf, and the stunty stumbled, live squigs sweeping over him.

Ratgob turned his attention to the gates, where a cadre of stunties with flaming poleaxes and fur cloaks had formed around the runefather, runes glinting evilly as they slowly beat back the tide.

He turned to Spookfinger. 'Now, *now*!'

The shaman raised his hands and, with a whoop fit to wake the dead, conjured a bolt of jagged, greenish lightning that blasted one of the fyreslayers from its nasty feet, beard burning, its flesh crackling with mad energy. The signal was taken up by other gits, and soon the cavern echoed with mad whoops.

From the tunnels came a beastly clatter, the clicking of claws on stone like a rain of arrows. Hundreds of segmapedes burst into the hall in a tide of roiling chitin. Spookfinger's loons had terrified the normally placid beasts into a wild panic.

The stampede shook the floor of the cavern, sending tremors through the rock. Ratgob thought he might have heard an answering rumble from deeper down in the caverns, but shrugged off the concern, too excited to watch the carnage to worry about a little quiver in the mountain.

The giant insects crashed into the stunty line, knocking even more into the pits. Ratgob had expected the stunties to flee before the stampede, but the fools stood firm even as the segmapedes crushed them by the score. Axes rose and fell, sprays of greenish ichor rising like flies from an old kill. One by one the segmapedes stumbled, their legs hacked away. Runes sparked as Runefather Thunas-Grimnir leapt upon the back of one of the giant insects and beheaded it with a single sweep of his huge axe.

'Show-off.' Ratgob's delight soured. Fresh stunty warriors poured through the broken gate, adding their numbers to the growing ring of steel. The momentum of their furious charge broken, the squigs shattered into smaller mobs, the duardin surrounding and hacking them apart one by one.

'Should I unchain the loons?' Spookfinger asked.

'Stunties can have the hall, we gots more surprises.' Ratgob shouldered past the shaman, risking a glance back. The lads had done good. The cavern was littered with duardin bodies, with even more wedged down in the squig pits.

Snarling, Ratgob scuttled for the tunnels, pursued by the deep rumble of stunty cheers. Let them celebrate, they would be weeping soon enough.

Those that survived, at least.

'Die, *thagi* filth!' The stunty's axe swept by close enough to ruffle Ratgob's robes.

The loonboss brought his moonslicer around to shriek across the sparking runes embedded in the fyreslayer's flesh. Although the duardin bled freely from a dozen such slashes, the wounds seemed to barely slow the maddened brute.

Another swipe from one of the stunty's axes almost took Ratgob's head. Eyes stinging with panicked sweat, he glanced around the tunnel. All around, terrified gits fled before the roaring fury of the fyreslayers. Bare-chested, their beards plaited with images of ferocious beasts, the stunties had come on in a wild, animalistic charge, runes flaring like a fresh blaze. It had been all Ratgob could do to convince the lads not to bolt at the mere sight of the duardin.

'Show yourself, creature!' Thunas-Grimnir's voice boomed from around the tunnel bend. Desperately, Ratgob shoved an unfortunate git into the path of the roaring stunty. The poor lad managed a single mournful screech before the fyreslayer's axe smashed him to the cavern floor.

Sprinting past a rust-scabbed vent, Ratgob breathed in the damp, heavy air, feeling strength return as the spores filled his lungs. The stunties were deadly, but they moved slowly, wary of more pits and snares.

Ratgob dodged into a side-tunnel and crawled along its twisted length, eventually spilling out into a nest of tangled pipes further ahead of the advancing duardin. Shriekstone gave voice to an echoing scream. A low vibration rippled through the mountain causing him to lose his footing. The tremors were coming more often and lasting longer, but Ratgob had bigger things to worry about than a little magma.

'They're almost to the vents.' The loonboss stood, hands on knees as he panted. 'Is the loonmist ready?'

'S'jammed.' Krudgit banged on a large bronze pipe, knocking loose showers of blue-green verdigris.

'No time for malingerin.' Ratgob straightened, ignoring the poisoner's irritated glare. The loonboss clambered from the network of pipes and further down the passage, to where a knot of lads were doing their best to restrain a dozen wild-eyed loons. Green foam dribbled from around the mad grots' gags, the ropes creaking and bulging as they struggled to break free.

'Dey comin'?' Rankfish staggered up. The foregit looked harried, and Ratgob noticed he was sporting a fresh black eye.

Ratgob nodded at the distant lantern flicker, broad-shouldered shadows crowding the gloom. 'Get 'em ready.'

Heavy chains were pressed into hands of the thrashing gits.

'Now, boss?' Rankfish asked.

Ratgob frowned. 'Hold.'

He could hear the stunties clattering down the tunnel, all boots and bluster.

Hold.

Their bestial helms glittered in the half-light: gryphons, bears, cliff snatchers, steelcats and more, the crests casting huge, ferocious shadows on the tunnel wall. At Ratgob's side, the foregit shifted from foot to foot, muttering.

Hold.

Ratgob could smell the oil on their weapons, hear the creak of harnesses, the miserable pant of stunty breathing.

'Cut 'em loose!' At Ratgob's scream, the lads cut the loons' bindings, sprinting away down the tunnel as the madcap-addled fanatics began to spin.

Ratgob scrambled back into the pipes before the loons could work up speed. He crouched behind a bronze tube to watch the fun.

The lead stunty raised a fist, the red-bearded ranks behind it grinding to a halt. Silence descended on the tunnel. The big duardin cocked its head to listen as a mad giggle echoed from the gloom. Eyes wide, he drew in breath for a bellow, already turning.

A huge iron ball swept him aside as if he'd been made of scrap. Seeming not even to notice, the fanatic continued on into the duardin formation. Stunties tumbled through the air, bowled from their feet or crushed wetly against the tunnel wall. Those in the front shouted for a withdrawal, but the air was too full of screams and laughter. Fyreslayers threw themselves to the floor or pressed tight against the walls to avoid the spinning loons, but, in the tight confines of the tunnel, there was nowhere to go.

A fyreslayer with a helm shaped like a snarling cave bear dived under one of the whirling chains to cut the legs from one of the loons, and the fanatic's huge ball went ricocheting down the tunnel, crushing another half a dozen stunties before rolling to a stop.

Further down the tunnel, a pair of duardin had become entangled in a chain. Although they struggled and swore, with each revolution the heavy chain grew tighter, until blood flowed between the links. With delight, Ratgob saw them slump and fall still before the fanatic spun off down the passage.

But there was only so much loons could do against so many. Two fanatics collided, their chains crushing them into a pulpy embrace. Another rebounded from the wall and was buried in the resulting avalanche of stone. More fell to blasts of magma, or were hacked down by stunties who seemed not to care it was death to charge the spinning loons.

Bloodied but undaunted, the surviving fyreslayers staggered to their feet. More than half their number lay spread across the tunnel floor, but the losses seemed only to make the stunties angrier.

'Shank me, dey'z still comin', Krudgit said. 'An' more from behind.'

Ratgob glanced down the tunnel, feeling his throat tighten at the sight of faint lantern light advancing from the other direction.

'We'd better bolt, boss.' Panic threaded the poisoner's voice.

'What 'bout the pipes?'

Krudgit gave the ancient duardin ventilation one last bang. 'S'no use.'

Ratgob shouldered past to peer up the corroded pipe, the clash of duardin blades sharp in his ears. This close, he could smell the musty scent of rotten fungus, hear the faint hiss as the overtaxed ventilation system tried to work air past the blockage.

With a curse, he shoved his moonslicer into the grate. The hooked blade rasped on ancient bronze as Ratgob stretched as far as he could. He felt the moonslicer sink into something soft.

The loonboss heard the boom of a magmapike, and a blast of hot lava splattered the stone a handspan from Ratgob's nose. He gritted his fangs as a scalding fleck burned a line across his cheek, and scraped with all his might.

'Zog dis.' Krudgit clambered back down the hole as a scowling, bearded face appeared beyond the pipes. Ratgob kicked at it, but the stunty ignored his shattered nose to grab the loonboss' ankle.

With a wet slurp, the mass blocking the pipe finally gave way, deluging Ratgob and the stunty with hundreds of dead snotlings.

The fyreslayers fell back with a curse as Ratgob clambered through the avalanche of tiny, putrefied corpses. The stupid blighters must have crawled in there to hide, or maybe some clever git had sent them up there to gum up Ratgob's plan. He shook his head as the rattle and chuff of duardin pumps echoed down the tunnel.

Thick, dark mist poured from the grates. Ratgob scrambled

down the grot tunnel as mist flowed down into the old duardin passage. He heard shouting from below, stunties hacking in the clouds of Krudgit's loonmist. The fyreslayers seemed dazed at first. They called to one another, but cries to dress ranks soon became confused shouts.

'Grobi, in the tunnels!'

'By Grimnir, they're behind us!'

'Kill the filthy skaz!'

Some duardin began blowing their horns while others pounded on drums, the rhythms sharp and erratic. Weapons clattered, angry oaths like sweet laughter to Ratgob's ears. At last, blinded and mad, the stunties turned on each other.

Ratgob only wished he could see the slaughter. Instead, he crouched in the grot tunnel and listened, bobbing his head to the sounds of stunties murdering one another.

Then came a shout from beyond the melee, a booming voice chanting in a language Ratgob did not recognise. Impossibly, golden light shone through the gloom. Scintillating, like glow-squigs reflected in stagnant water, it burned away the mist.

'Shake your madness, kinsmen!' Thunas-Grimnir's hateful voice rose above the clamour. 'Let the ancestors light your way.'

Ratgob could see the runefather, now. Surrounded by stunties in glittering helms, the king stood silhouetted by a swirl of fiery sparks. The circle of stunties raised their glowing braziers and struck them against the ground. There was a burst of painful light, and Ratgob was forced to turn away, hissing as bright after-images of duardin runes danced across his vision.

Slowly, the sounds of fighting died.

With a shake of his head, the loonboss clambered back up the gnarled tunnel. Forget Ratgob's lie about the Bad Moon; when he told the others how stunty tricks had dispersed the loonmist, he would be lucky to escape without a shank in his eye.

'S'time for somefin' big,' he muttered to himself. 'Somefin' *real* big.'

The slaves shuffled down the uneven stairs that wound down into The Pit. Shaved and gaunt, the runes prised from their flesh, the wretches were barely recognisable as duardin, let alone fyreslayers.

'Too slow.' Ratgob chewed his lip. 'Dose stunties'll be knockin' our 'eads in afore this lot gets in The Pit.'

Spookfinger peered over the lip of the old duardin cistern. 'Give 'em a prod, den.'

'And risk a scream?' Krudgit tittered. 'You wanna get et up?'

Spookfinger made a face, but offered no more advice.

'We need the slaves in one piece.' Ratgob paced across the gallery. 'How else we gonna lure in dem stunties?'

A distant boom almost startled the loonboss over the lip of the cistern.

'That'll be the vault door.' Spookfinger's mutter was just loud enough to set the surviving lads shuffling.

'This'll work – Bad Moon told me so.' Ratgob turned to glare at the few hundred grots gathered in the gloom of the tunnel – all that remained of his kingdom. 'It also told me to gut the first git who tries to nip off.'

'Not us, boss. Never.' Krudgit popped a vial of something blue into his mouth, crunching happily as blood dribbled down his chin.

Ratgob turned his back on the nutter. The stunties had backed them into a corner, occupying all the hold's central passages and collapsing every grot tunnel they could find – which, being duardin, meant *most* of them.

Still, the loonboss had one last knife up his sleeve.

Ratgob heard the stamp of boots in the outer hall, rising above the low, threatening rumble that had become almost constant in Shriekstone. The Bad Moon must have heard Ratgob's pleas, because the halls had not filled with magma, yet. Still, the stunties were moving slowly, taking time to clear each hall before advancing. They would not be caught in another trap.

Fortunately, this one would come to them.

'Dey're down, boss.' Throttle scurried around the edge of the cistern, Filthmiser close behind.

'Should be a sight.' Throttle flexed the long spidery fingers that had earned him his reputation as a master strangler. Behind him, Filthmiser chuckled wetly, the mushrooms growing through the holes in his rotted robes jiggling with each wheezing exhalation.

Ratgob peered into the mildewed darkness. He cocked his head, fluttering his fingers at the lads for quiet.

The Pit was quiet but for the occasional whisper of bare feet and the low rumble of snoring troggoths.

'Won't be long, now.' Krudgit rubbed his hands together, squinting at the flickering light at the far end of the hall.

'Get everyone back in the tunnel.' Ratgob nodded. 'S'time for the show.'

Duardin fanned out along the far side of the gallery, covering the various angles of attack, while teams of fyreslayers advanced cautiously towards the massive cistern, magmapikes at the ready. Fortunately, the light of their runelamps didn't reach the far end of the massive cistern chamber.

Rankfish and the lads scampered back down the tunnel, but Ratgob lingered with Spookfinger and Krudgit at the edge of the gallery. He noticed Thunas-Grimnir near the front. The runefather had exchanged his grandaxe for two smaller hand axes etched to resemble leaping leogryphs.

A snort reverberated from the depths of the ancient cistern, followed by a grumbling mutter.

The duardin held back, confused. Some with magmapikes took

cover behind fallen masonry as their brutish brethren clashed axes together.

'Dey ain't gonna fall for it.' Spookfinger gave a low chuckle.

Ratgob hissed the shaman to silence. The loonboss gripped his moonslicer tighter to hide his shaking hands. If the stunties backed off, Ratgob was as good as shanked. This was it – his last scheme. If there was any time for the Bad Moon to extend its Clammy Hand, it was now.

The first screams echoed from below – voices, *fyreslayer* voices, crying out in pain and terror.

'Stunties won't abandon der own,' Ratgob said with more conviction than he felt. 'You'll see.'

'S'pose I will.' Spookfinger's grin held no humour at all.

Ratgob could see indecision in the runefather's grim scowl. Thunas-Grimnir's gaze flicked from The Pit to his warriors and back again. Finally, with a growling curse, the runefather pointed an axe forward.

Ratgob almost fainted from joy as the stunties advanced.

The first ranks lobbed torches into the cistern, falling back while the magmapikes took up positions around the edge and sighted down into the dark. There was a moment, quick as an indrawn gasp, as the duardin took in the terrifying sight below. The chamber seemed almost quiet as Ratgob revelled in the stunties' horrified expressions.

A lumpy hand plucked one of the fyreslayers from the rim of the cistern.

The boom of a magmapike shattered the unnatural stillness. Everything seemed to happen at once – some duardin firing down into The Pit, others dodging back to reload as their axe-wielding companions pushed forward to provide cover.

The troggoths rose from the darkness in a blood-maddened frenzy. Their gnarled claws cut divots in the stone, rock flowing like thick mud. Thunas-Grimnir's bellowed commands were lost amidst the roars of the enraged trogghorde.

No sooner had massed duardin fire brought down one troggoth, than another would heave itself from the jagged mouth of The Pit. A lucky blast of magma burned away one troggoth's face, but the beast seemed not to notice. Blindly lumbering forward, it scattered duardin like pebbles with swings of its massive stone club.

Another troggoth was engaged by half a dozen fyreslayers, the runes on their heavy axes flashing red in the gloom. They cut at the troggoth's legs while it growled and stomped, but duardin steel proved no protection against the full weight of the enormous beast, and the stunties were crushed to bloody ruin.

Thunas-Grimnir charged into the fray. Dire oaths on his lips, he leapt to bury his axes in the stomach of a huge troggoth, scaling the beast's chest as it reeled back. Stony hands closed about his chest, but the runefather tore his axes free in a spray of gore and hacked down at the troggoth's wrist.

Ratgob made a sour face as Thunas-Grimnir's blade bit deep into the troggoth's rocky flesh. It snatched its hand back, yowling like a scalded squig, but the runefather only shifted to hack the beast's head from its scabby shoulders.

Fortunately, several of the troggoths the duardin had downed earlier slowly staggered to their feet, flesh knitting around bones the colour of wet shale, and the runefather was forced back.

A flash of brilliant light made Ratgob wince as one of the stunty's rune-pounders joined the battle. Chant cutting through the din, the duardin raised his smoking staff, the beginnings of a fiery sigil etching itself into the air.

A troggoth loomed behind the duardin. It frowned down at the jabbering stunty, then leaned over and smashed him flat with the palm of its hand. Light streamed between the troggoth's fingers, making the beast squint. With a frown of intense concentration, it scooped up a great handful of stone and simply folded it over the unfortunate stunty.

Ratgob could not restrain his delight as the fyreslayers retreated before the furious trogghorde. He could see Thunas-Grimnir waving his axes, but even the runefather seemed unable to deal with the onslaught. Troggoths kicked through the fleeing duardin, occasionally stooping to cram a screaming stunty into their mouths.

Ratgob should have known it was too good to last.

As the duardin scattered, so did the troggoths. Some pursued knots of running stunties, while others lumbered into the darkness beyond; a few even turned to climb back down into The Pit, blinking sleepily.

'Zoggin' idiots!' Ratgob slammed the butt of his moonslicer against the ground.

'Boss.' Krudgit nudged Ratgob, pointing to where a few hulking troggoth shadows were making their way around the chamber towards where the grots stood.

With a disgusted curse, Ratgob turned away from the slaughter. His plan had been perfect, but bigger was not always better.

'What the Bad Moon tellin' you now?' Spookfinger's words dripped with scorn.

'Never you mind.'

'Sure, *boss.*' The shaman spoke the last word like a curse.

Ratgob caught the slightest glint in the corner of his vision. Through reflex alone, the loonboss spun away just in time to avoid Spookfinger's dagger.

'A knife inna back?' Contempt iced Ratgob's words.

The shaman grinned. 'Well, it *is* poisoned.'

'You, too?' Ratgob glanced at Krudgit.

The poisoner offered an apologetic shrug, then tossed a vial to Ratgob. 'Plenty to go 'round.'

Ratgob snatched the poison from the air, then dropped flat as the shaman crooked a knobby finger at him. With a fizzling crack, a bolt of sickly-green lightning flashed above his head, leaving blackened streaks on the tunnel wall. Before the shaman could conjure another blast, Ratgob scrambled to his feet and leapt at Spookfinger.

'Enuf of yer lies! Touched by the Clammy Hand? Touched by lungrot, more likely!' Spookfinger met the loonboss' charge, his dagger darting like an angry blisterwasp.

'I've got dose stunties right where I want 'em!' This close, Ratgob could not bring the blade of his moonslicer to bear, so he gave Spookfinger's face a good thwap with the handle.

'Oh, come off it!' The shaman staggered back, eyes watering as he dabbed at his bloody nose. 'Shriekstone's lost – there ain't no future for you, not 'ere, not anywhere.'

Ratgob didn't bother with a response – the shaman was right, but it hardly mattered. Only stunties worried about the future, gits took things as they came.

The hook of Ratgob's moonslicer opened a wide gash on Spookfinger's leg. The shaman toppled with a shriek, hands clamped on his oozing calf.

'So, dis is it, boss?' Spookfinger looked up at Ratgob. 'After everyfing, you jus' gonna cut me up?'

'Not me,' Ratgob said, with a nod at the approaching troggoths. 'But I reckon dey might 'ave different plans.'

Ratgob scurried back into the shadows, Spookfinger's despairing cry lifting his spirits. He eyed Krudgit. 'I should feed you to the trogs, too.'

The poisoner spread his hands wide. 'Don't fink they'd bite, boss – I'm too bitter.'

Ratgob snorted out a laugh. Krudgit had betrayed him, true, but a little double-cross now and again was only natural. Besides, he still might need the poisoner.

Ratgob nodded at Krudgit. 'C'mon den.'

The two grots scurried down the hall. Spookfinger's screams were little relief to the heaviness threading Ratgob's chest. He was as good as shanked – if not by Krudgit then by some other canny git. Ratgob was done as High Creeper. Finished. Not even worth a glance from the Bad Moon.

Now, was *definitely* the time to run. But first, Ratgob just needed to grab a little something for the journey.

'You are not going anywhere, skaz.' Runefather Thunas-Grimnir the Unflinching stepped from the shadows of the treasure vault, one axe pointed at Ratgob's chest. The loonboss could see scores of stunties ranged in the glittering dark behind the runefather. All that remained of the fyreslayer host. Beaten, bloodied, their axes were chipped and their runes guttered like dying candles, but the hateful glint of their eyes burned brighter than ever.

There were mutters from the lads behind Ratgob – barely enough to form a proper mob, but still some of the most vicious loons Shriekstone had to offer. A few of the gits bolted for the vault exit, only to draw back as more fyreslayers emerged from the gloom, axes at the ready.

It was strange, being well and truly surrounded. Ratgob had expected terror, mad panic bubbling up through the cracks in his thoughts, but all he felt was an odd sense of relief.

'Did you think you could escape?' Thunas-Grimnir thundered, words falling like hammer blows. 'Skulk from my Magmahold like the filthy thieves you are? By Grungni's eternal eyes, did you think you could outwit *me*?'

'Outwitted you four times already, didn't I?' Ratgob shrugged. 'Figgerd one more couldn't 'urt.'

The runefather's face turned a delightful shade of purple.

Ratgob chewed his lips. Something had changed. There was an

absence in the air, an emptiness he could not quite place. With a start, he realised what was missing.

Shriekstone was no longer screaming.

'Yes, yes.' King Thunas' grin dripped with cruel promise. 'You hear it, do you not? The silence.' He thumped a fist against his chest. 'Lachad remembers its true masters. Soon you and your ilk will be naught but bad memories – thus to all defilers.'

Smiling wide, Ratgob spat upon the tunnel floor. 'Ow's dat for defilin'?'

With a roar, Thunas-Grimnir charged.

Ratgob retreated into the milling crowd of gits as he dodged the runefather's heavy, looping slashes. Thunas-Grimnir fought like a duardin possessed, strikes raining down. Ratgob ducked a wide cut, then threw himself down as the backswing almost took his head. The runefather's second axe would have buried itself in Ratgob's neck, except Rankfish chose that moment to leap at the fyreslayer, sharpened shovel stabbing for the stunty's eyes.

Thunas cut the foregit from the air with almost casual disregard, but Throttle leapt onto the fyreslayer's back, long fingers wrapping around the runefather's exposed throat. Krudgit flung a handful of puffshrooms at Thunas-Grimnir's face, while, giggling like loons, Magrot and Filthmiser tried to snare his legs with rope.

'That's right, lads!' Ratgob shouted. 'Bleed 'im good!'

The cave descended into confusion as the surviving fyreslayers charged to the aid of their king.

Surrounded, outnumbered and facing certain death, Ratgob's gits fought like cornered bush hydras. Ratgob saw stunties netted and clubbed to death, or reel back, clawing at their flesh as gits tossed handfuls of pocket squigs at them. Muted pops marked the explosions of puffshrooms, clouds of dark, stinging mist rising from the melee.

Feet tangled in rope, Thunas-Grimnir stumbled, and Ratgob

slashed at him, only to have his moonslicer rebound in a crackle of red-orange light as the stunty king's last runes flashed and went dark.

Wheezing, the runefather slashed the rope with one axe, then reversed the other to hack back over his shoulder and split Throttle's skull. Their snare broken, Filthmiser and Magrot scuttled away. Ratgob circled Thunas, searching for an opening, while Krudgit flung another fizzing vial at the duardin lord.

Thunas knocked it from the air, and the vial exploded with a pop of green mist, but the runefather was already moving, axes limned in sprays of crimson as he chopped into the poisoner's neck. Still giggling, Krudgit fell back, vials crunching as he flopped like a dying cave fish upon the slick tiles.

Ratgob's moonslicer carved a bloody line across the back of Thunas-Grimnir's left knee. The runefather stumbled, and Ratgob discarded his hooked blade to pounce on the duardin, dagger at the ready. He drove the blade into the stunty's ribs, twisting with both hands. It was a good dagger, filched from a stunty tomb deep in Shriekstone. Ratgob shrieked with joy as hot blood welled over his hands.

Thunas-Grimnir snarled, and Ratgob felt something dig into his thigh. There was no pain, only a dim sense of numbness. He gave the dagger one last twist, then pushed off to retreat, surprised when his leg would not bear his weight.

Glancing down, he belatedly realised he was short a leg.

The runefather tossed his axes aside to tackle Ratgob. The fyreslayer's horrible bulk bore him down, filthy stunty hands closing around the loonboss' throat.

Ratgob fumbled at his belt as his vision crinkled like rotting lichen, everything turning dull and distant. The runefather's grim face loomed like a hideous sun above Ratgob, seeming to fill the entirety of his sight.

The loonboss' fingers brushed glass, closed around the neck of Krudgit's vial. With a grunt of effort he twisted to smash the flask into Thunas-Grimnir's mouth.

The runefather blinked, dark green ichor dribbling down his chin. He shook his head as if to clear it, then gave a sputtering cough. The pressure on Ratgob's throat relaxed as Thunas-Grimnir tried to claw the poison from his throat.

Ratgob tried to go up on his elbows, but fell back, dizzy from blood loss. Teeth gritted, he craned his neck to watch. There was no way he was getting out of this, but there was *also* no way he was going to miss the show.

Thunas-Grimnir staggered to his feet. Spasms shook his muscled frame as he staggered about like a drunken troggoth. The runefather's beard was singed and wild, his eyes the deep orange of madcap dust. The duardin opened his mouth as if to speak, but all that emerged was a low, choking growl. He took a stumbling step towards Ratgob, then, like a great stone pillar, toppled forward and lay still.

Ratgob glanced around, satisfied. The surviving stunties were cutting up the last of his lads, but with a spark of pride, the loonboss noted there were as many dead duardin as grots, maybe more. What had started as a stunty horde the likes of which Shriekstone had never seen had dwindled to a few hundred tattered survivors.

'Murdering grobi.' A duardin shadow loomed over him, the muscled form blurring in Ratgob's faded vision. The stunty raised an axe. 'At last, our oath is fulfilled.'

The loonboss lay back, waiting for the blade to fall.

It began as a mutter, a chattering call that seemed to bloom in the back of Ratgob's mind. At first, he thought it was the blood loss, but slowly, a voice emerged from the mad babble, four words formed from the giggles and shrieks of a thousand, thousand grots.

The fyreslayers looked around as sickly yellow-green light bled into the cave, seeming to congeal the very air. From deep in the tunnels there came a low, threatening rumble, followed by a crackling roar that seemed to fill the entire cavern. In it, Ratgob heard the slap of feet on stone – many feet. Shrieks and cackles echoed from the gloom, mad chants, indistinct at first, but growing clearer by the moment.

'By the ancestors…' The stunty glanced around. 'What new foulness is this?'

The loonboss drew in a great, rasping breath – his last, he knew now – and grinned up at the duardin.

'Da Bad Moon will avenge me.'

As if to echo his words, the mountain began to scream once more.

THE SERPENT'S BARGAIN

Jamie Crisalli

Laila wriggled into the hole dug deep under the hut she called home. The hole was little wider than her hips and she yanked the stone cover over the opening, sealing her in a womblike darkness. Small holes the size of an old Pelos coin let in air. Thin roots tickled her freckled skin and the smell of Ghyran loam smothered her nose. A cache of water and bread in a sealed clay pot sat between her bare feet. In her shaking hand, she clutched a small leather bottle on a string around her neck.

Raw screams and exultant roaring filtered down to her in that tiny hollow. And other, more obscene sounds as the fiends went about their horrid joys. Of all the places in Ghyran, the followers of the Needful One had come to her village of Varna. The new palisade had not kept them out, nor had any fighter that they possessed.

Up above, the hut door banged open and she started, her heart racing.

A man moaned and licked his lips.

'Not much sport here,' he said, his voice melodious.

'This is the first settlement in weeks not tainted by those reeking pus-bags,' said another. 'So, I'd enjoy yourself while you can. These little people are entertaining enough.'

Something crashed over, shards of pottery scattering across the floor. And they talked about what they had done and would do if they found someone. Shuddering, Laila clamped a callused hand over her mouth and pressed herself deeper into the dirt. Her mind shrinking away from the memories of her husband's tortured last moments years ago, Laila worked the stopper out of the bottle and a dusty smell like dead flowers filled the air. She would not die as he had.

Inside was a poison called Blood of the Wight; it was not painless but it was lightning quick. Her mother had given it to her when she was a child and told her to keep it with her even when she slept. There were numberless things worse than dying.

With a hiss, the raiders went quiet. A shadow crept over the breathing holes, sniffing. Laila put the bottle to her lips. Then a shrill hollow tone wended over the town, reverberating in her head.

'Is that a retreat?' one asked in disbelief.

'I would watch your forked tongue unless you want to be the cure for Lord Zertalian's ennui,' said the other. 'Clearly he wishes to save this place for future amusement. So let's go.'

Ceramic crunched under foot and the door banged shut. Yet, Laila could not move. She stayed, holding the poison to her lips, staring at the dirt wall, trying to breathe quietly. Only a buzzing tension remained, as if her head were full of bees. What if it was a trick and they had not left, instead waiting to pounce? No, it was better to stay in here with poison than risk that fate. Even as her sturdy legs cramped and her lips went numb, she held still. Then a familiar voice called her name.

'Stefen!' she called, her voice ragged.

Laila crammed the stopper back into the bottle and clambered out of her sanctuary. Then she paused.

Her home was wrecked, her meagre belongings tossed about and broken, her food stores spilled and trampled. Still, she was lucky – only her things had been touched by the seekers. She would burn it all as was tradition with tainted things. Hopefully the elders would spare the hut itself or she would have to move in with a neighbour during winter.

Stefen rushed in, his dark eyes wide.

She embraced him, trembling and choking back tears. He was an old childhood friend; they had gone on to their separate lives when he had become a hunter and she had married Jonas.

'It's all right, they're gone,' he said, pulling her close. Stefen was tall and well built, though the Rotskin pox had left him with scarred, pallid skin, ruining his good looks. A clutch of scrawny birds swung over his shoulder, along with his snares and bow.

A wash of cold fear rolled through her as the gossip of the raiders rattled in her brain.

'Are the elders still with us?' she asked.

'Yes, they were spared,' he said.

'They need to know,' she said.

Without waiting to see if he followed, she rushed out into the bright light of the Lamp. The palisade gate dangled as men worked desperately to wrench the doors back into place. Homes burned, releasing sweet smoke and pale flames as ashen-faced neighbours watched, making no move to put them out. Others wandered aimlessly, their clothing torn and eyes utterly vacant, while some desperately called out for missing loved ones. Horror seeped through the very air as if some malign spirit had made a home in every hut and heart, a final curse bestowed by the fiends. No doubt it would linger for years.

Laila walked, eyes seeing but unable to understand it, same as it had been then. The horrid memories edged into her mind and she forced them away. Jonas was long dead, praise Alarielle.

By some miracle, the stone elders' hall had not been touched. Some speculated that it was once a temple devoted to a forgotten storm god. Perhaps that was why the fiends avoided it.

Inside, the place was stifling hot, the fires burning high to warm old bones. Yet, the crowd was more meagre than Laila had expected. The hall guards were gone to help with the gate. At the far end, sat in a loose half-circle, were the elders, some hunched and withered, some grey and still robust. The old altar loomed behind them.

'We will rebuild and mourn as we have always done,' Uma said, her voice like a creaking door. 'The dark ones never stay. The seekers will move on and leave us be.'

The other elders nodded. As always, they acquiesced to the ancient crone. Laila suddenly hated the old woman and the sycophants that surrounded her. Of course they felt that way; they sat in the heart of the village surrounded by stone and armed guards. Did they even know what happened out there? No more than they had after the last raid by the seekers.

'No, they won't,' Laila said, her tone cold. 'They're coming back.'

The silence sharpened and Laila blushed as all eyes focused on her. Uma's face crumpled, her eyes narrowing.

'What do you mean?' Uma said.

'They're coming back?' another man said.

The crowd bubbled with alarm, looking around as if the dark ones were going to lunge out of the walls.

'Two of them came into my house while I was hiding,' Laila said, wrapping her arms around herself. 'They were summoned by their leader early. They said that they would return.'

Another rumble of discontent. If Uma could have killed Laila with her gaze, she likely would have.

'I agree with Laila, we can't wait and do nothing,' Stefen said behind her.

'What would the youngsters suggest?' Uma said. 'That we fight them?'

Laila stammered, her thoughts churning. She had no solution to the problem that she had presented. Then an idea popped into her mind. A dangerous endeavour, but better than the alternative.

'The Fair Ones in the Valley of the Oracle's Eye,' Laila said. 'They help people if the foe is right. Is that not correct?'

The crowd murmured. The Fair Ones. Some said they had earned this name because they were beautiful. Others claimed they were hideous, with snakes for hair, and cursed those who did not flatter them. What the legends did agree on was that the Fair Ones hated Chaos more than anything else, especially the followers of the Needful One.

Uma snorted. 'You are not serious,' she said. 'The valley where they dwell is a place of madness and they are themselves not remotely human. The Fair Ones fight on their own terms and no one else's. You are a fool.'

'Says the old woman who counsels that we wait for those beasts to return and finish what they started,' Laila snapped.

Uma blanched, her thin skin turning whiter than the wisps on her head.

'Out! I will not tolerate your stupidity a moment longer,' Uma said, snapping a finger at the door.

Laila spun on her heel and pushed through the crowd, out into the smoky air. Inside the hall, the arguing escalated. Although there was a harvest to bring in, no one wanted to go outside the walls if there was the slightest chance that the fiends were waiting for them. Cries echoed, questioning why they did nothing. Others called for the villagers to resettle elsewhere. Uma shouted back with all the ferocity in her old bones.

'And she calls me stupid,' Laila muttered to herself.

'She's afraid, nothing more malicious than that,' Stefen said. 'This isn't like the pox walkers. It's worse. I should have been here.'

'You would have just got yourself killed, or worse,' Laila said. 'We need to get help from people that can fight. Uma is right, we can't defend ourselves against that.'

'I can lead us to the valley,' Stefen said. 'I've been to the borders anyway.'

'Really, you've seen it?' she said. 'That's forbidden.'

Stefen blushed sheepishly and nodded. 'Once.'

'You will not get there alone, especially if the fiends are still out there,' a stranger said in a hard, growling accent.

They both spun about. A man stood before them in leather and bronze plate. His skin was tanned and aged and he was built heavily with a round gut that spoke of a steady diet of beer and meat. That he was creeping into middle age indicated either luck or skill, likely both.

'Who are you?' Laila said.

'Ano,' he replied, as if that explained everything. When they continued to look at him in silence, he added, 'I worked for the merchant, Antton. I hope that if I help you, your village will let me stay over the winter.'

'What we're talking about doing is dangerous,' Laila said, suspicious.

'I heard, but what that old woman is suggesting is worse,' he said. 'What you described sounds like something that the fiends do. They wait for your guard to fall. And they can wait a long time. Then they strike.'

While Laila did not trust the stranger, when standing against the Chaos hordes all pure humans had to stick together. What few untainted humans remained.

'The real question is, will Hadlen let us out?' Stefen said.

Laila winced; the reeve was stubborn at the best of times. 'We have to try,' Laila said. 'He might be persuaded.'

Stefen smiled tightly. 'Yes, and lightning men will fall from the sky and kill our enemies.'

They snickered at the old child's tale and made their plans. They delayed as much as they dared, speaking to the few close friends that they knew would keep their peace. With the watch so tense, sneaking out would be a challenge. Carefully, they gathered their supplies – a few loaves of hard bread, dried beans and smoked meat. Then at the light of dawn the next day, they walked to the back edge of the village where the midden heap lay next to the wall. It smelled of rotten grain and human waste; however, there was a gap in the palisade where the beams had rotted and they slipped out into the greater world with no one the wiser.

'So this is how you kept escaping,' Laila said.

Stefen grinned as he brushed off his hands. 'No one ever looked.'

As they walked around the village and onto the road, they saw not a single corpse. Just dried bloodstains and spatters of clear fluid like the trails of slugs. Strange perfumes lingered in the air, faded but potent enough to tickle the nose. Crows fluttered out in the fields, squawking at each other.

Stefen took them off the road towards the east, into the thinning forest. A deep layer of leaves rustled underfoot. Overhead, the skeletal trees rattled in the wind. The glow of the Lamp dimmed with the evening, while the Cinder Disc glimmered, already small and red with the autumn.

It felt almost unnatural to be moving away from Varna. The trees seemed to hide sinister threats, and Laila waited for some pale horror to come pelting out at them. Out here, the urge to leave struck her as impulsive while in the town it had felt brave. Had she misheard the raiders? Was Uma right? With a start, Laila realised that she had never been this far from the walls.

'Second thoughts?' Stefen said.

'How do you do it?' she said. 'Leave Varna I mean.'

'One step at a time,' Stefen said, smiling.

They walked on, the shadows growing long. Stars flickered into being and the night birds started to warble to each other.

'What about you?' Laila said to Ano. 'How did you come to travel?'

'It's tough to do,' Ano said. 'But there are advantages.'

'Like what?' she said.

'Being paid in coin is good,' Ano said.

It was practical, yet there was a mercenary attitude to his response that she did not like.

'We can't pay you in coin,' she said, hoping to gain a clearer sense of his motivation.

'No, but a bed for the winter is priceless,' he said. 'Besides, I could not help my employer.'

She let the subject drop when he looked away from her with a cough.

They travelled for several days, the forest twittering and breathing around them. It had not always been so. Once upon a time, this entire woodland had been a mire of maggots, rot and corpses. Then something had changed. Some said it was just the way of nature to reassert itself after a time. Others said it was a blessing from Alarielle, waking from her long slumber. Still others whispered that it was the Fair Ones that had freed the region of its decay.

Laila found herself dreading the night. Her sleep was long in coming and when she finally drifted off, nightmares haunted her with horrifying blends of past and present. The fiends, all wearing the manic sweaty face of Jonas, chased her through the fields. They always caught her and then cut her apart, ecstatic breathing echoing in her mind. The shadowy pain remained after she bolted awake, lingering in cramping muscles and unmarked skin.

Just as Laila began to think they were going the wrong way, Stefen spotted a coiling vine growing under the dense boughs of a great tree. It was black, like the night void when no other heavenly bodies lit the sky. Laila had never seen such a colour in nature before and marvelled at the glossy black leaves.

'Don't touch it,' Stefen said. 'Most things in the Valley of the Oracle's Eye are venomous.'

'Are you sure you can get us there?' Ano said, shifting his weight.

'Normally this is where I turn around,' Stefen said. 'If we just keep walking, the landscape will guide us. Though it will be dangerous in ways that are unfamiliar to us.'

'We should be more cautious now,' Ano said, gripping his spear. 'Pay attention. Watch your backs. I will take the rear.'

'Why?' Laila said.

'Because I have the feeling that the beasts out here do not attack from the front,' Ano said with a sardonic smile.

Laila shivered. The shadows seemed even deeper and more threatening than before. As they moved eastwards, the land grew bleak. The trees shrank, their limbs struggling upwards. Blood-red leaves coated the earth, filled with worms that slithered alarmingly under Laila's bare feet. Above them, the Lamp grew fat and orange as if seen through a veil of ashes. Animals became quiet and unnatural, with deep black coats, bloated white eyes and long spidery limbs. The world of Ghyran changed, tainted by whatever miasma leaked from the Oracle's Eye.

They trudged onwards until the Lamp suddenly winked out and darkness fell, a blackness so complete that it hurt the eyes. Laila stifled a scream. The night had never come on so fast back at Varna, not even in the depths of winter. A clammy chill rushed in, cutting through their clothes. The sort of cold that would slowly kill if allowed to.

'Light,' Ano hissed. 'Now.'

Leaves rustled under foot as Ano shifted around.

The shadows watched them. This she knew. She felt their gaze lingering on the skin. Something whispered past her and she flinched. Shadows touched her hands, coiled around her legs and brushed her cheeks, light as cobwebs. She stayed still, even as a scream threatened to escape her throat.

Instead, she focused, her ears straining. The whisper of cloth, a soft grunt, a light rattle of stone. Something fell into the leaves. Stone clacked against stone. Sparks flared, stinging her eyes. Then the crackle of fire. The hiss of retreating things.

'Hold this,' Stefen said, handing her the torch before putting an arrow to the string of his bow.

'Where is Ano?' she said, looking around.

Their hearts hammering, standing in the little circle of light surrounded by blackness, they realised that their best fighter was gone without a struggle. How could he have not made a sound? Neither dared to call for the man. Laila crept to the edge of the light, as if she were looking over the side of a boat into a dark sea.

'Ano, say something,' she hissed, then her toes brushed something heavy and wooden.

Ano's spear lay where he had dropped it. There was nothing else. Not a drop of blood, nor a shred of cloth. Not even the leaves were disturbed. With a start, she looked up, expecting some beast but there was nothing but blackness.

'Don't make a sound,' Stefen said, then turned his back to the light and walked out a few paces. Unblinking alien eyes peered from the gloom, disappearing and then reappearing somewhere else. He raised his bow, drew and waited. Then he loosed and something hissed in pain out in the darkness. That he could see anything amazed her.

'We should move, that's not the only thing out here,' Stefen whispered. 'We may be in some creature's territory and it will leave us alone once we're gone. At least that's what I hope.'

Some might have called her and Stefen cowards for not looking for Ano. However, death came quickly or sometimes not fast enough. He was already lost and she would not risk her own life for a corpse.

Laila nodded jerkily, shaking from the fear and cold. She picked up the heavy spear though there was no way she could wield the thing. The idea of fighting was not comforting: more than likely she would die. Still, better that than simply giving up. They moved on, searching for shelter of some sort.

Laila wrapped her cloak about herself. She had thought the greatest danger was the fiends waiting outside Varna; once past them, she imagined that the venture would go smoothly. Guilt crept over her. This journey was her idea. Ano would not have been out here if they had not gone. But what choice did they have, given what they knew?

They needed an army, and if Ano had died to give them that, then his death was not in vain. Yet if the darkness could take Ano, what hope did they have of reaching the valley?

Eventually, the pair found a small ditch within which they took shelter, building a roof of branches over the top and then a fire to stave off the chill. Laila did not sleep, every noise emphasised by the unnatural darkness. The rustling of her clothes, every small cough, even her breathing seemed loud enough that all the world heard.

Dawn came on weak and cold, the air thick with grey vapours. They helped themselves to some beans and bread, then moved on. The earth became hard and stony, the trees shrivelled and the undergrowth thickened with pale white plants that shrank back when touched.

'We're definitely moving down,' Stefen said.

Grey hills rose on either side, shrouded in mist. Laila felt she was walking into a prison that she could not escape. Yet, her nightmares whipped her on. What dangers compared to what the fiends promised?

They walked on and then the rocky earth gave way to a smooth stone street, like the ancients had made before the Plague Times. Tall statues of women loomed on either side. But their proportions were strange, too tall and thin as if they had been stretched out. They wore scandalously little clothing and brandished swords as they silently charged towards an unseen enemy. Laila shuddered at their screaming faces and wild hair. The place seemed abandoned, yet every eye followed them as they passed.

Ahead of them, impossibly tall towers hove out of the mists, clawing up towards the heavens like a clutch of brambles. Laila had never seen anything so vast made by the hands of mortals. Set in the side of the nearest was a huge set of doors that stood open, guarded by another pair of stone warrior women. From over the doors, an idol with a screaming face watched them, grasping a downturned sword in one hand and something small and dripping in the other.

'Maybe this was not the best idea,' Stefen said. 'We should not be here. This place is not for us.'

She found herself nodding in agreement.

'We can't,' she said, more to herself than him.

'That statue is holding a heart in its fist,' he said, drawing an arrow from his quiver.

Laila paced around on the threshold, her fists balled up, trying to summon up her courage. One part of her wanted to yell at him for strengthening her fears, while another part wanted to leave and never return.

'I know what they will do,' she said, her voice shaking. 'I can't let that happen to me or anyone else. This place is terrifying, but not as bad as being in that hole, knowing what they do.'

She looked at the black opening and steeled herself. With a deep breath, Stefen stepped forwards.

'No, not you. Just her,' a hoarse man's voice floated to them out of the darkness.

They both froze like rabbits caught out by a fox.

'And no weapons in this holy place,' the voice said.

Laila swallowed. Reluctantly, she handed the spear to Stefen and then stepped over the threshold. A stifling silence enveloped her and when she looked back, the outside world was hazy and dark. Stefen was little more than an ink blot on a sheet of paper. Pale blue torches guttered, merely enhancing the deep darkness that settled in every corner. The ceiling loomed far above her, arched and covered in sharp, jagged runes. It made the old temple at Varna seem like a hovel.

'Go on,' the voice said.

She caught sight of a gaunt face in the dark, the eyes two black pits. Then it vanished into the gloom.

What kind of place was this? How could a darkness this deep exist? And was this one man all there was? No place this grand stood empty and unprotected. Yet the silence was so deep, and the place so empty. What if this was merely another grandiose ruin?

As she walked deeper, her eyes started to pull phantasms out of the black air, leering faces, flying serpents and skeletal men riding gangling horses.

A glutinous bubbling sound caught her attention and she moved towards it. As she walked closer, the air grew thick with incense and a sweet, coppery stench like cooking blood sausage. A strange altar revealed itself – at least, she thought that it was an altar. Two flights of stairs wound their way up to a vast cauldron held by a statue of a straining man. Steam rose from within the huge vessel. Looming over it was the same idol she had seen above the door. Yet this one was covered in thick red enamel, burnished gold and glittering gems. Its eyes burned crimson and seemed to follow her with predatory focus.

Something stirred in the cauldron, fluid sloshing over the side. A great coil rose, like a leviathan breaking the surface of the sea. Then a small green snake crept over the side, black tongue flicking. She cocked her head, puzzled. Another serpent and then another slipped over, peering at her with unnerving, single-minded interest.

Laila took a step backwards. Why would anyone put a snake colony in a cauldron? And what else was in it? Instinct rattled through her, the overwhelming need to run. There was a predator in here, one large enough to kill her.

Then a bright light leapt to life from her left, stinging her eyes. A woman's voice, deep and rough with wisdom, spoke softly. Whatever was in the cauldron settled back like a dragon lulled to sleep.

'I would come towards the light, young one,' the voice said. 'My sister is not friendly to the curious.'

Laila blocked the light with her hand and stepped towards it, feeling her way with her toes. She stumbled when her feet touched earth and a soft fragrant wind sighed through her curls. With watery eyes, she looked around at an outdoor garden, the surrounding walls gleaming like black glass.

All the plantings, neatly laid out in vivid clusters, were venomous: Strikeweed, Neolinem and Grave-eye. And those were just the ones she recognised. Other plants and trees whispered in the wind, dark and spiky or pallid and ghostly. Even the grass under her feet had a purple cast to it. Above her, the Lamp was shrouded, though still brighter than the blackness within the temple.

In the centre of the garden stood the most beautiful woman she had ever seen. Now Laila understood why they were called the Fair Ones.

The woman resembled a human being only loosely. Long and

thin as a blade, she moved with an airy grace, like a great cat. Her pointed ears peeked through her black hair and her skin was dark as a doe's eyes, without blemish or scar. A jewelled leather cloak hung off her slim shoulders and underneath she was nearly nude, though Laila doubted she felt any shame in it. Two strange blades hung from her hips, more like torture instruments than weapons of war. Yet it was her face that was the most unnerving. While her expression was gentle, it was at odds with her sharp black eyes and thin, cruel lips.

Next to the aelf was an elaborately carved table, upon which rested a stone bowl etched with sharp runes and the familiar idol in miniature.

'We have not seen one of your kind in many years,' she said, her accent hissing through the human words.

'Generations, ma'am,' Laila said, her voice scratchy with nerves. 'I am Laila. I represent the village of Varna.'

The woman's eyes narrowed and her smile deepened. No human expression, that. It was like seeing a sicklecat smile.

'I always forget how short-lived you humans are,' she said. 'So, Laila of Varna, do you know who we are or have even your legends forgotten us?'

Laila opened her mouth but then realised that she could not in fact answer the question. Certainly not to this woman's satisfaction.

'Only in the vaguest terms,' she said. 'We know that when the great enemy comes, you will fight for us.'

'For a price,' the woman said, with a tremor in her voice as if she were trying to repress some strong emotion. 'Let us move beyond simple legends, shall we? My name is Cesse, and this is a temple of the Khelt Nar, a sisterhood devoted to the defeat of Chaos under Khaine's holy guidance.'

'So you are a holy order?' Laila said warily.

'Precisely,' Cesse said, her voice bright with fervour. 'We are dedicated to our faith and that is enough.'

'And if you operate on faith, what is this price then?' Laila said, sensing something was off.

'The price is that of blood. Blood buys blood,' Cesse said, drawing a dagger from her belt.

Laila took a step back.

'Please, I will not kill you,' Cesse said, flicking her hand dismissively. 'You have a need of our skills. You need us to kill your enemy. What is this enemy?'

'They worship… um… they worship…' Laila started, then she took a breath and looked up at the sky. 'The Needful One. The Beckoning Prince.' Yet Cesse looked at her, one thin brow arched in confusion. '*Slaanesh,*' she mumbled finally, looking at her feet.

Heat crept into her face at her blasphemy, at speaking that abominable name. She looked up and recoiled. Cesse stared at her, every muscle standing like a cord under her skin. Seemingly unaware, the woman slowly drove her blade deep into the table, the wood creaking. The pleasant mask was gone, leaving a hate that shivered through the aelf's limbs and etched her face into a scowl of furious cruelty.

'Hear my words, human. We will not rest until your dread enemy is slain,' she snarled, her voice a terrible rasp. 'We will kill them without mercy. None of them can be allowed to live.'

Laila fought the urge to run, holding herself still as Cesse wrenched the dagger from the table. Seeing Laila's expression, Cesse's eyes narrowed in suspicion as if sensing some weakness.

'Do you not want them all dead?' Cesse said, her black eyes feverish.

'Yes, of course I do,' Laila stammered.

Cesse smiled. 'Oh, I see. To be as ignorant as you are now. You do not know what they do. You do not know the thing that lurks in the darkness and eats at their souls.'

Cesse's focus turned towards some inner turmoil, her eyes dark and dull. A profound hate flickered there, a self-loathing that was all-consuming and burned eternally. A shame that ever boiled, a pain that never eased, a hurt that never healed. What caused it, Laila could not guess. However, she did not want to be around when that storm of emotion turned outwards.

'You will kill them for blood?' Laila prompted. Now that she said it out loud, it seemed insane. What would a holy order want with blood? What was the significance?

Cesse tossed her head, her black hair shimmering, coming back to the present.

'Of course, that has always been the agreement,' Cesse said. 'And what is blood compared to the tortures that await you if you do nothing?' Cesse leaned across the table. 'Trust me when I say, the agonies and slow death that you envision are only the beginning. It is not just the body that they devour.'

'Whose blood is it?' Laila said.

'Yours, I assume,' Cesse said. 'Who else's?'

Laila blushed. It seemed easy enough.

'Why?'

'All of creation moves at the beating of a heart. All things from the strongest godbeast to the stars themselves. Nothing can be outside it. The heart and the blood it moves are the most sacred of things.'

Laila nodded. 'I agree on behalf of Varna. You will kill the raiders in return for blood.'

'Excellent, now we can begin,' Cesse said, gesturing that Laila should stand opposite her at the table. Then she began to chant, her words like the rattling of swords and spears. The aelven woman sliced the dagger across her palm without even flinching, as if she had done this many times before. Blood leaked into the bowl. Then she crooked a long finger at Laila.

Yet Laila hesitated. Then she shook herself. What was a little cut compared to what those creatures did to their victims? She thrust out a hand. Cesse took it, her skin feverish, and then quickly slashed open Laila's palm. It burned like hot iron and Laila tried to jerk away, but Cesse held her fast until her blood fell into the bowl. At last Cesse released her, still chanting.

Now the blood began to seethe, filling the air with coppery smoke. Shadows crept among the shrubs and flowers. Cesse's voice rose to a shout, darkness seeping around her body like a serpent. Then she clapped her hands together, the sound like thunder. Laila stepped back towards the door. The air became dark, vile and oozing, catching in her throat and lungs, crawling over her skin like spiders. Cesse's eyes were pits of the blackest spite, her hands dripping blood and gloom.

'It is done,' Cesse said. 'You will have our blades, our magic and above all our hate. All is yours for blood yet spilled. Now go, this place is no longer for you!'

Laila did not need to be told. She fled, the shadows hurtling after her. As she burst through the hall, something hissed and roiled up on that dread altar. Laila ran on, things catching and plucking at her clothes and hair. She bolted under that fearsome archway out into the sickly light.

'Stefen,' she yelled, slowing her breakneck pace only slightly. 'We're done. We need to go!'

He was not there. Only the spear, a broken arrow and an ominous spatter of blood remained.

'Stefen!' she screamed, looking around frantically.

The shadows boiled out of the temple, hissing like vipers.

Laila ran as fast as she could. Like any nightmare, it could not catch her if she did not look back at whatever it was that snarled and snapped at her heels. She reached the edge of the forest and hurled herself through the trees without pausing. The seething shadows grew distant and then retreated as if the brilliance of Ghyran was not to their liking.

Once she was certain that she had left the creatures far behind, she dropped to her knees and wept. Never had she imagined that Stefen would perish. She had always thought that it would be her, that Stefen would be the one to carry back the news of their success. After all, she was just another farmer and he was a hunter that went out in the wider world.

Why had she lived while he had not? As if in answer, the cut in her palm leaped to life, stinging like an envenomed lesion. The wound seeped a clear fluid, and the skin surrounding it was a sickly grey. She tore a strip of cloth from her frayed tunic and tied it around the torn flesh.

This done, Laila set off towards home, tormented at night by nightmares and pain, and driven on by terrors of fiends and predators during the day. Sometimes, out of the corner of her eye, she glimpsed thin pale men on dark horses slipping through the shadows. She wondered if she was going mad.

It was twilight on the third day when she came within sight of Varna, long shadows reaching across the fields. A familiar sickly-sweet smell tickled her senses. Had she been too late? Was that grim bargain all for nothing?

Exhausted fear leaped through her and she pelted out across the fields of red-tinged grain. She half expected some terrible shriek or that shrill tone to echo from the trees, but there was nothing.

The gate was already closed when she reached it. She banged on the wood and called out for someone to have mercy and open it, though she knew that they should not. They would leave her out here to survive the night as best she could before opening that door.

Then the gate creaked, opening just enough to let her in. She rushed through the gap and crashed into something solid.

'Laila,' Hadlen said, slowing her down. 'Where have you been? Where is Stefen?'

One of the other warriors took off, running towards the great hall, shouting that she had returned.

She shook her head and told Hadlen what had occurred in a soft voice. Yet, she found herself obscuring details, even as the story spilled out. She lingered instead on Stefen, on his skills, on his calm. As she finished, she noticed a commotion coming towards her.

Uma. Of all the people in Varna, the last person she wanted to see was Uma. Laila had no stomach for the crone's displeasure after everything that she had seen.

'You were forbidden from doing this, Laila,' Uma snapped as she shuffled up to them.

'What would you rather have happen?' Laila said. 'That we just sit waiting to be slaughtered by the worst that this world has to offer? By those beasts. You know what they were going to do to us.'

Laila glanced around. To her surprise, some of the others crowded around rumbled in agreement. Still, many clearly sided with Uma, their faces set hard as stone.

'You know not what you have done,' Uma said. 'Time will tell. The legends say to be cautious of the Fair Ones. Who knows what they will do in the end.'

'They are going to kill all those fiends for us,' Laila snapped, jabbing a finger in the old woman's direction. 'We might learn that we don't have to be so afraid any more.'

It was an empty thing, grasping at surety in the face of Uma's doubts. It was as if the old woman were plucking Laila's own secret worries from her head, when Laila desperately wanted the bargain to work out. Uma had not seen Jonas' body or heard his last wheezing breath. Sometimes the lesser evil was all that remained.

'I doubt that,' Uma said, turning away from her. 'There is always something to fear.'

Uma shuffled away, her back bent more than Laila remembered. Her supporters went with her, scowling.

Exhausted, Laila excused herself when the others pressed in with urgent questions. She stumbled into her house and hurled herself into bed. Yet her nightmares continued, dreams of shadows chasing her through endless halls while the aelves' bloody-handed god loomed over her with burning eyes. Sometimes, Ano and Stefen were with her and they were always devoured by whatever beast ran in the shadows.

As Laila returned to the familiar rhythm of her old life, she remembered the bargain with ever greater unease. She was missing something. But what? Cesse was sinister certainly, but had given her word in front of her god. While that god was no Alarielle, he was still a deity that had rules that were binding. So why did it feel like something had gone horribly wrong?

The days turned into a week and then two, autumn cooled and the rains started in earnest. Fear of famine set in; their stores were lean as much of the harvest had rotted in the fields. Stefen and Ano's funeral came and went, bleak and routine like all the others before it. Normalcy never returned. The cut in her hand would not heal; instead it constantly broke open and bled, the skin ashen and dry. Likewise, the vivid nightmares also continued, an unending torment.

Her neighbours treated her differently, either greeting her with cool politeness or pointedly avoiding her, making holy signs as they did so. Rumours that she was cursed began to circulate. Never had she felt as alone as she did now, surrounded by familiar faces, none of whom trusted her as they had.

Then late one night, a high musical tone sounded through Laila's dreams, reverberating through her bones. Dazed, she opened her eyes as another call went out, louder than the last. Laila clamped her hands over her ears as the sound pierced her skull like a butcher's pick. The horn-blower was real; worse, it was out in the fields. The fiends were outside the walls.

The cut began to itch, then to throb. She clutched her hand tight and felt warm blood. She stripped off the soaked bandage and searched for another. As she looked, another horn call went out, different than the first. Brassy and eerie, it shivered up the spine and set the heart racing. Then there was a high, keening howl.

The Fair Ones had come.

She wrapped her hand and glanced at her bolthole. Disgust at her fears and nightmares rose. She had to see the creatures die. Maybe then she would be free from the monsters that stalked her dreams and the memories of her husband's death. The Fair Ones had promised to kill them all, why not see them fulfil that promise?

She paused. The sounds from the battle filtered through to her, high ululating screams, roars of elation and the metallic bang of weapons meeting. It was almost musical in its own way, rising and falling by some rhythm that she could not discern.

Even as the pain crept up her arm like venom, she stepped outside and looked up at the cloudy sky. No, not clouds. Shadows. They weaved through the sky as though they were living things, tinting the Cinder Disc into a colour like heart's blood.

She climbed the wall to where Hadlen and a couple of warriors stood and looked out with them.

The scene was grim.

Out amongst the rotten grain, a great jewelled chariot lay crumpled like a dead beetle. Clustered about the wreck was a group of heavily armoured men, if one could call them such, bunched up with weapons turned outwards. At the centre was a tall, lithe creature with an elaborate helm, shouting in a silvery voice. All about them, shadowy women probed at the raiders' defence, thin spears piercing through hardened armour, others tearing at shields with hooked blades. A final, bloody last stand.

Something flew out of the trees on the wings of a drake and circled above the battle. Then it dived down into the heart of the raiders like a hawk. The defensive knot broke apart, revealing a flickering dance between the Chaos leader and a monstrous winged aelf. Blows lashed between them and, for a moment, it looked as though they were equal. Then the aelf skewered the leader through his jewelled breastplate, ending the beast's life.

The winged woman was not the only monster. Other aelves with the bodies of serpents weaved among strange crystalline statues that glittered in the half-light, frozen in mid-flight. Still other warrior women flickered after their fleeing enemies, snaring them with barbed whips or lopping off limbs with long daggers. The crack of breaking bones, the chanting of women and the screams of dying things drifted out from beyond the trees. A strange fire burned out there, throwing up dense, ruddy mist. The stench of blood was so thick on the wind that it gummed in the eyes and throat.

Never had Laila imagined that their defence would be so ugly. Yet did those creatures not deserve it? Did evil deserve evil? Yes, they did. Maybe now, Jonas would no longer haunt her dreams with his screams and pleading.

As they looked on, a shadow walked down the road. It was Cesse. Below them, she stood, strong and cold. A bloody sickle gleamed in one of the aelf's hands, while in the other was that magnificent crested helm. No, not a helm, a head in a helm. She lifted up the gruesome trophy, blood dripping from the severed neck.

'We thank you for this glorious slaughter, which we have carried out in your name,' Cesse said, her voice quivering with a cruel elation. 'This creature will trouble you no more. Now, whose blood shall it be?'

'What? I gave you what you wanted,' Laila said. 'I gave you my blood.'

Cesse blinked and dropped the head into the dirt. All the other aelves stopped and looked towards the village as one. The shadows paused in the sky as if frozen and then seeped downwards like black snow. Out in the forest, something rumbled and that dread altar rolled forwards of its own volition out of the trees, the cauldron the source of that terrible smoke. Around it slithered some terrible thing, a vast serpent.

'It pains me that your kind are so forgetful,' Cesse said, a hint of amusement in her voice as if she were revealing the punchline of a joke. 'You spoke for all, therefore you are all. Your blood stands for your village's obligation to us. Do not worry. We will not take the strong from among you, only the weakest from each household. The ones that you will not miss. Given the state of your harvest, you would not be able to feed them anyway. In time, you will be grateful for the lack of useless mouths. Just as it was before.'

'She cannot be serious,' Hadlen said. 'Laila, you could not have agreed to this.'

'I didn't,' Laila stammered. 'That was not what we agreed to.' She leaned over the wall. 'I gave you blood.'

'No, you sealed the agreement with your blood,' Cesse said. 'A few drops is not enough. Did you really think it was?'

Laila frantically searched her memory for some misstep, some loophole, something. Then a single moment leaped out at her.

For blood yet spilled.

It had been right there in front of her face. She had thought that the phrase referred to the enemy. But no, it had been her own people. That could not be right. She looked at the others, who glared at her with the frightened anger of those dragged into a situation not of their making. She had to fix this.

'The whole point of this was so that the defenceless would live,'

Laila said. 'If we could have done it ourselves, we would not have needed you.'

Cesse cocked her head, her sharp brows furrowing. 'I do not understand your motive. We have laws. We do not move our forces on behalf of the weak without payment in blood. The weak must be culled from the strong so that the strong may continue unburdened. If you do not give, we will take what we are owed, no more, no less.'

Cesse did not – no, she could not – understand. She wasn't human. It was inevitable now. Dozens were going to die because of Laila's naïveté, her idiocy. There was now nothing that she could do. There never had been. Someone was always going to kill them; she had merely chosen a different foe.

'You are like the fiends, like a reflection of the Lamp in a lake,' Laila said.

Cesse's face twisted into a depthless fury that no human could know. All the self-loathing and hurt turned outwards. She leaped into the air with a shriek, her cloak falling away, wings like those of a great dragon snapping free. The monstrous aelf crashed into Laila, slamming her off the wall. Laila experienced a long moment of weightlessness before she hit the ground, the breath blasting from her body. Breathless and throbbing with pain, she lay there.

Shadows flitted past her, the gate groaned open and the aelves shrieked in. They bolted right for the hall and the villagers scattered like startled birds from a nest, fleeing in terror. It mattered not, they died all the same: the infirm, the aged, the injured and the unlucky.

Cesse crouched nearby, a fleshy tail flicking, her wings loose over her back, watching the slaughter.

'Please understand, this is not purposeless or merciless,' Cesse said, calm as if the screams mattered to her not at all. 'We build a better world. One that is strong enough to stand against not only the destruction of the flesh but also the entropy of the soul. Illusions like justice and fairness allow weakness to fester. Killing the weak is merciful to the strong.'

Laila pressed herself onto an elbow, still trying to suck in a breath. Pain flared in her palm and then was gone as if it had never been. She looked down. A thin scar was all that remained of the wound.

'The bargain is complete,' Cesse said, straightening up. 'Now you are strong and will survive.'

Cesse leaped into the sky, her wings hitting the air. In the space of a breath, she was gone. They were all gone as if they had never been. Light washed over Varna as the shadows lifted, revealing a village of sorrow and corpses, of wailing and death, of curses and recrimination.

And Laila wept.

A TITHE OF BONE

Michael R Fletcher

A single ox-fat tallow candle lit the room with a flickering yellow light. It stunk like burning hair.

The Chaos lord Markash, Champion of Tzeentch, paced the confines of his chambers, the floorboards groaning beneath him with each step. At eight feet tall, clad in monstrous plate armour, jagged barbs of razored steel jutting at every angle, he towered over the sitting scribe, Palfuss. Wisps of black flame flickered about the armour, guttering and surging. Palfuss had heard that they changed colour based on Markash's mood, but in the year he'd followed the colossal warrior, he'd never seen anything other than deepest sable.

Each inhalation rumbled like an iron forge, each exhalation twisting the air before the lord's closed helm with its heat. Palfuss had never seen the man – if that's what he still was – without his armour, and was well prepared to believe he slept in it. If he slept at all. Curls of gritty smoke leaked from the joints. He was once told that Markash lit campfires by breathing on the wood.

At the time Palfuss had laughed. Now, sitting in the great Champion's presence, nothing was funny.

'Destiny,' Markash said, his voice the deep, bone-rattling bass of an avalanche, the crunch of dry snow beneath an elephant's foot.

Scritch, scritch – the sound of a sharpened quill on parchment as the scribe wrote the single word and hurried to describe the voice.

'Tzeentch, the Raven God,' said the Champion. 'The Changer of Ways. The Architect of Fate. Chaos solely for the sake of chaos. Beautiful, seething potential, free of shackles. Lord of destiny, god of change. *My* god. He is always different, ever-shifting, never the same twice. To see him is to lose yourself to the glory of madness. He is the unpredictable dance of flame, the crash of ocean waves. They call him ruinous.'

Scritch, scritch, scritch.

'The philosophers say,' the Chaos lord continued, sunken eyes of red fire glaring out from within the cavernous depths of his helm, 'that destiny is nothing more than an idea, that it has no basis in reality.'

Scritch, scritch, scritch.

'Delusion, they call it.' The bloody eyes blazed bright as an armoured hand curled into a massive fist.

Markash laughed, or maybe grunted in scorn. Palfuss couldn't tell. Was the Champion even capable of such human emotion?

'The philosophers are wrong,' said the lord. 'It *is* real. Tzeentch *makes* it real. He decides. He shapes. He destroys.' He gestured to where his sword, Ktchaynik, a daemon-bound blade too heavy for a mortal man to lift, rested against the wall. Ktchaynik breathed violence, tainted the air with hunger. 'Is it not beautiful?' asked the Champion.

Palfuss dared say nothing.

'Iron purpose,' continued Markash, 'wrapped in destructive rage.' Slick smoke coiled like writhing snakes from his clenched

gauntlet. 'The feel of that blade, cleaving through flesh and bone…
that is the feel of destiny. Blood, painting the air…' he drew fine
traceries with his other hand, 'the look. Torn bodies, gutted oppo-
nents, the stench. The feel of Chaos working within your veins,
twisting you, writing the god's plan in your very soul. These things
are destiny.'

Palfuss wrote fast, dipping the quill in the ink pot when the
characters grew faint. A score of already sharpened feathers lay
ready and waiting. He would not miss a single syllable.

Markash focused on the scribe, and Palfuss felt his bladder
loosen.

'What do you think, scribe?'

A direct question. He had to answer. Swallowing, he stuttered,
gathering his thoughts. 'Philosophers speaking of destiny is like
deaf people discussing music, or the blind critiquing art. They are
ill-equipped to grasp the concept.'

Markash stopped pacing. Blazing orbs of fire dimmed to slit-
ted embers as the lord studied the scribe. 'Indeed.'

Palfuss felt the single word shake his ribs.

'Is one born with a destiny,' said Markash, offering no further
comment on the scribe's assertion, 'or is it something only the gods
can create? Is it nothing more than potential, something anyone
might possess, or is it rare, something special?'

Head down, Palfuss wrote fast.

Markash resumed pacing, the heavy planks of the floor bowing beneath his weight. 'One man is destined to be great while
another is destined to be a farmer. Yet does destiny – one not
derived from the gods – care about scale? Can one be destined
to step in a puddle or stub a toe?'

Unsure if the Champion joked or asked a valid question, the
scribe remained silent.

'You've heard of Ammerhan,' said Markash.

Palfuss nodded without looking up, quill *scritch-scritching* against the dry parchment. Ammerhan, a legend among Tzeentch's Champions, came this way two years ago. With an army at his back, he'd been commanded to conquer Knazziir, drive out Nagash's influence. He hadn't been heard from since.

'He was a great man,' said Markash. 'I would have said he had a great destiny, a god-granted destiny.' The Chaos lord almost sounded wistful, as if remembering a better time. 'He taught me to fight. He carved the weakness of humanity from me, cut holes in my soul and filled them with the eternal glory of Chaos.' The Champion glanced at the scribe. 'Was it Ammerhan's destiny to die out here on the edge of Nagash's domain?' He grunted a deep laugh. 'It matters not. It is my destiny to succeed where my teacher failed.'

Palfuss wrote, capturing every word, throwing in occasional descriptors when the lord paused.

'Nagash thinks death is everything,' continued Markash, ember eyes scanning the room as if searching. 'He believes all things end in death, and that this means his triumph is inevitable. He's a fool. His very nature – his dependency on necromancy – blinds him to the reality. Death is nothing more than another aspect of change. And Chaos is change personified, the gorgeous manifestation of impermanence. Not everything dies. Gods are proof of that. But even gods change. In the end, there can be only Chaos.'

Approaching Ktchaynik, Markash reached out a massive fist to grip the pommel. Hefting the blade, he examined the daemonic runes inscribed there, tracing them with the armoured fingers of the other hand. Sparks arced between sword and man, leaving purple slashes across Palfuss' vision. The scribe had heard that a thousand souls had been sacrificed to bind that daemon. The stench of burnt meat and sulphur filled the room.

'It is,' the Champion mused, 'an interesting conundrum. No

matter what destiny is – outside force, something built by strength of character, or sheerest delusion – in the end it means nothing.' He sheathed the daemonic sword, and Palfuss' ears popped as the pressure suddenly changed in the room. 'Ammerhan had a destiny and yet he is gone. And so destiny, like all things, answers to change. Chaos is everything!'

Nodding, the scribe scribbled the last few words and waited, pen poised, for the lord to continue.

Markash stood silent, motionless like a statue, smoke snaking from his armour in sinuous coils.

The scribe wondered if he'd been forgotten. Sweat dripped from his brow and stung his eyes. His lips tasted of salt when he licked them nervously. Had he been dismissed? Should he leave? But he hardly dared breathe, much less rise and remove himself from the Champion's presence.

'As a boy,' Markash finally said, voice barely a whisper, the raw scrape of granite on granite, 'I dreamed of holding a sword. As a young warrior I dreamed of being a Chaos knight. As a Chaos knight I dreamed of being Tzeentch's greatest Champion. And now I dream of–'

Someone banged on the door, interrupting him. 'Something odd, my lord,' came a voice from the hall. Palfuss recognised it as Stayn Lishik, the highest ranked Chaos knight in Markash's retinue.

The ember eyes blazed bright as if fed a gust of fresh air from a forge bellows.

Palfuss darted a look at the sole window in Markash's quarters. Darkness. Morning was still hours away.

'Odd?' rumbled the Champion.

'The dead have come, my lord.'

Palfuss blinked. That was hardly odd. The corpses returned every week as if begging for punishment. Out beyond the walls of Knazziir, this reeking dung heap of a city Markash had conquered in a single evening of glorious war, great heaping piles of bones swarmed with crows and fat flies. Sometimes the men would leave one of the animated dead semi-functional and then bury it in corpses, taking bets on if and when it would manage to struggle free.

You had to pass the time out here on the frontier somehow, Palfuss mused, and it seemed harmless enough fun.

Markash nodded and his eyes returned to their usual smouldering burn. 'Then we'll kill them again. Re-kill them.' He turned on Palfuss. 'What do you call it when you kill something that's already dead?'

'Uh...' offered Palfuss. 'Destroy?'

The Champion studied the scribe, and Palfuss swallowed a lump the size of those bulbous toads you found out in the swamps. The voice beyond the door saved him.

'My lord, these aren't normal dead.'

'Are they any better with words than my scribe?'

'Actually,' said Stayn Lishik, 'yes, they are.'

Markash strolled to the wall so he might see these 'odd' corpses. Stayn Lishik followed a step behind, his plate armour clanging and squeaking where Markash moved in perfect silence.

There was, Palfuss saw, something in Stayn's eyes – a soul-deep anger. He hurried to keep up.

Markash cut through the courtyard by the city gate. Over one hundred slaves to darkness gathered there, checking arms and armour with the grim confidence of hardened veterans. No cowards here. Over and over, through countless wars and campaigns, the Champion's followers had proven themselves among the very best Chaos had to offer. Under his leadership, these warriors had cut their way through ten thousand dead in the last month.

Palfuss checked the horizon and saw no hint of morning. Hours from dawn, and already the damp air stank of sweat and leather, oil and steel. Another hot one, no doubt. The muted clank of iron echoed off stone walls. Out here he couldn't write, but made note of everything, every sound and smell committed to memory.

For the last year the scribe had followed Tzeentch's Champion, chronicling his exploits. He did his best not to wonder what happened to the woman he had replaced. There were rumours. Torn apart by ravenous corpses, limbs ripped free and brandished like prized trophies. Eyes plucked forth by some twisted dead thing that immediately popped them in its own gaping sockets, as if one might harvest the living for parts.

Shaking the thought off, Palfuss recalled how some had – quietly, and never when the Champion was within earshot – called Markash crazy when he announced that he would take Knazziir, claim it in the name of Chaos. It's too close to Nagash's domain, they said. He'll never hold it. You'll die there, they told the young scribe.

Palfuss had shrugged. If that was what it cost to be this close to greatness, to get the chance to chronicle even a brief moment of the Champion's life, he would gladly pay it.

Not only had Markash taken Knazziir in a single night, putting the city's rulers to the sword and bringing the shining beauty of Chaos to these broken peasants, he'd also held it for a month since.

Not a week after that first bloody night, a corpse, unusual for its expensive finery, strode towards the city. Terrified, the newly appointed town-master, some fat slob stinking of the weird food they ate here, claimed it was a collector coming for bones. Or something. The Knazziiri spoke a strange dialect. Palfuss spoke the language, but not well.

'What kind of bones?' he'd asked the town-master.

The answer had something to do with soup. The scribe had done his best to explain it to Markash, who'd grunted, uncaring.

Either way, it hardly mattered. Talast, the Champion's pet sorcerer, burned Nagash's undead servant to ash before it reached the gate, and everyone had gone back to killing and otherwise spreading Chaos.

'Where is Talast?' Markash demanded.

'Busy, my lord,' said Stayn Lishik, darting a glance at Palfuss.

The sorcerer often imbibed huge quantities of mind-altering substances as he clawed at the fabric of reality in his search for power. Even Markash would hesitate to interrupt one of his experiments.

Reaching the top of the wall, Palfuss stepped forward to peer through the murky night air. There, at the gate, stood a host of dead. But where most of Nagash's creatures were shambling ruins, these were thick and strong, composed of clean bone. Leaning forward, he squinted down at them. A legion of warriors stood with foul swords clutched in fists of raw sinew. Broad shouldered, bones thicker than Palfuss' thighs, they wore armour that looked suspiciously like a mockery of Markash's Chaos plate.

Having seen more than his share of corpses, Palfuss had a pretty good idea what a man looked like if you peeled away the flesh and muscle. And this wasn't it. Their twisted bones were knotted as if someone had skilfully knitted them together. Like ivy. The joints were wrong, too. Bulbous. Insectile, almost. He locked the scene in his memory so he might later capture it.

Behind the warriors stood a monster constructed of bone and steel, all melted together like some metallic corpse-beetle. Long scythes, polished bright, had been melded to its misshapen limbs. It had too many damned legs, each one backward-jointed, like a spider or a chicken twisted inside out. Flesh hung in raw ropes, glistening as if they'd been pulled from a fresh corpse. The thing bore huge baskets upon its spine and ribcage, strapped in place with coils of hardened cartilage. Black crows and fat green flies swarmed the baskets. Every now and then something wet and pink stabbed out from somewhere within the torso of the creature to snatch a bird from the air. Flesh and feathers were stripped away in a heartbeat, the dripping bones either tossed into one of the baskets or thrown aside. More dead things lurked behind the beasts, hidden in the dark.

'What in the name of–'

Markash raised a gauntlet, interrupting his chronicler.

The Champion stared down at the dead, and they stared back up at him, empty eye sockets like holes in the world. There were clearly several types here. Some stood with strange weapons held at the ready, while others, apparently unarmed, scanned the gathered living as if judging their value. A cancerous grey-green smoke writhed around a pair whose faces, stretched as if in horror, bore only smooth bone where their mouths should have been.

All this the scribe memorised.

For once the fat flies were silent. No *scree, scree* echoed through the night.

For one mad moment Palfuss was glad he was up here and they were down there, with a good thick wall in between. He shook it off. There was nothing Markash couldn't kill. He was Tzeentch's Champion, a man of destiny.

The tallest of the dead stepped forward, a gaunt corpse of indeterminate sex, cloaked in robes of bright jade at odds with its pale bone. It bowed low, arms crossed, damned near curtseying. A spark of sickly green fire glowed from deep within its orbits.

'We have come,' it said, voice like the grave, damp like putrescent flesh sloughing from a bog-drowned corpse. 'To collect.'

'Collect?' Markash called down, sounding more curious than anything.

'Bones,' said the corpse, drawing the word out, spectral eyes turning up to examine those on the wall.

That putrid town-master had said something about this. Why would the dead want soup bones? Did they eat? Were these the chefs for some deranged necromancer?

Markash waved at the piles of shattered bones littering the killing field beyond the wall. Countless thousands of dead had been broken there. Splayed ribcages, denuded of flesh, clawed at the sky like reaching fingers spread in supplication. 'Bones.' He almost sounded amused, though Palfuss had trouble attributing such a human emotion to the Champion.

The corpse in green hesitated, and the scribe could have sworn its brow, skin chafed to bleached bone, wrinkled.

'For the Tithe,' it said, bowing again, as if in apology, though it was the sort of overly polite apology of someone embarrassed *for* you. '*Fresh* bones,' it said. 'Bones for the Tithe.' Long fingers, those of an artist, drew graceful circles as if the thing sought to sketch its intent in the air.

Palfuss stole a glance at Markash, wondering what he was thinking.

'Stayn,' said the Champion. 'You have the city until I return.'

A dark greed crossed the knight's scarred features, gone before the scribe was sure he hadn't imagined it.

'Open the gates,' commanded Markash. 'We'll destroy them all.'

Again the corpse bowed, though this time seemingly in thanks, as if it somehow were getting exactly what it wanted. 'Good bones,' it said, studying Markash. 'Good bones.'

Trooping back down the steps, his Chosen warriors falling in as he passed, Markash marched to the front gate, waving at the gatekeeper.

Stayn remained behind, standing on the wall, gazing down upon the dead with a measuring look.

Wood and iron rose as Markash approached. The rattling clank of metal, the groan of damp wood, and the grunt of men cranking the wheel.

Palfuss slowed as he approached the gate, hesitant to leave Knazziir's safety.

'Come,' Markash called over his shoulder. 'Bear witness.'

Swallowing his fear, the scribe hurried to follow Markash and his retinue of warriors into the night, attention darting as he tried to drink in every detail. No time for fear, he would witness, as commanded.

The dead waited. They hadn't moved, hadn't shifted.

The jade-clad corpse nodded, a slight tilt of barren skull. 'Many bones. Such a fine Tithe.'

Markash drew Ktchaynik and it sung a keening note of triumphant rage. Reality, savaged by its mad will, warped about the blade, giving it a twisted corkscrew appearance. For a score of strides around the Champion the grass died, turning brown as the colour leached away, individual blades curling into dry husks. The ever-present greasy green flies wobbled in mid-flight and then spiralled to the ground, their tiny souls snuffed by the ravenous blade.

The dead flinched back.

Black fire crawled across the Champion's armour, smoke leaking from every joint, bright eyes like blazing rubies piercing the damp heat of the night.

Destiny.

'As a Chaos knight,' Markash had said, 'I dreamed of being Tzeentch's greatest Champion. And now I dream of–'

What could such a man dream? Palfuss reeled at the thought.

Did Markash dream of attaining daemonhood? Did he dream of leading Tzeentch's own dark legions?

One of the larger corpses strode forward, raising its sword in greeting and challenge. No one else moved. Not the dead. Not Markash's loyal troops.

MICHAEL R FLETCHER

Palfuss took it all in. The squelch of heavy steps on damp ground. The rot-stench of piled corpses. The furnace roar of the Champion's breath.

Markash nodded greeting, one warrior acknowledging another.

The two closed, circling. They feinted, testing the range and their opponent's reactions. The dead warrior moved with grace and precision. Light on its feet, like a dancer – perfect balance, utter calm.

Were it smarter, Palfuss thought, it would have feigned the jerky, shambling awkwardness so typical of the dead, and then surprised the Champion.

When it finally lunged, foul sword stabbing forward, the scribe was still startled by its speed. The damned thing *had* been moving slower than it was capable of.

Batting aside the attack, Markash cut the thing down, cleaving it from shoulder to hip so it fell in two directions.

The gaunt jade-clad corpse who had first addressed them straightened, that green fire deep in its gaping sockets surging brighter in what probably passed for surprise among the dead.

'Destroy them,' commanded Markash.

Roaring their battle cries, his warriors charged the fell host.

The corpse in the green retreated into the illusory safety of the dead warriors, and Markash cut down another corpse, Ktchaynik screaming its glee.

It was a slaughter. But not the slaughter Palfuss anticipated.

The lumbering beetle-like beast scythed through Markash's Chosen, massive blades cutting men and women in half. Limbs like seething tongues flicked from within its carapace to catch the dying as they fell. The bodies were spun, some still screaming, as the writhing tongue denuded them of flesh, shucked the bones like an angry child with a head of corn, and tossed the raw and dripping remains into the baskets on its back.

Destiny.

Palfuss knew a moment of nervous almost-fear.

'No,' he whispered.

Markash, servant of Tzeentch, Architect of Fate, had a destiny. The dead did not. So the scribe told himself, as he stood rooted, bearing mute witness, unable to move.

Screaming voices rang out from behind, and Palfuss turned to see the gate fall back into place, leaving Markash and his handful of elite warriors trapped outside.

Stayn Lishik grinned triumphantly down from atop the wall.

The sounds of battle echoed from within the city, and the scribe knew they'd been betrayed. The Champion would deal harshly with Stayn once these dead were destroyed. His screams would last weeks.

Markash faced a new opponent, a bipedal, four-armed creature with an oddly misshapen skull. The uppermost arms bore long swords of heavy steel as if they were the lightest feathers. The two lower arms worked in tandem to wield a monstrous barbed spear of hooked bone. The creature wore a carved bone mask displaying the savage grin of a warrior.

He knew that face. But from where?

So teasingly familiar, but so out of place.

Markash fought, spinning and slashing, stabbing and hacking. Moments of purest ballet pierced with savage flurries of vicious violence. The thing hooked Markash's sword with two of its blades, dragging Ktchaynik aside so the spear could lash out in a disembowelling thrust. Twisting, he avoided the worst of it, but still felt a line of agony tear his side. It had slashed through his Chaos plate as if it were nothing.

It pressed the attack, feinting and stabbing, sword carving wicked patterns of death – somehow strangely familiar – into the screaming air.

The grinning mask.

Those familiar patterns, learned as a youth, drilled into Markash over and over by–

Everything clicked into place.

Ammerhan, the Champion who trained him all those years ago.

Again Ammerhan tried to entrap Markash's blade, but this time the Champion was ready. It had been years since the two had duelled, and Markash had learned a lot in that time. Twisting Ktchaynik, he sent one of his opponent's swords spinning away, and lopped off that arm.

Grind, *click*!

The thing's lumpen skull rotated and Markash faced a new mask, this one depicting the face of an aelven warrior caught in mid-scream. When it attacked, sword shearing through daemon plate as if it were the softest cotton, and opening a long wound in Markash's thigh, the Champion realised he faced an entirely new opponent.

He fought.

All around his warriors fell, cut down, stripped of flesh. Some bones were collected, thrown into the baskets. Others were tossed contemptuously aside, unworthy. The roar of battle became screams of terror, became the wet sucking of flesh pulled from bone, became the harsh sound of Markash's own breath, the snarls of his pain and the ringing of steel on steel.

In moments he was alone, surrounded by the dead. Only his scribe stood, unmolested, ignored by the dead, witnessing.

Hundreds of faces watched from the Knazziir rampart, Stayn Lishik at their centre.

This couldn't be Markash's destiny.

Parrying a low spear thrust, hidden by a stabbing feint at his eyes from the remaining sword, Markash hacked the head of the spear from the bone shaft.

Grind, *click*!

He faced a new warrior, a mask bearing the chiselled jaw and smug superiority of a Sigmarite Champion, with an entirely new set of skills.

Markash laughed.

'I don't care how many faces you have, I'll best them all!' he roared at the thing.

It stabbed him in the gut with the tattered end of the spear, splintered bone tearing his insides, and he shattered another arm at the shoulder.

Flesh was nothing.

Blood was nothing.

Markash was naught but war.

Grind, *click*!

Another mask, this one a cold-eyed woman. The remains of the spear spun in its hands and all of a sudden Markash faced a weapon master skilled with a quarterstaff. It lashed out, crushing his daemonic plate, leaving deep dents. The sword followed, wielded in a weird fencing style with fanciful flourishes like high-court calligraphy.

Markash fought, parrying attacks, staggering back as the thing followed, weapons spinning and flashing, writing notes of pain in his flesh. He bled from a score of wounds, left a trail of blood.

The dead watched, waiting, making no move to aid their four-faced warrior.

One last face.

This was not his destiny. He was Markash! Someday he would join the ranks of Tzeentch's greatest daemon princes!

The staff spun, cracked him in the ribs, snapping one like a dry twig; spun again, and shattered his left knee.

Markash roared again and staggered, half kneeling in the bloody muck. Each breath felt like a hot knife driven into his lungs.

The four-faced corpse stabbed at Markash, and he caught the sword in his armoured fist. Twisting the blade aside, he felt it slice through his gauntlet, severing his fingers – a terrible moment when the last of the strength in his grip failed. He drove his sword into the fourth and final face.

It stood transfixed, shivers running the length of its body.

'Destiny,' Markash said, tearing Ktchaynik free.

The dead warrior collapsed.

Still kneeling, Markash raised his sword in victory, spitting blood and bits of broken teeth at the watching dead.

The corpse in jade robes stepped forward. It now bore a viciously curved scythe. 'Good Tithe.'

Then it sliced Markash's head off with one smooth and effortless swing.

His skull bounced once in the soft earth and then came to rest, one cheek against the cool muck. His fingers lay littered before his eyes like pale, undercooked sausages thrown into a midden pit. How long had it been since he'd seen his own flesh?

Markash blinked at them, mouth moving. Somewhere out of sight, something geysered blood into the air and then toppled over with a wheezing, wet groan.

His body.

Blood puddled about his face, filling one nostril and turning his vision red.

Blink.

One of the dead noticed the scribe, strode to the unmoving man, and cut him down. A snaking tongue flicked from the monstrous beetle-like beast, collected the dead scribe and began shucking him of flesh.

Destiny.

No.

* * *

Movement.

Swinging movement.

They're carrying me, thought some deep part of Markash, some dwindling spark.

Opening his eyes, he saw that long limb-tongue or whatever the hells it was flick out and curl around the ankle of his headless corpse. He watched it drag his body closer, lift and rotate it about, peeling away the armour.

Where was his sword? He wanted it.

Armour gone, it stripped meat from bone.

Unable to escape into death, held at this teetering precipice between life and unlife, Markash was forced to bear witness to the harvesting of his loyal followers. He watched gaunt dead sift through the grizzly remains, choosing bones by some alien metric he couldn't understand. He saw men and women ground into meal, a sodden porridge stained pale pink, and be remade.

Some were used to repair damaged undead warriors, applied like a salve, or twisted into limbs to replace those lost in battle. Some were whole new constructions, towering beasts, giant corpses built from the bones of scores of fallen men and women.

And all the while Stayn Lishik watched from atop the wall.

Markash saw his own bones reduced to sludge and shaped to create new limbs for the four-faced warrior he'd battled. Hanging there, vision swaying slightly as whatever held him by the hair moved, he bore mute witness as they hacked Ammerhan's mask from the once-again-whole warrior and tossed it aside.

Finally, they remembered him and he was brought closer. A great hand gripped his face, twisting it until the bone of his skull gave with a crack. Beyond pain, Markash finally lost himself to the nothing.

The Bonereapers of Ossia.

Markash knew them now.

The Mortisan Boneshapers, the master craftsmen who took the raw material collected by the Gothizzar Harvesters, those huge beetle-like beasts, and crafted weapons and warriors. The Mortisan Soulreapers, the mouthless corpses, harvesting the animus of Ossia's enemies. The Mortisan Soulmasons, deciding what purpose to bend each soul towards, veritable surgeons.

They carved apart the idea of Markash and found much of use. A lesser soul they would have turned to meal – soul porridge – much as they did the bones, and rewritten; painting something new by combining the harvested ideas of many. In Markash they found something special, something rare and worth keeping: his blind faith in himself, in his abilities, and in his god.

Iron loyalty.

Faith is but an idea, and the Soulreaper cut the idea of Tzeentch from Markash, left the shape of it intact, a hole in who he was. It then filled that hole with a new idea: Nagash.

It also found another, stranger idea at the core of the man. Destiny.

Standing over the Necropolis Stalker it intended to meld Markash with, the Soulmason considered its options.

It could remove this foreign idea, but it wasn't sure what to replace it with. Leave a hole in the idea that is a man, and the man cannot be complete. That, in part, was the strength of the Ossiarch Bonereapers. Though made from many souls and the bones of dozens, each Mortek Guard was still a complete idea. It knew what it was, where it belonged. It knew its loyalties and its purpose. But the shape of this idea, this *destiny*, was unlike any the Soulmason had previously seen. What could fit such a hole? Digging, it found the idea itself was created to fill an even deeper hole, a wound from far back in Markash's past.

In the end, it left the idea. It was too integral to that which made Markash useful. To such an ancient soul as the Soulmason, the concept of destiny was pathetic, the kind of self-deceit the living were so fond of. There was only one fate. In the end, all things would share in it.

Death and destiny.

The two words meant the same thing in the Ossiarch tongue.

Markash woke.

Strong. Stronger than he'd ever been. Faster too. Unencumbered by sad flesh and muscle, scrubbed clean of life.

A warrior. Battle writ bone-deep.

He shared the body with three other mighty souls, united in purpose, existing in perfect tandem. One carved bone mask of four. Though he couldn't see it, he knew the face it showed.

And there, a dim spark in the background, lurked Palfuss, the scribe. Harvested, his bones and soul had been deemed worthy of use. Fragments of him existed within the living corpse.

I witness, said that spark, still clinging to purpose. *I still witness*.

A Necropolis Stalker, one of the Ossiarch Empire's elite shock troops, Markash understood his own place and purpose. To war against the enemies of Nagash. Bring them death.

It was a glorious purpose!

As a Stalker, he was a near-invincible warrior. Each mask was that of a champion, a peerless warrior. Face a style you could not defeat, or one better countered by one of the other masks, and a different soul stepped forward, took charge.

That– No. That was wrong. Someone else in charge?

Why hesitation? asked Ghaanmast, who was once the First Sword of an empire long since fallen to dust. *We have task*.

And they did. Collect the Bone Tithe. Nothing could stop them. The Tithe was everything, a holy command from Nagash himself.

And yet…

Ossiarch Bonereapers moved around him, each bent to its task.

They marched to collect the Tithe, tireless bone legs moving at a pace no mortal could match for long. The Mortek Guard advanced in flawless formation – individuals, yet capable of fighting with impossibly unified precision. The Gothizzar Harvesters followed behind, their tongues lashing out to ensnare birds and any wild-life that dared approach too close. Most of the bones were useless, tested and tossed aside.

Markash remembered this land. Hot and damp. Leather rotting so fast the armourers could barely keep up. Anything not magi-cal or daemon-bound rusted. Insects everywhere. Biting, stinging, sucking, pestering. Those fat green flies swarming everything, get-ting in your eyes and mouth, tasting like rot. They still swarmed, but as a thing of clean bone he was of little interest. When they did land, he noticed nothing. No tickling of little legs at the cor-ners of his lips and eyes. If it was hot or damp, he felt none of it. Not comfortable, just… existing. Such things were distractions the dead did without. Purity of purpose.

The warrior most suited to defeat an opponent takes the fore, said Markash.

He sensed the confusion of the others. There was nothing to discuss. They were one, servants of Nagash. They moved as one. Even though they took turns being in control, they fought as one. They would do whatever was needed, their individual desires unimportant.

And yet…

Something niggled, an idea. The memory of a memory.

Markash knew his old life, understood what he had been, why he had fought. No need to carve away the past and all its valu-able lessons when you can carve the idea. He remembered his loyalty to Tzeentch and cared nothing. He remembered wanting to be Tzeentch's greatest Champion, hungering to rise through the ranks, to achieve true immortality.

All pointless nothings.

Ossiarch he was forever. If he fell warring for Nagash, he'd either be rebuilt, repaired or replaced. Such was the way of things, and the way brooked no questions.

That hunger was gone.

And yet...

I defeated you, said Markash. *I fought all of you, and I won.*

Ammerhan was gone, cut away, replaced by Markash.

Destiny.

Death.

To the Ossiarch, they meant the same thing.

He remembered thinking about destiny. He would have laughed, if such things mattered.

I found it.

Found what? asked Ghaanmast.

My destiny. I am the best of us. I defeated you all, and any opponent who could defeat me would beat any of you even faster.

They were one, served one purpose. They could not argue because he was correct. He had defeated them all. He was the best of them.

Markash knew then he would always be the mask that faced the world. It could be no other way. It was his destiny. He would rise until he commanded the Necropolis Stalkers. He would be the greatest of the Bonereapers. He would bring down the false gods, the pretenders. He would lay their flayed corpses at Nagash's feet.

I still witness. Palfuss. A thin thought at the edge of existence.

It was, decided Markash, only right. The scribe would see it all, remember it all.

Today he would collect the Tithe as was his sacred duty. But this was only the beginning.

Heaped mounds of pale bone littered the ground. Glistening flies buzzed around the shreds of stubborn meat. The crows, having learned their lesson, wise in the way of death, fled when they saw the Bonereapers.

The nearest Mortisan Boneshaper sniffed at a pile as they passed. 'Inferior,' it said. 'Unworthy of the Tithe.'

Ahead, Markash recognised the fortified wall of Knazziir.

He remembered dying here. Somewhere, his fingers lay in the mud. How long ago had that been? As a flensed soul, he had no concept of time. Was it days? Years? Longer? Studying his hand, he saw it was complete. His, but not his. Familiar and different.

Faces atop the wall looked down. Damp with sweat, fear and disgust. He grunted an almost-laugh. This wall was nothing. The Ossiarch would tear it down, collect the Tithe by force if necessary.

What funny? asked Ghaanmast.

I died here. He didn't care if the First Sword understood.

Atop the wall, a man pushed to the front of the crowd. He wore the plate of a Chaos knight, daemon-bound, wrapped in foul sorcery. Poking over his shoulder, the pommel of a great-sword. Ktchaynik, Markash's sword.

Markash recognised the man. Stayn Lishik, the Chaos knight who'd betrayed him.

'We have no bones for you!' called Stayn.

'Decent bones,' said the Mortisan Boneshaper at Markash's side. 'Acceptable Tithe.'

The Soulmason, dressed in robes of jade, the green smoke of harvested souls swirling about its ankles, nodded. 'The soul is flawed, but usable in some lesser beast.'

The Soulmason opened its mouth to call out to the mortals above, but Markash stepped forward, interrupting it.

'We have come to collect a Tithe of Bone.'

A rustle of confusion swept through the Ossiarch host. The highest ranked of the Bonereapers, a Soulmason was never interrupted.

Stayn laughed. 'Open the gate! Let us see these foul dead back to their graves.'

Markash, amused that this fool would repeat his own foolish mistake, awaited the warrior's arrival.

When Stayn strode from the city, sword drawn, teeth bared in a confident grin, Markash met him in single combat. And took his head.

Blood and screaming.

Churned mud and spilled guts.

The Gothizzar Harvester, that enormous armoured beetle, chopped through the wood-and-iron gate with a monstrous scythe, and the dead poured in.

The wall was nothing.

The knights of Chaos were nothing.

The Ossiarch had come to collect their Tithe.

Death and destiny.

One word.

And Markash had found his.

BENEATH THE RUST

Graeme Lyon

The Rusted Wastes stretched out before Borri Kraglan.

The name was appropriate. The landscape was the colour of rusted iron, something that made Borri instinctively uneasy. No self-respecting duardin, particularly a Kharadron of Barak-Nar, would ever allow rust to mar any of their equipment. The reason for the colouring had become clear as soon as Borri and her fellow endrinriggers had started to excavate the area.

In the realm of Chamon, metal infused everything in one way or another. There were forests of silver trees that shed golden leaves in the autumn. There were oceans of mercury and molten lead. Further out from the realmsphere's core, where the magic was wilder and the laws of nature more malleable, great creatures of living metal stalked the landscape like technological marvels of a bygone age. Here, in the Rusted Wastes, the ground itself was like solid iron.

That was what made their discovery all the more perplexing.

'You had no idea this was here?' she asked her companion, looking up at the impassive mask he wore.

'None,' replied Ferram Drakesbane, shrugging. As he did, the great golden frames on his back stretched, and wings of the purest light briefly flared, haloing his armoured form. 'I would not have thought the daemon-worshippers capable of such a feat.'

'We can't be sure it was them,' said Borri. 'It was fairly deep beneath what used to be their camp.'

The Kharadron Overlords had retrofitted a drill cannon from one of their sky-vessels into an excavation tool – much to the consternation of the ship's captain – and used it to begin digging in the area the Stormcast Eternals of the Sigmarite Brotherhood wished to build their Stormkeep. To their surprise, they had been beaten to it. Beneath a deep layer of ironearth, they had broken through into an existing tunnel, nearly losing the drill and its operator in the process.

'How far down does it go?' Drakesbane asked.

'Far,' Borri replied. We sent some arkanaut privateers down to see if it was a limited space. They say the tunnels reach a huge shaft that goes down a considerable way.'

'Can it be filled? Or covered and ignored?'

'Probably…' Borri mused. 'We can certainly cap it and cover it, and work the foundations on top of what's there. But my worry would be *why* it's there. Did the tribe who lived here build these tunnels? Were they there already? And in either case, they must have a purpose. They're definitely artificial. You can see from the–'

The Knight-Venator held up a hand. 'I trust your skills, my friend. Now I must trust to mine. I will lead an expedition into the tunnels and discover their purpose.'

'Aye, that sounds like a plan,' Borri said. 'Will ye be needing a wee hand down there? I mean, you Stormcasts are good in a fight and all, but you don't know tunnels like a duardin.'

'Have you spent much time in tunnels, my friend?' Drakesbane asked, amusement behind his words. 'I wouldn't think there are many in the wide skies of the realms.'

'Aye, well, maybe we're not quite as used to tunnels as some of our distant kin, but still. A duardin is a duardin.'

Drakesbane nodded slowly. 'And what payment will your people expect for this service, Borri Kraglan?'

Borri cleared her throat. Under the dictates of the Kharadron Code, she could, and almost certainly should, ask for remuneration for such a potentially perilous task. The Admirals' Council back on Barak-Nar had been very clear that this entire expedition was about forging relations with the Sigmarite Brotherhood. Still, it never hurt to push for a little more.

The Stormcast Eternals had appeared across the Mortal Realms in recent decades, bringing the wrath of the God-King Sigmar to those who followed the Dark Gods of Chaos. They had fought the Realmgate Wars, dealing the so-called Everchosen a blow that had sent him back to his infernal fortress to lick his wounds. And more importantly, they had opened near-infinite new avenues for trade, and resources that the Kharadron Overlords could exploit.

The Sigmarite Brotherhood had chosen to situate themselves here, on the shores of the Stratis Skull, where lines of power apparently converged. From here, the constellations of Azyr, the Celestial Realm, could be most clearly seen in the night sky. Drakesbane had explained that they were used for the divinations of the Stormcasts' Lord-Ordinators. They were going to be a new power in the region, and the Kharadron sky-port that allied most closely with them would reap great rewards. Barak-Nar had been quickest off the mark, offering resources and expertise to the Sigmarite Brotherhood in exchange for future favour – as well as a hefty retainer in precious substances. They had a reputation to maintain, after all.

'I think this would necessitate an amendment to the existing agreement,' she said at length. 'An extra twenty per cent on the payment should suffice. Besides, who knows what trouble you might get into down there?'

'This is a terrible idea,' grumbled Harek Steelfist for what Borri thought might be the hundredth time. The arkanaut captain was at the front of the group of Kharadron Overlords who had ventured into the tunnels. Winged Stormcast Eternals had offered to carry them down the long shaft, but Harek had refused, insisting that the arkanauts rapelled down. It had been a long and awkward journey, and combined with the perceived slight from the Prosecutors' well-meaning offer, he had been left even less happy than usual. His mood hadn't improved since. Even Mala, his life partner, hadn't been able to cheer him up, and that was rare.

Borri glanced at Mala, who floated alongside her, held aloft by the portable aether-endrin that all endrinriggers used. When they were performing their duties keeping sky-vessels in working order, the aether-endrins allowed the duardin to float around the ships, ensuring they could make repairs without having to dock at a sky-port. In battle, they allowed the Kharadrons to get above their enemies and strike with rivet guns and aethermatic saws. Harek had complained that the tunnels might get too tight for them, but Borri and Mala had argued that if that was the case, they would also be too tight for the Stormcast Eternals who accompanied them. Harek had grudgingly agreed to wait and see.

'Harek seems in an even worse mood than usual,' Borri said quietly.

Mala's face was hidden behind her helmet, but Borri was sure she was smiling as she replied. 'You'd think he'd be happy to get his privateers into action. He's spent the last month complaining this duty was too boring. He's never happy.'

She laughed, and Borri joined her. This was a familiar refrain. For as long as Mala and Harek had been together, Harek had always had something to grumble about. And yet the way he smiled when he looked at Mala showed that he really was happy. And he made Mala happy too. As her best friend, Borri appreciated that, though she did wish she could see more of her friend, outside of engagements like this one.

Harek's habitual grumpiness had its uses though. It came from a place of wariness, and that made him a good arkanaut captain. He kept his privateers ready for action – and that could be invaluable here. The tunnels so far had been deserted, but there was no guarantee they would remain that way.

'How could those blood-worshipping filth have dug all this?' Harek asked no one in particular, knocking his fist on the smooth wall of the tunnel, which stretched to five times the height of a duardin.

'They may not have,' answered Drakesbane. The Knight-Venator walked alongside Harek's arkanauts, his immense wings folded at his back and bow held loosely in one gauntlet. A large bird the colour of the night sky rested on one shoulder, its gaze fixed firmly ahead. His Prosecutors, a trio of Stormcast Eternals with a smaller wingspan and hammers, had ranged ahead to try and get a feel for the layout of the tunnels. 'This region was settled in the Age of Myth, before the coming of Chaos. The forebears of your own people excavated much of the lands around the Stratis Skull in search of minerals.'

'So these could be duardin-made?' Mala asked.

'That makes sense,' grunted Harek. 'Too sturdy to be dug by any men, let alone the daemon-lovers.'

Borri felt a surge of anger at Harek's casual dismissal of the work of men. While it was true that even the work of Sigmar's most skilled human smiths was no match for that of duardin, saying so in their company was impolite at best. The Kharadron Code was very clear that insulting employers wasn't a good idea, at least before payment had been made in full.

Borri's thoughts were interrupted by a flash of light from further along the tunnel. It was a Prosecutor flying towards them at speed.

'My lord Drakesbane,' the Stormcast said, her voice issuing from her mask with a metallic rasp. 'We have engaged enemy ahead. Bloodreavers, in great numbers.' She turned and flew back the way she had come.

Drakesbane turned to the duardin.

'I expected a handful,' he said thoughtfully. 'If they are here in numbers, there must be a reason.'

'I thought such savages would have stood and fought when we took their camp,' Harek grumbled. 'Maybe it's the cowards of the tribe.'

'Savage they may be, but I have rarely crossed blades with a cowardly servant of the Blood God,' Drakesbane said. 'There is more going on here.'

The Knight-Venator's wings spread and he took to the air, pulling an arrow of purest starlight from his quiver and nocking it to the bow. His star-eagle lifted off from his shoulder with a loud caw and sped in the direction from which the Prosecutor had come. Drakesbane followed, and Borri pushed her aether-endrin to maximum to keep up.

She heard the battle before she saw it. The unmistakable roar of bloodthirsty cannibals and the clash of blades on armour was drowned out only by the boom of thunder as Prosecutors hurled celestial hammers into their foes.

Borri rounded a corner to a scene of carnage. The tunnel was no wider here than elsewhere, and the press of unwashed bloodreaver bodies made it feel positively claustrophobic. Drakesbane had joined the Prosecutors in battle. He was moving fast, loosing arrows from his great bow with unerring accuracy. Each shot felled a Khorne worshipper, the star-forged missiles striking hearts or heads. Yet for each bloodreaver that was killed, another five seemed to take his place. Around him, Prosecutors hurled celestial hammers, each one hitting with the force of a meteorite before dissolving into celestial light, leaving only ruined bodies.

Though the tunnel was huge by duardin standards, the men stood tall enough to strike at the Stormcasts as they swooped overhead. So far, their sigmarite armour seemed proof against the crude axes and swords, but weight of numbers would bring the Prosecutors down like falling birds in time.

'Let's get stuck in,' Mala said with relish.

Borri looked back, another surge of irritation passing through her. Harek and his privateers were so slow.

'Aye. Let's go,' she said, activating her aethermatic saw and speeding towards the enemy. She dived straight into the closest and brought the saw down, carving messily through flesh and bone. The bloodreaver spasmed, the muscle reflex driving his axe into the arm of a comrade, who roared in pain and fury and lashed out at Borri. She tried to dodge the blow, but it came too fast. At the last second, Mala's saw blocked it with a resounding clang. She followed up with rapid-firing shots from her rivet gun, and the Khorne worshipper fell back. Mala swept forward and took the brute's head from his shoulders.

'Thanks,' Borri said, and Mala rounded on her.

'Watch yourself! Recklessness like that could get you killed,' she snapped.

Borri was taken aback. Mala had never spoken to her like that. The shock quickly turned to anger, but her reply was interrupted by a shout from behind.

'Arkanauts, form up!'

Harek had arrived. He ordered his warriors forward, and the privateers joined the fray.

It was brutal, bloody work. With the duardin wading into the thick of the enemy, Stormcast and endrinrigger alike had to be more careful where they placed their blows. The armour of the privateers was sturdy, but the sky-suits beneath, which simulated the rarefied atmosphere of Barak-Nar to which the Kharadron Overlords were adapted, could be easily pierced by a stray rivet or the impact of a celestial hammer.

Though it was absolutely normal for endrinriggers to have to be so careful when their fellow Kharadrons fought below them, Borri found the need to do so here profoundly irritating. She silently cursed Harek as she fired a stream of rivets past him, ruining the face of a bloodreaver who was finished by a blow from an arkanaut cutter moments later.

She pushed the resentment down and busied herself with killing Chaos worshippers.

One of the brutes came at her, an immense axe swinging at the globe of her aether-endrin. It deflected from the hardened metal, the blade notched, and Borri was rocked back by the force of the blow. She fired her rivet gun and the shots went wide, tearing through another bloodreaver, who was fighting one of the Stormcasts. Borri cursed as the barbarian in front of her roared and raised his weapon high to strike. She fired her rivet gun again, and this time found her mark. The rivets tore the human's face apart, leaving a lumpen mass of bloody flesh over a grinning skull. It took him long moments to realise that he was injured, and the axe came down. It sliced through armour and sky-suit and into Borri's shoulder. She dropped the rivet gun as pain coursed through her.

She lashed out instinctively with her saw and finished the bloodreaver, who fell with blood pulsing from a ragged wound in his chest.

'Give that to your god,' Borri muttered as she gingerly felt her shoulder. The wound wasn't deep – the armour had robbed the blow of most of its momentum. She moved her arm, testing the pain. She would live, and still be able to fight. She picked up her rivet gun and looked around.

She grudgingly admitted to herself that the privateers' arrival had helped to turn the tide. Though they still massively outnumbered the forces of Order, the bloodreavers had been forced to focus on the duardin in their midst instead of the celestial warriors above them. Finally, they were realising through whatever red mist clouded their perceptions that they couldn't win the fight, and started to fall back.

'Come on, let's follow and finish them!' Mala shouted furiously.

'Prosecutors, after them,' Drakesbane ordered, still firing arrow after arrow into the fleeing warriors, each one replaced in the quiver by Azyrite magic as soon as it was drawn. 'The rest of us will regroup here.'

His fellow Stormcasts followed his order, advancing after the bloodreavers until both were out of sight. Mala followed them, ignoring Harek's calls for her to stay with the group.

The Knight-Venator landed lightly, and Borri approached him.

'Why hold us here? We should support Mala. The more of us taking the fight to them, the better,' she snapped at him. He gazed at her, the stern visage of his mask impassive.

'The Prosecutors have the speed to harry them as far as is required. Neither you nor your privateer brethren can say the same. It was the logical choice.'

'Logic be damned! We want to finish the fight!' snarled Harek, who had joined them.

'Stay out of this,' Borri snapped. 'It's between me and Drakesbane.'

'You're not in command here, Kraglan,' Harek replied.

'No, I am,' Drakesbane said, his voice booming. 'And I would know where this animosity comes from.'

'It's coming from Kraglan here not knowing where her boundaries lie,' Harek said. 'In battle or in life.'

'Or maybe it's about Steelfist sticking his nose in where it's not wanted,' Borri shouted, fury surging through her.

'You feel great anger, Borri Kraglan?' asked Drakesbane levelly.

'Aye, I do. Can you blame me?'

'And you, Harek Steelfist?'

Harek turned and punched the tunnel wall, an answer in itself.

'There is something more at work here,' Drakesbane said. 'A malign influence working upon you all.' He turned and watched the privateers for a moment. Borri followed his gaze. Her fellow duardin were clearly as irritated as she was, restive and on the edge of brawling.

'You must fight the urge towards anger,' Drakesbane said, his voice loud and clear. Something in it washed over Borri, and she felt the haze of anger lift from her. 'This is some machination of our enemy. Their lord uses anger and fury as weapons as surely as his followers use axes and swords. Do not allow it to overwhelm you.'

'Th-thank you, Ferram,' Borri said, shame now flooding her to replace the rage. 'I can't believe I… Harek, I'm sorry.'

Harek simply glared at her and turned away.

The shame grew. It was true that Borri loved Mala. Perhaps more than she'd ever been willing to admit to herself, let alone say aloud. She cleared her throat.

'Why weren't you affected, Drakesbane?' she asked the Knight-Venator.

'The lord Sigmar plucked me from the realms, destroyed my mortal form and reforged my eternal soul into something better. With that comes protection from the works of the Dark Gods. It is a rare influence that will affect a Stormcast Eternal. Would that all servants of Order could say the same.'

'Think you're better than us, do you?' spat one of the privateers.

Borri turned on him. 'Shame on you, Kareg Half-fist,' she said. 'Control yourself!'

'Don't you speak to my warriors like that, Kraglan!' bellowed Harek. Suddenly he was in her face, his stylised face mask clashing against hers. 'They are mine to discipline.'

Anger rose again, and Borri snapped, 'Then actually discipline them!'

'Enough!' bellowed Drakesbane, and the red mist receded again.

Borri stepped away, taking deep breaths.

'We don't know what we'll face as we continue,' the Knight-Venator said. 'But there is a dark power at work in this place, and I doubt my Prosecutors and I can do so alone. We need you. All of you. Set aside these squabbles and work together, or whatever is at work here may be the undoing of us all.'

Chastened, Borri nodded, and looked into the tunnel before them as the Prosecutors returned, their great wings carrying them swiftly towards the party. It took Borri a moment to realise what was wrong. Harek voiced it first from where he stood against the far wall.

'Where's Mala?'

None of the Prosecutors had seen Mala taken, but it was the only explanation.

'She wouldn't have run off by herself,' Harek argued furiously. 'Even with this… whatever it is working on her, she's not stupid.'

Borri agreed, but the constant ache of irritation she felt towards Harek, and the anger she harboured towards herself for not ignoring Drakesbane and going with Mala, prevented her from saying so.

The Knight-Venator had counselled that they should continue. It was their best chance, he said, of finding Mala, as well as the source of the influence working upon the Kharadron Overlords. The tunnels took them steadily downwards. The further they went, the harder it became for Borri to let go of her anger.

'This influence must be fought,' said Drakesbane softly. 'It is the only way to save your friend.'

'That's easy for you to say. We don't all have mighty Sigmar's gifts to help us,' Borri said, venom in her voice.

'No, you don't,' Drakesbane said with irritating calm. 'Would that we had a Lord-Castellant here, to bring the light of Sigmar to you. As we do not, you shall have to simply try harder, Borri Kraglan.'

He moved on, leaving Borri at the back of the group, seething with misplaced rage. She followed quietly, trying to fight back the feelings.

They continued for some time, until the passageway came to an abrupt halt. Before them was a stretch of blank stone wall, as smooth and finely finished as any of the rest of the tunnels they had passed through.

'What's going on?' Borri said testily, floating over the throng of arkanauts and gently touching down next to Harek.

'A dead end,' Harek said through gritted teeth. 'Either we've come the wrong way or those lanky blood-drinkers back there were all that's to be found.'

'There is more,' said Drakesbane firmly. 'Something is working its influence on you. It must be found and eradicated.'

'How do we even know it's something else?' one of the arkanauts shouted. 'It could be you doing this to us!'

For a moment lightning seemed to flash behind the Knight-Venator's bone-white mask. The privateer drew back, muttering something that might have been an apology. Drakesbane turned back to Harek and Borri.

'My Prosecutors are sure that every other passageway is a dead end, and this is the true path. I trust their judgement. There must be a way through. If these tunnels were duardin-crafted, could there be some subtle enchantment or wonder of engineering hidden here?'

Borri moved towards the dead end and began studying it. She vaguely registered that having this to focus on made it easier to avoid the anger.

'There might be something here,' she said, tapping on the wall with the butt of her rivet gun. 'I'll need some time to survey it.'

Borri gave the wall a thorough examination, noting imperfections and irregularities. As she covered the whole thing, her heart sank. There was nothing that was obvious to her.

'If there is some hidden magic or mechanism here, we can't find it,' she said at length. 'Maybe if we had a specialist in ancient runic enchantments–'

'Well we don't,' said Harek angrily. He stomped forward and punched the wall in frustration. To Borri's astonishment, it began to move. With the sound of grinding rock, a section of the wall simply moved aside to reveal a short passage that widened out into a chamber.

'What did I do?' Harek asked, clearly as puzzled as Borri.

The duardin looked to Drakesbane, whose gaze was fixed on the newly revealed entrance.

'It responded to anger,' he said. 'This is troubling. The servants of the Blood God eschew sorcery, but their priests are capable of great craft, and their prayers to their god do not go unanswered, though the costs are high. There must be something of great value here. We need to be very careful, my friends.'

'We're past time for careful,' bellowed Harek. 'Privateers, move in!'

The arkanaut company came to order and marched in unison down the short corridor and into the chamber. Once more, Borri felt anger and contempt for the idiot her friend had chosen to spend her life with. How could he be so foolish as to rush in after what happened to Mala? For that matter, how had he been careless enough to let her rush off in the first place?

She followed the privateers in, not bothering to activate her aether-endrin. As she passed through the corridor and into the chamber beyond, she felt her anger increase. Harek would pay for everything. She would make sure of it.

Borri stepped inside and saw more carnage. The chamber was huge, the ceiling shrouded in darkness far above them. The walls here were different from the passageways they had navigated. The stone was dyed red, and marked with infernal runes that hurt her eyes and made her head swim. At the chamber's heart was a large altar. It was twice her height, and the runes that marked the walls were replicated on it, in patterns that made bile rise in her throat.

Atop the altar, unconscious, was Mala, and around it were the fresh corpses of half a dozen bloodreavers, killed by Harek and his privateers. The captain was finishing the last, his cutter embedded deep in the human's guts. He pulled it out and turned towards her.

'Help me get Mala down,' he said gruffly. Borri activated her endrin and floated to the altar, gently lifting Mala and laying her on the chamber's blood-slick floor.

Harek knelt beside his partner, looking worried. Borri felt anger flood her again.

'What were you doing, you fool?' she demanded. 'Drakesbane counsels caution and you march in here without so much as a thought for the safety of your warriors?'

'I told you before, Kraglan, my privateers are my business,' Harek growled. 'Keep your nose out of it, and out of my partnership while you're at it.'

'I would if I thought you were any good for her,' Borri said, giving in to the anger. 'All you've done is take her away from me.'

'Jealous wretch,' Harek said. 'I've had enough of you!'

The arkanaut captain raised himself and swung around, his cutter scything towards Borri. She ducked back just in time to avoid the blow, and activated her aether-endrin again, quickly rising out of reach of Harek's blows.

'You won't get away that easily,' he said, reaching for his pistol. Borri didn't give him the chance. She hurled her aethermatic saw at him. Harek ducked out of the way, his half-drawn pistol falling to the ground, and the saw continued past and struck the altar. The aether-powered blade embedded itself in the ancient stone near the base. Slowly, a great crack rose upwards from where it impacted, splitting the altar in two. The runes on it flared brightly, as if great energy were being released, then blinked out one by one. Slowly, the two great pieces of stone fell, and a piercing shriek emerged. Borri reeled back as images of anger and bloodshed, even more acute than before, flashed through her consciousness.

Humans in furs, bones woven into their hair and beards, beat one of their kind to death with crude wooden clubs. A dark-cloaked aelven assassin slipped between shadows and silently slit her target's throat. A woman walked in on two people entwined in lust and grabbed the nearest heavy object, beating them both to death as they screamed in terror and agony. In the midst of battle, a duardin with a flaming crest rising above his head swung an immense axe indiscriminately, cutting down friend and foe alike, lost to a blood-rage.

Each vision was more intense than the last, and with them came pain, as Borri experienced not only the violent anger of the perpetrators, but the pained deaths of their victims. Murderer and murdered, all at once. She screamed, rage and agony mixing into a potent brew that flowed through her, robbing her of anything beyond the increasingly violent scenes. It lasted an eternity, until she felt a hand grip the arm of her sky-suit and a voice piercing the haze.

'Fight it,' said Mala, and Borri opened her eyes. She was on the ground, her aether-endrin deactivated. Mala, now awake, knelt beside her, and beyond her, Borri saw a scene of carnage that was nearly the match for the visions that had assailed her.

Most of Harek's arkanauts were dead, their broken and bloodied remains littering the chamber. Those that remained, Harek among them, stood in a ragged line, battling something huge and nightmarish. It stood many times the height of the duardin, towering over even the Stormcast Eternals that circled it, hurling their celestial hammers. It was roughly the shape of a man, but wrong in every aspect. Its limbs were too long, the joints bending at unnatural angles, and its flesh was the colour of rich, arterial blood. It was clad in ornate armour, layered plates of brass marked with the same sigils that had adorned the altar and which covered the walls. The creature carried a great axe, its edges so infernally sharp that Borri thought it might be able to cut the very air.

'What… what is it?' she breathed, the sheer terror the beast instilled in her crowding out the anger and pain that had been her consciousness for what felt an eternity.

'A daemon in thrall to the god of blood,' intoned a voice from above her. She looked up to see Ferram Drakesbane firing shot after shot at the creature. All were on target, but most dispersed into light before hitting the daemon, as though it were protected by some invisible barrier. Those that reached it punched holes into armour, or penetrated flesh that re-knitted and healed in seconds. 'It manifested from the ruin of the altar. It is a creature of power, a prince among its vile brood. We must stand together,' Drakesbane continued. 'Are you fit to join us, Borri Kraglan?'

'I did this,' Borri said, the horror of her actions hitting home. 'I released it. I…'

'It wasn't your fault,' Mala said quickly. 'The thing we were feeling, it was this, getting in our heads, making us angry. It wanted us to fight, to destroy each other.'

'Mala Steelfist is correct,' Drakesbane said. 'But this has given us our chance for victory. Now that it has manifested, it can be defeated and sent back to the hells from which it came.'

Borri stood and checked her weapons. Her rivet gun was holstered by her side, but her saw... It was by the shattered remains of the altar.

'I'm with you,' she said.

She activated her aether-endrin again and rose into the air. Pulling her rivet gun, she spat white-hot projectiles into the daemon's chest. Like the Knight-Venator's arrows, most of them melted into nothingness before hitting home, but some got through and began to pock the thing's breastplate with holes. Mala rose up and joined her, their combined fire drawing the daemon's attention. It turned to them, and a sinister snarl crossed its bestial features. It turned, kicking an arkanaut privateer into a wall as it did, and began to cross the chamber towards the two endrinriggers. One of the Prosecutors flew in front of it, and the daemon lashed out with its axe, bisecting the winged warrior. The Stormcast Eternal vanished into a stream of light, which sped upwards and vanished with a crack of thunder.

The daemon advanced, and the two Kharadron split, each moving around it in a different direction, continuing to pepper it with rapid-firing rivets. It swung its axe towards Borri, who pulled back, the blade missing her by mere inches. The daemon turned towards her and swung high. She couldn't get out of the way quickly enough, and it caught her aether-endrin. Borri quickly pressed the release catch, and she fell to the ground, rolling away as the endrin exploded. The daemon reeled back, roaring with primeval fury. Borri curled into a ball as razor-sharp metal shards peppered the area, then pulled herself up and ran towards the altar, scooping up her abandoned aethermatic saw. Without the power from the aether-endrin, it was just a blade, but gripping it made her feel better.

As the daemon recovered, Borri took the chance to run towards Harek and his handful of remaining privateers.

'How do we kill it?' she asked, and Harek shook his head.

'I don't know,' he said irritably. 'We're barely scratching it. Even the Stormcasts aren't making a dent. The only thing that really hurt it was your endrin exploding.'

Borri looked up towards Mala, who was darting around in the air firing rivets at the daemon, the remaining two Prosecutors swooping about her, hurling their thunderous magical hammers.

'I have an idea,' Borri said. 'But it's desperate.' She didn't wait for Harek's response, but turned and ran towards the daemon. It was distracted by the warriors in the air, so she aimed low, slicing across its leg with her saw as she passed. It looked down, and swung its axe towards the floor, but it was a slow and obvious blow, and Borri dodged it with ease.

'Mala,' she shouted, 'come with me!'

Mala glanced over and flew down as the three Stormcast Eternals redoubled their efforts, hammers and arrows striking the daemon.

'What's happening?' Mala asked.

'We need to use your aether-endrin,' Borri said. 'Set it to overload, turn it into a bomb.'

Mala nodded and lowered herself to the ground. She released the aether-endrin and together they pulled it behind the much reduced line of arkanaut privateers.

'Buy us some time,' Mala said, and Harek nodded, ordering his remaining warriors forward to fire at the daemon with their arkanaut pistols.

Desperately, the pair of endrinriggers began to adjust the controls on the device, disabling venting valves and setting the power to beyond the safe maximum.

'How do we get it over there?' Mala asked.

'I'm taking it. I'll get up-close and make sure the daemon's as near as possible when it detonates.'

'How will you get away?'

Borri looked at her, and shook her head.

'No!' Mala said. 'There has to be another way.'

Borri grabbed the aether-endrin, which was starting to emit a high-pitched whine, and ran towards the daemon, shouldering her way past Harek.

'Watch what you're… Wait, what are you doing?' he asked.

'She's sacrificing herself to try and stop the damned thing,' Mala said.

'Stupid…' Harek growled and started forward. He grabbed Borri's shoulder and pulled her back. The aether-endrin fell from her arms and rolled towards the daemon.

'I thought you'd be happy to see me gone,' Borri said icily. 'That'll keep me out of your partnership.' Harek glared at her, saying nothing.

'We have to get the endrin to the daemon somehow,' Borri said.

'Allow me,' came a voice from behind her. She turned to see Drakesbane scooping up the aether-endrin. 'When I die,' he said, 'I will be reforged in Sigmaron. I will return, so my sacrifice will be little compared to yours.' He nodded to the duardin and took to the air, flying directly into the daemon. The endrin detonated, and Borri shielded her eyes from the blast. For a moment, everything went silent, the explosion so loud that it drowned out all noise. Then she heard a scream of absolute rage. Looking up, she saw the daemon still standing. Its armour had been torn to ragged strips, and its unnatural flesh wasn't much better, gaping holes revealing a brass mockery of a skeleton and thick cords of muscle where organs would be in a true living creature.

'Get it!' Harek bellowed, and all the duardin opened fire. The remaining Prosecutors did likewise. The daemon staggered forward under the onslaught, swinging its axe with wild abandon. Borri jumped back out of the way, but she saw that Harek wasn't going to be so lucky. The axe swung towards him, and horror filled Borri at what was about to happen.

That horror turned to abject grief as Mala pushed her partner out of the way, and the axe hit her. Its preternaturally sharp edge cut through armour, sky-suit and flesh, and Mala fell, split nearly in two. From the angle at which she lay, and the way she twitched, Borri knew that there was no saving her. She screamed in pain and fury, and on the edge of her perception she heard Harek doing the same. Unthinking of the consequences, she advanced, just as a celestial hammer from a Prosecutor struck the daemon in the leg.

The daemon fell, and Borri raised her aethermatic saw to impale it. Beside her, Harek did the same with his cutter. Both blades were driven deep into the daemon's chest as it fell onto them, and as they pierced what passed for its heart, it died.

Its bonds to reality cut, the daemon began to collapse in on itself, shrivelling into nothingness. Silence fell in the shrine. Borri turned to Harek, but he was already moving towards Mala. Towards what was no longer Mala.

He knelt beside her corpse and cradled it, great wracking sobs taking him. Borri knelt beside him and placed a hand on his shoulder. He pulled away violently.

'Don't touch me,' he said in a low voice. 'Don't you dare. She's dead. My partner, the mother of my children, is dead, and it's your fault.'

'My…' Borri didn't know what to say. The venom in Harek's voice shocked her. It was worse than it had been at the height of the daemonically induced rage.

'Blowing the thing up was your plan. You did this. If you hadn't, she'd still be alive.'

Borri found her voice, and her anger once more. 'We'd all be dead. It was the only way to hurt it. It would have killed us all.'

'I wish it had,' said Harek bitterly. 'At least then I wouldn't have to live without Mala.'

He turned and walked away, leaving the body of his partner, Borri's oldest and best friend, behind.

Borri remembered little of their return to the surface. The months that followed passed in a haze. True to his word, Ferram Drakesbane returned from beyond death, and he grieved with Borri and with Harek, though separately, for the arkanaut captain refused to be in Borri's presence where it wasn't entirely necessary.

Priests of Sigmar were brought from Azyr to cleanse the site of any lingering traces of the Khornate taint. With the foundations secure, construction of the Stormkeep continued. Borri buried herself in her work, crafting defences for the fortress that would keep it safe from the many threats that lurked in the Rusted Wastes.

As she worked, Borri considered her future. When this undertaking was complete, she decided, she would resign from the Endrineers. She would never again be able to walk the halls of the academy on Barak-Nar where she and Mala had learned their trade together without feeling the pain of loss. Her skills would be useful to any sky-vessel's captain seeking crew, and in time she could advance through the ranks to captain her own ship, and maybe even command her own fleet as an arkanaut admiral. She could travel, see the realms.

Perhaps, in time, she would travel far enough to escape her grief.

THE UNLAMENTED
ARCHPUSTULENT OF
CLAN MORBIDUS

David Guymer

'Graunch Festerbule is with us.'

Rattagan Borkris listened with an idle ear as a pair of skaven-slaves fussed over his cassock. His assistant, Underdeacon Makulitt Pus of the Presbyopic Wilt, was an unctuous rodent with teeth the colour of gold pried from Shyishan soil, black gums and a muzzle with one side drooping lower than the other, bestowing a permanent frown as though he were assessing the value of another skaven's organs. He was, as Borkris' keen sense of smell could confirm, much beloved of the Horned Rat. He stood with only a slight hunch, garbed in a long-sleeved black cassock with varicose piping. The rat servants busied themselves about their master.

Rattagan Borkris.

Malfeasant Superior of the Church of Gnawing Ruin.

Spiritual overseer to a million unworthy souls, twoscore lairs spread like a necrotic rash across the Realms of Metal and Death.

His robes were vestal white, as befit the lord of a great diocese of ruin, the emblems of the Great Corruptor and the one hundred and sixty-nine Verminlords that served that aspect of the skaven's schizophrenic deity covering the garment with gold stitching. Even the gnawholes around the trailing hem had been re-stitched with thread of so close a colour match that only the keenest of eyes amidst his dim-sighted race could have spotted the difference. It was raiment to bankrupt a warlord clan and make the eyes of a lesser priest water. It announced him as the unholiest of unholies, a high priest and lector of Clan Morbidus, and a skaven who commanded the ear and whiskers of the Horned Rat himself.

He stared through the warpstained windows of his high tower as a slave threw a tatty white cloak over his shoulders. Rain scratched at the glass. Green lightning and machine fire lit the horned belfries and gnawing spires of Blight City.

'Sequeous Rank is bought and bribed for,' said Makulitt. 'Milketan, Sithilis, Verukik – all have taken-snatched your offer. Ureik is under Festerbule's claw and will scratch, as he does. Perish and Wastrett are loyal to you.'

Borkris squeaked, unimpressed, as the ratservant moved in front of him to affix the collar buckle.

Loyalty, even amongst the pestilential ranks of the faithful, was not the same thing to the skaven that it was to other races. It meant that Rank, Perish, Wastrett and the rest had been bribed, threatened and cajoled for so long that they could no longer smell the distinction between their own self-interest and that of Borkris' coin purse. Their churches espoused a variation of the Withered Word that was no more at odds with his own than that extolled by the more excitable zealots in the farthest flung parishes of the Gnawing Ruin. But if he had a warp-token for every skaven that had snatched with both paws, tail crossed behind their back, then he would be rich enough to buy the high throne of Azyr, never mind the archpustulency of Clan Morbidus.

A second slave forced a jewelled mitre over his ears. He wriggled his brow until it sat properly.

'Go on.' Borkris' voice was a cultured squeak, blessed with a bubbling hoarseness that spoke of his high favour. He waited.

Makulitt remained painfully silent.

'Is that all?'

'Eight scratch-votes, your unholiness,' said Makulitt. 'Nine if you add-count your own.'

Borkris resisted the urge to turn and cuff him. To do so would have unsettled the teetering armature of arm rings and signets so painstakingly arrayed and forced the slaves to begin again. He was not one to fret over his property's inconvenience, but tardiness he would not tolerate. 'The Lyceum of Lectors numbers twenty-one. Fool-fool! A majority of twenty-one is eleven. With all my wealth you cannot bribe-buy two more scratch-votes?'

'Two times the backing of Hascrible, or of Dengue Cruor, your unholiness. Persuade one of them and the archpustulency is yours.'

The slave working on Borkris' collar nicked a dark red bubo on the underside of his muzzle with a claw. The slave gagged, swiping at the emitted flatus with his paw before going stiff and dropping dead at Borkris' footpaws.

Borkris sighed and fastened his own collar. He chose to take it as a positive omen. The Horned Rat scurried in nefarious ways.

As archpustulent he would be a claw's length from the primacy of Clan Morbidus. In time, perhaps, even a seat on the Council of Thirteen. A touch on the Black Pillar. A sup of the life-elixir. He preened as staccato lightning brought the warp-stained glass to life, a chiaroscuro of light green and dark, scenes from the First Withering as retold through the Withered Word. And after that? He would see out the Final Withering with his own half-blind eyes.

The thought of Dengue Cruor or, better yet, that bell-waving fanatic, Hascrible, elevating him to so lofty a standing at the Corruptor's right paw was a pleasing one.

'Is it yet known how Archpustulent Heerak Gungespittle died?'

'Not yet. Not yet,' said Makulitt. 'The sextons are still trying to determine which of the archpustulent's wounds was fatal. I do wonder why so many would want-crave so lofty and... *exposed* a position.'

Borkris gnawed thoughtfully on his tail before answering. 'Slave-thing.'

The second skavenslave scuttled around. His muzzle was inclined so far that, if not for the curvature of his spine and pronounced skaven hunch, he would almost have been looking backwards. He was naked apart from a grubby loincloth and a leather collar, his pelt lice-ridden and mangy, and pock-marked with scabs. Borkris closed his paw around the slave's bare throat. The creature's breath hiked, but he made no effort to resist. The abject's fear-musk brought saliva trickling through Borkris' fangs.

'This is why,' he said, and then he pushed.

The warpstained glass behind the slave shattered, the sound of raining shards immediately gobbled whole by the tumult and the hunger of Blight City's insane machinery. The capital of skavendom in the realms was a teeming metropolis of a billion souls, the true Eternal City, gnawing on the roots of Order from a cosmic plane neither truly within the Realms of Chaos nor a part of the great hierarchy of the Mortal Realms. The ungodly engines that had dragged the city to that limbic nether-realm continued to rumble on, belching waste magic into the air, triggering city-wide quakes and only *very* rarely causing the first and last of the realms' great cities to sink deeper into the dark strata of the universe. Over all that, Borkris still thought he could hear a faint squeal of terror falling further and further away before ending in a pathetic, hopelessly distant *smack*. Then again, it might just have been one of the Skryre clan assembly lines stalling.

'As archpustulent I get to push-shove whoever I want through whatever I like.'

'Who here can squeak-say of the Withered Word?' Hascrible, The First Claw Broken of the Scratching Ruin, sprayed the table that was his pulpit with spittle. 'There are those in this unwholesome covenant who do not know-smell the Word. I see around me the opulence and idolatry that abounds!'

He was speaking rhetorically, of course, as the Corruptor spake unto Grey Seer Salasqueek.

Id est – he was lying.

Hascrible was blind.

He had not been born to the Clan Pestilens, littered instead to a warlord clan of no significance, but the fever that had burned through his body and taken his sight had cracked his brain open for the Word of the Corruptor. That plague had been the prelude to an attack by Clan Morbidus and he, half dead though he was, had been taken by the plague monks and enslaved. In the spore mines of Sour Pit he had preached. To himself. To the breath ghost he left hanging in the cold air. To the *clang* his pick made on the rock. And then – because what else was there for a slave to do but listen? – to his fellow chattels. Hascrible had killed the slavemaster that had sought to silence the Word and had eaten him. After that his following in the mines had grown large enough to be considered a Congregation of Filth within the internecine hierarchies of the great clan.

It was not, though, recognition that he sought. No. Nor the validation of his former slavemasters. No! The crackling in his chest and the fiery maledictions of his joints were all the acclaim he required, for they were the gift of the Corruptor. He had no ambition of his own, but if his god wished for him the archpustulency – which he surely did, for why else would he bid this avatar of his will to pursue it? – then it would surely be done.

'You!' He pointed into the congregation at random. 'Squeak to me of the Withered Word! The rat so chosen hesitated, and Hascrible stabbed his claw elsewhere before he could find his voice. 'What of you? You! You!'

He could not see them, but he could smell them. He could taste their zeal. Their hunger for the Final Withering. It was a tingle as of dark magic on his whiskers. He felt as they did, smelled as they did – a simple monk in a pestiferous habit and tattered cowl, crusted slavemarks and spreading cankers there on the sloughing flesh of his muzzle for all to see and judge his piety.

'The Word is fever! The Word is madness! The Word is poison and lies, for the lesser pieces of the Horned Rat are jealous of the Corruptor, and so he plant-seeds lots-many falsehoods in the minds of his faithful. But not to me. Not Hascrible!'

He raised his staff, the horned bell housed at the top with a bronze emblem of the Splintered Temple clanging. The creaking protestations of his spine were, most assuredly, the manifested impatience of the Corruptor.

'Your leaders have lost scent of the foetid path. Their noses are filled instead with gold and realmstone and earthly treasures. They have become numb to the blessed reek of his foulness.'

A sea of angry chittering surrounded Hascrible.

'Anoint one of these false prophets in the unctures of the archpustulency and Clan Morbidus will be surpassed by Clans Septik and Feesik within the year!' The outrage of the congregation grew more shrill. Hascrible's screech rose to match it. The acid taste in the back of his mouth was, without doubt, the fetor of the Corruptor, eager to be sprayed across the Mortal Realms. 'We will be ejected from the Council of Thirteen, become a shadow of those messiahs of ruin that brought the germ-spore of Clan Morbidus from the world-that-was, left to scavenge over the scraps of our lessers. Such will be the Corruptor's punishment of your masters' failure!'

Hascrible's sermons had never been for the mighty. Partly this was practical. The mighty seldom wanted for anything he could give them. But there was strength in numbers too, power and a certain thrill in exerting the true will of the Horned Rat through the furry masses of the laiety.

'Whisper in the ears of your fellow monks. Squeak to the clan-servants. And your slaves. Squeak the truth to your priests and your abbots. Let them know-smell in your gathering the mind of the Horned Rat, for you are many-many and they are few. Hascrible of the Scratching Ruin! Archpustulent Hascrible!'

Delirious squeals and the discordant choir of bells and chimes broke out across the eating hole, but Hascrible's sensitive ears alerted him to the sounds of a fracas at the back of the crowd. While fighting was *technically* forbidden within the walls of the Morbidus clan stronghold during conclave, there were any number of loopholes relating to blasphemous squeaking and apostasy that the inventive skaven mind could contrive. Most therefore resorted to scratching and hissing, only accidentally misplacing a knife in someone's chest when they thought they could get away with it.

He cocked his head towards the sound.

'Ruin gnaws!' one rat snarled.

'Ruin scratches!' another chittered.

Hascrible sniffed at a wafting scent, the inside of his nostrils shrinking from it like blasphemous parchment from a naked flame. He sniffed again. Wightrot. He knew it well, though it was only a smell. An incense so potent it was said to be capable of inflicting ague and shivers on the dead. Cut from the ethereal bark of dead forests, it was fabulously rare and fabulously expensive. The ignorant and the vain saw a censer of wightrot as a mark of prestige, and the Horned Rat knew that there was no dearth of ignorance or vanity in the upper echelons of Clan Morbidus.

'Rattagan Borkris!' he guessed. Or perhaps not, for it was not coincidence that had caused the rotgrubs in his brain to wriggle and bite until he had taken *this particular* eating hole between Borkris' lairs and the Lyceum chambers for his church. 'Come-stay. You and your priests. Listen-hear the true Word of the Corruptor and side with me!'

Borkris' disdain squeaked from across the eating hole. 'You will be exiled, Hascrible, not elevated. If you are not made archpustulent here then you and your church are soon to be purged. You know this. If you were not as mad-cracked as you are then you would know that you will *never* be made archpustulent.'

Biting and pushing, the malfeasant superior's guard made a path for him through the congregation.

'Never say never,' Hascrible hissed. He held out crooked arms for a pair of burly monks to lift him from the table and onto their shoulders. He pointed after his departed rival. 'To the Lyceum.'

The eating hall erupted with the sounds of squeals and furniture breaking the moment that Hascrible was out of sight.

'Pustiss Ventik. Lord-Brewer of the Shrivelling Pox.'

The Lyceum burrows were a temple to the Great Corruptor, gouged from the sub-basement dinge of the Splintered Temple, the Blight City acropolis of the Morbidus clan. Bits of broken claws stuck out of the walls, and there were smears of diseased blood on the panels and triptychs where the slaves had continued digging with their fingers.

'Gastrule Skabes. Provost-Warden of the Excremental Feast.'

The cornices and clerestory were celebrations of tarnish, mould and verdigris, lesser decorations lurking amidst the gilt like rats, unaware of the awful majesty that loomed colossal overhead.

The ceiling fresco was the last masterpiece of the visionary, Glotto. *Visions of the Final Withering*, as it was known, had been the work of his disciples, painted after the skaven artist's death using the fluids of his own diseased organs. Sigmar dissolved in lightning. Nagash succumbed to decay. Alarielle withered within a dead forest. Grungni drowned in the molten metals of his own forge. In a band of painted marble around the lower tier of the dome, the nine gods of Order succumbed in hideous and inventive ways to the divine malfeasance of the great four in the band above, while above them all, filling the dome's apex, the Horned Rat gnawed at the stuff of the Mortal Realms in glee.

A dark-veined slab of marble, shaped by the devotion of skaven teeth and claws and installed with the strength of the faithful, sat beneath a mottled ciborium. A mildewed altar cerecloth lay across it, the grey material speckled black with dead insects and eggs. Behind it, an elaborate triptych of gold and mica, burnt sienna and skaven faeces showed the Great Corruptor ascendant over the lesser personalities of the Horned Rat.

To either side of the altarpiece, a plague furnace was tended by a hooded mutant. Standing somewhere in stature between a monk and a rat-ogre, the mutants were the results of the Morbidus priesthood's spectacularly unsuccessful attempts to use disease and arcane alchemy to siphon some of the wealth generated by the Moulder clans' breeding programme. The hulking creatures tended their fires with a rare single-mindedness, and resilience to disease. When the Lyceum of Lectors came to its decision and the doors of the Splintered Temple were again unbarred, then the sexton-general would squeak for the furnaces to be fed with greenvile and with cankerwood, and with the new archpustulent's own befouled robes, so that the pilgrims in the burrow-plazas beyond the stronghold's walls might be flooded with toxic smog. Any skaven lacking in their tolerance to disease would, of course, die in horrific agony, but the faithful would know that a new arch-pustulent had risen to lord over them.

'Graunch Festerbule. Most High Supreme Patriarch of the Carrion Blights.'

A heavily built skaven in a steel cuirass and a helmet with a crown read from an enormous ledger, spread across the hunched backs of two kneeling slaves. Sexton-General Crassus was a brute of a rodent, a lay-member of Clan Morbidus and so beneath the labyrinthine hierarchies of priests, but charged with the maintenance and defence of the Splintered Temple and thus of supreme eminence within its walls. At the sexton-general's call a priest in a dust-grey cassock with venous piping and an elaborate bone-effect mitre and crosier raised his paw. Crassus gnawed on the tip of his quill and dutifully scratched Graunch's name into the ledger.

The roll call went on.

Borkris watched, arms crossed over his wiry chest, paws burrowed into the voluminous sleeves of his cassock, as rivals, flunkeys and nobodies alike declared themselves. Underdeacon Makulitt had assured him of the votes of eight of them, and it would be his underling's spleen if they failed to deliver.

'Priestmonk Hascrible of the Scratching Ruin.'

Hascrible raised one crooked paw. Crassus squinted down his long snout as he scratched down the lector's name. Borkris' lips pulled back into a sneer. Hascrible looked as though he had snuck inside to scrub a fresh layer of filth onto flagstones before anyone important recognised his presence. As pathetic as the monk's devout zeal was, it did seem to endear him to the masses. It was commonly remembered by beggars and slaves like Hascrible that the gullet of the Horned Rat awaited all, but the Word also spoke of the amusement he drew from those whose strength and cunning saw them climb over the backs of their litter-brothers. A frothing lunatic the monk most clearly was, but ignorant of the lies and hypocrisies of the Withered Word he could not be.

No one clambered over the bodies of so many rivals by being stupid.

For that reason Borkris had always assumed the bell waving and the frothing at the mouth to be elaborate theatre to enthuse his congregation, but his probity had, in recent days, proven frustratingly genuine.

'Dengue Cruor. Bilious Sage of the Extirpated Way.'

Crassus looked up from his ledger.

The priests shuffled amongst themselves as if to shake the elderly plague priest like dandruff from their ranks.

The sexton-general drew back enough lip to expose a yellowed fang. 'Dengue Cruor?'

'He is not here,' someone squeaked.

'I have not seen-smelled him since first bell prayers,' squeaked another.

Wastrett Spleenrot, Pox-Abbot of the Ghurish Spreading, tittered, hacking up something corrosive and spitting it onto the flagstones. 'The old-thing probably died in the night.' He smeared the gobbet under his footpaw. 'At long last.'

'And where is Bilemaster Drassik?' said Hascrible.

Everyone looked to the priest beside him.

Drassik, Bilemaster of the Church of the Scales of Pungeance, belonged to the small group of priests mad enough and poor enough to scratch their vote for a maniac that would be the doom of them all. And with Borkris' only other genuine rival for the archpustulency, Dengue Cruor, similarly absent, the supporters of the Bilious Sage might not be so unwavering in their support.

Borkris preened. The Corruptor bared his throat to him this day.

'They are late, and we all have other duties to attend in our own realms,' he said. 'We should vote-scratch without them.'

Dengue Cruor, also known as the Verminable Cruor, or the Bilious Sage of the Extirpated Way, was in his burrow-hole in the meridional wing of the lower dinges. Drassik was there also, although, unlike the aged verminable, he was strapped to a table.

'The Church of the Scales of Pungeance will make sourblight from your flesh and pudding meal from your bones, old-thing!' The table legs rattled against the floor as the priest again decided to waste effort on breaking the leather belts holding him down. The priest's diatribe had veered between fulminating threats and promises of hellish vengeance, but he reached for an inarticulate squeal as Cruor picked up an enormous pair of metal cutters. 'Verminable! Maker of plagues! Whatever you want-wish is yours! Warptokens? Slave-meat? My scratch-vote. It is yours. All of it. Take it. Take-take!'

Cruor struggled to open the cutters. Despite the care he devoted to all of his tools, it had rusted. It was the price one paid for lairing in Blight City, for entropy was to the Realm of Ruin as heat was to Aqshy or darkness to Ulgu. It had not always caused him such difficulty, however. He was getting old. That was the real problem. Invigorating diseases and elixirs of his own concoction had strengthened and sustained him for many centuries, but age was finally starting to wear him down. Finally, he managed to wrench the cutters apart, wobbling the heavy tool towards Drassik's snout.

'No! No! No-no!'

The priest thrashed like a cocooned slug.

Snick.

'Arrrrrgh!'

A single whisker dropped from between the scissoring blades. Cruor plucked the hair from Drassik's chest with the claws of his forefinger and thumb. Drassik panted something nonsensical. He stared at the severed whisker with an idiotic blend of incredulity and relief. Ignoring the priest, Cruor twisted around on his stool, his tail slithering around its legs.

A brass alembic had been spread across a pair of tables, several stools and one precarious stack of books. The pot bubbled over a blue alchemical flame, filling the burrow-hole with fumes. Cruor removed the glass lid and dropped the whisker into the pot. It dissolved instantly into the liquid within. His assistant, a bronze-furred whelp called Gagrik, stirred the contents with a huge glass paddle. Despite his self-conferred title of poxmixer augustus, Gagrik was dressed not in the priestly cassock that was his due, but in an apron, mask and a pair of thick leather gloves. He hunched over the bubbling pot atop a platform of nailed-together stools and lengths of shelving.

'One whisker of plague priest,' Cruor muttered under his breath. 'Taken...' Cruor turned his attention back to the priest, foraging with one paw amongst the assorted implements strewn across his workbenches.

He found a paper knife.

'That is it. Yes? You will let me go now. Yes? Most verminable sage. Most blessed of the Horned R–'

Cruor ran the knife across the priest's throat. A bloody froth gurgled up from the neat wound, the priest jerking once more in his restraints. As if freedom would come as any kind of relief to him now. His jaw hovered open and shut before falling open for the final time. Blood continued to squirt from the priest's neck, but it was slowing. His red eyes began to turn pink. Cruor frowned over him. He poked the priest with the knife. Drassik did not respond. Cruor pounded on the priest's chest, bringing a splutter of blood and a damp gargle from the priest's lips.

The verminable nodded to himself, satisfied.

'Taken exactly thirteen breaths before death.'

He turned away from the corpse to study the bubbling alembic, adjusting the formulations in his head as he watched the evaporated fumes rising into the condenser.

Unlike his fellow lectors, Cruor had no church. He commanded no armies and had conquered no lands. Despite all of this he knew that he had personally delivered more apostates, both skaven and not, to the belly of the Corruptor than the other twenty members of the Lyceum combined. This he knew. He knew that they knew it too. And it was not because, at over five hundred years of age, he was *older* than the other twenty members of the Lyceum combined. His mastery of alchemy and pox-magic was unrivalled in Clan Morbidus, and over the centuries the increasingly deadly potions of his genius had been the death of millions.

He was one of very few skaven still alive who had experienced the Age of Blood, when the triumphant legions of Chaos had turned on their erstwhile skaven allies. He had seen plague lords and lectors who had sought to ingratiate themselves with champions of Tzeentch and Nurgle, only to be thrown onto the proverbial sword. But Cruor had survived. He had hidden, he had brewed his poisons and he had prospered.

Sigmar's warstorm had been the best thing to have befallen the skaven race since the days of the First Withering. Suddenly the other gods – traitorous, savage Khorne in particular – were weak and the Horned Rat again had shadows in which to lurk and scheme. Such was the Corruptor's way. To take advantage of other's vicissitudes, to exploit unwitting catspaws like mighty Sigmar in securing the future dominion of the skaven race.

Such was also Dengue Cruor's way.

He just needed to live long enough to see it.

'Grated horn of a Great Unclean One,' he muttered, sprinkling a claw-pinch of the exotic powder into the alembic.

The mixture in the crucible turned a sour yellow. Bubbles broke the surface with increasing vehemence, and the brass vessel began to rattle against the table. Cruor turned one side of his long face to the glass to study the reaction more closely.

'Forgive this unworthy interruption, master.' Gagrik swayed on his footpaws, dutifully stirring the mixture in spite of the bubbling pot banging against the frame of his platform. 'But should you not quick-soon be joining the Lyceum?'

'Do not speak-squeak. Fool-fool!' Cruor glanced up, another claw-pinch of ground plague daemon horn at the ready. 'The Lyceum does not meet for three bells yet.' He sprinkled the second titrant into the mix. The brass plating around the alembic began to bloat, a sickly foam frothing through the imperfect rubber seals. He touched his soft nose to the froth and blinked at the giddy spike of acridity it drove up his snout and into the back of his brain. He shook his muzzle. 'Pleasantly caustic.' He reached again for the powder jar.

'Forgive me, oh verminable one. But it is now.'

'Now?'

'Yes, master.'

Cruor pondered. Could he really have allowed so much time to scamper away, unnoticed? Age slowed even the nimblest of minds in the end, oh yes, it did. He would need to remember to wind the pocket bell-chime that he kept in one of these drawers. Perhaps he should take on a second assistant to tidy up and keep time for him...

'I am too busy to spare myself now anyway. You know I hate-loathe the fuss of liturgical matters.'

'Yes, master.' The hint of a sigh in his underling's voice. Cruor decided to be gracious and overlook it. Taking on one new assistant would be onerous enough.

'These things are never done-settled at the first assembly. By the time they have argued the first vote and Hascrible has demanded a recount we will be done-finished. I will be robed-ready to rejoin them when they return from recess.' He snickered. 'Yes-yes, I will be ready.'

'But what if–'

'Even I cannot be in two places at once.' As he spoke, he rummaged through the clutter of his workbenches, finally spotting what he was looking for and reaching over Drassik's body to snatch it up. It was a glass potion bottle with a metal screw-cap lid. In it was a roundworm the size of Cruor's middle claw. It was curled up, apparently sleeping. Cruor shook the jar and it uncoiled like a spring trap. Cruor tittered as a suckered mouth squealed down the side of the bottle where Cruor's eye was, its segmented body bristling with spines. 'Or can I not?' He unscrewed the bottle, picked the roundworm up in his claws and dropped it into his mouth. The worm splattered under his blunted teeth, the texture meaty and the taste pleasantly vile.

As he chewed, he picked up a bronze-bottomed pan that he used for the cooking of poisons and spat into it.

He squeaked a word from the one hundred and sixty-nine phrases of power, then carved a rune into the brown splatter in the base of the pan. Then he spat out what was still in his mouth, along with an unhealthy gobbet of saliva, and smeared the lot over the bronze surface, obliterating the rune. What remained in its place was a mucoid smear-pattern that slowly ran into an image. *Priests in jumbled gilt and jaded finery, stood beneath the great clerestory of the Lyceum burrows.* The gungy fluid continued to run. The image moved. *A pair of rat-men in sexton robes move amongst them. One carries scratch-quills. The other parchment scraps. A third stands by the altar with a bucket. The priests stick together, like clanrats on a battlefield, as the sextons pass their consignments around. All except one.*

Borkris.

The whelp.

The malfeasant superior of the Gnawing Ruin looked more than usually smug. Cruor snorted. As if all the wealth in the Realms of Chaos could make a golden bolus thick enough to save his soul from the belly acids of the Horned Rat come his time.

He would have liked to hear what the priests were saying or, better yet, to smell the tell-tale emanations of their musk-glands, but he saw through the eye of Gastrule Skabes. The identical twin of the worm he had just consumed had burrowed into the provost-warden's eye and curled up there to feed off his optic juices and lay its eggs, a procedure so excruciatingly painful that the plague priest probably did not even recall it being inflicted upon him.

With half an eye on the silently moving image, Cruor watched the first drop of virulent yellow-green liquid swell from the dripper of the alembic. He snapped his claws for a vial and, when it was handed to him, bent to hold it patiently under the growing drop.

Oh yes. Soon, the life-elixir of the Council would be within his grasp. Soon, he would be ready.

What was the old verminable's scheme?

Hascrible scratched at a particularly ripe gift from the Corruptor, nestled on the lobe of his right ear, as the Prater of the Foulsome Crucible made his claw-scratch. The priest glanced over both shoulders before scrunching up the parchment roll and tossing it into the bucket. And then, under the sextons' unwavering gaze, he ate the scratch-quill. Hascrible heard the bones crunch as they went down.

Cruor was testing the loyalty of those who had pledged him their votes. Yes. That had to be it. His absence would tease out those who would remain loyal, even without the old rat's breath on their necks, from those tempted to chase after their own ambitions. But how? How! How could he know? Each priest scratched the name he favoured on a strip of parchment, which would then by bundled into a ball and mixed with the others by the sextons. Even the quill would then be destroyed.

Hascrible was young for one so riddled with ailments and plague, but he had seen two elections in his time as a high priest of contagion.

He had seen a priest attempt to cheat by scratching a rune onto his own parchment that had changed every other scratch-mark on parchment that touched his own. Unfortunately for the unanimously elected priest, the one mark that had not been altered was the rune itself. The priest had, of course, protested his innocence, and the sexton-general had acknowledged that such a ploy would indeed be an ingenious way for another priest to rid himself of a rival. Crassus had therefore executed a third of the Lyceum at random and ordered a recount.

A rather surprised Heerak Gungespittle had been elected archpustulent from a thinned field of candidates immediately thereafter.

Hascrible gave his ear one last devotional scratching. He did not need to resort to such risky deceptions. His faith and energies went instead to the dark claws of the Horned Rat. *He* would guide the minds and the paws of his children, and *he* would ensure that Hascrible's mark was made on their parchment, even if they were misguided enough to wish another there in its place. Yes, he would.

All praise the Great Corruptor!

Graunch Festerbule prodded him in the back with the butt-end of his crosier. Bone chaplets and pale torques jangled against the morbid obesity of the priest's cassock.

'You were squeaking to yourself,' he said.

'I was not.'

'It sounded like you were chanting.'

'I was *not*.'

'He was chanting!'

Hascrible sensed the spreading of an anxious quiet as the sextons glanced his way. 'I was praying, you gas-bloated oaf-thing. Because the Horned Rat does not listen-heed to your chitterings does not stop a true child from begging his ear.'

Festerbule bristled. 'Infecund whelp. When you nurture your pet blights in the nighthaunt kingdoms of the glass veldts or the unfeeling lands, you come-scurry to me and squeak-tell of your favour. Until then, you may lick the pus from my claws.' The priest's arm swung back.

Someone grabbed his wrist before he could rake his claws across Hascrible's snout.

Hascrible sniffed, but he could not make out who it was. The sexton-general, if he was lucky. *If the Horned Rat favoured him*, he corrected himself, preening in the warm glow of his piety.

'The Most High Supreme Patriarch of the Carrion Blights apologises for his outburst,' said Borkris. 'These auspicious surrounds, the excitement of the occasion – it is all too much-much for one accustomed to the Realm of Death. Perhaps you and he can chitter-pray together when this session is concluded.'

Hascrible bobbed his head.

The sextons seemed to relax, withdrawing themselves to the clerestory walls. The fear-scent in the chamber thinned.

'There is nothing to forgive,' he said. 'The Horned Rat is a permissive and uncaring god. So should we be.'

Crassus took the bucket of scratch strips from his underling. He started to pick out names, his muzzle moving up and down as he read the marks to himself, then again as he scratched them into his ledger. Hascrible could hear the scarred rat's teeth clacking together. He shuffled from footpaw to footpaw, muttering homilies of corruption under his breath. What would he not have given for the chance to read the sexton-general's lips? Why, oh why, had the Horned Rat needed to take his sight? Could he not have claimed his bitter taste instead, his sense of cold, the prickling in the nape of the neck when another skaven lurks in the dark? Not that he would ever question who or what the Horned Rat took to devour. No. Of course not. Never! He turned his nose to sniff the priests to either side of him. Their musk was as tense and as fearful as his own must have seemed to their noses. Not that he was at all anxious, of course. The Corruptor favoured only one rat, and his name was Priestmonk Hascrible of the Scratching Ruin!

'The first scratch-votes are counted,' said Crassus, managing to make his voice snarl as though the consummation of that sacred duty had caused him to crack a tooth. 'Rattagan Borkris has nine marks.'

A chittering of consternation and surprise broke out amongst the gathered priests. Borkris himself gnashed his fangs in frustration at falling short by a whisker's margin. With Cruor and Drassik absent that left nineteen voting lectors, and ten a winning count. Hascrible wriggled on the spot, closed his blind eyes, another prayer scuttling its way towards the pricked ears of the Horned Rat.

'Dengue Cruor has four marks.'

'What?'

Hascrible stamped his footpaw on the ground and lashed his tail. The crunching of bones and the arthritic flare in his ankle was, most definitely, the choler of the Corruptor himself. How could a high temple full of so-called priests be so deaf to the squealings of their god?

Crassus ignored him. He squinted down his snout at his ledger. 'Hascrible has three marks.'

'This is a travesty!' Hascrible squeaked. 'An outrage!'

'Silence-close your muzzle, Hascrible.'

'Who said that?' Hascrible sniffed the air and turned his ears, but whoever it was was staying wisely quiet now.

'Salvik Rakititch has two marks,' said Crassus.

The rust-furred priest from Aqshy seemed as startled as everyone else.

'No one else has any marks. You have not elected an archpustulent.' The sexton-general made it sound like an accusation as he closed his ledger.

Hascrible's fury – incubated in his breast on behalf of the Great Horned Rat, naturally – bubbled over. 'I demand a recount!'

The priests groaned – the only collective action the Lyceum would ever knowingly undertake.

'Every time,' said one.

'Never sniff-smelled a sorer loser,' said another.

'Bad enough an archpustulent has to fail-die every few years to make us do this again.'

'Agreed,' said Borkris. 'We all have our diocese to attend. The Corruptor's designs for the Mortal Realms suffers for want of our guidance.'

A dozen priests nodded in agreement.

'This is as much a part of the Corruptor's scheme as the wars for the realms,' Hascrible protested. 'I say count-tally the marks again. Crassus made a mistake. Either he cannot read or he cannot count!'

From being closely jostled by half a dozen priests, Hascrible suddenly found himself alone in an empty space in the middle of the burrow-hall. He gulped. The watery feeling in his bowels was, quite understandably, the ire of the Horned Rat at his doubting the indestructibility of the true of faith.

The sexton-general was silent a long time.

Then he reopened the ledger with a snarl.

'Very well. *One* recount.'

Elaborately flocked plague priests spilled from the Lyceum's burrow-doors like birds released into a mine. Some flew straight into the waiting cages of their guards, others fluttering off together to darkened burrows to plot and scheme and to decide how best to extract personal advantage from the coming rounds of voting. Borkris hoped that his demonstration of support would be enough to persuade a few more waverers. Assuming Cruor and Drassik remained absent, then all that stood between him and the arch-pustulency was one scratch-mark more.

He watched Salvik Rakititch disappear into a pocket of burly plaguevermin before departing through an upward sloping tunnel. The lay warriors were clad in rusted half-plates patched over with scraps of cloth. Their heads were tonsured and they carried heavy maces in baldrics, shields bearing the device of the Flame that Withers.

One more scratch-mark.

One.

Borkris summoned Makulitt with a curt snap of the tail. The underdeacon had been waiting outside of the Lyceum with Borkris' own gaggle of priests, guards and paid cronies, and scuttled in behind his master as he swept after Rakititch.

At first, Borkris assumed that the priest was returning to his own burrows. Each of the twenty-one lectors had their own grace and favour burrows within the Splintered Temple. Those who lacked the ambition to assume the mantle of archpustulent for themselves, and preferred to avoid the skulduggery that occurred between votes, would often bolt themselves inside until the decision was made. It would have surprised Borkris to discover that the Aqshyan was such a rodent. His reputation for violent conversion said otherwise, and anyone who would dare vote for themselves, never mind command the support of another, was surely not one to cringe and squirt the musk of fear when destiny reared its horns. That had seemed to be the priest's destination, however, until his entourage had scurried him onto a branch to the left and started ascending again.

The tunnel opened up, after a few minutes, to what looked like a wine store. Huge metal vats stood off the ground on spindly wooden legs. Like pregnant beetles armoured in brass. The air was rancid with the taste. Corrosion leaked from the ancient drums. Every so often, one of them issued a tortured groan. Another tunnel led off from the chamber but, unlike the way in, this one had a door across it. That door was locked, and guarded by a pair of sextons. They were heavily armed with helmets and metal shields, their mail covered by frayed surplices. One carried a halberd, the other a wicked-looking morningstar. The door must have led to one of the outer warrens, for the import of wine. The warrens of the Splintered Temple were as interconnected with those of Blight City below ground as they were above.

Rakititch turned as Borkris and his company entered behind him, a hulking plaguevermin to either side. Borkris frowned at that. He was certain that Rakititch's entourage had numbered almost a dozen when he had walked into the storeroom.

With a threatening squeak, the other ten plaguevermin stepped out from behind the wine drums. The warriors stood with their shields raised, paws near to where their maces lay in their baldrics – although, a beady eye apiece on the phlegmatic sextons at the chamber's far end, none of them had yet drawn. Makulitt squeaked in alarm. The underdeacon and his subordinates huddled into a tighter knot of bodies, glancing nervously between the well-armed plaguevermin and their master.

Borkris reluctantly tilted his muzzle, giving Rakititch a flash of throat.

'Are you so afraid-scared of what I have to say that you run-scurry to the sextons?'

The Aqshyan priest shrugged. His fur was the colour of rust, or dark sand, swaddled in umber robes and yellow piping. An incense burner nestled against his chest on a neckchain. It made him resemble a miniature plague furnace, his head wreathed in smoke.

'He who fights and runs away...' began the priest.

'Lives to flee another day.' Every littered runt knew that old rhyme. It descended from those who first fled the world-that-was, or so the litter-mothers said. 'I am not here to fight-kill.'

'Good-good.' Rakititch lifted his muzzle towards Borkris' underlings. 'Then they have nothing to squirt the musk over.' Borkris waited for the Aqshyan to order his plaguevermin to back off, but he did not. He just stood there, waiting, back hunched, arms folded in his cassock sleeves, slowly disappearing in a thickening red cloud of incense smog. 'If you have come to persuade me you are the Horned Rat's favourite rat then do not waste your time-breath.'

'You think the Corruptor favours another?'

'I think he does not take favourites.'

Borkris tittered. 'Of course he does. A slavemaster has favourites. Or a breeder of rat-meat will become fond of the rat cunning enough to avoid the block. But his mind is vast, his attention span short. He leaves us to pick our own favourites and expects to be pleased with our choices when his gaze again returns.'

'Your reputation for usury and perfidiousness precedes you even into Aqshy, Borkris.' Rakititch cocked his head. 'I see-smell it is all true. If it were not, then the gossips would have surely squeak-talked instead of your... *agility* with the Withered Word.'

'To use a thing properly you need understand the thing. Creatures like Hascrible do not see. Even the Eshin clan killer learns first how a body works.'

Rakititch snorted, conceding. 'What do you want, Borkris?'

'Your scratch-mark, of course. And I want to know-smell the other who voted for you. With you I have ten. With both I have eleven, and a majority of the Lyceum even if Cruor and Drassik return.'

'I know not. It was a surprise, even to me.'

Borkris gnashed his teeth. Annoying, but not unexpected. 'Then squeak your support of me before the next vote, and whoever it was may follow.'

'Why would I?'

'You know you cannot win for yourself. Not with two scratch-marks. Better to back the winner. Is it minerals or jewels from Chamon you want?'

The priest pulled a face.

'Rare spores from the deserts of Shyish?'

'You insult me, Borkris.'

'A virulent crusade in the Realm of Fire, then! Yes-yes! With you, Salvik Rakititch at its head. As archpustulent I could command it. All the land it covers would be yours to despoil. All the glory would be yours to bargain with the Horned Rat for the fate of your soul come the Final Withering.'

Rakititch paused in thought.

He was still thinking when the head of one of his plaguevermin exploded.

Everyone turned as the armoured warrior sank to his knees, a fuming metal ball lodged in the ruin of his neck. A monk in vomit-brown robes dragged the flail back on a heavy chain. His nose was dripping, smearing his habit and his paws with copious quantities of virulent snot. Foam flecked the tattered edges of his hood, red madness gleaming from its depths. The nearby warriors were already starting to choke and die.

'Plague censer!' Borkris shrieked.

The censer bearer opened his toothless mouth and squealed, monks and warriors boiling up from the plague cloud that filled the tunnel behind him.

Hascrible screeched a challenge as he scrambled after his warriors. It was not cowardice that made him last into the storeroom, oh no, for he was a favourite of the Horned Rat and feared neither decrepitude nor death. His wizened muscles and arthritic joints were, quite obviously, the Horned One's way of ensuring he entered the fray at exactly the time that he was supposed to. He felt a glow lurking in the mucous-filled caverns of his chest, a choke-response that, he was almost certain, had nothing to do with the nurglitch vapours currently circling through his respiratory system and devouring the plaques blocking off the inside of his lungs. It was destiny! The focused intensity of the Corruptor's interest in him and him alone, nurturing and curating the many ailments of his life, much as the jovial grandfather was said to do with his own favoured creatures. Providence had brought him here. Yes, that was it. Providence!

He scuttled into the melee, crouched low, hidden by the incense pall, his normally keen senses of smell and sound confused by the anarchy of combat, questing the path ahead with his bell-staff.

He found a body.

His tail patted it down while he sniffed at the air. Robed. Hooded. A staff. *A priest.* One of Borkris', judging by the finery. He was spread-eagled, face down, blood still oozing from the eyes and nose. That and the occasional rattle of breath told Hascrible that the priest was still alive. Hascrible's tail coiled around the dagger in his cincture, then stabbed it into the priest's brain through the soft meat of his throat. Hascrible felt only joy, for the priest's final jerk was, as plain as the scent of blood, the last futile effort of his soul to evade the damnation of the Horned Rat's jaws. This was, after all, the Corruptor's work he did here. Rattagan Borkris had schemed to pervert the Horned One's great will. It was a wrong that the faithful would see righted. Crassus would understand, he was sure, once Borkris was dead and unable to answer Hascrible's charges of blasphemy.

An armoured warrior ran at him.

In the chaos of sounds and smells, vibrations and tastes, the first he knew of it was the scrabble of claws on stone. Then the hiss of breath as a weapon was drawn back. A lesser rat would have frozen, panicked by his blindness in such a sensory din, but not he. Not Hascrible. His blindness was the great paw of the Horned Rat upon his brow.

Hascrible raised a claw and pointed it towards the sound. He chittered a word that brought a cluster of rancid blisters to the tip of his tongue, and a beam of withering energy stabbed from his claw. The charging rat-warrior was vaporised. A mace-head and some rust flakes clattered to the ground, the sound of their falling muffled by the robes he had been wearing. Hascrible sniffed. He wished that he could have seen that. But such were the sacrifices demanded of the faithful.

With a sigh he lowered his still-tingling claw, squeaked another challenge and scurried off in search of Borkris.

A plague-shrivelled wretch from the stronghold's slave stocks stabbed at Borkris with a spear. The thrust was weak, the paws that guided it malnourished and barely strong enough to keep a grip on the shaft much less drive the point through skaven flesh. Borkris twitched aside, catching the spear as it slid across his shoulder, and then yanked it from the slave's paw as he rammed a fist into the prominent lump of bone between stomach and chest. The slave doubled over, spraying Borkris' cassock with spittle, and Borkris broke the spear over his head.

Raising his paws in line with his snout, Borkris snarled.

The altercation had knocked his armlets askew.

Sliding his right arm into his cassock's left sleeve, he drew out a long, curve-bladed shamshir. This was why lectors so often lingered with their arms folded into their sleeves. For the comfort of a concealed blade. He was tempted to reach into his right sleeve as well, but decided that, in such an enclosed space, that would be unwise.

His hired thugs and Rakititch's plaguevermin were fighting back hard against Hascrible's followers, but the waves of foaming zealots had forced them back into the storeroom.

The priestmonk's entourage, as with everyone else's, had been restricted to a dozen. Twelve plus one amounted to the unholy numeral of the Horned Rat, but the true objective was to create a field even enough to discourage overt treachery. But Borkris had seen for himself how Hascrible had been spreading his message amongst the clanservants and slaves of the Splintered Temple, and there were even a pawful of monks in the habits of other lectors amongst his fighters. They outnumbered his and Rakititch's guards several-fold, and those were the kind of odds that would lend spine to even the most enfeebled of slave warriors.

The plague censer bearer, however, was down, coughing up an orange froth in the midst of a ring of rapidly bloating skaven corpses.

Borkris would take the fanatic's death over the alternative, but he suspected that Hascrible's task for him had already been accomplished. Half of Rakititch's warriors were in that pile, and most of the rest were coughing up their insides even as they fought off three, four, five times their number of foes.

And *those* were odds to make even the proudest of the Corruptor's crusader-knights waver in his certainties.

Borkris spied a priest of the Gnawing Ruin scrambling up the wooden legs of one of the wine drums. The priest launched himself upwards, grabbing hold of a rivet, claws digging into the metal, while a pair of spear-armed slaves stabbed at his whipping tail. A monk wearing Hascrible's filthy brown threw away his sword to climb after him. Muttering a loathsome incantation, Borkris claw-scratched a rune of decay into the air and blew it towards the drum. The rivet the lackey had been clinging to burst, firing the screaming plague priest across the burrow-hall on a sour jet and slamming him against the vat on the opposite side of the chamber. Corrosion spread from the broken rivet and into the surrounding metal. It thinned, flaked.

It turned black.

Acrid wine gushed through the sickened metal, sweeping away the monk that had been clambering up the vat's wooden legs, and crashing over Hascrible's slaves. The flood flattened the followers of the Scratching Ruin, slicking the flagstones with communion foulness and imposing enough of a lull for his cronies, under Makulitt's urgent squeakings, to pull back and regroup.

Watching Hascrible's minions slip over the wet stones brought Borkris a brief gnawing of amusement before the sounds of an entirely separate battle drew his attention.

The sextons had entered the fray.

The temple warriors butchered whatever happened to fall in their path, entirely without consideration for allegiance. As Hascrible's monks and slaves greatly outnumbered everyone else, for the time being that predominantly meant them. They swamped the two sextons in fur and froth, but the warriors fought as a genuine pair. Another skaven might – on the very horns of the Corruptor – swear to do such a thing, only to shrink from it or conveniently forget in the heat of battle. Not these two. They watched each other's backs, without even the momentary hesitation of whether to stick a knife in there. They defended each other, killed together, while every other rat in the burrow-hall was busily fighting for its own hide. They were, in effect, unstoppable. And they were coming directly at Borkris. He doubted it was for his own protection.

He still remembered the election of Gungespittle.

He turned towards the entrance.

The emptying wine drum had pushed back the censer-bearers' lingering fumes to reveal Priestmonk Hascrible's dripping host in all its foulness. The zealot himself was towards the rear, hunched over and sodden through, his off-brown robes stained purple. He was shaking his muzzle, banging his ear as if to force wine through to the opposite side, pausing every so often to sniff at the air. The wine fumes seemed to have confused his nose.

Borkris bared his teeth.

He had not started this fight. Assuming he could evade the sextons, then he could prostrate himself before Crassus and claim self-defence. Kill Hascrible and victory was as good as his.

Rakititch breathed in his ear.

'Who says I cannot win the archpustulency on my own?' he hissed, and then punched a previously concealed sword of his own through Borkris' back.

Hascrible pulled his claw out from his ear. He was certain he recognised that scream. A grin peeled his lips back as it came again. Borkris. His ears pivoted and he cackled at the brief snatch of conversation he managed to pick up over the melee. Borkris and Rakititch were fighting each other. The Horned Rat bless skaven perfidy! He was about to order his warriors to withdraw – those of them sane enough to heed a simple command at any rate – and let the two plague priests kill one another, when a crazed screech split the air. He sniffed, but all he got was wine vapour. He could hear squealing, dying, fighting getting closer. He snarled, scratching at a wart between his blind eyes.

'What is happening?'

'*Underdeacon Makulitt!*'

And suddenly Hascrible saw. He didn't *see*, of course, Corruptor be praised, but he *saw*. Caught between Hascrible's rotten host and the sextons, Borkris' minions were fighting the way only trapped rats could.

Hascrible turned in the direction of the voice that had answered. He could neither see the monk, nor smell him over the pungent wine, but was confident enough when he reached out that he would find a pawful of habit to drag the underling into the path of the frenzied underdeacon's charge.

The monk shrieked as Borkris' frantic underlings ripped him to shreds.

The Horned Rat's will had been done.

All praise to the Great Horned Rat!

Snorting wine from his nose and banging on his clogged ear, he turned tail and fled.

Borkris fell to the ground as Rakititch pulled his sword out of his back. The flagstones took a tooth. He snarled. If there had been a single nerve in his body not sick with plague or encrusted with scabs then both the impalement and subsequent blow to the muzzle would undoubtedly have been extraordinarily painful. But the Corruptor's priesthood were a tough breed. Even those of Borkris' ilk, who preferred to hold their paws above the day-to-day business of the death of all creation. He crawled along the ground from the Aqshyan priest, his breathing sucking in through one lung. He could hear it hissing out from the other, gurgling through the blood that was ineffectually plugging the hole in his back.

Rakititch pounced with a snigger and rammed the sword through his shoulder, hard enough to crack the metal but not before enough of it had penetrated the stone to pin Borkris to the floor. Borkris shrieked. That broke enough of him to hurt. He turned to look over his ruined shoulder, some morbid need inbred into the Clans Pestilens to sniff every blessing and pick at every scab.

It was not a sword at all, but a leather gauntlet with a quarter-tail-length fist spike. Rakititch wriggled his fingers out of the glove, causing the wound to stretch and tear. Borkris chittered in annoyance, but the diseases that had been calcified into the bone were already in his bloodstream, busily killing anything that might have caused him further agony. Smoke from the Aqshyan's incense burner wreathed his muzzle, eddy patterns snaking about his snout and muzzle so that he no longer resembled a plague furnace so much as a bale taurus of the azghor duardin. Or perhaps that was just the necrotising infections that Borkris' injuries had flushed into his brain, making him see the hated foe that he had crossed so often on the battlefields of Chamon and in the consular burrows of Blight City.

'You squeak-say I cannot be archpustulent alone,' Rakititch hissed. 'But when word spreads that I killed you, your followers will quick-soon become mine.'

Borkris snarled. The pain was already dulling, and the degradation of his brain from within was proving a rhapsodic experience. 'You think Hascrible is not already telling everyone that *he* killed us both?'

'But I am not dead-dead.'

'Not yet.'

With one eye, Borkris glanced towards the sextons. Just a pawful of panicking slaves left between them now. Rakititch turned rigid. His mouth opened to squeak a protest, even as his eyes roved the burrow-hall for a way out.

'Deliver this morsel to the Corruptor,' said Borkris. His neck swelled, his jaw broke, and a torrent of corrosive gases rushed from his distended mouth. Rakititch had been crouched over him. The bilious flood dissolved his sword arm and the rest of his body from the chest down.

Everything above that took a little longer to die.

'May he be… sated… when I arrive.' Borkris spat out a gobbet of acerbic phlegm, cackling, gasping for breath even as the butt of a sexton's halberd cracked his temple and knocked the consciousness out of him.

The atmosphere in the Lyceum was quietly resentful, the echoes of the occasional muffled squeak gobbled up by the rotunda's nightmarish frescoes. Wastrett Spleenrot was missing part of an ear, Verukik a paw-shaped patch of fur along his snout. Almost all had rips to their robes, cuts and plague blisters they had not possessed before. Borkris glared at them, one-eyed. The other was swollen shut. His head and body was a bundle of pointed sticks glued together with pain and a liberal slathering of skalm. His whole body rattled when he breathed. None of his former supporters risked standing too close. It might have been wariness of the heavy eucalyptus reek of the skalm, but he did not think so. None of them would even catch his eye. They gathered around Hascrible like flies late to the midden.

Having claimed responsibility for the killing of Rakititch, the maiming of Borkris and the disappearance of Drassik for good measure, the priestmonk looked outrageously pleased with himself.

Borkris did not care anymore.

A maniac like Hascrible would last five years at most. Borkris did not think he would survive even as long as that. He would generously give him three months before a senior cleric of good sense pushed him off a building. They would all be back here again in no time. He could wait.

He glanced to the old priest at his right.

Verminable Cruor was the only rat in the chamber, the sexton-general and his warriors excluded, who did not look the worse for wear. And perhaps that had been the full extent of the old rat's ploy after all, for compared to his bedraggled and exhausted kith-rats he looked resplendent in a blood-red cassock, gold fascia, chaplets and a horned mitre. He carried as well an ornate stave, and small censers breathed out puffs of yellow-green fumes as he scurried. Where the other lectors were too mired in smugness or self-pity to do much beyond twitch and chitter, he seemed too anxious, or perhaps excited, to keep still, skittering hither and thither and wafting a trail of caustic vapours all around him.

He had every right to be agitated.

With Hascrible about to be elected archpustulent he was set to find himself in the same unpleasant hole as Borkris. Perhaps the old poxmaker would be nervous enough to consider an alliance. Borkris preened stiffly. Yes. Perhaps this need not be considered a defeat after all. A delay in his ambitions at best.

Before he could consider the matter further, Crassus cleared his throat.

The sexton-general stood before the altar, framed by the blotched pergola of the ciborium. A heavy sword hung at his hip. His claws drummed on the cracked device of the pommel. 'You will now vote-scratch again.' An over-the-shoulder snarl sent sextons scurrying towards the lectors, parchment, buckets and quills in paw. 'Will anyone squeak-talk to the Lyceum before the scratch-count is made?'

A few eyes flicked towards Borkris. Guilty, some. Fearful, almost all.

He was weak now, they knew, but he would not always be so.

He shook his head.

Hascrible bared his teeth. 'Nor I. Let us vote-scratch.'

'I would squeak before we vote.'

There was a rustling of cassocks and a popping of joints as everyone turned from the altar towards Dengue Cruor.

Crassus thrashed his tail. 'Speak-squeak.'

'You all should vote for me,' said Cruor.

Hascrible snickered. 'You, old-thing? Why?'

Cruor sighed. 'How I despise the intrigue of this burrow-place.' At least one lector rolled his eyes. 'So I will be simple-quick. You should vote-scratch for me because all in this chamber have been infected with splintergut. With a little help from Drassik, of course.' He flicked one of his belt censers with a claw and tittered as the closest priest scuttled back from him in alarm. 'A most virulent plague.'

Borkris felt a ringing in his ears.

Everybody else was quiet.

'Onset is fast-quick and death quite painful,' said Cruor. 'So painful it will follow your soul to its afterlife.' He withdrew what appeared to be a pocket bell-chime from beneath his fascia and studied it, counting under his breath. 'I suggest you vote quick-quick.'

'This is outrageous,' Borkris hissed.

He looked to Crassus, but the sexton-general appeared to be at a loss for how to respond.

'I submit gladly to the Corruptor's plagues!' Hascrible squeaked, straightening to his full, hunch-backed height. 'I survived the blistering scalepox before even hearing of the Withered Word. Do your worst, verminable, I say.' The priests started to shuffle away as though the priestmonk was personally contagious. 'Vote-scratch for me. All who scurry in the Corruptor's shadow will be spared!'

Borkris' eyes narrowed.

Hascrible had to know something that the others in the Lyceum did not.

No one was *really* that zealous.

Yes. He saw it now. Hascrible and Cruor were in league. He could not believe he had not sniffed it before. Cruor's absence from the first vote had allowed Hascrible to scare off Borkris' supporters, allowing Cruor to re-enter, unsullied, and steal the archpustulency with this farcical deceit. He wondered what the priestmonk had been promised. The life-sustaining secrets of his alchemical concoctions? The recipe for plagues that had ravaged the first nations of the Mortal Realms before the awakening of the gods, known now only to a scholarly few? Yes. That had to be it. How else would he have bribed a fanatic that cared not for Borkris' wealth? Borkris cursed his fixation on his own prize and that he had not deduced all of this for himself already. This was a trick. There was no plague. Splintergut indeed. Whiskers of a plague priest? Horn of a Great Unclean One? Extract of nighthaunt and an unshed raindrop from the high clouds of Azyr? Preposterous!

'Only a rat cunning enough to smell through such a blatant deception is fit to lead Clan Morbidus.'

He drew the shamshir from his left sleeve, and with the same left-right arc, struck Cruor's head from his shoulders. Blood sprayed towards the ceiling, as though its final act was to strain towards the Horned Rat at the apex of the dome, as the verminable's body collapsed.

The lectors squealed in terror as Borkris lowered the blade.

He regarded them smugly.

'What did you do?' squeaked Festerbule.

'You have killed us all!' said Rank.

'There is no plague,' said Borkris, as though explaining the Withered Word to a fool. He pointed a claw at Hascrible, but the accusation he had been about to level disappeared in a tirade of increasingly painful coughs.

A muscle in his stomach that he did not know he had, clenched. Something semi-liquid and foul-smelling trickled down the inside of his thigh as he doubled over with a squeal.

Onset is fast-quick and death quite painful.

'Great Corruptor,' he moaned, as groaning lectors began to crumple to the ground. 'No-no...'

'What is happening in there?' Gagrik hissed.

'I do not know.' Makulitt pressed his ear to the door. 'I cannot hear anything.'

'They have been in there a long time.'

'Maybe they are praying,' Makulitt said hopefully.

'I heard something hit the floor.'

'I am sure they are fine.'

'We should check.'

'And interrupt the unholy ruminations of the Lyceum of Lectors?'

Gagrik hesitated. The poxmixer augustus was clad in robes that were almost laughably plain. Half his whiskers had been singed off and one eye drifted lazily, constantly weeping from too much time staring into his master's concoctions. 'A sniff then. Just to be certain.'

'The door is bolted from the inside by the sextons.'

'Just try it.'

'You try it.'

Makulitt looked over his shoulder. The lackeys and lieutenants of Perish and Skabes and Festerbule and all of the other high priests milled behind them. It was quite clear that they were happy for Makulitt and Gagrik to settle this amongst themselves. Makulitt cursed his misfortune. If not for his injuries in the battle against Hascrible's zealots then he would never have allowed himself to be manoeuvred into so exposed a position.

'Fine then,' he hissed. 'We do it together. On three. One... Two...'

Gagrik and Makulitt pushed together. To their surprise, the door opened. Something on the other side resisted, but nothing so unyielding as a bar across it.

Makulitt pushed harder.

The door opened fully.

The body of the sexton that had been slumped against it slid onto the floor.

He was still holding the locking bar in both paws, but had apparently died before he had been able to open the door. And he *was* dead. The pale glaze over his eyes and the coolness of his fur was confirmation enough for Makulitt, his lack of breath another, but there was a very *living* pain in those eyes still. It was subtle, slow, but, moreover, Makulitt realised that the corpse was actually still writhing in pain. He raised his snout to take in the rest of the burrow-hall. Heavily robed bodies lay slumped over the ornature. The sexton-general was draped across the altar, covered by his mangy scrap of cloak. Even the mutants that had tended the plague furnaces were dead, the fires nibbling away at their skin, burning darkly on the voided contents of their vast, corrupted bowels.

The underdeacon squeaked in alarm, covering his snout with his cassock sleeve as the diarrheal stench reached him.

He was a priest of plague, an acolyte of the Corruptor and proselyte of the Final Withering, but the malady at work was something horrifying that he knew instinctively he wanted nowhere near him. Here was a plague straight from the codicils of the Libers

Pestilent, certain martyrdom to any but the most malefic priest or champion of Nurgle.

'So… who does that make archpustulent of Clan Morbidus?'

The gaggle of underlings in the corridor behind him quickly shuffled back.

'I vote-squeak for Underdeacon Makulitt!' Gagrik squealed.

THE SIEGE
OF GREENSPIRE

Anna Stephens

Brida Devholm, captain of the Freeguild company Lady's Justice, watched with dismay as the most incompetent of her new recruits staggered, fell and landed hard on the stone courtyard that made up the ground floor of the watchtower known as Greenspire. The barrel he was carrying slammed onto the flagstones and split, and a cascade of fine black powder spilt forth over him and the stone while clouds of it plumed into the air.

Brida leapt back on instinct. 'Careful, idiot,' she shouted. 'You want to blow us all up? That's gunpowder! Why not just strike a spark while you're at it?'

It was no use. Kende had hit his chin on the top of the barrel as he went down and was sitting in the drift of gunpowder, bleary-eyed and spitting blood from a bitten tongue. 'Sorry, captain,' he managed. He made it to his knees, upended the broken barrel and began scooping the powder back into the hole cracked into it, scraping handfuls up off the stones.

Brida ran forwards and snatched the barrel from him, spilling more onto herself and the ground with the violence of the move-ment. 'By the Lady, are you stupid?' she demanded, despite the clear evidence confirming her suspicion. She pointed at the ground as he blinked up at her, confused. 'That powder's con-taminated now, full of dirt and dust, your blood and sweat, stone chips even. You've just mixed it with the pure still left in the bar-rel.' He stared at her, still not understanding, and Brida cursed him silently.

'Do you know what happens when you put dirty gunpowder in the firing pan of your musket? Either it doesn't fire, leaving you unarmed against the hordes trying to claw your guts out of your belly, or it backfires and blows your damn hand off. Which would you prefer, Kende?'

Kende wiped blood from his chin with a blackened hand and scrambled to his feet. 'Um, neither?' he ventured.

Brida nodded. 'Neither. Good choice. Now think what would happen if you loaded it into the breech of a cannon.' She cursed again as she peered through the split wood and gave the barrel a tentative shake, judging its weight. It had been full. She groaned and gave it back to him. 'Congratulations. Your first month's wages are forfeit to enable me to purchase more powder, though it's any-body's guess when the suppliers will be back this way. And don't even think about complaining.' She stared him out and Kende closed the mouth that had been about to utter something very unwise.

'Shovel the rest of it back in there and then mark up the bar-rel with chalk so we know not to use it in the weapons. Might be we can sprinkle it in some of the traps out front, add a lit-tle excitement for when the beasts come again. And then sweep this yard – I don't want a stray spark setting my company alight because the ground's dusted with gunpowder. And then report for night duty – no, I don't care that you've just pulled a day shift.

And try not to fall over your own feet next time, yes? Alarielle knows what you'll be like in an actual fight.'

The torrent of orders and abuse withered the man like a tree before Nurgle's rot and he nodded, mute, his black-stained face slack with chagrin. Brida bit the inside of her cheek to stop herself saying more, and sighed. She shouldn't be too hard on him; he'd been a farmer before a tzaangor warflock from the Hexwood took everyone he loved and he swore to end his days fighting them. The problem was, he was doing a damn fine job of trying to take Lady's Justice and Greenspire with him when he went.

His was a common enough tale in Verdia and, truth be told, she knew a thing or two about that driving need for vengeance and where it could take a person. She just had to hope Kende could learn weapons easier than he could carry barrels of gunpowder across a flagstoned courtyard. And he wasn't the only one. The last skirmish had left her company under-strength, and they'd replaced the dead with a dozen raw recruits – some barely more than children, the others merchants or farmers like Kende. A dozen who didn't know which end of a sword was safe to hold. One, Raella, who'd discovered she didn't like heights and cried every time she stood watch on the third level, spending most of her time with her eyes screwed shut and clinging to the guard wall until they prised her loose and sent her down to the ground floor again.

A muscle jumped in Brida's jaw, but she managed to keep her frustration trapped behind her teeth as Kende resumed funnelling wasted powder into the barrel. He'd learn or he'd die, all of them would; that was the way of it out here on the Emerald Line, which stretched from Fort Gardus to Hammerhal-Ghyra. Brida's concern was that they didn't take too many seasoned soldiers with them into death.

Above, Greenspire's bell rang the changing of the watch, and Brida left Kende to his task with a final reminder to bathe and change before going near any naked flames. She jogged up the stairs to the top floor of the tower and marched a brisk round of all four sides. This evening the approaches from the Hexwood were clear, although there was a tangle of vine crawling out from the treeline towards them, already closer and thicker than it had been at dawn. Brida rubbed a weary hand across her face. The Lady of Leaves would need to be propitiated and placated before they could hack away the vines; left untouched they would strangle Greenspire, cracking the strong stone foundations and tumbling it into ruin, leaving a gap in the Emerald Line through which the beastkin and tzaangors of the Hexwood could launch attacks.

'A captain's work is never done,' Brida muttered under her breath, though in truth she wouldn't have it any other way. Her hand found the thick gold ring hanging from its cord around her neck and she squeezed it, feeling the reassuring weight and warmth of the metal – more habit than reminder of all she'd lost to bring her to this point. It wasn't often she thought of her life before, but Kende's earnest incompetence and the hesitant, awkward actions of the other recruits brought back an old pain, one never fully healed.

She was relieved when Drigg, her duardin second-in-command, appeared at her side and the memory rolled like a corpse in a river and submerged again. It'd be back, it never left her for long, but hopefully not tonight to steal her sleep. 'All quiet?' Drigg asked. He'd been awake for a couple of hours and already knew the answer, but she appreciated him asking. It signalled the formal transference of power from her to him for the night watch.

'Too quiet, and for too many days,' Brida said. 'I don't like it.'

Drigg laughed, the sound rusty and low in his throat, and shifted the double-headed axe hanging from his belt. 'You wouldn't like it if Sigmar and Alarielle themselves came down here and proclaimed the war against Chaos over, the enemy defeated, and all of us able to go home to peace.'

The corner of Brida's mouth twitched. 'I'm a careful sort,' she acknowledged.

Drigg shook his head. 'You say careful, the rest of us say suspicious and untrusting. And this is a duardin speaking. Careful is what we do.'

Brida glared at him for a long second, but there was no heat in it. 'It's strange how often the two sentiments can be confused. Check floor two for me, would you? Orla reported an issue with cannon one, something about the vent hole being blocked, so I've ordered crossbow emplacements set up at each corner. I know, I know, I'd have told you earlier if I'd known earlier. I didn't. You'll have to tinker with it in the morning, we can't risk moving it now. Even a visual deterrent's better than nothing. Oh, and Kende's pulling a double shift – or maybe a triple if I decide he's on duty tomorrow as well, so keep an eye on him. He's greener than springtime and clumsier than a one-legged tzaangor, but he needs to learn, and fast.'

'Because you have a bad feeling?' Drigg asked.

'Because I have a bad feeling, and because he's fouled an entire barrel of gunpowder,' Brida confirmed. 'You have the watch, lieutenant.'

Drigg saluted and stepped back. 'I have the watch,' he confirmed formally. 'So you can take your bad feeling off my wall,' he muttered, and only their long familiarity allowed him the privilege – and then only when no other soldier could overhear. Drigg and Devholm, backbone of Lady's Justice for twenty years. Other than Brock, Orla and a couple of others, the only surviving members of the company from back when it was formed. Years and battles and deaths and horrors they'd been through, saved each others' lives more times than she could remember, and she'd never once got Drigg to admit her bad feeling had been right. He always insisted it was coincidence.

She listened to his footsteps retreating along the walkway, the crisp commands as the watch was handed from the day to the night units. The wind hummed around the watchtower, warm and pleasant and vibrant with life – and, every so often and only from the west, tainted. The tiniest breath of foulness, there and then gone so fast she almost couldn't detect it. But there.

Brida's scarred fists clenched on the waist-high guard wall and though she was now officially off-duty, she didn't move. There was something wrong.

There was something coming.

The watch changed again at dawn and Kende was found asleep at his post. So was Raella, who should have been preparing the meal that would end the night watch's shift and begin the day watch's. Instead, all of them went hungry for an extra hour while she frantically stoked the ovens and baked, in some cases burned, the bread and scalded the porridge. It was poor fare, and it put the whole company in a mood.

Brida was staring through an arrow slit at the tangle of vine, taller than she was now and closer than ever, when Drigg brought them both to her. He was shame-faced and furious in equal measure – the night watch was his duty, so the failure was also his. He offered to endure the recruits' punishment along with them, in a voice loud and clear that carried across the yard and brought everyone within earshot to a halt. Those recruits who'd managed to stay awake muttered to the more experienced Freeguilders, surprised and a little awed by Drigg's offer. Their respect for him grew, but Brida knew if she agreed, their opinion of her would fall.

She turned him down, but she had no choice but to punish the pair, smacking her spear shaft across their backs three times each and driving them to their knees, welts and bruises springing up on their skin. It was worse than they'd anticipated though less than the proper flogging they deserved, and both shouted in pain; Raella begged to be allowed to resign from the company.

'No. You signed up for a year and a year is what you'll give me. We're under-strength and I can't afford to lose you. You're going to learn to be a soldier, and a damn good one at that.'

Raella burst into tears again and ran for the kitchens. Brida didn't like punishing her soldiers, but Lady's Justice was a tight-knit company, a hard and disciplined company, and over the years they'd all received punishment for similar infractions. Brida herself had the scars that told of her own insubordination back when she'd been a grunt.

Just because Kende and Raella were new and still grieving whatever horrors had led them here, that didn't mean they got a longer rein than the rest of the company. And best to find out Raella's mettle – or lack of it – now than when they were beset by the worshippers of Tzeentch. Lady's Justice didn't break and run. Raella had broken already and Brida couldn't afford sympathy for the woman. Her job now was to take Raella's broken pieces and fit them together into something hard and sharp – a weapon. She hoped she'd have enough time to do it before the next attack.

'We're on the frontier, Kende,' she said. 'We're part of the thin line between Hammerhal-Ghyra and the Hexwood, between civilisation and Chaos. Between joy and despair, and life and death. We're here to prevent what happened to your family from happening to everyone in the realm. I have to be able to trust you and know that you'll follow my orders, that I can depend on you. At the moment I can't. You have ten days to prove me wrong. Shadow Lieutenant Drigg, learn from him, and for the Lady's sake try and stay awake.'

He didn't ask what would happen after ten days. He didn't argue and he didn't beg for leniency or even promise to do better. He just gave her a sloppy salute and walked away too fast for dignity. She watched him go, frowning, wondering if she'd made a mistake. Perhaps it would be better to cull him and Raella now, cut the rot from her company before it had a chance to spread. He'd been sullen, and there was no place for resentment in Lady's Justice. No place for anything except dedication to the cause and belief in the Lady of Leaves.

Twenty years as a soldier had taught Brida much, and she knew with bone-deep certainty that Kende wasn't going to make her believe in him in ten days. But what else could she do? She needed him. She needed them all.

The beastkin attacks had been increasing in frequency of late, increasing in cunning too, which worried her more. Greenspire's neighbouring watchtowers, Highoak and Willowflame, had both reported growing pressure from skirmishes. Couriers were vanishing on the roads strung along the Emerald Line, and the green alchemical flames that burned day and night at the top of each tower were changing to red to signal attacks more and more often. Even on a clear day, the flames were all that could be seen through the miles separating each tower, and usually by the time Lady's Justice had marched to the aid of a red-crowned neighbour, the attack was over.

Part of Brida longed for a full-scale battle, a chance for all the Freeguilders to unite to crush the enemy. This probing of the Line worried her. It suggested an unexpected intelligence guiding the horde's attacks.

Mostly, those dazed and lucky few who survived an attack fled to bigger towns and cities, abandoning their farms and orchards to scrape a living on the streets or as labourers in the sky-docks. Only a very few found the courage to transform their loss into fire and join the Freeguild. Lady's Justice had been under-strength for half a year before Kende and the rest were finally allocated to them and Greenspire. Even if they'd each had the resourcefulness and skill of five soldiers, they would not have made up the shortfall. And if Kende's anger or Raella's timidity infected the other recruits… Brida's gut wound another notch tighter.

'I should have meted out their punishment,' Drigg said from behind, and then yawned wide enough to swallow a cannonball. 'They slept on my watch.'

'No, better they hate me and respect you. Kende's going to need a lot of babying – I've given him ten days – and you're better at that than me. Help him but push him wherever you can. I'll put Brock on Raella – his charm and encouragement might work better on her. We need them all, and none of them are ready for anything except feeding to monsters.' She slapped him on the arm. 'Go on, fix that cannon for me and then get some sleep – we'll speak again before dusk.'

Brida found Drigg at noon. He was hunched over the cannon in his workshop following a complicated hour spent with rope, tackle and pulleys lowering it from the second level to the courtyard, then trundling it into the sooty, alchemical-smelling gloom. The duardin leapt to his feet when Brida's shadow fell over him, and she noted the instinctive dart of his hand towards his axe. A cold weight settled into her stomach.

'Look at this,' he grated. She advanced and took the object he handed her, then looked from it to where he was pointing on the cannon and back again. Brida had always preferred spears and swords to cannons and muskets, but that didn't mean she didn't understand artillery.

Air hissed through her teeth. 'Someone's spiked it?'

'Yes, and done a good job, too. It was sitting flush with the vent, barely visible. On casual inspection it looked fine. Whoever's done this didn't want us to realise we couldn't fire her until we needed to. Say, when we came under attack.'

Brida met the duardin's deep-set eyes. 'You're saying we've a traitor in Lady's Justice?'

'I'm saying it's taken me most of the morning to bore out the spike without damaging the vent. We'll still need to test-fire a few balls and I won't allow anyone near it when I do in case she blows. I don't know who spiked it or why, but after I'm done here I'll be checking the other cannons and the muskets too. I'll be checking firing pans and barrel rifling and everything else I can think of.'

Sweat prickled at Brida's hairline. There was a joke in there somewhere about how he thought her untrusting, but there was nothing funny about the situation. 'You check the cannons, I'll check the rest. Then get some sleep, that's an order. I need your eyes sharp for the enemy.' She gestured. 'Outside Greenspire – and maybe inside it.'

Drigg nodded and bent to the cannon without another word. She left him to it, striding back out into the bright day with suspicions blackening her heart.

She spotted Brock and called him over, reassured as ever by his easy competence, his ready smile. If she was the head of Lady's Justice, Brock was the heart, and his return from Fort Gardus had given them all a boost. A joke and a wink at the right time from him solved most disputes before they escalated, and his easy reminiscences of mistakes made when he first joined up served to reassure the recruits that they, too, could get better with practice.

'What do you think of the new lot, sergeant?' she asked as she led him to the armoury.

'About as useful as you'd expect, captain,' the tall man said. 'Though they're having much the same issues even at Fort Gardus, if that's any consolation, as well as along the Line. Too many youngsters and old folks, not enough steady hands. That Kende's a waste of uniform and I wouldn't be surprised if Raella poisons us all.'

Brida gave him a sharp look. 'Can they be trusted?'

Brock's eyebrows shot up. 'Trusted? That's a strange question, captain. They're young and they're nervous, but they're decent enough. Why do you ask?'

They ducked inside before she answered. 'Someone sabotaged cannon one. Spiked the vent. I trust the rest of Lady's Justice with my life – gods, most of them have saved it at least once, you included – but the recruits? That's a different matter.'

Brock's mouth was hanging open, but he snapped it shut and thought. Brida reached for the first musket in the rack and let him. Slow and steady, was Brock. No point in hurrying the man. She checked the firing pan and cocking mechanism, peered down the barrel.

'I haven't noticed anything so far. I mean, Kende's useless, but I'd have said he was harmless, too, before this. He was stationed by the cannon yesterday – could he have done it then? Would he even know how to spike a cannon? I can fetch his records, check his background.'

Brida selected the next musket, repeated her inspection. 'Vinetown, down west. A small agricultural town that provided wheat, oats and barley to Fort Gardus. Attacked and destroyed by tzaangors eight months ago. Kende was one of only a dozen survivors.'

Brida made a point of knowing the histories of every one of her soldiers. For the longest-serving members of Lady's Justice, their histories were hers and as familiar as the feel of her spear in her hand. She'd learnt the stories of the recruits as well, but they didn't open up to their captain the way they would to a friendly, easy-going sergeant, and Brock had been on a supply run to Fort Gardus for pig iron when Kende and the rest arrived.

It wasn't Brock's responsibility to assess the recruits, of course, but over the years she'd come to rely on his judgement and now she needed it more than ever. 'Work your charm with Kende and the others,' she said as she picked up another musket. 'Let me know if anyone seems off to you, but don't make it obvious. You know the drill.'

'Yes, captain,' Brock said. 'I won't let you down.'

Brida found a smile for him. 'You never have.'

Drigg and a team of ten had manoeuvred the cannon back into place, and he'd checked the other two as promised and found everything in perfect working order. It was mid-afternoon before he'd tumbled into bed in the small room in the officers' barracks. Brida could hear his snores from where she sat outside, checking the supply lists in the shade away from Ghyran's fierce sun. Even after twenty years, the sound amused and infuriated her in equal measure.

'Captain?'

'What is it, Orla?' she asked the gunner.

The short woman's freckled face was pale despite her tan. 'Three day watch taken sick, captain. It's coming out both ends, if you get my meaning. They're in the infirmary.'

I wouldn't be surprised if Raella poisons us all. Brock's words rang in Brida's head as she shoved the papers onto her desk and weighed them down with a mug. 'What have they eaten?' she demanded. 'Who made it?'

Orla stepped back from Brida's vehemence. 'Nothing, just the same as the rest of us and we're fine. Do you want–'

She was cut off by the sight of Raella running from the kitchen. Brida's hand went to her spear, but then the woman was on her knees in a corner vomiting. 'Bring her to the infirmary,' she said, and ran for the building herself.

Over the next hour fourteen more soldiers arrived, until there were no beds left and the room stank of vomit. 'Heatstroke?' Brida asked Tomman as Raella sipped from a cup and promptly threw it back up again. The physician shook his head. 'Poison?'

'It seems most likely, but the method of ingestion is unknown. Perhaps they've touched something smeared with it, or–'

But Brida wasn't listening. 'We all ate the same, yes. But you and I haven't drunk from the water barrels on the levels. Orla?'

The gunner shook her head and patted the waterskin slung over her shoulder. 'From this morning,' she said.

Brida slapped a fist into her palm. 'That must be it. Orla, go and wake up Drigg. Brock, with me. You too, Tomman.'

The sergeant hurried after her and they met Orla and a bleary-eyed Drigg in the courtyard. 'We're low on gunpowder, a cannon gets spiked, and now my soldiers are taking sick,' she said to the huddled group. 'Tomman, I need you to test the water barrels on each level for poison, then the well – day shift will have been drinking a lot in this heat. Brock, Orla, see anything suspicious around the barrels or well in the last couple of hours?' They both shook their heads. 'Damn. Fine, Drigg and I will begin questioning–'

The bell on Greenspire's third level began to ring. 'Attack, attack from the Hexwood. Warflock, some hundreds!'

Brida exchanged a horrified look with Drigg. 'All hands,' she said. 'Tomman, get those samples, then Orla, confiscate the barrels. Brock, cap the well. Tomman, do whatever you have to to get the sick on their feet and ready to fight. Powders, potions, I don't care. Just do it, and then find or create me a clean water supply. Fighting soldiers are thirsty soldiers.'

Freeguilders began sprinting to the armoury for muskets, powder and shot. Others stumbled from the barracks, cursing and fumbling with the buckles of their armour. Dusk was beginning to pool in the sky. Brida looked at the duardin, her mouth dry.

'Crimson the flame.' Drigg blinked away the last of his fatigue and broke into a run for the nearest stairwell.

Brida snatched up her spear and took the stairs two at a time, cracking her knee into the wall at the second level turning, and cursing as pain spiked through her leg with every step. She was breathless when she reached the third level and sprinted onto the allure, craving water now she knew she couldn't have it.

The sight that met her eyes dried her throat even further. Tzaangors, their beaks and horns sheathed in steel and reflecting the dying light, raced across the open ground bearing jagged weapons. Beastkin, twisted giant wolves and maddened bear-things with too many teeth, too many claws, thundered alongside.

Brock reappeared. 'Well's capped, captain. And, I don't know, but does it seem a bit too convenient that Orla has a separate supply of water to everyone else on the day they're all getting sick?'

Brida blinked at him, uncomprehending for a moment. 'Orla? I've known her as long as I have you and Drigg!'

Brock wouldn't look at her. 'Of course, captain.'

Brida stared over the wall at the oncoming flock, but she wasn't seeing it. Orla was the gunnery sergeant. She knew how to spike a cannon. Could it be more than a coincidence? Had one of Lady's Justice walked into the arms of Chaos and agreed to betray Devholm and all the soldiers under her command? But why? *Why?*

'Captain?'

'Drigg, there you are. We've got enough powder for a dozen shots each, so get… What now?' A throbbing pain began behind Brida's eyes at the duardin's gloomier than usual expression.

'Flame won't crimson, captain. I've changed the alchemical compounds three times – she just keeps burning green. No one's coming.'

Brida looked up, as though she could see the fire through the stone separating them. 'That's not possible.'

'Sputters crimson for a heartbeat and then greens again. It's trying, the alchemy's there, but something's holding it back. I'd say we've some sort of mage in Greenspire. They've spell-locked the flame, bound it to something living. Or someone.'

'So we kill them and the flame crimsons?' Brida asked, biting back the urge to scream. No one was coming to Lady's Justice's aid.

'Theoretically. Need to know who it is first.' He stroked his beard. 'Come to think of it, I took Kende up there last week. He was curious, asked a lot of questions about the flame – how it changes colour, when we'd signal for help and how long it'd take to arrive. Thought we might've had a budding engineer on our hands until his recent lapses in discipline.'

Brida stared between her two officers and then out at the approaching warflock again, closing fast on their position. She didn't have time for this, but she couldn't let a traitor run around loose in Greenspire, either. She sucked air through flared nostrils. 'Drigg, prime the cannons.'

The duardin blew out his cheeks. 'Orla's gunnery sergeant,' he began, and Brida rounded on him.

'And right now you're one of only two people I trust, so you're gunnery sergeant. Get to it.'

Drigg stepped back from her fury and saluted, then clattered down the stairs without a backward glance, giving no indication of what he thought of her implication.

'Brock, get me Orla and Kende, now.'

The warflock had reached the broken ground and pit traps dug into the rich soil around Greenspire. She had to make this fast. *Please don't be Orla,* she thought as she waited, the tower humming with activity and shouted orders, the controlled panic of a company about to come under attack.

Orla, Brock and Kende arrived at her position. 'Captain? You don't want me on the cannons?' the woman asked, a wrinkle of confusion between her brows.

'Where were you both when people started getting sick?' Brida demanded, turning from the enemy picking their way through the maze. The cannons would open up any minute now, the crossbows when they reached the marker flags that signalled they were in range.

Orla's frown deepened; Kende just looked confused. 'On watch, captain. As always. Forgive me, but didn't we have this conversation in the infirmary? I haven't drunk the water.'

'I was counting supplies with Raella in the kitchen before she felt ill,' Kende said.

'Who replenished the water barrels?' Brock demanded. 'It was you and Raella, wasn't it? And you oversaw it, Orla.'

'I did,' the woman said with stiff indignation. 'You saw me. You watched me do it. What are you saying, sergeant?'

Brock glanced at Brida as though that settled it. Perhaps it did.

'You're both relieved of duty and will be confined to the cells to stand trial once we have repelled this attack,' Brida said heavily. It didn't sit right with her, but they were fast running out of time before the enemy was at the very walls of Greenspire. And the cannons still weren't firing. 'Put your weapons on the floor and step back, keep your hands where I can see them.'

'Captain,' Orla tried, but Brock muscled in between them and wrenched the spear from her. Kende threw his to the stone and put his hands up, his habitual confusion drowned beneath fear. Fear of her, or of discovery? Or of the hordes coming to tear them to pieces?

'Get them out of here, sergeant,' Brida snarled. She didn't turn her back until the trio had vanished into the stairwell, but as soon as they were gone, she ran to the middle of the allure and leant down to see the gun emplacement at the corner. 'Drigg! For the love of the Lady, fire! They're nearly on us.'

The duardin looked up at her shout, then around the men and

women standing in tense silence on the wall. None were working the cannon. He pointed to the gunpowder barrel and drew his finger across his throat. 'All of them,' he shouted back.

'Get up here,' Brida roared, instead of the curses that crowded her throat. 'Crossbowmen and archers, start loosing in volleys as soon as the enemy breaches the marker flag. No let up. Independent firing when they're twenty feet out.'

'What in Sigmar's name is going on?' she hissed as soon as her lieutenant arrived. 'We lost one load when that fool Kende smashed it. Didn't he mark it up like I said?'

'There's flour mixed into every barrel, captain. Put that in a cannon and you blow up the cannon. Dropping them on the warflock is about all our artillery's good for now.'

Brida gaped at him, her mind a momentary fizzing blank. *How? Why?* Then she forced herself to think, to plan some way to save her company. 'Get back up to the flame. I don't care how you do it, but crimson it. We're not going to outlast this attack without aid or artillery. Barricade yourself in there, Drigg,' she added, squeezing his forearm, 'and Alarielle guide you.'

'The defence?' Drigg asked, already backing away.

Brida hefted her spear. 'I've got the defence.'

Bows and crossbows were taking a toll among the warflock, finding the joins in armour and punching through them, the ground shuddering beneath the thunder of running feet and falling bodies. The demi-wolves and half-bears, though, shook off the missiles as if they were stinging insects, leaping across the pit traps and sharpened stakes, gaining ground. Without Drigg, Brida was everywhere, running between the second and third levels, shouting down to the ground to ensure the gates were fully braced.

She looked for Brock, couldn't find him, and hoped Orla and Kende hadn't resisted. She was torn between wanting it to be them so they were locked away, and hoping it was all some horrible series of accidents. A small, ugly voice in her head told her to execute them both now. If it was one of them, their death would release the spell-lock and the flame would crimson. She pushed it away and focused on repelling the attack.

The beastkin reached the walls, the still-green glow from above glistening in their eyes and teeth. They roared their pain and hate and madness, and they began to climb.

'Crossbows, down into the beasts. Archers, take the tzaangors!' Brida screamed. Greenspire seemed to rock under the impact of mutated flesh, and she stepped back, let an archer take her place at the wall and spun to look into the courtyard. Three figures sprawled in their own blood in all the indignity of violent death. 'What the–'

She raced for the stairs, threw herself down them two at a time and came out into the courtyard. She whirled around, looking for enemies, but saw no one but Brock at the main gate.

Brock at the main gate.

She ran even as she processed his actions, realised he was clearing the barricade and tearing back the bolts that would let in the enemy. The gate shook as it was charged from outside. '*Brock, no!*' she screamed as the awful realisation dawned. He'd fooled her. He'd fooled them all and damned them all.

He turned as if in a dream, exultation glazed across his face. 'For Chaos!' he yelled, and slipped the last bolt free.

Icy fury rose like a hurricane and Brida channelled all of it into the cast of her spear. The weapon hummed through the air and punched into her sergeant's chest, snatching him from his feet and pinning him to the opening gate. He never lost his expression of adoration. She followed the spear and shouldered into the gate with all the momentum of her sprint, digging her boots into the stone and heaving. Seconds later, Tomman the physician joined her. He didn't push, but darted his arm around the opening gate and threw a handful of pellets. The pressure from the other side lessened and now he did lend his strength to hers. 'Quick-sleep,' he panted, 'slow them down a bit.'

'Gate breach!' Brida bellowed, so loud her lungs hurt and Tomman winced. Shouts of alarm from above told her that soldiers would be sprinting down the stairs to help, and across the wall above the gate to rain death on the monsters seeking entry.

It wasn't enough. The pressure on the gate returned and then increased, and Brida and Tomman were shoved back. Shoulders and thighs burning, Brida gritted her teeth and pushed, but the beastkin had the momentum now.

She met Tomman's eyes. 'Count of three, run.'

'We have crimson!' a voice from above blared, and Brida felt a sliver of hope. Brock's death had broken the spell-lock on the flame, and Drigg had added the alchemical compounds to change the colour. It wasn't over yet.

'Stay alive, physician. Help's coming. One. Two. *Three.*'

They let go of the gate and sprinted away as the first half-bear tumbled into Greenspire, falling over itself as the pressure on the barrier released. Those behind clambered over it slavering and howling, each one big enough to tear Brida in half. She didn't give them the chance, hurling herself into the nearest stairwell behind Tomman and slamming the door and locking it. The stairwells were narrow and low to prevent the mutated giants of Tzeentch's hordes from entering. Though that wouldn't stop them rampaging through the kitchen, stores, armoury and infirmary. Anyone found alive in there soon wouldn't be. She had to save them.

She ran into Drigg on the second level. 'They're in.'

'I know. Got half the archers picking them off but there are more still piling through the gate.' He was cut off by a splintering crash and a chorus of desperate screams: a demi-wolf had taken down the door to the infirmary. Drigg directed arrows at it, but it was already too late. The patients were gone, torn apart in seconds as Brida watched in stunned, helpless silence. Ice swamped the fire that had raged in her blood, black and lethal, and Drigg took a step back when he saw her expression.

'You said drop the cannon,' Brida said, the rough edge to her voice all the grief she would allow herself. 'Drop it in front of the gate, crush those coming through so their bodies block the entrance.'

Drigg nodded once. 'Inside the gate,' he corrected, and she trusted him enough not to ask why, just ran for the cannon nearest the gate.

The gun carriage was wheeled, but it still took ten of them to get it moving while another two rigged a hasty pulley system from the hooks hammered into the roof. The tzaangors had cleared the last of the traps and were crowding in behind the warped backs of the beastkin at the gate. The fog of their stink was overwhelming, stinging eyes and clinging like slime inside mouths and throats.

The cannon rocked on its carriage and came free with a chorused grunt from those on the ropes. Brida helped guide it up over the guard wall and into position. She chanced a look down into the courtyard and came face-to-snout with a half-bear, talons dug into the stone blocks of Greenspire's wall.

'*Drop it!*' she yelled and the cannon vanished, scraping the bear from the wall and thundering into the mass of twisted flesh spilling from the gate. The end of the rope, smoking from the speed it went through the pulley, ripped across the side of Brida's head as it flashed past, laying open her scalp and cheek to the bone. She reeled back, blood sheeting, a screech of pain bursting from her.

There was a wailing-howling-roaring from below as beastkin flailed under the cannon's weight, spines cracked and pelvises shattered. They scratched at the flagstones and each other, straining to free themselves, their bulk blocking most of the gate.

Brida sagged against the wall and blinked blood from her eye, trying to formulate a plan that would see them survive until reinforcements from Highoak and Willowflame could reach them. All around the interior of the second level, the soldiers of Lady's Justice were shooting down into the mass of the enemy choking the courtyard. More half-bears were climbing the walls while a giant wolf was half inside a stairwell and straining upwards, arrows lodged in its haunches.

The mess at the gate began to writhe. Howls rose up as broken bodies were shoved aside and tzaangors began worming through the carnage, hacking any flesh that lay in their path.

'…powder.' Drigg's voice was hard to hear over the cacophony rising within and without Greenspire's walls. She turned. The duardin was roping four gunpowder barrels together. Soldiers were breaking open the lids of the others and throwing powder and the contaminating flour into the air over the attackers until a fine mist hung above the warflock's heads.

'Fire arrow,' Drigg snapped. Brida snatched up a bow, lit the arrow from the safety lantern and nocked as the duardin pushed the bomb over the edge.

Brida loosed. The fire arrow struck home when the barrels were just above the heads of the attackers. They exploded and so did the flour hanging in the air, a roiling fireball that sent those on the wall diving for cover and ripped the warflock to pieces. For a few seconds the world was nothing but noise and searing light and boiling air, and then it started raining blood and flesh.

The tzaangors who hadn't been killed outright were running or dragging themselves away, many falling into the traps and pits they'd avoided on the way in. Drigg set archers to harry them as they fled. Brida gave him a grim nod, handed off her bow and snatched a spear, then gathered a score of soldiers and headed for a clear stairwell. There were still disciples of Tzeentch in Greenspire and it was time for them to die.

The Freeguilders from Willowflame reached them first, when they were mopping up the last of the enemy and beginning to count their own dead. That included Orla and Kende, killed by Brock instead of imprisoned. Killed because of her short-sightedness, Brida knew, her trust in a man who didn't deserve it. Orla, a friend of decades, who'd never done anything but stand at her side and support her. And Kende, who hadn't been cut out to be a soldier but who'd died one anyway. Because of her.

Captain Sonoth sent half his company to harry the decimated warflock back to the Hexwood, and the rest began the ugly process of piling dead tzaangors and beastkin for burning.

'Lot of corpses considering your flame was only crimson a short while,' he said. 'How did they get the jump on you?'

Brida sat on the well cap while Tomman stitched her face. She'd been lucky not to lose an eye, though part of her ear was missing. She'd refused poppy extract for the pain – her penance for Orla and Kende, the scar a lifelong reminder that trust was a luxury she could no longer afford.

'We had a traitor,' she said. 'Sergeant Brock, a man I've served with for twenty years. Took a supply run to Fort Gardus and when he came back… fouled the gunpowder, poisoned the water, framed a damn good soldier and a recruit for it, and then opened the gate to let the flock in. And I didn't see any of it coming. I just let him back in and he nearly got us all killed.'

Sonoth's face hardened. 'And where is this sergeant?'

Brida met his gaze. 'I killed him, and my only regret is that I didn't do it slowly. Our flame was somehow spell-locked to his life force – when he died it changed colour. Either there's a Chaos cult in Fort Gardus or one of the Emerald Line towers between here and there chose evil and drew him in. But he's dead, so we'll never know.' She hoisted herself to her feet, groaning as wounds and aches made themselves known. 'Captain Sonoth, I'll be sending word up and down the Line about what happened here. Any new recruits, any veterans who leave your company for any period of time, especially if they're sent out alone, they need to be carefully watched on their return. Maybe even quarantined. Tzeentch's plans are subtle, but not even I ever considered something like this. We need–'

'Crimson on the horizon!' came the shout from above. 'Highoak, Gemfire, by the Lady, Dawnspike too! Captain… captain, they're all changing. Crimson along the line, far as I can see!'

Sonoth and Devholm looked at each other. 'Whatever warning you have, captain,' Sonoth said heavily, 'I think you're too late.'

GHOSTS OF KHAPHTAR

Miles A Drake

Her feet squelched in the putrid mud, pressed down by an unfamiliar weight. The hem of her dusky robe and much of her dark, glassy purple armour was caked in the necrogenous ooze. The noxious haze emanating from the landscape of rotting benthic matter grated at her lungs and burned her eyes.

The foggy currents of the aethersea that might once have brought comfort were stagnant, though she could still feel the ripples of movement cast by the exhausted strides of the namarti at her flanks, and the lethargic circling of her rakerdart. The latter emerged from behind the immense, bleached ribs of a rotting murkwhale, whose skeleton she strode through.

'Heel, Ionian,' Akhlys whispered.

The rakerdart did as it was bid. Its scales had turned a hypoxic purple.

'It won't be long now,' she said, mournfully stroking the rakerdart's dorsal fin with a gauntleted hand.

Death was everywhere, splayed out across the seabed. The decay made a final banquet for millions of chitinous scavengers, who glutted themselves on the rotting world they once flourished in, even as they slowly asphyxiated beneath the wilting, purple radiance that pierced the eerie haze.

She closed her eyes as another beast thrashed behind her. The last fangmora.

Hardening her resolve, she turned, seeing the ragged band file into the colossal ribcage of the murkwhale.

The namarti, several dozen in number, paused, listening to the dying eel. Their once lithe and imposing figures had given way to slumped exhaustion, and the runes on their foreheads, once glimmering with the light of stolen souls, were dull and muted. Several of them carried stretchers bearing comatose compatriots wrapped in damp, saline gauze.

Her gaze panned over to the convulsing fangmora, whose scales showed a more severe discolouration than Ionian's. A trio of akhelians knelt beside it. Two held it down, easily overpowering its weak spasms. The third, the beast's bonded master, removed his helm and drew his helsabre.

With a single word of deliverance, he opened the beast's throat with the inward curve of his blade. A flood of purple sprayed, misting in the air for a moment, caught in the aethersea's stagnant current, before condensing to sink into the mud.

The akhelian stood, head bowed, helm clutched in the crook of his arm. His regal poise had faded, and his expression showed a blank, hopeless void. He turned as Tethyssian, the tidecaster, approached. The isharann's loose robes were weighed down by caked mud as he drew back his cowl. He regarded the dead fangmora, before looking up to its former master. 'May I speak the Rite of Severance?' he asked, his voice solemn and tired.

'For what?' The akhelian stared blankly at the tidecaster, his voice barely a whisper. 'There are no ebbing tides to dispatch the beast's spirit upon. The sea is dead. And so is that which was bound to me.'

As an isharann, Akhlys knew the rite bore no true sorrow. The akhelians shared no emotional bond with their enslaved beasts. But it still held significance.

Tethyssian's lips tightened. 'Ceremony and tradition, Saturiandi. What we once took solace in are the only truths that can keep us whole through this nightmare. We must preserve the nobility of our forebears, lest we slip further into the abyss of soulless pragmatism.' His reprimand was as loud as he dared, given the danger that might still lurk in the fog, but it was enough for the others to hear. It was addressed to everyone.

Saturiandi turned away from Tethyssian, leaving the carcass of his eel behind. 'We can afford no sentiment that does not help our immediate survival,' he spat.

'That is the current to oblivion,' Tethyssian scolded. 'If we abandon what is ours, what purpose is there to our salv–'

The akhelian wheeled around, his pale visage flushing a furious grey. 'Salvation is an end unto itself!' he hissed. 'What was the purpose of the death of our ocean? What was the purpose of the destruction of our encla–'

'Enough!' Akhlys stepped forward, thudding the butt of her talúnhook onto the shell of a rotting ammonite. 'You will draw more of the thrice-cursed vermin down upon us if you continue bickering. And our enclave is *not* dead. The Laebreans came to our people's aid. They will have saved many.'

Saturiandi spared her a half-glance. 'Yes, but that doesn't exactly help *us* now, does it?' he hissed, before moving on.

Akhlys turned to follow the akhelian. She could understand his pain. The dying defenders of the Amoch-túr pickets they'd returned to had told them that the death toll had been catastrophic, regardless of the Laebrean intervention.

Glancing back at the namarti, Akhlys could see the same pain written in their stances, even if it was more muted. Most of the namarti had left their kin behind in Amalthussanar when they'd been selected to join Akhlys' raiding party. Ironically, that selection might have saved them, though many would never know what happened to the kin they'd left behind. The receding sea had cut off the route to the Laebrea Basin, as well as any attempt to search for their lost kin.

But there was nothing Akhlys could say to balm their woes. She could heal their flesh and reinvigorate their souls, but she was no tru'heas. She could not heal their wounded psyches. All she could do was remind them of their purpose, and lead them to deliverance.

As the exhausted caravan ascended the slow incline of the Silence of Songs, the death and decay rampant on the vast mesobenthic plain only sapped the ebbing vigour from the tattered band further.

And worse, the place held a certain, solemn significance to the idoneth. It was where the murkwhales came to die. Their great migrations had once carried them through the dark seas of Shyish, and when their ancients passed through the Khaphtar Sea to come to their final resting grounds, they provided the idoneth sustenance in the form of the chitinous parasites that clung to them.

Akhlys had always marvelled at their songs, lonely and sombre. Her enclave lived in near total silence, fearing to utter any noise, lest it draw the teeming shoals of drowned dead down upon Amalthussanar. Thus was the dirge of the murkwhales the only music her people could readily experience.

But now that was gone... forever.

Their remains were scattered about amidst the noxious fog, the ominous shapes of their colossal skeletons overgrown by thickets of huskworms. Once, the worms had bloomed like violet flowers, nourished by the leviathans' corpses, but now, their macabre beauty had decayed, having long degenerated into masses of crimson, viscera-like ribbons.

Amidst the husks, the pale, spindly carcasses of the carcinarians that had once pruned the worm colonies with tender grace lay scattered about, twisted in the agony of their last, asphyxiating moments, and making banquets for flocks of squawking, razor-beaked bloodgulls.

Things shambled about in the putrid haze. Vile, barnacled cadavers loped alongside the bones of ancient mariners and the bloated husks of the verminous filth that had died during their attempt to infest the draining sea. Flocks of spectres drifted in eerie gyres, their anguished howls carrying across the dead wind, and many times, the idoneth were forced to change course, to avoid the attention of the dead.

'The putrid sun allows no rest...' Tethyssian muttered as they marched, glaring up at the purple gleam above. 'It is the Soul Collector's abhorrent will made manifest that such dark animation is breathed into the husks of the dead. If *he* can sift through the memories of those we have claimed, I wonder what secrets he might glean of our people... now that the drowned are exposed.'

It was an unsettling thought. The Khaphtar's raiders, and all of the enclaves of Shyish, took extra care to carry those whose souls had been taken down into the murky depths with them. They left nothing for the Soul Collector's agents to interrogate. But no longer... Now he would know. The draining sea had ended their secrecy.

'The bones of our chorrileum are open and bared to his gaze,' Akhlys replied bitterly. 'The memories of those we have taken will tell him no more than what he already knows. I can only hope the other seas have not met a similar fate...'

'Surely not,' the tidecaster said. 'The Amiritanni Ridge will prevent the Laebrea Basin from draining, and the Bleached Isthmus ahead separates us from the Great Quagmire. I merely wonder if your hope is justified. Do you truly believe the Mor'phann will take us in?'

'They must,' Akhlys said grimly.

Tethyssian shrugged. 'I do not know. We broke currents with them because they refused to contact the other enclaves. Do you truly believe they will break their isolation now?'

'I have to,' Akhlys said. 'What other hope is there?'

Tethyssian sighed. 'None, I'm afraid.'

'The Bleached Isthmus is not a wide landmass. We can cross it in but a single tide.'

Tethyssian inclined his head. 'Of course, but such a journey won't be without its own peril. The Revenant Kingdoms hold the isthmus. We will need to tread carefully.'

'I'm well aware,' Akhlys muttered. 'The shores ahead were my reaping grounds, remember? I will lead us through.'

Tethyssian nodded again. 'I have faith in you in that regard. I merely...' He paused, thinking how best to phrase something controversial. 'I merely wonder if you underestimate what lies beyond that. *If* we reach the Great Quagmire and find the Mor'phann... *if* we can convince them not to kill us outright... they will demand a tribute in exchange for their protection.'

'I'm well aware,' Akhlys said again, coldly.

'Perhaps, if we encounter more of the thrice-cursed vermin along our route, or are forced into conflict with the humans of the isthmus, I might suggest saving the souls you harvest.' He gestured at the doused lantern she carried.

Akhlys had removed it from her helm, and fastened it to her belt. Without the aethersea's buoyancy, her crested anglerhelm had become too cumbersome to wear. She'd left it behind leagues ago.

Turning her gaze to Tethyssian, Akhlys' lips curled into a snarl of distaste. 'That would mean the death of many of the namarti who were weakened by the vermin's sorcery.'

Tethyssian's features tightened, and he lowered his voice. 'I know. But without souls to barter with, I fear we will be turned aside by the Mor'phann... at best. You must consider thi—'

'No,' she said flatly, before increasing her pace and leaving the tidecaster behind.

She would sacrifice much to ensure the survival of her people, but to endure whatever trials lay ahead, they would need every namarti ready to fight.

It was hours later, when the caravan began its climb up the continental rise, that they encountered more remnants of the thrice-cursed vermin that had doomed their enclave. Akhlys saw the shape of one of their vile engines ahead, its hull gouged open on the rocks, and was overcome by the tide of bitter memories, fresh and painful in her mind like a festering wound.

Her raiding party had been ascending the rise, several hundred leagues from Amalthussanar, when Tethyssian had detected the shifting tide. When he'd worked out that the sea was draining, the decision to return to the enclave to learn of what was happening was unanimous, and so her band abandoned its task of gathering souls, and began the journey home.

They did not make it, however. Perhaps if the increasingly powerful currents hadn't made the journey across the abyssal plain so difficult, they might have arrived in time to join the evacuation. But they hadn't.

They'd barely managed to reach the floating Amoch-túr pickets before the verminous ones attacked in their rattling submersibles. The toxic wakes of their infernal contraptions, and the devastation wrought by their techno-arcane weaponry, halved the strength of Akhlys' warband.

She'd learned of what was occurring in Amalthussanar then, from one of the dying akhelians that had been part of the Amoch-túr phalanx. The Laebreans had come to evacuate, and, according to the warrior, had somehow managed to distract the dredge-fleets the Soul Collector had sent to investigate. She'd also learned that the currents had grown too powerful in the hadal channels surrounding the massive seamount the enclave was built atop, and that attempting to reach the city, *or* the Laebrea Basin itself, would be suicide.

With no other option, Akhlys had given the order to make for the *second* nearest idoneth settlement, the great Mor'phann city of Mor'drechi. All that stood in their way was the relentless pull of the draining currents, and the tide of drowned dead that were caught in them.

It had almost been a relief to exit the waters, for at least that granted the idoneth a reprieve from the harrying vermin sub-mersibles that had trailed them since the pickets. That was about the only mercy they'd been granted since it all began.

The wreck of one such submersible hung impaled on two jagged, rocky spires that protruded from the muddy substrate below. It had clearly run aground as the ocean bled out beneath it.

The machine was dotted with crude stabilisation fins and strange dome-like lenses across its hull. Protrusions of coiling metal, ending in greenish crystals, jutted from its prow, and a secondary cupola clung to its spine like a metallic tumour. Debris and bloated, waterlogged corpses were haloed around it, and Akhlys scrunched up her nose at the stench of decay and acrid fur.

'Disperse! Seeker shoal!' she commanded.

The namarti fanned out, adopting a wide formation that would allow their acute, but range-restricted senses to cover the most ground. The akhelians searched the bodies in a more conventional manner.

'Find me any wretches that still live,' she called again, surveying the area. The souls of vermin were sour, sickly things. They provided only a paltry spark of nourishment to the namarti. But now, they'd need every morsel, no matter how revolting.

If any of the vile creatures still lived within the submersible, they would be unreachable. She was not about to send anybody inside it, as the vehicle's gaping wound leaked a glowing green slime that sizzled into the mud below.

Eventually, the leader of her reavers, the Icon Bearer Akmaeon, returned. His face and upper torso were badly scarred with old lamprey bite marks, and he was something of a grizzled veteran – a fierce, old namarti at the end of his current.

'Nothing...' he said dourly.

Saturiandi snarled in agreement, emerging from behind the vehicle. 'Not a twitch of whatever passes for life in any of these cancerous wretches...'

'Then we move,' Akhlys commanded. 'Before something else animates them...'

She saw the namarti slump just a little further. Several of their wounded might not survive the journey without reinvigoration.

But there was nothing to be done. She gave the call to advance, sparing another glance at Ionian, who drifted lethargically in her wake, its scales even more discoloured. With a swish of her hand, she sent a ripple through the dead aetheric currents, calling her raker-dart from the asphyxiated trance it had fallen into, and pressed on.

Hours passed, and the incline and lack of buoyancy taxed the idoneth further. For all of Tethyssian's exhausted efforts, the aethersea had receded to an almost imperceptible shroud. The air was dry and grating.

The first of the namarti to die from soul-enervation passed but a scant few leagues beyond the wrecked submersible. Tethyssian administered what rites he could, and cast the unsouled husk of the thrall face down into a hastily dug trench in the mud. The other namarti listened, before paying their respects, touching two of their fingers to the emblazoned rune on their foreheads.

With grim resolve, Akhlys bid the band onward, for the route to salvation shimmered in the distant mirage, periodically coming into view as a stinking squall blew away the haze. She could see the skeletal structures of the bleached coral forest ahead, high on jagged cliffs of broken basalt.

She gestured with her talúnhook so the namarti might feel the ripple of the movement. 'Salvation lies beyond the isthmus ahead. It is still leagues away… but that is but a paltry stretch in our journey.'

Tethyssian lent his words to hers. 'The humans of the Revenant Kingdoms dwell there. And that…' He panned his tired gaze towards Akhlys. 'That means there are souls for the taking.' That the barbs in his gaze did not translate into his words, for the sake of the namarti, was enough to make Akhlys give him a barely perceptible nod of thanks.

It was all that needed to be said. It was all that *could* be said.

With a wave of her hand, the respite was over, and the exodus continued.

But the suffering and loss of life did not abate.

Ionian faltered further up the continental rise, slumping into the mud with the ridge and towering coral-forest in sight. The rakerdart thrashed in the silt, frothing at the mouth.

Akhlys knelt beside it, drawing her ritual dagger. The hooked blade was fashioned from the fang of a kharybdean horror from the hadal trenches. She covered Ionian's form in a shroud of rotting seaweed, and the beast ceased its thrashing, the cool wetness of the decaying vegetation bringing its last comfort.

With a pang of sorrow, Akhlys drew her dagger across Ionian's throat. Its blood bubbled into the mud, and after a moment, its last shudders of life ebbed away.

As she had done so many times in the past, Akhlys quashed her emotions, forcing them into that deep black void in the back of her mind where all unwanted thoughts went to die. There was no place for grief. Ionian was just another loss. Just another scar to bear.

She stood, straightening her robe.

The namarti regarded her with cocked heads. She didn't know if they could sense her pain.

Saturiandi did, to some degree. He gave her a solemn nod.

'Come... we move. We're close to the isthmus now,' she said, hoping the strain wouldn't be evident in her voice.

But she didn't hear it. The numbness had already set in.

As they approached the cobbled strand ahead, under the cover of barnacled boulders and swirling mists, the twilight haze of Shyish's sun bathed the jagged formations ahead in a shimmering violet sunset.

Great gouges split the cliff face beyond, and Akhlys knew a warren of trenches, runnels and basins would provide some cover during their crossing of the Bleached Isthmus. A forest of pale coral splayed out above the dark stone bluffs, branching up like skeletal limbs, though most of it remained hidden behind the basalt cliffs.

Hissing a quick command to stop the party, she moved ahead with a small force to take cover behind a muddy escarpment several hundred paces from the strand.

Akmaeon, a trio of other reavers and Saturiandi joined her.

'That wasn't there the last time we came this way,' the akhelian hissed, gesturing at the rickety, whalebone bell tower that stood above one of the rocky outcroppings on the strand.

'No,' Akhlys agreed.

'The humans have caught on to our raids, then,' Saturiandi muttered.

Akhlys panned her gaze further down the rocky strand. More towers rose up at regular intervals, every several hundred paces along the coast to each side. All were manned.

She looked at Saturiandi. 'Bring up your ishlaens. We do this with blade and hook.'

Saturiandi gave a thin smile, retreating back into the caravan.

'We can fight,' Akmaeon said, his voice muted and emotionless.

'You are weakened, and robbed of your senses,' Akhlys rebuked. 'The humans *cannot* sound that bell. I need faultless precision, and for now, that is not something you can offer.'

The receding aethersea might have brought discomfort to the higher castes, but the namarti relied on it for their very perception.

Akmaeon bowed his head in deference. 'We will protect the others.'

Akhlys nodded as she calculated how best to approach the watchtower unseen. The setting sun cast long shadows that would be easily noticeable, but the mist was still dense enough that, with just a little luck, they could make a stealthy approach.

Moving forward, Akhlys and the akhelians hugged the strewn boulders and empty tidal channels, before crossing the final stretch of the cobbled strand to wait in the shadow of the rising bedrock. She'd caught glimpses of the sentries. They were stooped, and leaned on hook-bladed voulges. Their stance indicated fatigue.

She left her talúnhook leaning against the rock. It would be too cumbersome to climb with, or to fight with in confined spaces. Drawing her kharybdean fang-dagger and clenching it between her teeth, she began to climb.

The akhelians followed. But they were mostly a precaution, if anything. She could handle the trio of men atop the tower on her own.

Scrambling up, she hoped the moaning of the distant wind, and the shrill call of the bloodgulls overhead, would mask her ascent. Shifting to the tower's whalebone scaffolding, she easily hauled herself and her armour upward, her muscles taut with a strength derived from decades of harsh training and battle.

Once she reached the top, she all but vaulted the last rungs. The expressions of surprise on the sentries' faces gave her a cold satisfaction.

They were wretched-looking men, emaciated and clad in dark, oily rags decorated with frills of pale gull feathers. Two wore masks of driftwood, while the third's face was obscured by the skull of a doom vulture.

She lashed out with her dagger, opening the throat of the man closest to her. He fell, gurgling as he splattered crimson across the pale driftwood decking.

The one nearest to the bell reached for its cord, but Akhlys shoulder-slammed him, sending him crashing through the flimsy driftwood rail and plummeting to his doom on the rocks below. The third managed a shout of alarm, and raised his voulge to slash at her. But she lashed back with blinding speed, the hooked tip of her blade embedding into his chest before he could even bring his weapon down.

He slumped, gasping.

Saturiandi poked up from the scaffolding, and took one quick glance. 'It's done,' he said, amused, to the other akhelians below.

'Go back down.' He ascended the platform anyway. 'Good to see you're still quick,' he said to her, panning his gaze out across the landscape. 'The fools didn't build their towers in sight of one another. They thought bells would save them...'

But Akhlys wasn't listening. She had something to do.

Unfastening the lurelight lantern from her belt, she held it down over the dying humans.

Wispy, aethereal light began coiling from their writhing bodies like a phantasmal mist, seething up to whirl around Akhlys.

Saturiandi shuddered as the coalesced souls drifted around him. He couldn't see them, but he could certainly *feel* them. She imagined anyone could.

As the bodies ceased their agonised death throes, ghostly limbs raked at Akhlys with accusation, and she heard the distant cries of the men she'd slain. They screamed, helpless in anguish and confusion as the lurelight drew them towards it.

She didn't shudder.

Not any more.

With the spirits of the slain trapped in her lantern, Akhlys descended from the tower, pausing to collect the soul of the broken but still breathing man that had fallen, before having one of the ishlaens bring up the rest of her ragged band.

She watched them move up the strand, and guided them through one of the runnels in the rocky terrace that merged into a gouged trench in the cliff wall. Leading, Akhlys kept a hundred paces ahead of the others, backed by Saturiandi, Akmaeon and a pair of other namarti reavers.

The trench's basalt walls loomed above them, shrouding them in a near aphotic gloom.

Reaching a wider point in the narrow passage, Akhlys gave the signal to halt. The others quickly caught up to her, and she gave the word to allow them a few moments of respite.

Tethyssian emerged from the ranks just as Akhlys drew the lurelight once more. The lantern glowed faintly with the light of stolen souls.

The tidecaster's exhausted features scowled. 'You intend to–'

'Yes,' she said. 'This is not a discussion.'

The tidecaster sighed, but bowed his head in deference.

Brushing past him, Akhlys knelt beside one of the stretcher-borne namarti, wrapped in saline gauze. She began to peel the wrappings from around the namarti's face, revealing the visage of a young female; the raw burns of the vermin's accursed lightning weaponry marred her features as much as the dim, half-soul rune emblazoning her forehead.

Akhlys uttered an ancient cythai word, causing the souls within the lurelight to stir. Lowering the lantern over the dim rune, Akhlys uttered another word to coax one of the souls from the lantern, directly into the namarti's collar, where it rushed in to fill the gaping void waiting inside the namarti's psyche.

With a gasp, the namarti awakened. Immediately, the emblazoned rune began to glimmer.

Akmaeon knelt beside the female, holding her still as her senses surged for a brief instant. His hand over her mouth, he stifled her scream as the unfamiliar sensation of searing emotion and life blazed like a bonfire.

It quickly doused the energies leeched by the collar, lest they burn her out. As the fleeting sensation faded, the muted numbness that was the namarti's existence returned, and the female ceased her shuddering.

Akhlys watched in disconnected fascination. During that brief moment, she sensed the same will, the same impulse and identity that existed within the akhelians and isharann, if but for an instant.

The moment gone, Akhlys moved on to the next. She had

three souls, and there were almost a dozen enervated namarti that needed them.

Repeating the process with a male and another, younger female, Akhlys finished, moving back to the head of the caravan as the revitalised namarti borrowed spare weapons from their kin.

Akmaeon stood perfectly still as she passed, inclining his head ever so slightly.

The other namarti mimicked his motion.

She paused. The gesture was odd. The namarti knew their place. And they knew *her* place. They did not offer thanks simply because Akhlys had carried out a soulrender's ordained task. Such was as much for her benefit as it was to theirs.

But then she realised.

They knew.

They'd realised the souls she'd spent to revive three of their number might have been better used to bargain with the Mor'phann. And they'd realised that any bargain made would favour the isharanns and akhelians of the party, not the namarti.

They knew she'd sacrificed something for their sake. And that was a rarity for her caste.

She shook her head, and brushed past the namarti.

'There will be a small village in the basin ahead,' she said. 'If we cannot slip past them, we will need to silence them.'

Sure enough, the trench widened into a basin, several hundred paces across. At the far end, a cluster of immense coral structures rose – from giant reticulated brain corals, their shadowy recesses glimmering with flickering torchlight, to stacks of massive table corals, the spaces between the bone discs fitted with whalebone, driftwood and canvas. Behind it all, a knobby-branched fan coral spread its eroding limbs high over the settlement. Corpses were strung up from the limbs alongside shuddering, winged things, and the light emanating from within the structure had an unsettlingly pallid hue to it.

A network of tidepools and channels pockmarked the muddy flats of the basin. Several villagers, clad much like the sentries, walked on stilts, their long strides unhindered by the mud as they moved about, tending to the crustaceans and sponges within the pools. While they presented gaunt silhouettes in the dying light, the *other* figures scattered about the basin, armed with hooked voulges, were even more unsettling.

They were *too* gaunt. Too motionless.

Akhlys narrowed her eyes. 'Deathrattles,' she hissed to her scouts.

'Easy enough to sneak past,' Saturiandi whispered. 'It's the living that'll present the greater danger.'

'My reavers can end them,' Akmaeon said, his voice muted. 'Scent gives them away.'

Akhlys shook her head. 'No.' She gestured towards the fan coral. The *things* hanging among the corpses were gigantic bats. She had learned not to disregard them as mere creatures. They served as eyes to beings best left undisturbed…

'We must slip past, silently,' Akhlys said. 'If we awaken what sleeps here, we will lose many.'

'Wait for darkness…' Akmaeon began, before quieting. The namarti cocked his head.

Akhlys heard it moments later. Tapping.

The sound of stilts on stone, drawing near.

Gesturing for the scouts to take cover, she ducked into a gouge in the trench wall, seeing the namarti disappear into similar gaps in the rock while Saturiandi submerged himself into a pooled-up runnel in the trench's floor.

The intruders appeared from what must have been an unseen passage in the rock. There were three, dark garbed and bedecked with driftwood masks and gull-feather frills, just like the farmers. Their stilts gave them a close countenance to the strange straw men that the agrarian villages of the Morvirian Duchies left to guard their plantations.

Each carried a long-hafted billhook that they used as a third limb to stabilise their strides.

They stopped for a moment, whispering to themselves in their hushed tongue, before moving down the trench. While they might pass Akhlys' scouts without realising it, the others would not be so fortunate.

Taking a deep breath, she waited until they came into range.

As the third passed her, she emerged, her talúnhook flashing downward, its curved point biting deep into the collar of the man, sinking all the way to his sternum. Her lantern flared as the man quickly died. Wrenching her blade free, she faced the other two as they turned, shifting their grips on their billhooks.

One went down with a pair of arrows in his back as Akmaeon and another reaver emerged from a crack in the wall.

Saturiandi rose from the shallow water, bashing out the stilt of the remaining man with his shield, and delivering a spine-severing slash with his helsabre.

The clatter of wood and the thump of bodies echoed through the trench.

It was the only sound.

Akhlys glanced furtively into the basin. The farmers continued their toil. The dead kept their vigil.

With no further word, she began her grim work.

Moving back to the others, she transferred the stolen souls to three more comatose namarti before bidding them to wait. A short while later, the setting sun sank behind one of the bulbous corals, swathing the entire basin in shadow.

They crossed then, and Tethyssian drew upon the paltry wisps of the aethersea to further cloak their movements in a sparse, gloomy fog. He slumped further at the effort, but refused the assistance of a namarti to help him move.

Less hindered by the dead weight of their enervated kin, the survivors were able to slip around the edge of the basin easily enough, and entered another partially flooded trench.

Eventually, the passage opened up into a sinkhole, some forty paces wide. Stagnant brine flooded the area, and the fan corals jutting from the cliffs above cast strange shadows on the wall. A lone table coral shelf sported a driftwood shack, where a hooked net, stretching across the sinkhole, was anchored above. Several bloodgulls hung motionless, ensnared in the barbed mesh.

Akhlys was about to bid her scouts to tread carefully when a stilt walker emerged from a recess in the rock wall. In an instant, Akmaeon and his reavers drew back their already nocked arrows. But the human's weapon, a long metal tube chased in driftwood, decorated with gull feathers, was already drawn.

A bang, and the acrid stench of brimstone filled the air. One of the namarti fell, his chest mangled by a dozen wounds, just as Akmaeon's arrow found the stilt walker's throat.

The man splashed hard, with a gurgling cry. In response, two more humans emerged from the shack above. Both carried crossbows.

The third reaver's arrow took one in the shoulder before he could act. But the other crossbowman knelt and loosed a quarrel. The reaver fell, the projectile piercing her side.

The wounded human loosed, but his shot went wide.

At that instant, the brine pool shifted, and a trio of stinking, salt-encrusted carcinarians emerged. Their carapaces and spindly, gaunt limbs were bleached and hollow, and an unnatural violet glow gleamed from within them.

Akhlys advanced to intercept the reanimated crab-creatures as they scuttled forward.

With a hiss, she swung her talúnhook down in a deadly arc, severing one snapping pincer limb. The other clamped around her thigh, crushing with horrifying force. Her armour dented, but held. With a gasp of pain, she thrust out with the butt of her polearm, pulping its long, opaque eyes and cracking its exoskeleton.

It reared up, lashing out with its barbed secondary limbs, forcing Akhlys back. With her leg still caught, she almost tripped. Bashing again, the impacts of her polearm caved in the front of the carcinarian's carapace, and it collapsed. The crushing grip broke, and Akhlys pulled her leg free, sloshing through the brine towards the second carcinarian, which was busy dragging one of the fallen namarti into the pool.

The third had latched onto Saturiandi's shield with one pincer, but the akhelian was busy hacking off its other limbs with his helsabre.

A heavy splash resounded as the wounded crossbowman on the table coral fell into the pool.

Akhlys swung wide, her hook puncturing through the side of the carcinarian attacking the namarti, severing one leg. She pulled, wrenching it off its victim. Gritting her teeth, she kicked, her sabaton crushing its mandibles as it snapped at her with both pincers.

Thrusting with her polearm, she kept it at bay, as Saturiandi, finished with his beast, rushed in to hack into its shell. It collapsed after a trio of fierce swings.

Catching her breath, Akhlys looked up. The other crossbowman sat, slumped, transfixed by the pair of arrows embedded in his chest.

There was no further sound.

When she was certain the danger had passed, Akhlys pulled aside the hem of her long robe to undo the fastening on one cuisse. Prying off the ruined armour plate, she grimaced as pressure released from her pulverised thigh muscles.

She took a moment to lean on her talúnhook.

'Akhlys…' Saturiandi began, concerned.

'I'll live,' she hissed through gritted teeth. 'Even in death, their size ill belies their power.'

Saturiandi gave a knowing nod, holding up his shield. The metal rim of it had been twisted by the wrenching force of the beast's pincers. 'Clever,' he said, regarding the now motionless carcinarian corpses. 'Hiding the dead beasts in the flooded ways. I wonder how many more we've managed to avoid thus far?'

'Indeed,' Akhlys returned, wincing as she put weight on her leg. Such creatures had *not* been present during her last raids in this region. 'We'll have to be wary of other pools from now on. More of these sentry beasts might be scattered about.'

Satisfied that her wound was little more than an annoyance, Akhlys unfastened her lantern, holding it up as the wispy soul of the dying stilt walker coiled towards it, even if the dead man on the coral ledge would be out of reach, and the soul of the crossbowman that had fallen had already been pulled away by the ephemeral, deathly gale that perpetually swept across Shyish.

There was no saving the first namarti. The wound inflicted by the human weapon had been grievous, and his chest was a ravaged mess of metal shards. But that wound paled in comparison to what the carcinarian's pincer had done to him. His leg was shattered, and blood and marrow leaked from the hideous wound, diffusing into the burbling brine pool.

She *could* revive him, but it would be for naught, for such a wound would not heal without *far* more extensive care. He would be crippled at best.

Akmaeon knelt beside the mangled reaver, his fingers feeling over the wounds.

'He's gone,' Akhlys said solemnly.

Akmaeon nodded. He understood what Akhlys was and was not capable of, perhaps better than any of the other namarti in the band.

'Sleep, kin of the silent soul…' he whispered mournfully, as he touched the rune on the fallen namarti's forehead, before doing the same to himself.

He immediately moved to the other wounded reaver, who knelt in the brine pool, struggling for breath. The quarrel had pierced one of her lungs: a minor wound, by comparison, even if it would be fatal if left untended.

'One soul…' Akmaeon said as he inspected the wound with touch alone.

His voice was muted, but Akhlys could tell it was a plea. A plea for her to expend another precious soul to heal his wounded kinswoman.

She didn't respond, but limped over to the gasping reaver with sloshing strides. She knelt to remove the projectile from the namarti's ribs, twisting the head so that it slipped out more easily.

To her credit, the namarti did not cry out, though her features bleached in shock.

Akhlys spoke the word to coax a soul from the lantern, and guided it into the namarti's collar. But instead of letting it pass into the soul-void within the namarti, she uttered a second ancient word, redirecting the energy into the namarti's physical flesh.

Forced into material form, the latent potential of the soul's lifespan condensed into a single moment, burning out its energy to accelerate the healing process to impossible speed. Organ, muscle, sinew and skin knitted shut as though months of natural healing had occurred in a matter of moments. Through the namarti's torn vest, Akhlys saw the wound vanish, replaced by nothing more than a raw, livid scar.

With a gasp, the wounded reaver convulsed for a moment, before slumping. Akmaeon knelt to help her rise, turning his head towards Akhlys. While his expression was a placid mask, as was typical for his kind, he inclined his head ever so slightly.

That was when Tethyssian and the others arrived. 'Were you ambushed?' he exclaimed, out of breath, as the rest of the party fanned out to search for other threats.

Akhlys shook her head. 'Not really,' she hissed. Her leg still hurt furiously. 'But such an accidental engagement was bound to happen.'

'They'll have heard that… *noise*,' Tethyssian said.

Akhlys nodded, and began to usher the others along with greater urgency.

'The body…' Tethyssian gestured at the dead namarti. 'They might learn–'

'They already know,' Akhlys reminded him. 'Leave the dead. One more corpse left to the Soul Collector's agents won't grant him any more secrets.'

With no further sentiment, they moved on. The namarti touched their fingers to their rune-marked foreheads as they passed the body of their kin.

Thankfully, the idoneth didn't encounter any immediate reprisal, or any further patrols, and eventually, they emerged into a basin far larger than the first they'd snuck through.

Fields of pale, calcified reeds were arranged along muddy irrigation channels, and strange, slimy growths protruded from several pools, encaged by hanging gull-nets. The gulls hopped about, squawking and bickering over what little pickings they'd found in the mud.

In the distant gloom, torches illuminated a massive complex of reticulated brain coral, and a huge cluster of hollowed pillar corals that loomed like a castle above, its towers connected by rickety rope bridges. Tattered pennants flapped above as swarms of bats, some of unnatural size, circled.

The largest of the towers, soaring high over the settlement, was decorated with an effigy of whalebone and driftwood that resembled a leering skull, topped with a high mitre cap of segmented bone. Baleful blue flame flickered within the icon's empty eye sockets.

'The twisted countenance of the Soul Collector…' Tethyssian muttered with distaste. '*He* watches with burning eyes. He hungers and he hates.'

Akhlys ignored him, and focused on the more tangible threat. 'We need to move quickly,' she said, noting a formation of stilt walkers gathering before a cavernous portico carved into the pillar-castle like a yawning gate. A host of disturbingly gaunt figures emerged from that darkness, their strides eerily synchronised.

'A response force,' Saturiandi hissed. 'They'll see us if we try to pass.'

'And they'll find us if we stay,' Akhlys said dourly.

'Then we must fight,' Tethyssian whispered. The calm in his voice was clearly forced.

Akhlys shook her head. 'What do you feel, Tethyssian?'

The tidecaster regarded her, confused.

'The tides,' Akhlys said. She'd started to feel a cloying dampness settling on her skin not long ago. She wondered why the tidecaster hadn't. Perhaps it was the numb exhaustion.

'I…' Tethyssian closed his eyes, and then opened them again. 'I hear waves. I feel currents. Weak and fleeting. Distant, but…'

'Then we're near to the Quagmire,' Akhlys said.

'Yes,' Tethyssian agreed. 'The Khaphtar's current is dead, but I can feel another.'

'How far is it?' Saturiandi asked, his voice eager.

'I cannot say,' the tidecaster returned. 'I am unfamiliar with the Quagmire's currents. They feel... oily and alien.'

'Akhlys?' The akhelian looked to her.

She shook her head. 'I've raided this landmass thricefold, but this township is as far as I've come. What lies beyond is unknown to me.'

'So what?' he asked, warily regarding the mustering formation.

More figures marched out from the dark gate, cloaked and armoured, but still moving in disturbing unison.

A humanoid shape, tall and lithe, descended from amidst the bats. For all the familiarity of its form, it possessed a set of membranous, chiropteran wings, which vanished disturbingly into its billowing cloak as it landed.

'We move,' Akhlys said. She knew what that creature was, and in no way, shape or form did she wish to encounter it. Regardless of the cold dread prickling at her skin, she kept her voice calm and collected. 'If we can reach the Quagmire in time, we'll be able to avoid them. If they spot us, then so be it. We can outpace them.'

'But they'll know these warrens...' Tethyssian protested.

Akhlys' face hardened. 'We have no choice. They'll find us here, or they'll find us somewhere down the current. The closer we get to the Quagmire, the better our chances.'

'I am in agreement,' Saturiandi said, drawing his helsabre.

Tethyssian took a deep breath, and nodded. 'Yes, I suppose this is the only course left to us. May the currents favour our passage, and befuddle our foes,' he whispered. 'May the ghost of Mathlann bless us.'

Akhlys nodded, though she shared none of Tethyssian's sentiment for ceremony. Mathlann was dead. The only god they needed to worry about now was the one that wanted to exterminate her people.

With no further word, she led the way into the basin.

* * *

Keeping their heads low, and moving through the bone-reeds, the idoneth advanced as quickly as they could. Akhlys led, with Akmaeon and a pair of other reavers, to scout the easiest path. The namarti were forced to shoot the bloodgulls that nested on the nearby rocks several times, lest they take flight and squawk in alarm.

Halfway across the basin, while the band stalked through the pale reeds along the edge of a muddy, crab-infested irrigation trench, a flight of shrieking bats whipped overhead. The idoneth ducked low, hoping to avoid their attention, but a shrill call from some manner of horn echoed up from the village, and immediately, as one, vast plumes of bats suddenly took flight, erupting from caves in the basalt cliffs to join the swarm swirling around the pillared castle.

Akhlys poked her head above the reeds. She saw the stilt walkers advancing, their loping gait unhindered by the muddy terrain.

Flocks of pale bloodgulls squawked in alarm, taking flight in every direction.

'Protective shoal!' Akhlys shouted, waiting for the rest of her people to form up before leading the close-formation retreat down into the nearby trench.

With several namarti still comatose and borne on stretchers, the idoneth were slowed, and their progress was further hampered by the difficult terrain of shattered coral bone and boulders. But quickly enough, Akhlys realised that the trench would work to their advantage. The bony fan structures above prevented the swarm from descending in full force, forcing the bats to trickle in through the narrow gaps in the coral.

The vicious, fanged creatures shrieked, latching themselves to the namarti with their hook-fingered wings, before sinking their dagger-fangs into bare flesh. Several of the creatures landed on Akhlys, and she slowed, ripping one free and crushing its wing with her gauntlet.

Another attempted to bite at her throat, crawling up onto her pauldron, but she tore it off and stomped it under her boot.

With a snarl, she reached to pluck one from Akmaeon's back even as he pulled two more free of his torso. She spun, deftly arcing her talúnhook through the air to bisect a pair of the shrieking vermin.

One of the namarti fell, covered in half a dozen of the creatures, his throat gushing crimson.

She didn't have time to help. The stilt walkers were not far behind.

Scything sweeps from the lanmari blades of the namarti thralls, and deft slashes from the akhelians' helsabres, cut down dozens of bats each moment, littering the ground around them with twitching, black-furred corpses. A deafening bang echoed, and another namarti fell as the lead stilt walker shot his firearm into the tightly packed idoneth. Several reavers were capable of loosing arrows in the midst of the chaos, but most were intercepted by the seething swarm. One of the stilt walkers fell, a lucky shot in the ribs piercing the fingerbone cuirass he wore.

And then, suddenly, Tethyssian's voice rang out above the carnage. He sang the Rite of Effluvial Torpor, the syllables of the ancient cythai tongue echoing through the trench. In an instant, the moisture-laden air seemed to freeze, and an unearthly, frozen mist billowed out to coat everything, living or otherwise, in a thin film of hoarfrost.

To the idoneth, the sensation was unpleasant, as their parched skin became beset by a blanket of icy cold. But for the bats, it was worse. They fell like a thick black rain, collapsing to the frozen stones. Most writhed about, wings and ribs broken by the impact. Others were able to crawl away, their movements sluggish and weak.

The stilt walkers backed off, and Akhlys saw Tethyssian, his robe covered in thin icy crystals as he held out both arms.

The mist blew away moments later, as a gust of air, disturbed by the sudden heat vacuum, swept through the trench. But unaffected as they were, the idoneth made short work of the bats that still lived, stomping and skewering those that attempted to flap away and rejoin the swarm above.

'The sea... is returned!' Tethyssian called, his voice strained from the effort of pulling such a powerful current so far. 'The Quagmire is near!'

'Salvation is close!' Akhlys took up his triumphant cry, taking a moment of satisfaction in seeing another volley of whisperbow arrows scythe into the retreating stilt walkers. Several tumbled and fell.

But she quickly realised they wouldn't have long before the bats returned. Even now, the creatures billowed up, like some abominable smoke plume overhead.

And worse, through a gap in the fan coral above, she saw a figure, standing atop a narrow spire-coral that loomed over the trench. The bat swarm whipped about it, disturbing its long, tangled hair and tattered black cloak. Its skin was ghostly pale and its eyes seared a malevolent crimson. It pointed with a single, gnarled talon, directly at Akhlys.

Staring up at the figure for an instant, Akhlys gestured back at it with her talúnhook, her lips curled into a snarl.

And then, without a further word, she turned, following the rest of her kin down the trench.

Several hundred paces further, the idoneth emerged from the gloomy canyon into a wide, rocky valley. Hollowed, knobby coral structures, converted into crude dwellings, dotted the entire area, and the surrounding slopes had been carved into terraced pools, lined with gull-nets. Stilt-walking farmers milled about, carrying flickering lanterns as they drew the nets over the terraces for the night. They quickly fled upon seeing the idoneth emerge from the trench.

Ahead, down the gradual slope of the valley, close, labyrinthine formations of brain and column coral obscured what lay ahead, but a cool, oily smell wafted up on the wind.

Akhlys couldn't see what lay behind that, but she knew immediately. A comforting dampness set on her skin, and a sparse fog misted up around them, coalescing at hip level into a dark, sheeny layer that rippled with their movements.

'The aethersea floods!' Tethyssian called, the vigour of hope returning to his voice. 'The Great Quagmire is close!'

'One final eddy,' Akhlys called, glancing up at the bats that crested the cliffs behind them.

Ahead, the flickering torchlights within the labyrinthine structures belied hidden threats, waiting for them, and the tapping sound echoing from the trench behind signified the pursuing host.

'Move, now! Through the coral warrens ahead,' Akhlys called, hopping from boulder to boulder, the comforting buoyancy alleviating her fatigue.

But the swarm still circled overhead, following them from above. While Tethyssian's evocations of freezing mist seemed to keep the smaller bats at bay, larger shapes emerged from the shrieking mass.

With a beat of monstrous leathery wings, a host of abominably large chiropteran horrors swooped low, emitting a chorus of debilitating shrieks as they slammed into the idoneth with savage force. Akmaeon fell, knocked flat as one of the beasts raked at him with its claws. He rolled away, disembowelling the creature with his keening dagger.

Another swooped down at Akhlys, but she scythed its wing off, sending it crashing into the rocks with pulping force. Snarling, she lunged forward to cleave through another's skull that had knocked down one of the ishlaens.

The idoneth instinctively circled up: a protective shoal to ward off predators. But Akhlys saw what was approaching. The stilt walkers and the armoured undead were not far behind. And the winged, humanoid figure soared above them, the bats haloing it as though it were the eye of their maelstrom. Its whispers echoed across the basin, eerily merging with the cacophonous shrieks of the chiropterans. It descended to perch atop the highest of the pillar corals ahead.

Suddenly, gaunt, tattered figures armed with billhooks and sickles emerged from the structures around them.

The enemy was closing in on all sides, urged forward by the enthralling force of the creature above.

'Disperse!' Akhlys shouted, breaking back into a run down the slope. A dense shoal was easily slowed and overwhelmed by sustained attack.

Risking a glance behind her, she winced as a stretcher-bearing namarti fell, her throat opened by a giant bat's fangs. The gauze-wrapped, comatose reaver rolled onto the rocks as a second bat descended upon it to feast. The other stretcher bearer attempted to intervene, but was quickly scythed down by another shrieking creature.

Akhlys could do nothing. They had lagged behind.

'Keep moving!' she roared, seeing several namarti slow to assist their kin.

There was no time to aid the wounded.

Akhlys cleaved a landing bat down in front of her, spinning in mid-run to shear off the wing of another that swooped towards Akmaeon. The namarti's whisperbow sang its hushed song as he ran, its arrows leaving distorted trails in the aetheric fog, and spitting plumes of misting black blood from the bats they struck.

A series of cracks rang out behind them, as several stilt walkers fired their powder weapons on the move. But none found their mark in the refracting haze of the aetheric mist.

The swarm of smaller bats extended tendrils of itself down towards the idoneth, but most simply fell to the ground, ice crystals blanketing their forms as their movement was reduced to a lethargic crawl.

Akhlys noted how each of the swarm's attacks was directed specifically at Tethyssian's position. 'Protect the tidecaster!' she called to Saturiandi.

He complied, flanking Tethyssian with another akhelian, savagely carving the swooping bats from the sky with their helsabres.

The aetheric fog became more dense, and the onslaught faltered, the distorting mist playing havoc on the creatures' echolocation, allowing the idoneth to approach the dense, coral-bone labyrinth further down the slope.

They almost made it.

But then, a whole host of hostile movement erupted from the warrens ahead, cutting them off. Black-clad humans emerged alongside deathrattle warriors, the latter covered in strange kelp-fibre funerary shrouds and driftwood fetishes.

The flanking forces of stilt walkers and animated skeletons approaching from the terraces reached them at precisely the same moment. It was *too* well timed to be a coincidence.

'Forward!' Akhlys snarled, lashing out with her talúnhook to decapitate an oar-armed skeleton, before sidestepping the thrust of a rusted guisarme from a bone-masked mortal. Her riposte impaled the human through the jaw, and her lurelight flared brightly as the escaping souls began to swirl around her. She led the push, deep into the coral warrens. The passages became narrow, carved alleys between the brain and stack corals, and every hole in the walls or rope bridge overhead seemed to unleash more enemies, living and dead.

Akmaeon and his reavers, their quivers empty, cut into the assailants with their keening daggers, severing the sinuous joints of the undead and opening the arteries of the living. The thralls required less finesse, shearing off limbs and spilling entrails with their brutal lanmari blades, while the akhelians reaped a savage toll of their own, their helsabres spraying crimson and shattering bones.

At their centre, Tethyssian unleashed surges of black, aetheric water, coalesced directly from the dark mist that billowed from him. The waves slipped harmlessly around the idoneth, but tore at their foes from below, sucking them down into the oily gloom. While most of the undead rose again, only hindered by the arcane riptide, many of the humans did not resurface, succumbing to the overwhelming terror of drowning.

Akhlys moved like a spectre of death, her talúnhook seeking out the mortal foes, and ending them with scything sweeps. She let the others deal with the undead, and her lurelight flared bright as ghostly apparitions swirled around her, pulled from the dying humans.

She stooped beside a fallen namarti, the cordon of thralls around her warding off the attackers with wide, sweeping strikes, allowing Akhlys to coax one of the stolen souls into the fallen warrior.

The hideous wound raking his chest fused shut in an instant, and Akhlys stood, holding out a hand to pull the namarti to his feet.

Continuing the advance, she saw a human wearing a mask of stitched-together gull-skulls emerge from a gap between the stack corals, impaling another namarti through the chest with the point of his guisarme.

With a snarl, Akhlys rushed in to behead the human, just as another pair of namarti positioned themselves to shield her from the other attackers charging from the adjacent passages. She knelt to heal the next fallen thrall.

In the confined space of the coral labyrinth, the onslaught was hindered, as fighting was constricted by the narrow passages, and the bats struggled to find the space to make their swooping attacks. But the restricted movement hampered the idoneth as well.

Several namarti fell, too far back or too grievously mangled for Akhlys to heal. And she saw one of the akhelians dragged from his feet by a guisarme hooked into his armour. Several more humans seemed to rise up from the corpse-strewn ground, covered in blood as they descended upon the thrashing akhelian with nothing more than their fingers and teeth.

Akhlys saw the baleful violet glow in their eyes... and the fatal wounds that had felled them previously.

Emerging into a wider, staired thoroughfare, Akhlys looked up to see the tattered, black-cloaked figure standing atop one of the higher stack corals that loomed above the labyrinth. Strands of ghostly violet light descended from the figure to pull many of the fallen humans back onto their feet, regardless of the mortal wounds they'd suffered from the idoneth's blades. Other strands descended into the piles of shattered bones that had once been deathrattle warriors, forcing the broken skeletons to crawl back together and rise again.

Slowed by the endless tide of foes, the idoneth's progress had been hampered enough to allow the forces that had pursued them all the way from the previous hamlet to finally catch up. The armoured deathrattle warriors led the charge into the rear of the idoneth band, menacingly descending the thoroughfare's steps, while the stilt walkers lagged behind to fire their missile weapons over the heads of their unliving allies.

Akhlys saw immediately that these undead were different. They were not the rickety, animated bones that swarmed them from the warrens; instead they were armoured in ancient laminar lined with fingerbones, and bedecked with tattered cloaks and frills of gull-feathers. Each wore pauldrons and a vulture-skull mask decorated with twisted driftwood branches, giving them the illusion of wearing crowns of bleached horns. They all but resembled the animated husks of what Akhlys assumed might be these townships' long-dead chieftains.

They carved into the namarti rearguard with hook-bladed swords that trailed pale flame.

As Akhlys pulled back from the front to assist, the dead rose in their midst, animating with frightening speed to strike the idoneth from within their formation. With a frustrated roar, Akhlys tore into them with hook and fist, dismay surging as the undead butchered the last of the stretcher bearers, and cut off the retreat of the rearguard.

'Akhlys!' Saturiandi called, just behind her. 'They're gone!'

He was right. There was nothing to be done.

She turned, leaving those namarti to their fate, hoping their sacrifice would buy the rest of them time. Glancing around in frustration, Akhlys saw that only half her people remained.

As the staired street descended between rising basalt formations beneath a massive, building-sized arch of spindle coral, Tethyssian unleashed another billowing surge of freezing mist into the rabble blocking their path.

It stiffened the enemy's movements, slowing them enough to allow the idoneth to hack a clear path through.

But the undead behind them continued to advance, cleaving through the last of the rearguard as Akhlys moved with the akhelians to intercept them.

'For the Khaphtar and the lost!' she cried, sweeping her talúnhook forward. It was parried, and deftly riposted by the undead chieftain. Though she leaped back, the hook-bladed sword smashed into her armour, sending her sprawling down the steps.

Saturiandi took her place, and dropped the ancient chieftain with a trio of lightning-fast helsabre slashes.

It was immediately replaced by two more.

Stumbling into the rocky wall of the alley, Akhlys heaved, feeling broken ribs under her dented cuirass. Leaning on her polearm, she barely ducked under the beheading sweep of another warrior.

She saw Saturiandi fall, the ghostly edge of a chieftain's sword beheading him even as he pummelled another down with his shield.

The remaining akhelian cried out, avenging his kinsman by cleaving down his slayer. Several namarti moved to assist, one lashing out with a crescent-headed axe to bring down the chieftain assaulting Akhlys. Another namarti pulled her back, away from the battle.

'You must… live,' he said to her, desperation marring his muted voice.

A crossbow quarrel, loosed from the stilt walkers further back, took the namarti straight through the eye.

Akhlys gritted her teeth in rage as the reaver fell, pulling back as another pair of namarti intercepted the advancing chieftains, giving their lives to cover her retreat. Exhaustion and pain weighed her down, but as she turned, she saw the first glimmer of hope…

Out beyond the stair only a few coral structures remained as the labyrinth thinned, rising up from a wide, rocky strand. Runnels and jagged boulders dotted the empty strand beyond, sharing space with numerous fishing boats, roped to barnacle-encrusted pillars.

Beyond that, an endless expanse of oily black water beckoned, shrouded in a dense, dark fog.

'The… the ocean! The Quagmire!' Tethyssian called, raising his krakigon-headed staff in triumph. 'We are sa–'

A black shape landed on him, flattening him against the rock. Membranous wings vanished into a tattered, voluminous cloak, and dark hair whipped about like the tendrils of a thrashing oktar.

The tidecaster's tortured scream was cut short as crimson sprayed around him, misting into the lapping fog-waves for an instant, before condensing into droplets and splattering to the muddy stone.

In an instant, Akhlys felt a staggering weight threaten to topple her. The namarti stumbled, debilitated, as the frigid mists began to quickly dissipate in the dead wind.

The slender creature rose, deflecting a namarti's sword with a cruel-bladed sickle before raking open his abdomen with a taloned claw. Akhlys saw the creature was vaguely feminine in form, but its jaw was elongated, revealing rows of blackened fangs. Crimson was spattered all over its face, and it shrieked, its sickle flashing with unnatural speed to dismember another attacking reaver.

It darted straight towards Akhlys, who only barely managed to bring up her talúnhook to deflect a decapitating slash.

'Soulless abomination!' Akhlys roared, a strength born from cold, vengeful fury drowning her fatigue and pain.

She riposted, twirling her staff in the attempt to skewer the creature with its hooked blade, but it darted around her, its sickle raking into Akhlys' shoulder, puncturing up beneath her pauldron. The blade's serrations caught agonisingly in her flesh and the kelp-fibre cloth she wore beneath her armour, causing it to slip from the creature's grip as Akhlys turned. She thrust the butt of her polearm into its throat, sending it gasping back, slamming into the wall of the staired street.

A namarti rushed it, distracting it by thrusting his keening dagger up into its ribs. Akhlys saw it was Akmaeon only a moment before the she-creature backhanded him down the stairs.

The battle continued to surge around them as the voulge-bearing stilt walkers and the undead chieftains closed in, having cut through the second rearguard.

Only a dozen of her people remained.

'So close...' Akhlys gasped at the pain. The sickle blade was still embedded in her back. She shook her head. She would not fail now. She *could* not...

Lunging forward, she attempted to hook the creature's skull, even if the movement tore muscle and sent spasms of fire across her back. The creature sidestepped, recovering from Akmaeon's attack, though the namarti's dagger was still firmly buried in its chest.

Akhlys whirled, bashing it away with the haft of her talúnhook, and it backpedalled up the stairs, disappearing into the advancing undead ranks.

Akhlys turned and ran, stumbling as she reached the rocky strand below. Akmaeon had risen and waited for her. He'd seized an akhelian helsabre somewhere along the way. For a namarti to carry such a weapon was unheard of, but for now, Akhlys was thankful for his pragmatism.

'Close,' he said.

'I know,' Akhlys gasped, agonised.

The namarti reached to remove the sickle blade from her shoulder, but she twisted to brush him off.

'Later,' she hissed.

The other survivors, all namarti now, were already further ahead. The swarms of smaller bats descended like black coils from the sky to harass them, but with salvation so close, they ignored the verminous creatures. Even so, she saw one namarti fall.

In a staggering, pain-wracked run, she paused long enough to bring her lurelight over the fallen namarti. A quick surge of converted energy brought him to his feet, as Akmaeon slashed the bats away.

The undead weren't far behind them.

The freakish, slender creature burst from the pursuing host, swooping forward on its chiropteran wings, eviscerating the namarti Akhlys had just saved.

Lashing out again, it raked Akmaeon across the chest, sending red sprays spattering across the mud. Akhlys thrust out, bashing it back before twirling her polearm around in a decapitating arc. But it leaped overhead, landing behind her to tear its sickle blade free from her shoulder.

The force tore Akhlys' pauldron clean off, and ripped open her flesh. With a scream, she fell, her talúnhook tumbling from her grip. She rolled, seeing the creature rear up to deliver the killing stroke.

Akmaeon tackled it, bowling into the abomination, shoving it back and slashing open its chest with his helsabre.

Three other namarti joined him, descending upon the thrashing, shrieking horror.

They'd come from the group ahead. They'd turned to save her.

Crawling away, Akhlys found her talúnhook, and rose, stumbling with the dizzying sensation of shock and blood loss, as well as the unfamiliar absence of the aethersea. 'Move!' she gasped.

The namarti backed away from the thrashing creature. Its clothing had been shredded, and black, vile blood oozed from its ghostly pale flesh. It had clearly been a woman once... Now, Akhlys didn't know *what* it was.

And she didn't much care either. A downward slash, bearing all of the strength she had left, impaled the point of her talúnhook directly into its skull.

It stopped shrieking, and stopped thrashing.

It slumped, and in an instant, its skin, flesh and bone crumbled, disintegrating into ash that quickly began flaking away in the dead wind.

Akhlys collapsed, sliding down the blood-slick haft of her weapon to sink to her knees.

The bats, many of which were still attached to her and the namarti, flitted away in a panic, and the undead, so close to catching them, stopped, suddenly becoming motionless, as though confused. The stilt-walking humans slowed, staring in disbelief.

Akhlys' vision greyed. Her blood was everywhere, drenching her left arm and side.

She felt the namarti pull her... lift her.

She gazed up into the sky. The sun's light had faded. The darkness above was cloaked in the noxious haze that the Khaphtar Sea's death had created.

After a few, almost serene moments, as she felt her life ebb away, the lapping touch of oily waves began to caress her skin. The pain faded as the light dimmed. The muted voices of the namarti became distant, and she couldn't even muster the strength to see just how severe her wounds were.

As silent numbness claimed her, a violet shimmer washed over her vision. As the mirage of dancing, dying light rose above, she realised it was the oily sheen of the surface. After all that had happened, she could scarcely remember what that looked like...

Akhlys allowed herself a thin smile as she felt the black depths of the Great Quagmire pull her into its unfamiliar, but comforting embrace.

BOSSGROT

Eric Gregory

'It's the wrong way, innit?'

Gribblak opened the visor of his helm and squinted through the rain to survey the valley. His skrap was an avalanche before him, but it was falling in the wrong direction, falling *back*, a tide of grots and squigs and troggoths crashing towards Gribblak and the safety of the foothills.

His cave-shaman, Oghlott, fidgeted. 'They's leggin' it, boss.'

'I en't told 'em to leg it.'

'All respect,' Oghlott said, 'they's bein' chopped to bits.'

Gribblak's visor creaked down over his eyes again. He left it down this time, stared at his shaman through the eye-slits. Oghlott was a keen enough shaman, but given to glumness. Now and then he needed some conviction slapped into him. Gribblak smacked the other grot's back.

'That's rot. They's just got to shape up.' He cupped his hand around the grille of his helm and shouted, 'Go back, you half-gitz! Shape up and go back!'

The dusk light was muted behind the clouds, and the freezing rain was picking up, turning to sleet. Out of the roiling clash bounded a clump of squig-riders, the grots clinging to their panicked mounts. Squig-breath fogged the air, and the beasts crashed through the outlying yurts of the enemy encampment like red fists pounding muddy slush.

That looked mighty fine to Gribblak. Smashing the camp, driving the roving 'umies away from King Skragrott's territories – it was the whole point of this raid on the valley nomads. These weren't even the cleverest 'umies. A bunch of blood worshippers, by the look of their banners. Fools enough to worship the mess inside 'emselves; fools who had wandered too far into Skragrott's claim.

So why was Gribblak's skrap running away?

He glanced aside at Oghlott. The shaman clutched his robes tight against his body, anxious or cold or both. Braids of roots and cave-fungi swayed from his neck as he shivered. Maybe…

'Give us a Dincap,' said Gribblak.

Oghlott's frown deepened. 'Why–?'

Gribblak snatched a deep purple mushroom from the braid around the shaman's neck, opened his visor and swallowed the fungus whole. The moment the flesh of the Dincap touched saliva, it began to vibrate.

His throat thrummed and his guts shook as he swallowed the mushroom in a gulp.

Being a boss was about words. Anyone could see that. The boss-gods of the realms – the bloated pus-bag gods and big rat gods and shiny gold git gods – you didn't see them out here scrapping. You didn't see them at all. They were stories. They were words in the heads of their warriors.

The big bosses knew how to put the right words in the heads of their mobs, and that was why they won. That was Gribblak's way, too, and it had got him this far: boss of Gobbolog Skrap.

And it was going to take him further. Maybe Gorkamorka had taken a bite out of the Bad Moon, but Gribblak was going to eat the whole thing.

He was going to be the boss of gods.

'OY!' he shouted, and his voice reverberated down the valley. The Dincap's vibration in his stomach and chest and throat gave him the voice of a hundred grots, the voice of a riot.

'OY!' he shouted. 'LOOK 'ERE.'

In the muddy, rain-lashed valley below, the stampede of his skrap slowed. The eyes of his grots turned up to him; even the cave-squigs hesitated and turned around, confused. Now that the fighting slowed and Gribblak commanded the attention of the valley, he could see that the 'umie nomads looked up to him, too, clad in their crimson armour and furs, axes and butchers' knives in their hands. A thrill of pleasure ran across his scalp.

Look at 'em all, looking at me!

Gribblak imagined how he must have appeared to these common grots and 'umies, his lunar helm gazing down like the Bad Moon itself. Proper majestic.

'YOU LOT,' he thundered. 'SHAPE UP AND SHOW 'EM WHO'S BOSS!'

The grots of the skrap looked back and forth amongst one another. Now Gribblak raised an angry finger towards the enemy line.

'AND *YOU*. COWARDS! SEND YOUR BEST AND I'LL GIVE 'IM A POINTY ENDING.'

The entire valley seemed to hesitate as Gribblak's words echoed. The sleet drummed against his armour, and satisfaction welled in his chest.

This was how you did it. This was how fights were won. You didn't need to go down in the mud and actually stab an 'umie. Inspire your skrap, goad the other side, and watch the show – that's how gods did their business.

And then it stormed out of the fog of dirt and snow and flesh: the 'umie blood-boss.

It *had* to be the boss. Its armour was stained the colour of sunsets, and steam rose where the rain fell on its skin. It rode a beast like nothing Gribblak had ever seen, metal and sinew clenched around hellfire; the eyes blazed, and slag-spittle dripped from the jaws. The warboss' axehead burned, too, an otherworldly crimson borne aloft like a torch. A wreath of skulls hung around its neck.

The 'umie clutched a wriggling grot by the waist – a fanatic still gripping his ball and chain. The blood-boss raised the grot to its mouth and tore his head from his neck, then hurled the limp body aside and emitted a garbled, throaty scream.

The hooves of the beast burned the ground where they fell. The blood-boss crashed through the skrap's already tattered line and made straight for Gribblak.

'Leg it,' he squeaked, and his tinny alarm echoed across the valley. 'LEG IT!'

The blood-boss stormed past a troggoth, and the troggoth's arm – still wielding a stalactite plucked from an old lurklair – whirled into the air. Squigs scattered from the front lines, screeching their distress and bounding into the hills. And the sleet turned to hail.

Gribblak ran. He was already unsteady, breathing hard inside his helm as the ponderous thing bobbed with every step, but now he was slipping in the mud, and pellets of ice threatened to knock him flat. 'Oh please oh please oh please,' he panted, and his own voice thundered all around him, 'OH PLEASE OH PLEASE OH PLEASE–'

The cave mouth was close. From his perch in the crags of the foothills, he could wriggle into the damp, dark safety of his caverns. Squeeze his way into a narrow passage where no fire-eyed 'umie monstrosity could follow.

But the blood-boss was quick, and Gribblak couldn't turn his head to see how close it was. He couldn't see much of anything, ahead or behind. He was almost to the cave mouth, wasn't he? He tried to blink away sweat and sleet. The ground was shaking, or he was – then something *massive* slammed him in the back and he went skidding through the mud.

'*Please,*' he screeched. 'I en't boss of 'em! Don't kill me! I en't bossgrot!'

And his throat vibrated, and his helm thrummed, and the words sounded all through the quicksilver valleys in the northern reaches of King Skragrott's claim:

'PLEASE! I EN'T BOSS OF 'EM! DON'T KILL ME! I EN'T BOSSGROT!'

He hardly knew he was talking, at first, he was so lost in his terror. He wanted to move, to run, but he was frozen where he lay. Was he dead? The rain drummed on his armour. He heard his own words playing around him, his own begging, and another voice, too.

'Shut up!' said the voice. 'Just a squig.'

Gribblak looked up at his cave-shaman. Grimacing down at him, Oghlott gripped his arm and hauled him upright. 'Up,' he hissed. 'Shut up and run, go!'

He ran. And as he scrambled towards the cave mouth, an echo of his begging chased him:

'I EN'T BOSSGROT, I EN'T BOSSGROT, I EN'T BOSSGROT...'

A lot of bosses liked to boast that they'd never taken a shanking, but that wasn't Gribblak's way. You had to reckon your losses, he said, in order to know who to blame.

Once the shakes had died down and he felt fit to hold court in his Reckonin' Room, Gribblak set his Gobbapalooza to work up a ledger of the damage. Oghlott recited the totals:

A full two dozen fanatics. A contingent of snufflers. Seventeen squig hoppers, and most of the squigs. Two Dankhold troggoths. One gargant named Hurg. A coterie of stabbas that no one actually remembered joining the skrap, but whose remains were present and who had definitely themselves suffered a stabbing.

'And,' Oghlott finished, 'morale.'

The boss and his counsellors sat around the fossilised toadstool that served as a round table. Luminescent mould lit the lair a sickly blue.

'Who?' Gribblak asked.

Oghlott hesitated. 'Wot?'

'The last one. Whoizzit? Mor–'

'Mor-*ale*.' Oghlott pursed his lips. 'The fightin' feelin' in the mob.'

Gribblak frowned and rubbed his eyes. 'Is these the gitz I got to hold Skragrott's claim?' he asked no one in particular.

Several of the Gobbapalooza – his shroomancer and scare-monger and boggleye – exchanged glances. Hazzlegob, the scaremonger, munched absently on what looked like a small bat's wing. He stuffed the wing through the mouth-hole in his Glareface mask, which was painted to make him look like the primal enemy of all grots: the great burning face in the sky, bright-death incarnate, Glareface Frazzlegit.

'I got to show the Loonking I'm *keen*,' said Gribblak. 'Show 'im I got this skrap in hand. But they got no stick-it-to-it, do they?'

'No stick-it-to-it,' repeated Hazzlegob glumly. He was the only one who answered, but he didn't seem entirely attentive.

Gribblak had tried to be a good boss, a kind boss. A lot of grots wanted to rule with an iron claw, to command fear and timid obedience, but that wasn't Gribblak's way. If you lived on your skrap's fear, you'd lose everything the second someone scared 'em more. What you wanted, what you *really* wanted, was unqualified adoration. Or failing that, some grudging respect. Gribblak thought he'd done right and proper by his mob – he gave 'em a place in the deep and dark, let 'em carouse a bit in between raids...

But maybe he'd gone too easy on 'em. Let 'em get soft. Some of these young grots hadn't seen real scrapping since they were wee spores, and perhaps not even then. The moment they hit a band of blood-drunk 'umie daemon-worshippers, they turned tail and ran.

'We got to get 'em fit and fighty,' said Gribblak. 'If you fall off the squig, you got to get right up, stab it in the eye and show it who's in charge. We got to throw 'em back in a fight.'

Oghlott the cave-shaman glanced across the table at the members of the Gobbapalooza. 'Once we heal up, build the mob back up a bit–'

'I en't talkin' later. I'm talkin' now.'

The chamber was quiet. The glowy moulds flickered.

'Now,' said Oghlott.

Gribblak smiled. He expected his counsellors were feeling pretty awestruck by his boldness of vision.

'It's got to be now. Give 'em a win 'fore they got time to get all mopey 'bout tonight. And 'fore Skragrott gets wind we took a shanking, starts to think we's less than keen.'

'When,' said Oghlott carefully, 'is *now*? And what fight do we got to throw 'em into?'

Gribblak felt such a surge of pride in his new plan that he spread his arms in a flourish of revelation.

'Tonight! The Glinty Crown!'

King Skragrott's territories had steadily expanded since his founding of the loon-city Skrappa Spill and the vast outlying network of lurklairs in the Yhorn Mountains. But in the northerly reaches, his Gloomspite hordes had hit a snag.

On the peak of Mount Pizmahr: a fortress hammered into an iron mountain of Chamon. Mob after mob and skrap after skrap had laid siege to the fastness, and each had been repelled. Not just repelled, but decimated. The fortress was cold and silent and flew no banners – no grot knew who held it, or why. But whenever a skrap approached, the massive cannons on the ramparts thundered, and even the finest mobs were broken.

A great Glinty Crown on the peak of Pizmahr, its cannons winking a taunt in the light of day. And a prize that the King of Grots hadn't yet added to his pile.

If he could give Skragrott the Crown, any little missteps or embarrassments would be forgiven, forgotten. Surely he'd ascend to the ranks of the king's most favoured generals alongside the likes of Izgit or Warrblag. The skrap would get its pep back – everyone would win!

'No,' whispered Oghlott.

The cave-shaman usually had a downcast look to him: tired or dour. But his demeanour was changed now. He met Gribblak's gaze, and his tone was resolute. Some decision seemed to have worked itself out behind his eyes.

Gribblak blinked. 'Wot?'

'*No*,' Oghlott repeated, more firmly this time.

'You en't allowed to say no,' said Gribblak, more puzzled than angry.

''S sayin' no. The skrap'll riot. You try to send 'em on some deathwish blunder 'fore the moon has set on the *last* rout, these gitz'll tear you limb from limb and eat your tongue to shut you up. They'll rip us *all* up just to be safe.'

The moulds on the wall brightened, as if in response to Oghlott's raised voice. Gribblak sat back on his toadstool stump, aghast.

'They'd never. They adore me. Even the meanest gitz got some grudgin'–'

'They do *not* got some grudgin' respect for you,' Oghlott spat. 'Not before, and sure as Gork's fist not now. Not after the raid on the Corroded Hills, not after that awful sortie with the stunties and the time we lost a lair to some tree-aelves. Not after you ran squealing from the 'umies where any git could hear...'

The memory floated up out of his guts unbidden: *Please! I en't boss of 'em! Don't kill me! I en't bossgrot!*

He shook his head to dislodge the words. The valley had been noisy. No one had paid him any mind.

'Stop talkin' rot,' he said. 'This skrap is mine. I built 'em up with my own hands. I know what's best for 'em, and they *know* I know what's best for 'em.' He stood up. 'You lucky I don't shank you.'

Oghlott looked to the assembled Gobbapalooza, and all save for Hazzlegob – who had fallen asleep – nodded their support.

'We's all tried to do our jobs,' said Oghlott. 'But if we got to stop you to do right by the Loonking and the skrap, that's what we goin' to do.'

His counsellors stared at him, unified and obstinate. The mould-light flickered again, and each of their eyes glowed red in the dark.

Gribblak had been afraid of a great many things in his day, but never his own Gobbapalooza. None of them were very fighty taken alone, but together they commanded an awful brew of shroom-spells and hallucinations and danksome magics. He backed out of the Reckonin' Room slowly.

'*You en't boss,*' Gribblak hissed. 'Y'hear me? By sun-up you'll see. I'll take the Glinty Crown and this skrap'll call me bossgrot and cheer. Mark my words. By sun-up.'

And with that, he turned and ran from his own skrap.

He needed a disguise.

In battle – or *near* battle – Gribblak was unmistakable. The plates of his prized boss-armour were layered with growths of war-fungi, and the bright yellow lunar helm put him a head above the other grots. The get-up always made him feel a bit more like a boss: he stood tall and heavy and looked out from behind the face of the Bad Moon itself.

But the armour was also a bit of a pain. The helm was cramped and unsteady, and its visor wouldn't stay up. The vambraces were sufficiently heavy that he had to grunt and strain to raise his arm and point at stuff, especially as a battle wore on. And while the crop of mushrooms growing across his armour were appealingly colourful and helped clear his head for wily tactical calculation, they also smelled like the troggoth dung in which they had been cultivated.

When the skrap was at ease in their lurklair, Gribblak wore a different sort of dress: robes and sashes of the finest make a grot could get, dyed the colours of squig-skins and glow-moulds. Around his neck he wore the fangs of Chamonite ore-beasts bigger than gargants.

So he was always unmistakable.

Gribblak hurried away from the Reckonin' Room and through the windy lurklair passages that led to the common grot-holes. Puke pooled on the ground, and the leftover parts of half-eaten cave wyrms were strewn about everywhere, as if they'd been hurled at the cavern walls. The stench of both mixed with spilled brew.

Gribblak knew the skrap got rowdy, but this was ridiculous.

At his feet he found a grot passed out with his arms wrapped around a stalagmite, his black Moonclan robes splayed around him.

Aha, Gribblak thought.

With his new, pilfered hood pulled low over his eyes, Gribblak made his way through the tunnels of the lurklair and into the Ruckus Pit. The gitz had spent an inordinate amount of time equipping the chamber with massive kegs built into the walls. Everywhere, stalagmites were festooned with shroom-chains. Glowing spore-dust drifted through the air, giving off a faint light. Teeth and chunks of bone fashioned into dice littered the ground; the stench of bodily waste was thicker, and grots were passed out here and there in heaps.

Ordinarily, the noise of the Ruckus Pit echoed through the lurklair at all hours. But the mood was subdued now – a low music of mutters punctuated by the occasional bitter laugh.

If Gribblak knew one thing for certain, it was that his skrap adored – or grudgingly respected – him. And though he couldn't fathom why Oghlott and his band of back-stabbers would believe otherwise, he was going to have a mighty fine time showing them just how loyal his gitz could be.

In disguise, Gribblak would walk among his ordinary grots. He would speak with them of their hopes and dreams and plant the rumours of a glorious plot soon to unfold at the hands of their boss. Then, when the ground was prepared and the time was right, he would reveal himself as Gribblak and announce, with maximum drama, the siege of the Glinty Crown.

He couldn't wait to see the look on Oghlott's face.

Doing his best to walk like a common grot, Gribblak approached a cluster of gitz gathered in a circle. It looked like they were playing some dice-chucking game. As he came closer, he could make out fragments of the grumbled conversation.

'–fine and good but I'd pull out his tendons, to start.'

'Tendons. Mm.'

No one paid Gribblak much mind as he joined the circle. The dice-chucking game, he found, wasn't quite a game. Instead, the grots were trying to prod two runty squigs into a fight by half-heartedly throwing bone-dice at them.

A lot of bosses liked to mix with the common grots when they weren't fighting – have a few mouldroot brews, act like a regular git – but that wasn't Gribblak's way. You could pretend all you liked, but the fact was your leaders had one job, and your front-line grots had another. Maybe you could buy cheap affection with a shared drink, but a proper boss cultivated real love, real power, real command, all by drawing lines. Gribblak knew he was right about that – it was all the proper gods' way – but it meant he hadn't spent much time talking to his mob.

'Howzit 'ere?' Gribblak asked. He tried to sound like his idea of a common grot, and a little inebriated. 'You's drinkin' anyfink good?'

No one answered for a while. The smallest grot fidgeted with an emblem of the Bad Moon. 'Just the swill wot's left,' he said. He looked up at his friends and resumed the previous conversation. 'I 'spect *I'd* work up a kinda grinder for 'im. Put 'im through nice and slow, turn 'im into a kinda paste.'

A grot with one eye nodded approvingly. 'Nice one, Vork. We oughta put you in charge.'

'I heard a rumour,' Gribblak broke in, 'dat da boss has some kinda proper plan to put Gobbolog Skrap on top. Right where we's belong, eh?'

The one-eyed grot paused mid-throw, narrowed his remaining eye. 'Aye. Right where we belong. What's your name?'

Gribblak hesitated. 'Hob… blangle,' he said. 'Hobblangle.'

Vork grunted. The one-eyed grot threw his dice, caught one of the tiny squigs on the head. It squealed and flopped into the other animal, but they didn't seem to want to fight. 'I'd like to hear what the boss'll have us do now, then.'

'Well,' Gribblak said, 'I 'ear he's keen to take a *big* prize. Maybe even da Glinty Crown.'

'I'll bet 'e is,' snorted Vork.

'Reckon 'e aims to give us a win. Show us we's a sharp lot of–'

'You boys remember,' Vork interrupted, 'when we lost a lair to those *trees*? Trees in a cave. I never.'

The others laughed darkly.

'We get shanked,' Vork sighed. 'Over'n over, we get shanked.' He shook his head and threw his Bad Moon emblem at the larger of the runt squigs. The medal smashed the beastie's head and left a luminescent pink goop on the cavern floor.

'Aw, c'mon, Vork,' someone said.

Gribblak tried not to let his consternation show. With this group of grots, at least, he was going to have to be a little more inspirational than he'd anticipated.

'I wonder,' he said, 'wot you's hopes'n dreams are – for after we take the Glinty Crown?'

'Y'know,' said the one-eyed grot, 'we was just talkin' through that. Rankar here was thinkin' we oughta tie the boss' arms and legs to four squigs and send 'em all running to the four winds. And I like that for a dream, but I'm really intrigued by Vork's put-'im-through-a-grinder idea.' The one-eyed grot stared at Gribblak, his eye unblinking. 'You?'

Gribblak shivered. 'I want a drink,' he said quietly.

Vork grinned. 'I'll bet.'

Trying not to look too out of sorts, Gribblak backed away from the circle and hurried deeper into the Ruckus Pit, pulling his hood further over his head.

His thoughts wheeled like he'd eaten a bad toadstool. That was proper seditious talk from the dice-throwers. But it was just six gitz, right? Six gitz didn't make a skrap. And these front-line grots were notoriously unreliable. You had to watch 'em every second.

In the farthest corner of the Ruckus Pit, where it was darkest and most danksome – and where the largest keg stood – Gribblak spotted his top bounder trio, known in the skrap as the Squigwind. Between the three of them, they'd been riding for six seasons, which was a prodigious and frankly improbable amount of time for anything to survive mounting a squig. The Squigwind was held in awe by the rest of the skrap – given all the best grub, the best grot-holes, the best trophies (though it had been some time since the skrap had occasion to take trophies). They were exactly the sort of voices Gribblak wanted to hear, and wanted to speak for him. Respected. Influential. With the Squigwind behind him, the rest of the skrap was sure to fall in line and march on the Glinty Crown.

The trio sat along the spine of some long-dead subterranean beastie. The nominal leader, Ralgog, smoked an elaborate pipe of stunty make and stared at nothing, while the spore-twins Habble-grob and Grobblehab played a pilfered snare drum and lyre, or at least thwacked the instruments at intervals. The thwack-song was slow and disjointed and unpleasant to the ear, but – perhaps on account of the musicians' status in the skrap – no one complained.

'Oi!' Gribblak called, waving to the Squigwind. 'Howzit 'ere, bounderz?'

Ralgog didn't look at him. 'Zog off.'

It had been a good long while since anyone had told Gribblak to zog off from anywhere. For a moment, he was speechless.

'I got – I mean, a rumour's goin' round y'might want to hear,' he managed.

The bounder Grobblehab slapped a discordant twang of irrita-tion from his lyre and threw it to the ground in anger. 'They said *zog off*, didn't they?'

'Now you stopped Grobblehab playin',' Ralgog growled.

'I–' Gribblak started.

'*I want to hear the music,*' Ralgog spat. 'Go away. Or I'll gut you.'

It was as though something in the air had gone rank and thick and bitter, and every grot Gribblak talked to had breathed it in. But that only made his plan more important. He resolved to stand firm.

'Rumour is,' he pressed, 'boss is goin' to lead us on a siege of the Glinty Crown 'fore sun-up.'

'Ahh. I see what's goin' on here.'

Gribblak froze. 'You do?'

Ralgog waved away Gribblak's rumours like a faint odour. 'Don't y'worry, little grot. He tries anything that stupid, we'll feed 'im to the squigs.'

'I 'spect we'll feed 'im to the squigs anyway,' Habblegrob added in sing-song, banging the drum to each syllable of *an-y-way*.

'It's past time,' Grobblehab agreed.

Somewhere in Gribblak's head, a voice was beginning to scream, and he wasn't sure he would be able to shut it up. He could feel the shakes starting up again, and he was desperate not to let that show – inside his robes, he gripped his own wrists and tried to hold himself together. The Squigwind was just a bunch of big-headed gitz with mouths full of rot, he told himself. Their pride was bruised; they didn't mean what they said.

'You en't really goin' to feed 'im to the squigs, though,' he said quietly. 'You wouldn't. He's the boss.'

There wasn't a chance for the Squigwind trio to respond. Into the Ruckus Pit marched a grumbling, clattering, stomach-turning procession. Flanked by two Dankhold troggoths – one missing an arm – and their attendant trogg-herders, Oghlott and the Gobbapalooza entered the chamber, banging a piece of scrap metal like a bell.

'OI!' Oghlott shouted, Dincap-amplified. 'NOW HEAR THIS. GRIBBLAK WANTS TO MAKE US FIGHT AGAIN TONIGHT. HE WANTS TO SEND US TO THE GLINTY CROWN TO DIE. BUT WE EN'T GONNA STAND FOR IT. WHO 'ERE THINKS 'IS TIME IS UP?'

The grots in the Ruckus Pit roared their approval.

'Grind 'im up!' shouted Vork.

'Let's feed 'im to the squigs!' called Ralgog.

Gribblak couldn't stop the shakes now. His whole body trembled; his hands shuddered in his robes. The screaming voice in his head made it hard to think straight. *This skrap is mine. I built 'em up with my own hands.* Were the words in his head, or was it his own voice screaming?

Gribblak hurried towards the lurklair tunnels farthest from his back-stabbing cave-shaman, and for the second time that night, he fled from the grots he was meant to command. And all the while a voice screeched, *You'll see, I'll show you, you'll see.*

Frantic, hands shaking, he tried to strap the vambraces to his wrists. Latch the greaves. Usually he had someone to help him with his armour, and these irksome echoes kept sounding in his head:

I en't bossgrot, I en't bossgrot, I en't bossgrot...

Stupid. Gribblak tried to shake away the past. Fumbled the last armour-strap through its loop and put on his moon-helm.

You'll see, he thought. *I'll take the Glinty Crown and this skrap'll call me bossgrot and cheer.*

The armour-stash was quiet, except for the shifting, slobbering sounds of nearby squigs in their paddocks. All the grots were in their holes, licking their wounds, or else plotting revolt with the Gobbapalooza. Gribblak took up his slicer and made for the stables.

He was still shaking, and his thoughts were still a storm, but Gribblak moved with a new clarity of purpose. He opened the stable gates and stepped towards the sound of gnashing in the dark.

In the Gobbolog Skrap, a bounder of the Squigwind was held in awe for riding an ordinary cave squig and surviving the season. But there were madder and more deadly mounts.

Among many of the skraps most favoured by King Skragrott, it was customary for bosses to keep a mangler: two giant cave squigs chained together. Each of these monstrosities had grown to the size of a troggoth, or larger, and together they were a tide of destruction, two hungry disasters that hated one another.

Up to now, Gribblak hadn't actually ridden his mangler. But now was the time. He was boss. This was his place. He opened the cave-mouth gate, then opened the paddocks.

What followed was a blur. The darkness filled with thundering squig-flesh; Gribblak grabbed hold of a rein and held on as the mangler squigs rammed into the walls of the stable, smashing the other paddocks and releasing the rest of the smaller cave squigs.

Then the mangler jerked in the opposite direction and they were outside, tumbling at an absurd velocity through the Yhorn foothills, night air whipping Gribblak's skin.

Summoning all the strength in his shaky limbs, Gribblak climbed the leash and seized the harness and goad atop the larger of the mangler squigs. They touched ground and then leapt, again and again, creating a jerky, bobbing rhythm. Muddy slush flew as they bounded forwards; trees snapped and branches scritched across his helm. Gribblak looked above and below, looked for anything to guide him.

And there it was: the Bad Moon.

The grinning light shone down and lit a path towards Mount Pizmahr and the Glinty Crown. Gribblak exhaled in awe, then renewed his grip on the harness and goaded the mangler squigs north, towards the Crown.

For a wonderful moment, they answered his reins, or at least moved in the direction he harassed them into moving. He soared through the night under the light of the Bad Moon, and he raised his lunar helm high, and in spite of the madness and sick-making speed, his shakes stopped.

This was it. The peace of perfect command. This was where he belonged. He fixed his gaze on the fortress atop Mount Pizmahr and grinned.

Then, with a *crack*, muzzle flashes lit the face of the mountain.

The Bad Moon fell behind the clouds, and fire streaked at him through the sky.

The cannons on the ramparts of the Glinty Crown thundered, and it was as if an entire mountain were shooting flame at him. A shot must have hit the larger mangler – it yowled and surged forwards when it touched ground, somehow faster and angrier than before.

The fortress grew closer, closer. He could make out torches on the ramparts – what looked like 'umies.

They were moving too fast. His eyes teared up; he couldn't see. Another shot cracked, and it must have stopped one of the manglers this time. He lost his grip on the harness and now he was in the air, hurtling faster than he'd ever moved, tears in his eyes and his stomach in his throat, a lone grot in the night sky.

He woke to the sound of 'umies.

There was an ugly cadence to their speech. Their words were like stones in a wall, dull and neat and all in line. But you could catch the gist of 'em.

'–a single rider?' said one voice.

'I shouldn't think so. I have encountered the creatures a great many times, and I have never known them to act alone.'

'Perhaps it was inebriated.'

'Oh, indubitably. But I'll guarantee that more of the filthy little sots are to follow.'

Gribblak was face down on damp straw. Night breeze still cooled his skin in the spots his armour didn't cover. He got to his knees, blinked, opened his visor, looked around.

He was under the stars, still. The sky was purpling to dawn. Underneath him, a thatched straw roof. The roof was inclined, and he had to work to keep his footing as he stood.

Below lay... well, it looked like an 'umie village. He'd seen – and razed, or *tried* to raze – plenty of little townships like this back in his early raids as boss, back before everything went to rot.

The first voice was speaking again. 'To be frank, lord, I am uncomfortable firing the cannons while the instrument is tuning. The crew report… strange sights. Faces in the powder, lord. Tongues in the cannon fire.'

Gribblak looked out over the village. It wasn't quite the same as the 'umie settlements he'd seen before, now he looked closer. The buildings were crowded together, leaving only a web of narrow alleys between them. The village was surrounded by thick walls and cannon emplacements. And in the centre of the settlement was a vast machine of rings and spheres, twice again the size of the house he stood atop, golden and seeming to speak to every sense at once, shine-hum-vibrating and leaving a copper tang in his mouth and nose. Understanding struck him all at once.

The Glinty Crown. His mangler had hurled him into the Glinty Crown.

Alone.

Gribblak crawled to the edge of the thatched roof and glanced down at the owners of the voices. The 'umies were both covered head to toe in silver armour and red regalia, but what really seized Gribblak's attention were the blastas and fire-sticks strapped to their belts and backs. He felt the shakes starting to return. These were some of the most heavily armed 'umies he'd ever seen. Soldiers in the same armour marched through alleys across the village, fire-sticks at the ready.

'Your objection is noted, captain,' said the 'umie with the biggest feather in its hat. 'I will report your crew's sightings to the battlemage. But I recommend that you master your discomfort. It is unlikely that the Collegiate wizards will interrupt the night's trials on the Orrery.'

'Yes, lord.'

The 'umies parted, and Gribblak exhaled. He looked up to the Bad Moon for reassurance, but the sky was empty now. No grin, no guiding light.

And that was about right, wasn't it? Coming here had been stupid, stupid. He couldn't break a fortress himself. His whole skrap couldn't have survived the first thirty steps of a march on those cannons.

Oghlott was right. He was a git. He'd never been bossgrot, not really: he was a stupid git, and grots had listened to him for a while, and now they didn't.

He was a stupid git whose luck had run out, and he was on his own.

Gribblak whispered a plea to the Bad Moon. 'Let me live,' he whispered, 'let me get outta here, and I'll just take what I get forever after. But let me live.'

The night was silent, except for the shine-hum-thrum of the golden machine and indistinct 'umie orders in the distance.

'Right,' said Gribblak. He was on his own.

First, he needed to get off the roof. Then he could sneak through the alleys, make his way to the top of the ramparts, avoid the gunnery crew, and climb down Mount Pizmahr.

He took a deep breath.

Below the edge of the roof, about a body-length down, was a cart full of straw. Gribblak scooted over the edge of the roof feet first, kicking to find a foothold on the cart. He misjudged the step, slid off the edge, hit the cart and fell onto the cobbles of the alley with a loud clang of armour on stone.

'What was that?' came the voice of the 'umie with the big feather. Gribblak scrambled under the cart as its footsteps neared. Four more pairs of feet followed shortly behind, and Gribblak watched the armoured boots approach.

'I saw one. One of the little sots. I would swear on it.'

'Heads and fingers steady,' said the 'umie boss. 'We *cannot* have any stray fire, understood?'

The boots stopped by the cart. Gribblak bit the insides of his cheeks and gripped his wrists and tried to stop himself shaking, fearful of his armour ringing against the cobblestones.

But it didn't matter. Slowly, the captain peered under the cart. There was nothing for it.

'Yaaaaa!' screeched Gribblak, and leapt out at the captain. He grabbed the 'umie's head and gripped its helmet; the 'umie stumbled backwards, dropping its weapon and batting at its own helm. The other soldiers raised their fire-sticks uncertainly.

'*Do not fire!*' the captain shouted. 'Do not fire! Hit it with the stock! Get it off me!'

Gribblak dug his armoured claws into the captain's eyes, eliciting a scream from the 'umie, then hurled himself from its shoulders to the spot where it had flung its fire-stick. The weapon was a lot to lug, but he could just manage to carry it with both hands. The 'umie soldiers decided to disregard their captain, spraying fire all around Gribblak as he rounded the corner and dived into another alley.

Which way were the ramparts? He tried to remember the view from the roof, but he couldn't quite place himself. He passed what looked like a blasta-stash, an 'umie mob-hole. In one doorway, an armoured soldier blinked and reached for its fire-stick as Gribblak raced past. The line of 'umies in pursuit was growing.

He weaved left and right, zigged and zagged. Where were the drink-houses, the game-houses? He'd seen plenty of 'umie villages. There should have been big, dumb uggos stumbling out of taverns and puking in the streets. There should have been swindlers and night's-watch and angry card games and midnight music – all the messy life that turned to screaming when a Gloomspite raid caught a town unawares in the dead of night.

Instead, the Glinty Crown was all soldiers marching in rows and that awful shine-hum-thrum. Where were the spore-'umies and wrinkly-'umies? What kind of village was this? There was something wrong about the place. He thought again of stones, dull and all in line.

He emerged into a courtyard, and realised he was running the wrong way entirely. Before him was the great golden spinny machine, all spheres and rings. *Orrery*, the 'umie captain had called it. Around the instrument were gathered 'umies in robes of black, adorned with astronomic patterns in gold. The robes almost reminded him of a common Moonclan grot's.

The Orrery was bright-loud-heavy. The copper tang sharp on his tongue. The robed 'umies turned to regard Gribblak, and their eyes blazed white.

In the centre was a light as bright as death and hot as annihilation. He swore he saw eyes in the fire, eyes and a gaping mouth. He saw his scaremonger's mask before him, and every scare-story he'd ever heard as a little spore-git returned to him at once.

'Glareface,' he whispered.

Gribblak raised the fire-stick and shot at the Orrery. He wasn't sure what happened next. The recoil knocked him on his back and dislocated his arm. The muzzle-flash was light and thunder but it was also a face, and the face vomited more faces, which vomited more faces. The faces weren't grot or 'umie or anything else that made sense, and they licked the world with tongues of fire. He was pretty sure the fire-stick wouldn't have done that in a normal place, but somehow it didn't seem all that strange here, now, in the loud-heavy-bright aura of the Orrery.

Behind Gribblak, his 'umie pursuers opened fire. Their muzzle flashes made faces, too, and bright hairline cracks opened in the spheres of the Orrery, in the faces of wizards. The light in their eyes and mouths shifted from white to a pulsing rainbow.

The world was breaking. Gribblak got up, spun around and dived under the legs of his pursuers, back into the dull, cold alleys of the Glinty Crown. Gritting his teeth against the pain in his arm, heaving his armour forwards with every step, Gribblak did what he did best:

He ran.

In the wake of Gribblak's flight from Gobbolog Skrap, Oghlott was left with no choice but to abandon the lurklair. The paddocks were smashed and the tunnels were swarming with squigs, so the surviving grots made their way outside, into the foothills. It was the first real moment of cheer the skrap had shared in ages. The troggoths were grumpy to be awake, of course, but the grots laughed about Gribblak's flight and the various means by which they would kill their old boss when they found him.

For his part, Oghlott was almost gratified by the necessity. Of *course* Gribblak had ruined the lurklair as he left it – *of course*. Further proof that the Gobbapalooza made the right choice in deposing him.

For the first watches of the night, the craftiest grots fashioned effigies of Gribblak and entertained themselves by flattening or shredding or burning or eating them. They scanned the horizon and kept half-joking watch for Gribblak, should he attempt to return. Some discussed who would be the next boss, glancing sidelong at Oghlott, who was careful to make no claims on bossdom. He had an idea that the leadership of the skrap ought to arise out of common agreement, but he was still working out how to put this to a mob of boisterous, intoxicated gitz.

As the night wore into morning, the grots of Gobbolog Skrap grew less boisterous, but more intoxicated. They'd started eating more potent mushrooms out of boredom, and many watched the horizon purple in a bleary stupor. Having nothing better to do, and having plenty of choice fungus on his person, Oghlott joined them.

And then something strange happened. The sky bloomed, its purples unfolding all at once into blues and pinks and reds and greens, a rainbow corona that expanded to encompass the sky.

In his fungal haze, Oghlott couldn't be sure for how long this unfolding in the sky carried on. It might have been minutes; it might have been hours. Then, as abruptly as the colours had opened, they collapsed into a single point on the peak of Mount Pizmahr. The Glinty Crown erupted in a column of flame that made a false daybreak.

Yelps of fear arose from the grots who were awake. Oghlott shielded his eyes.

It was late, and he was severely inebriated, and time shifted tricksily. An hour might have passed, or a night. At first, the cave-shaman thought he was hallucinating. But no, there he was, trudging through the woods towards him:

Gribblak.

One arm hung limp at his side, and the other lugged an 'umie fire-stick. The visor of his moon-helm was broken off, the yellow paint was scorched. The bonfire of an 'umie fortress burned on the mountain peak behind him.

He staggered towards Oghlott, panting hard, and hurled the helm from his head. The grot underneath was bloodied and squinting through a puffy eye, but it was unmistakably Gribblak. Oghlott looked back and forth from Gribblak to the ruins of the Glinty Crown to Gribblak again.

'You was right,' Gribblak gasped. 'I en't bossgrot. Never was. It oughta be you.'

Much of the skrap was passed out, but the ones who were awake and gazing at the horizon drifted closer to see what was happening. The scaremonger, Hazzlegob, left off chewing the head of an owl to stare at Gribblak.

'I en't interested in fightin' or runnin' no more,' said Gribblak. 'So you know. You don't got to hunt me down. I'm finished.'

Hazzlegob swallowed part of his owl. He removed his mask, briefly considered the crude Glareface scowl, and pointed at the blaze on Mount Pizmahr.

'You do that?'

Gribblak looked back at the destruction and frowned.

'Oi!' said Hazzlegob, sudden and sharp. A nearby pile of grots startled awake. 'Boss 'ere's burned down the Glinty Crown all by hisself.'

More of the skrap began to gather. 'I never seen Skragrott do nuffin' like that,' one said.

'I never seen a herd of troggoths do nuffin' like that.'

'You 'member those rumours in the Ruckus Pit?' said a one-eyed grot. 'I 'spect we got it wrong. I 'spect the boss was sayin' he'd take the Crown on 'is own.'

'If 'e can do that, 'e oughta take the crown. The real one.'

The talk was moving too quickly for Oghlott to follow properly. Gribblak seemed to feel the same, looking confusedly from speaker to speaker.

''Ere's to the boss–'

'Down with Skragrott–'

'The Bad Moon's high!'

'Give 'im a crown–'

More and more grots gathered, staring at Gribblak and the horizon in awe. The little grot looked helpless in his armour, dragging his 'umie fire-stick. In his numb fungal haze, Oghlott wasn't sure what to feel. Despair? Relief? Resignation? What he did feel, as the skrap chanted around him, was an unnameable brew of the three. Snufflers and bounders and herders and every other sort of grot stomped over the effigies they'd made earlier to get a look at their returned leader.

'Hail Gribblak!'

'High King of Grots–'

'Touched by the Bad Moon–'

'Hail to the bossgrot!'

The mob cheered, and behind Gribblak, the sky burned. He looked questioningly at Oghlott. 'I'm bossgrot?'

The cave-shaman shrugged.

'I *am* bossgrot,' he repeated, and it wasn't a question this time. Gribblak surveyed the assembled mob, squared his shoulders, stood a little taller and raised his voice. 'I killed the Glareface, y'know. Got 'im right in the eye.' He grinned.

'D'you want to hear the story?'

ASHES OF GRIMNIR

Michael J Hollows

They were surrounded by death. Death clouded the heavens in ash. Death stalked them at every turn. The duardin of the Ealrung lodge knew death, and they were not afraid.

Runesmiter Thorrok held aloft an urn, cast in the Temple of Fire itself, and uttered an oath. He tipped the golden vessel and dust landed on his runemaster's brow. It coated Orrag-un's beard and arms, giving his unarmoured skin the sickly pallor of the dead. Around him, the bass tones of the duardin joined together in a chant. Now that the binding of ash had begun, Orrag-un led them, uttering the sacred words. He allowed his eyes to droop shut.

There was fire. It bathed his skin in its warmth, a comforting embrace. The heat haze was familiar, homely, but something was wrong. The fires raged in the forge, angry and vengeful. He stepped forward on cautious limbs, leaving the magmahold behind in spirit. Battle raged across the Ealfort, as it had done many times before. Its song called to him, and he felt the warrior essence of Grimnir stir within. This time the battle was different, wrong. Spectres flashed around the fort, passing through walls. The duardin couldn't pin down their attackers. Fyresteel rose and descended, axes cutting into the dead as they attacked, but it was not enough. Duardin fell where they fought. Scores of the undead battered at the gates with broken and rusting weapons. Ancient war machines, makeshift and rotting, catapulted lumps of fiery rock over the walls. A boulder smashed into his path, splintering into pieces, forcing him back.

The essence of a fyreslayer rushed past him, bare feet slapping on the stone pathway, and jumped axe first into a group of enemy revenants. Fyresteel swung with fury, hacking into the dead, before they outnumbered the berzerker, cutting him down. Ealgrum-Grimnir bellowed and led the charge. The runefather swung his latchkey greataxe with practised ease from atop the lodge's last remaining magmadroth, White-flank. A spectral general on a decaying horse attacked the duardin with a tarnished greatsword, before an enormous aethereal scythe manifested and swept the runefather aside, and he disappeared from view.

Orrag-un descended another staircase. They were going to be overrun and the Ealfort would fall if they could not change their fate. A creature, skeletal equine head leering beneath a dark cowl, lunged at him with a long and rusting glaive. He raised his runic iron to parry, but the stalker was quicker than its bulk would have suggested. He felt the blade pierce flesh and roared in despair.

His roar filled the magmahold as his essence was pulled back into the chamber. It had not been the vision he had been searching for. The Ealrung were used to relentless attack, and even in this rare respite they all dreamed of the next battle. However, Orrag-un had been searching for something else, not a warning but hope of salvation. Sweat broke out on his brow, but not from the heat of the forge at his back. He had seen the fall of the lodge, doomed to be overrun by the dead. He kept his eyes closed, breathing deeply, and resumed the chant. After a few seconds Orrag-un smelled that telltale scent.

He walked the ashen path, the ancient road that led from the Eal-fort back to the Ealrung's ancestral homeland. None had walked the path and returned. The landscape was covered in a thick fog, but through it he could feel the essence he was searching for. It called to him, a vibration, a siren song, a part of himself. He was Grimnir the wanderer, drawn towards a great barrow built atop a mountain. It called to him; as Grimnir, he was led to their salvation, a way to save the Ealrung. He climbed, the might of Grimnir lending his muscles strength. The essence called him on. He would not falter. This time he would not fail.

Orrag-un opened his eyes. He was back in the Temple of Fire, the lava bathing the chamber in an orange glow. With the light of the forge at his back, his body cast a long shadow across the assembled duardin, but the Ealrung had learnt not to trust in shadows. The magma was a part of them, and would one day turn all their bodies to ash, but the shadows would bring only death. When he had first become runemaster the chamber had been full, but they had lost too many since then. His eyelids drooped again.

There was ur-gold nearby. The smell was thick in his nostrils. Grimnir had climbed the mountain, had sought out his prize. Only a thin light of flame fought back the darkness of the barrow, but he did not need light to find his way. The ur-gold sang to him, the essence of Grimnir the warrior. He who was Grimnir and also not Grimnir. Wanderer and warrior both.

The skeletons of a long-dead mountain hold stared back at him, accusing whispers on the wind. He did not know how they had died. He could not save them now. They were beyond help, but he could save the Ealrung. There was a faint crack in the darkness, a volcano fire. It called to him as the ur-gold did, the light of a forge waiting to be given new life. It revealed its secret to him in the fires of the mountain. There was hope here, when there had been no hope before.

Orrag-un wrenched open his eyes, casting off the vision. The feeling of strength in his muscles died down to an ember as the essence of Grimnir left him. Yet still he felt strong. He felt hope.

Thorrok leant over to him. 'What did you see, runemaster?' he asked, eager.

'Grimnir. Fire. Ur-gold...'

'We must recover the ur-gold.' Ealgrum-Grimnir spoke from atop his obsidian throne. Varga moved through the others to gain a better view. Every duardin in the lodge joined the binding of ash. It was an important ritual passed down from their ancestors in the Ulrung lodge. Usually she would stand at the back observing quietly, but today she would take her rightful place. The rune-father's beard, daubed in a streak of white ash, was the longest in the room, and the Ealrung's latchkey greataxe lay across his lap. Braziers flickered and fire filled the forge. There was a crash as the runesmiter's apprentice, Ongrad, struck the gong. As it vibrated, the light of the forge reflected and shifted around the room, pulling at the shadows.

The binding of ash was over, and now they would decide what to do. It would be the runefather's decision, but Varga would make sure she played her part. She felt the lines of the fyresteel war-picks that hung at her side. They were perfectly weighted, a fine example of duardin craftsmanship. Soon she would wield them again; the dead would return and they would all have to fight. She longed to take the battle to the enemy, and whatever happened she would be ready. She would fight for their future.

Torgrum, first runeson, turned to speak. 'At what cost?' he asked his father. 'Nagash's legions wish to draw us out and away from the safety of the Ealfort. We cannot divide our forces like this.'

The runefather's laugh was hollow. 'For too long have we sat within the walls of our lodge, my son. If there is ur-gold to be

found, we must recover it.' Though he spoke only to Torgrum, his
voice travelled for all to hear.

'They will attack as soon as we have left the lodge. What of the
flamelings? Without the fyrds they'll be defenceless.' Torgrum
pulled at his long beard with one hand, its length almost equal-
ling the runefather's. It was about time that Torgrum set out to
make his own forge. He should lead the expedition, but Varga
knew he would never leave the Ealfort.

'Then we must send only what we can afford to lose. For the
good of all Ealrung.'

'You are suggesting we march to our deaths? Give up our lives
for the scant promise of more ur-gold? Who would lead such a
quest?'

Ealgrum-Grimnir nodded in the direction of the runemaster,
signalling him to speak. Orrag-un stood on the dais, daubed in
the ashes of the dead. The white powder covered his lined face,
his hair and his fists. 'Which of you will swear an oath and honour the lodge in finding the ur-gold?' he called. His voice was
deep, the groan of ancient wood.

Varga barrelled her way through the assembled duardin, feeling their anger at her slight. Her usual place was at the back, but
this time she would not be forgotten. 'I will swear the oath!' she
bellowed. 'I will find the ur-gold.' Once sworn, a duardin would
never break an oath except in death, and even then they wouldn't
do it lightly. She could feel the glimmerlust rising. The essence of
Grimnir called to her, as it called to all fyreslayers. They all felt
the need for ur-gold, even those with many runes. Some said that
only made the glimmerlust worse.

'You?' The runefather's laughter was like thunder, rolling
through the magmahold. 'Why you, my daughter, when I have
many sons?' He waved the slab of his hand in the direction of the
twelve duardin by his side.

'She has earned the right, runefather.' Groggni stepped forward to stand alongside Varga. From a flameling her uncle had always been more like a father to her. She had longed to be a part of his fyrd. 'She has trained with fyresteel and throwing axe. And I will lend my fyrd to her quest.'

'You have always been too sentimental, brother,' the runefather replied, a light chuckle on his voice. 'And I know that even if I tried you would not heed my warning. You will lead your fyrd from my gates whether I give you my permission or not.'

'Grimnir has given us a sign,' Varga interjected, hoping that invoking the name of their god would give her request the power it needed. 'I will do this.'

Ealgrum-Grimnir stroked his long beard and looked between the runemaster and his sons. It was the runefather's decision and they knew better than to argue. They would all be needed when the nighthaunt attacked again. Varga had offered them a way to maintain their defence and to find the ur-gold. She would not let them down.

'Very well then, *runedaughter*. Bring us news of the ur-gold, or take a toll in souls.' He looked at the runesons assembled beside him, and their beards bristled in dishonour. 'Go and succeed where your brothers have failed.'

Varga turned and stepped from the magmahold, leaving the shouts of her objecting brothers behind her. She had her oath-quest, and now she would need to prepare.

The great brass doors of the Ealfort banged shut behind Varga, the sound of hammer on anvil. A bas-relief of their god, Grimnir, looked out upon Shyish, a warning to their enemies. It was some time since the western gates had last opened, and time would pass before they were opened again.

As she walked onto the path, a large duardin was waiting for her. He was a head taller than Varga, and could have passed for a young manling, if not for the heavy beard that hung down to his waist and the thick shoulders of a duardin.

'Ardvig,' she greeted him.

'Runedaughter,' he said, in a growl. 'Ardvig's been waiting for you.'

Ardvig had so many ur-gold runes it was a wonder that they didn't drive him mad with glimmerlust. He was more ur-gold than skin, and even if they had more, she wondered where it would go. It was only due to the fact that the grimwrath berzerker was such a fearsome warrior that he had been afforded so much ur-gold.

'You need Ardvig's axe,' Ardvig continued. 'Soulbane will stop anything that attacks us.'

He lifted the double-headed fyresteel axe as if to emphasise his point. He would be a potent force no matter what weapon he wielded, but she was thankful all the same.

'You honour me, Ardvig. I welcome your strength.'

'There's no honour in waiting here to die. Ardvig pledges his axe to you, runedaughter. Give Ardvig something to fight and kill. Ardvig will not die in there!'

He pointed his large hand towards the Ealfort, roughly in the direction of the mausoleum chamber. Varga nodded, agreeing, and clasped his arm in a warrior's grip. It was as good as an oath between them. He would be a welcome addition to the group of ageing and forgotten duardin she had assembled for the oath-quest. He was the best fighter the Ealrung had, and her brothers would not be happy that he had defied the runefather to join them. She glanced back at the gate. 'Good,' she said, as she joined the others on the path. 'We will need you.'

As they walked, the sun was obscured by the thick cloud of ash that hung in the air like a funereal shroud. It cast a purple hue across the landscape, adding to the shade of the sands at their feet. It was impossible to tell the time of day, or for how long they had been on the path.

'Best not to look up, flameling,' Groggni said, trudging past. Even though she had long come of age, he had not stopped calling her that. Other fyreslayers mocked him for failing to found his own lodge, but Varga was close to her uncle. Having him nearby was reassuring, even when the rest of her family had abandoned her to this fate. She tried to push the bitterness down inside. Let it fuel the fire at her heart, and give her strength for the coming battle. She had been given command, and for the first time in her life she had warriors at her back. She would not let them down, even if they were a disparate and pathetic group. With Groggni, Ongrad the apprentice runesmiter, and Ardvig, they might just stand a chance of fulfilling their oath.

They followed the ashen path, the ancient road that had led the first Ealrung away from the Ulrung lodge. It had been some time since one of the Ealrung had walked this path. Her brother Grumgan had left years ago, searching for ur-gold. Like all fyreslayers he had wanted to find glory of his own, but he had never returned. His fate had only made the Ealrung more cautious, wary of the lands outside their fort. Varga hoped she would break that curse, that she would return with the ur-gold, victorious. They would rebuild the Ealfort, replenish the fyrds and fight back the enemy once and for all.

Her bare feet trudged along the stone and shingle path. No matter how careful she was, it was impossible to be silent. She stopped by a line of trees to check their way, and the fyreslayers behind her ground to a halt. The duardin that carried the heavy metal chests for storing the ur-gold placed them by their feet and stretched their back muscles.

'Which way, Ongrad?' she asked, looking back over her

shoulder. The young runesmiter seemed confused by the question. He glanced around as if to see who she was speaking to. He was a poor excuse for a duardin, just as expendable to the lodge as she was. In the eyes of the Ealrung he had failed as a runesmiter when Grimnir had shown him nothing during the binding of ash. In this moment she could understand why the others had not believed in Ongrad. His frame was small, his skin sickly grey even without the ash that covered it.

'We follow the ashen path,' he said, beady eyes searching ahead. 'And then… Then the way will become clear. I can already sense the ur-gold from here.'

'You can?'

He nodded eagerly. Varga looked over at Ardvig. The big grimwrath was staring off into the distance, eyes glazed. His nostrils flared like a trapped animal; he could smell something too. Perhaps the runesmiter wasn't so useless after all.

'I think we're going the right way,' she said, striding off. The others followed her in a loose formation, watching their surroundings. They walked for some time, the path rocky and broken. The sands, like fine shards of glass, cut into the fyreslayers' bare feet as they walked. The further they went, the wilder the landscape became. Near the Ealfort the trees had been burned and removed, so that their enemies couldn't hide, but here they grew as they pleased. Their ashen-grey bark flaked and fell to the ground as the wind blew amongst the thin trunks. If Varga didn't know better, she would have assumed they were dead, like everything else in this realm. But they had a strange life to them, never blossoming, but never quite withering away.

When she glanced at the woods, Varga was certain she saw shadows moving amongst the boughs, following them. But when she looked they were gone. It was only the faint breeze blowing around the leaves and bark. Even the wind quietened down when she looked. Every so often a carrion bird, with glossy black feathers and watchful eyes, landed on top of a branch and observed their progress. They were waiting for something to happen, and so was Varga. Her muscles tensed and she swung her shoulders to loosen the joints. The war-picks no longer hung at her sides. She wouldn't let them leave her hands. 'I don't like the look of those woods,' she said, looking back over her shoulder. 'There are fell beasts in there.'

'I wouldn't worry about that.' Groggni didn't even turn to look.

'No?' she asked, wondering why he looked so smug.

'No. You want to worry about that.' He pointed ahead of them and for the first time Varga saw the mountain they had been seeking. The fog swirled around its peak in a vortex resembling a single baleful eye. From the caves that dotted the surrounding hills, it looked as if it had previously been mined. It was the perfect home for duardin, a place where they could see their enemies for miles around. With some fortifications it could be easily defensible. It was less open than the Ealfort, and with luck it would also have a fire at its heart. She wondered why her people had not settled here when first they came to this realm.

'Ongrad?' The runesmiter jumped at the sound of his name. 'Is this the place we seek?'

'I… think so.' She had been following him, but now realised that he hadn't been leading them at all. 'My senses are confused, I can't tell for sure.'

Ardvig had already pushed ahead, leaving the ashen path behind. The young runesmiter followed the grimwrath, not wanting to be too far away from the safety of the big duardin. Varga shrugged at Groggni and followed them up the incline.

When they came above the treeline, there was a whisper on the breeze, threatening and malicious. It called to Varga, but she couldn't quite make out the words. The sound of chains interrupted the trudging of the duardin. At times it blended into the chink of their armour; at other times the sound reverberated as if coming from some forgotten tomb. It taunted their every step. They were supposed to fear it, to flee, but the fyreslayers would not be discouraged. They were fire and they brought death.

The breeze stopped whipping around them. It dropped suddenly, as if they were in the eye of the storm. The day grew ever darker, the purple sky resembling an angry bruise. The whispers became louder, almost-words appearing in Varga's mind.

A shout came from behind and Varga turned. A thick wall of cloud was making its way inexorably up the mountainside. It shifted and warped, changing shape as it came, threatening to materialise.

'Hold firm!' Varga called, as the first spirit coalesced from the storm. It was a whirl of rusted blades and tarnished chain. '*Kha-zuk!*' she cried. The nearest fyreslayer was hacked down by a savage attack before he was able to raise his weapon, duardin blood spilling onto the sands.

'Shield wall!' Groggni was trying to arrange his fyrd into a line, but the dead had caught them by surprise. Another duardin fell to a wicked blade before they could link their slingshields. Some of the fyreslayers preferred to fight with dual axes. They sought the cover of the shield wall as the spirits rushed around them. Others threw their slingshields with a war cry, but the spectres simply ignored them. A ghost sped for Varga. She swung her war-picks in an arc around her, having practised the move time and time again. The hooks would catch the enemy before the following hammerhead shattered their bones. Only, the spectre had no bones. Fyresteel disappeared through the thing as if it were mist. It screeched at her and lunged. Varga crossed her war-picks to parry the blow. It dissipated, passing right through her body.

For a second she could see its real, dead face, a mess of rotting flesh, thick maggots crawling under the flaking skin. Varga felt a wave of extreme coldness as the thing cooled her inner fire. In that moment she saw her own death. She was numb, as if her heart had stopped.

'Not yet!' she screamed, and attacked. Even if she couldn't hurt it, she could push it back into the waiting fyreslayers. 'For Grimnir!'

Chains clinked behind her. Varga turned, but too slow. Thick metal loops passed from the ghost's neck to its arms, ending in a round metal ball. The entire visage was transparent, until the chain hooked over Varga's neck and pulled. In that moment it had substance. Varga choked as the metal squeezed against her throat. She kicked out, but met no resistance. Stars flashed around her vision. She pulled the chain over her shoulder, but the spectre simply floated above her. Underneath its ghostly white cowl, a long-dead jaw laughed at her.

Hooking her pick in a loop of chain, she pulled. The links grew tighter around her throat, but her attacker came closer. She attacked with her other war-pick, aiming at the ghost's head. It hit home, smashing its skull apart. Now solid, it couldn't avoid the fyresteel. Soundlessly, it burst into black ectoplasm, covering Varga's arms.

She had only a brief moment to feel the soreness around her neck before the fight pulled her back in. Ardvig's skin blazed with light as his ur-gold runes burned in anger. The ghosts that got too close were either deflected by the blaze, or swept up in the grimwrath's fury. Soulbane whipped around in a blur, destroying a spirit, before bisecting a spectre behind. The axe appeared to be the most effective weapon against the dead, and they focused their attacks on him. Varga tried to hook a wraith with her war-picks as it swept by, but it was futile.

The shield wall backed up the slope, each step orchestrated by a shout from Groggni. The cloud closed in around them, obscuring their escape. Varga saw a spirit ahead of them on the hill, the image of a human female, tall and lithe. A Guardian of Souls. Its black cowl was tattered and frayed, and the rest of its body blended with the mist. A blackened, steel death mask hid its features in a mockery of life. Varga could feel some unseen link between it and the other spirits. It carried a lantern, illuminated with spectral light, and a sword that was flecked with ice.

Two wraiths swept past Varga, and she felt chilled to her core. The fire in her belly dimmed, as if quenched by the icy touch of death. Two zharr berzerkers, twin brothers, swung their brazierflails around in synchronised arcs. Every ghost the auric fire touched disappeared in a haze. The weapons were effective, but their numbers were limited. Varga's own weapons were almost useless against the spirits. The fyresteel would force them back, but it wasn't enough to destroy them. She would need to do something else.

'The witch!' she shouted, over the din and crash of battle. Varga plucked a throwing axe from her belt and flung it at the Guardian of Souls. It tipped end over end, and thudded into a rock nearby. The spectre hissed in response and raised its lantern, amethyst energy spilling from its globe. Another wave of ghosts pulled themselves out of the stone surrounding the fyreslayers.

Varga hacked at one with a war-pick. It split around the steel, unharmed, and went to attack another duardin. 'The witch!' Varga shouted again. 'Destroy their leader!'

'Trying!' Bezran, one of the twins, said through gritted teeth. He swung his brazierflail back and forward like a whip. A wraith that had been about to attack Varga burst into flames.

'With me!' she shouted, running up the hill. 'Ardvig, with me!'

Ardvig roared and charged, overtaking her easily with his long stride. There was glimmerlust in his eyes. They were glazed over like the unseeing eyes of the dead. It would be hard to stop him now. The big fyreslayer smashed a path of his own to the Guardian of Souls as the dead swirled out of his way. The ur-gold in his flesh glowed as he drew on the essence of Grimnir. Rusted weapons sliced at his flanks. He ignored them, blood dripping from his skin, congealing with the ash. He pushed on, raising his axe to strike. As the blade neared, the spectre leapt into the air, dodging and screeching.

The sound almost deafened Varga, but did not stop her charge. It was not expecting her attack, and the fyresteel was enough to force it back. The spectre wheeled to face Varga, raising its sword. The eye-slits in its mask glowed with amethyst power as it screamed at her. 'Soooon, you will be one of us.'

'I've met your kind before,' Varga said, crossing the war-picks in front of her. 'And I don't fear you!'

Ardvig attacked from behind, Soulbane's brazier burning with fury as it swung through the air. Obsidian blade met ethereal essence. Varga didn't wait to see what happened. She hammered at the spectre as Ardvig sliced from neck to centre. Varga spun on her heel, weapons striking out. The Guardian of Souls' death mask clattered to the floor as the body disappeared into mist. All that remained was a blackened stain in the sand.

With their leader gone, the other spirits began to lose their grip on the realm. Without her power they were more vulnerable to fyresteel, and the duardin dispatched them with angry strikes from their axes.

Groggni trudged up to Varga, checking his axe. 'You fought well, Ealgrum's daughter,' he said. 'Like a true berzerker. A flameling no more.'

'We lost too many,' she said, ignoring his comment. 'Fyrgun, Durgi and the others will never see the Ealfort again. And we still have an oath to fulfil.' She watched as the fyrd dealt with their own dead, their axes turned against their own. It was a gruesome but necessary task; the dead were no longer their kin – they were their enemy.

The mountain loomed above them, the renewed wind whipping at the low cloud as it swirled around the summit in a vortex. The purple glow of the sun made the peak look like a jagged, rotting tooth, each cave opening resembling a decaying cavity. A chunk of stone had been carved out of its side, avalanching down to leave a debris of boulders and revealing more caves. Varga could imagine Grimnir himself fighting on the mountain, carving away at the stone as he battled some other god. The wind was a chill on her skin, flecks of ash flying away on the air like the embers of a burning fire. She continued up the hill without calling to the others. Even if they owed no loyalty to her, she knew they would follow. The oath to return the ur-gold meant just as much to them as it did to Varga.

Groggni remained at her side, the fyrd following close behind. It was best to stay together rather than risk getting lost in the fog, but Ardvig pushed ahead, grunting. 'Grimnir calls Ardvig,' he said to no one in particular.

They entered the first cave mouth they found, eager to reach their goal. It would have been low for a human but the duardin easily walked upright, and there was plenty of room for them to walk side by side. The wind died down to a faint whimper. Inside, the cave smelled of damp, rot and mould. Water dripped down the walls in streams of green limescale. The darkness was almost complete. Varga would not have known the cave extended any further if not for the faint breeze that rose from the depths. They lit brands to guide their way, the flickering light adding to the braziers of their weapons and casting varying shadows on the walls.

'There are marks here,' Ongrad said from beside her. His voice was low, almost reverent, as he ran a hand along the stone. Runes and other symbols were scratched into the walls, hard to read in the gloom. Some told tales of past lives, while others were meaningless notches. They tailed off the further they went along the corridor, becoming illegible scribbles.

Ongrad fell back as they moved along, a silhouette in the light cast from his brand. They headed for the core of the mountain, where Varga knew her prize awaited. The cave ceiling grew higher as they descended into the mountain. Deep grooves ran through the stone, cuts from pickaxes as whoever had mined here had expanded the cavern.

'What happened here?' Varga whispered.

A crack reverberated around the depths as she stepped on something. A bleached bone lay in the rubble at her feet, abandoned.

'I guess that answers your question, flameling.' Even though Varga couldn't see her uncle's face clearly, she could hear the chuckle in his words. 'Now we know what happened.'

'Ardvig cares not.' The grimwrath's voice was a rumble as he pressed ahead. 'Give him an enemy to fight, runedaughter.'

They passed the skeletal remains of humans, duardin and even some that looked aelven. Long forgotten, they lay where they had fallen, staring at her as if pleading for help. There was nothing she could do for them now. Some of them were incomplete, skulls separated from the body and bones caved in by blade or hammer. Further along, there was a faint crackle in the darkness, a volcano fire. Its light pulled her forward through the mountain, promising so much. The ur-gold must be nearby; she could almost sense it. The fires of her heart were drawing her on, showing her their prize. The duardin relied less and less on the brands as they went.

Ahead, the cave network split into two archways. The larger of the two had runic inscriptions carved into the smooth stone that ran around its threshold, while the other was roughly hewn and bare. Both offered Varga a tantalising view of the orange glow at the centre of the mountain.

'Runesmiter?' she called, her voice echoing in the cave network like a thousand voices speaking, overlapping with one another. She thought she heard a voice call back to her, but it could only have been an echo. Ongrad appeared at her side, the brand he carried casting him in shadow. He turned back and forth as if he were trying to catch an unruly bat.

'Which way?' Varga asked. 'Which way leads us to the ur-gold?'

'Either way will do,' he replied, before lifting a pale finger and pointing. 'But that way is quickest.'

'Then Ardvig goes that way.' The big grimwrath shrugged and pushed past the rest of the fyreslayers. He lifted his axe and stepped through the smaller of the two archways, disappearing around a corner. The others hurried to keep up. The air became staler as they descended, and the smell of damp grew stronger. They were closer to the ur-gold now, hidden within the depths of the mountain.

'Something is wrong,' Ongrad said, whispering so as not to be overheard. The runesmiter had been walking beside Varga, but suddenly he stopped dead. He looked at the edges of the cave. The tassels holding his beard were coming loose as he worried at them. 'The ur-gold is all around us.'

There was a snap in the darkness, a sound like breaking branches. The skeletons they had passed began to move. Skulls cracked on dry joints, and empty eye sockets stared their way. She should have known better than to trust the dead.

'*Uzkular!*' she yelled, the sound multiplying as the fyrd called out. She crossed her war-picks in a guard, waiting for the attack. The first of the dead stood, joints clicking in protest. It grinned liplessly at Varga as its companions woke. It had no weapons, but reached for her with clawlike finger bones. It towered over her, leering with an unseeing gaze. She lashed out with her war-picks, catching ancient bones between hammer heads. A second swing smashed its skull, flinging it across the cave to dash against the wall. The rest of it clattered to the floor. Ongrad set about the undead with his hammer. Surprisingly fierce, he used his low centre of gravity to his advantage. Deadwalkers filled the cavern. Some had leathery skin, but the rest were nothing but bone, as if the winds had scoured them dry. One, the size of a duardin, reached for Varga with a rusting axe blade. Green light spilled from its sightless eyes. Apparently some of her people had died here, but she would not hold back. She would grant them the rest they'd earned.

It swung the axe at her, its jaw distended in a soundless roar. She blocked with a war-pick, but the blow forced her back. It was astonishingly strong for a skeleton. Whatever magic gave it life was powerful. It hacked again, and she barely had time to evade the attack. The rusting blade nicked her shoulder and she cried out in anger. They might be easier to hit than the spirits outside, but the undead outnumbered the fyreslayers greatly. Varga pushed forward, smashing one hammer blow down, then another. The skeleton's skull caved in and it fell to the floor. Varga was already moving on. Her war-picks crashed into the waist of an undead human and it disintegrated in fragments of bone.

Other creatures rose from the dead. They tried to claw at her, or lunge with weapons that now hung loosely in atrophied limbs. The fyreslayers destroyed them with fyresteel and fury, but still they came. A small group of the dead shambled forward from an unseen gap in the wall. Their silver gromril armour was blackened with age and coated with flecks of rust, entire pieces crumbling away. Varga could see through the small gaps in their armour, revealing glimpses of bone, the flesh upon it rotting. A few of them held tarnished bronze guns clumsily in gauntlets – irondrakes.

There was a roar of alchemical fury as the nearest fyreslayer was engulfed. The berzerker flailed wildly at the dead irondrake before falling to the dirt.

Varga hacked at the nearest, smashing through gun and wrist. The rusted metal crumbled into dust. It clawed at her with its remaining arm. It was cold to the touch, but it failed to make purchase. She attacked with her other war-pick, carving a deep hole in its faceplate. She saw no eyes beneath that gromril, yet the creature behaved as if blinded, its clumsy limb trying to find her in the darkness. She let Grimnir's fury course through her and knocked it down with another hammer blow, destroying its armour piece by piece until it moved no longer.

More dead attacked the fyreslayers. They walked forward, less unsure. Sickly-pale flesh was visible for their lack of armour. Orange crests of hair and long beards had fallen out in great clumps. Varga hadn't expected to see other fyreslayers here, especially not amongst the dead. They guarded the end of the cavern, blocking her from the volcano heart of the mountain, and the ur-gold they sought.

Their leader stood amongst the loose formation of dead warriors, twin fyresteel axes held arrogantly at its sides. Dead eyes locked with hers. There was recognition there. Somehow it retained some form of memory. It grinned a deathly grin, decaying lips peeling back to show broken and neglected teeth.

'Brother,' she breathed. The sound disappeared into darkness. Even though the face was pockmarked and rotting, she knew it. She had been a flameling when Grumgan had left the Ealfort. He had never returned. Now she knew what had become of him. His skin was pale, but not from the binding. Blood had leaked from his body, leaving a husk of his former self. She could no longer think of him as her brother.

She lifted one pick over her shoulder. 'Khazuk!' she roared as she charged the reanimated corpse. Fyresteel met fyresteel. Her brother disappeared in the melee. The nearest deadwalker parried her attack with an ancestral axe. Its blade was tarnished, but the strength in the duardin's limbs had not yet atrophied. It blocked her blows, one after the other, rocking back on its feet. But she was faster. There was no way it could keep up with her. She stepped back, feinting, and allowed the creature to press forward. The axe flew over her head as she ducked and forced her shoulder up into the deadwalker. It didn't budge, but she was already bringing her pick around. The fyresteel crashed into its head, causing a splatter of foul blood as it went down. Varga made sure it was dead with a pick to the brain.

Their small fyrd was vastly outnumbered. The fyreslayers fought like Grimnir himself, but it wasn't enough. Blood poured from various cuts on Varga's body, some of which she hadn't even noticed. The war-picks felt heavy in her hands. She pushed herself on; she would never break her oath.

Across the chamber, Ardvig, a blur of golden rune-power, exchanged blows with what had been her brother. The dead runeson didn't seem to care about his wounds; it seemed pain no longer affected him. Varga worked her way towards them, cutting down skeleton and deadwalker alike. It was like trying to climb a cliff. Each fight slowed her and added to her wounds. As she looked on, Grumgan landed an axe blow to Ardvig's stomach. The grimwrath doubled over in pain, clutching at the wound.

'Ardvig!' she called, reaching out for the big grimwrath. With a flourish the runeson sliced Ardvig's neck with his other axe, almost removing the grimwrath's head. Ardvig fell. Her brother grinned that cold grin in her direction, then stepped across the body.

Groggni rushed to her side, swinging his axes at the deadwalkers that surrounded them. The twin salamanders cast on his helmet blazed with golden energy as he attacked. They fought their way to the grimwrath as the fyrd formed a protective shield wall around them. When Varga reached Ardvig he was already dead. She stood over his corpse, for some reason wishing to protect it from the deadwalkers. As with her, sweat had washed the ash from his body, and all that was left was blood. They would miss his strength. The runes on his arms were still glowing, but the golden hue was fading. She closed her eyes, even as the battle still raged around them. She already regretted what she was about to do, but she had little choice. 'Ongrad?' she called, before reaching out and gripping hold of Ardvig's rune of strength. Her fingers curved around the metal, pushing into his still-warm flesh. The ur-gold burned her hand, but she didn't care. She pulled. At first the rune resisted, but then it came away with a flash of light.

'Ongrad? Now!' she shouted again, passing the rune to the blood-spattered duardin who'd appeared at her shoulder. He looked at the ur-gold as if it were a newborn flameling. The dead crashed into the shield wall. They were running out of time.

'No! I can't.' His eyes darted around them, searching for another solution. 'I'm no runemaster!'

'Do it, Ongrad. I believe in you. Quick, or this battle is over!' She checked to see if the shield wall surrounding them was still intact, then placed the haft of her pick in her mouth, biting down on the grip. She knew the agony would come at any second.

Ongrad hesitated, then slapped the rune against Varga's arm. The pain was intense, burning her flesh, but she felt its power. The runesmiter's hammer fell with the clink of metal on metal. There was a flash of bright orange light, and Ardvig's rune became a part of Varga. She would never forget the grimwrath. Hooking the war-picks at her waist, she picked up Soulbane. She could feel the rune's power flowing through her.

She moved into the fray and sliced to her left, gutting the nearest deadwalker. The axe was lighter than it looked, the power of Grimnir flowing through its haft. A skeleton shattered into a thousand pieces. The blade led her to the dead, as if the weapon itself were sentient, willing her to fight. And she answered its call. An undead duardin cackled in some approximation of pain as she annihilated its body with a heavy blow. It clawed at her ankles as she moved on and she crushed its head with the flat of her blade. Breaking the link with whatever dark power animated them was the only way to truly stop the dead.

As the press parted, she came face-to-face with what once had been her brother. His face was peeling, like molten wax. His body bore wounds from the fight with Ardvig, but it had not been enough to stop him.

'Enough,' she ordered, knowing it would have no effect. He raised his axes and swung at her with an agility she didn't remember him having in life. Soulbane took the blow and she kicked out at Grumgan. He stumbled back as her new-found strength flowed through her. The rune blazed with golden fire. He lunged again, but she used the curve of her blade to hook the axe. It flew out of his hands, clattering to the ground a few yards away. With his guard down, she brought the greataxe up, hammering the brazier at its core into his chest. The dead runeson caught fire, but still tried to return the blow. Her backward swing cut through flesh and the other axe fell to the ground, a dead hand still clutching its haft. Grumgan leered at her, trying to bite with blackened teeth. Varga pulled Soulbane back, gore dripping from its blade. She swung, letting the weight take it. With one motion, the blade severed head from neck.

This time she didn't need to catch her breath; Grimnir was with her. She set to work killing the other deadwalkers. Without their leader, they were no longer coordinated. Groggni appeared alongside what remained of his shield wall. They were covered in the gore and viscera of battle, but still they fought, pushing the dead back. The dark power was waning and some of the skeletons simply collapsed to the floor in pieces. The fyreslayers hacked apart the remaining dead as their numbers dwindled.

'Is this the ur-gold we came for?' Varga asked Groggni. 'It belongs to the dead.'

'No,' he said, shaking his head. 'We can't have come all that way for this.'

They had no other choice but to take the ur-gold from the dead. They would no longer need it, and it would help them live on through Grimnir. It would be melted down in their forge and made anew, as it had always been. The fyrd set about the grim task, filling their cases with the runes of the dead. Others searched the cave for any useful materials they might employ in the defence of the Ealfort.

As before, Varga was drawn to the end of the cave. Light filtered through the cracks in the stone, golden beams that warmed Varga even in the darkness. It pulled her on, stronger now than it had been before. The curse that had clouded the essence had lifted when its undead fyreslayer guardians had fallen. With Ongrad at her side Varga stepped forward. She hung Soulbane at her back and grabbed a pick from her waist. With sure hands she hacked at the stone, opening up the seams, light spilling out. 'Help me,' she called over her shoulder. Ongrad and a few of the others pulled at the rock, clearing it away. The light was almost blinding, but within minutes they had cleared enough space for Varga to climb through, followed by Ongrad and Groggni.

The gap led to a vast cavern, bigger even than the magmahold of the Ealfort. Lava spilled from a fissure, collecting in runnels that filtered off into other caverns either side of them. The walls were a mosaic of different minerals, spotted in gold that shined as the fyreslayers came nearer. The distant ceiling glowed like stars in the night sky. Varga pulled a piece of the gold free, selecting one that looked different from the others. She could feel the essence of Grimnir through it, his strength adding to the rune she had already gained, but she had to be sure. 'Ur-gold?' she asked, handing the lump to the runesmiter. He sniffed at it, then licked it, his pale tongue darting out like a reptile.

'Ur-gold,' Ongrad agreed, hesitating before he returned it.

There was more ur-gold than Varga had ever seen. Even had each of the duardin brought a chest, rather than the two the fyrd carried between them, it was more than they could carry. The Ealrung lodge would be rich beyond their wildest dreams, filled with the essence of Grimnir. They could use the lava to return their dead to fight at Grimnir's side, cremating their bodies in the fury of the fires. Ongrad would give the ceremony that fyreslayer tradition demanded before they returned to the Ealfort. Not for the first time, Varga was glad Ongrad had joined her.

'Come on,' she said. 'Grab what you can, and let's get home.'

The journey home was harsh; the ashen path seemed to go on forever. The fires of battle had dimmed in the fyreslayers and their losses weighed heavy on Varga's shoulders. She longed to get the ur-gold home, to fulfil their oath and bring hope to the lodge. She didn't know how long they had been away, as Shyish's purple sun never faltered. It stared down on them, always watching, doing Nagash's bidding. Winds harried them all the way, pushing against them, but the dead left the fyreslayers alone. Varga hoped they'd learnt from their last defeat, but she knew that was unlikely. You could never trust the dead; in Shyish they would always return. The whispers that had called to Varga since she had left the Ealfort haunted her, but she would not listen. They had only lies to tell her.

A keening sound pierced the air, soon followed by other voices, low and threatening, a hum of angry souls. Varga lifted Soulbane in her hands and worked her shoulders loose; she had known war would come again. Their fyrd was smaller now, but she would not be cowed. As they reached the treeline, the Ealfort came into view. As usual, smoke rose from the active volcano at the heart of the mountain, but something was wrong. Angry barks of thunder and lightning shot across the peak as if it were about to erupt. The smoke blackened as the fires raged at its core. The mountain was angry.

Varga had returned, but she was too late. She had spent too long on her quest and in her absence the Ealfort had burned. Nagash's legions had attacked, as Torgrum had warned. Dead spectres swarmed across the fortress like hunting bats, destroying everything in their path. They should have listened to his warning. Groggni's fyrd could have aided in the defence, along with Ardvig's axe. Now, the fortress was crumbling as the undead smashed everything they had against the stone. Varga had abandoned her kin to their fate, and now they were lost. She had failed them.

Varga moved, about to break into a run, but Groggni placed a hand on her arm. It wasn't a strong grip, but it was enough to make her think twice about getting closer. 'There's nothing we can do for them now,' he said, his voice barely above a whisper. She relaxed, allowing Groggni's hand to drop. The sounds of battle still raged in the distance.

'We have to do something,' she said, gesturing at the fort. 'They're our kin.'

A huge roar of defiance spilled from the Ealfort, reverberating down the valley. Only a duardin could make that sound, but then it was silenced, gone. If her father were still alive he would be first on the battlements, riding atop Whiteflank, but he was nowhere to be seen. She could imagine that roar coming from his throat, a final cry of despair as his lodge fell around him.

'There is no one left. We're too late.' Groggni refused to look at the Ealfort, but instead stared into Varga's eyes, imploring. If Ealgrum-Grimnir was gone, then her brothers would be next.

'There may be some,' she said.

'And what good could our little group do them? Do you want to add our bodies to that funeral pyre? We've already lost enough.'

Varga had never seen Groggni like this – there was a look in his eyes that she didn't like, the look of a flameling, wary and frightened. 'There's nothing we can do to save the Ealfort from that horde. All we can do is take the ur-gold and live to save the Ealrung name.'

Varga looked between Groggni and the ancient home of the Eal-rung. Flames licked at the battlements and there wasn't a single duardin to be seen. They were all gone, her father, her brothers, even Runemaster Orrag-Un and Runesmiter Thorrok. She had not yet fulfilled her oath, but they would have no use for the ur-gold now. Undead beasts prowled amongst the corpses, feasting. Soon they would come for Varga and her fyrd.

'We will forge another lodge,' she said, looking around at the group of duardin. Most of the fyrd was old and past their prime, but she knew now that they would fight for her. They would hon-our Grimnir till the end. 'And we will find more duardin to help us. One day I will return to avenge our kin. I swear that oath to you, in Grimnir's name. Until we return with ur-gold and rebuild the Ealfort, our oaths still stand.' She hefted Soulbane and started to trudge away from their home, not looking back. The fyrd fol-lowed in her wake as they set out on the ashen path once again, not knowing where they were heading. One day Varga would return, but before then she would need to find an army to fight at her side. Grimnir would provide.

BLESSED OBLIVION

Dale Lucas

'Shield to shield, brothers!' the Liberator-Prime barked. 'Close ranks the moment the refugees are through the lines!'

Klytos fell into formation, tower shield at the ready, warblade heavy in his gauntleted fist. He took a moment – the briefest of moments – to close his eyes and summon his last, fragmentary memories of the people he had loved in life.

A woman: sea-green eyes in a smooth, tanned face.

A newborn: small, impossibly fragile in his seemingly enormous hands.

An old man: face eroded like a time-worn cliff, tears on his filthy cheeks.

He stirred his memories before each battle, knowing that if he fell, he would next incarnate with even fewer of them dwelling inside him. He'd already lost their names, most meaningful details of the life he'd lived, even the smallest inkling of where or when that long-ago lifetime had unfolded. When next he was smashed and reforged upon the Anvil of Apotheosis, there was no telling what might remain, if anything.

That thought terrified him.

A jostling. Klytos opened his eyes. His fellow Celestial Vindicators formed a vast wall of shield bosses, gleaming blades and shining turquoise armour to either side of him. For days they had protected a massive refugee band effecting a desperate retreat across the Hallost Plains towards the sea, mere hours ahead of the trailing Khornate warhost. Now, at last, the servants of the Blood God bore down upon them.

They could run no further. It was time to make a stand, however desperate.

'Prepare to close ranks!' the Liberator-Prime shouted. Klytos' world was a storm of panic and terror as the refugees fled through their spaced ranks. As he often did, Klytos saw the ghosts of his lost loved ones in the faces of the mortals they now stood to defend: there, his wife, as a fleeing mother clutching her infant; nearby, an old man with a face like his father's – or was it his grandfather's? – hobbling along on a crutch. Phantoms. Echoes of a past that every death and rebirth took him farther and farther away from.

The last of the refugees – the lucky ones – were just about to pass through the massed ranks of the Stormhost. Out on the plain, scores of unlucky stragglers were overtaken by ravening Flesh Hounds or cleaved by bloodied hellblades.

The order came. 'Shoulder to shoulder, my brothers!'

The shield wall closed. A shock wave rippled through the Stormhost, Klytos and his comrades absorbing the impact of hundreds of charging, screaming bodies as the Khornate vanguard met them. Barbed spear tips and bloodied sword blades thrust and swiped at Klytos and his Stormcast brethren around their enormous shields.

Barely discernible above the tumult: 'Make them pay, brothers! Strike! Forward!'

The battle line moved as one, the shield wall crushing the forward ranks of barbarian marauders and lesser daemonspawn. Klytos lowered his shield, warblade thrusting and slashing, mowing a bloody swathe through his amassed adversaries. All was chaos and slaughter: a storm of churned soil, clods of torn-up turf, gouts of diseased blood, gobbets of hewn flesh, the deafening ring of steel upon adamant sigmarite. Klytos revelled in the carnage: it filled him with a dutiful calm.

Then, a blasphemy enormous and terrifying advanced from the surging fray: an Exalted Deathbringer, a tower of rippling, knotted sinews and taut, leathery skin the colour of dried blood. Tall and looming, it waded through the massed bloodletters and skullreapers clogging Klytos' vision like a man striding out of a rolling surf.

The monstrosity bore in its hands an enormous, double-headed axe. As it closed on the front rank of the Stormhost – on Klytos – it drew that axe back over its broad shoulders and began hewing, right and left, indiscriminately slashing down foul comrades and shining enemies alike.

Its monstrous blade split Klytos in two, and the holy lightning of Sigmar Heldenhammer stole him from the field of battle...

That night, the slaughter abated and the plain secured, the Stormhost established a perimeter around the refugee camp. Inside that perimeter, the mortals stoked cook fires, fed empty bellies with meagre provisions, tended the wounded and comforted the dying. A chill wind skated over the Shyish plain, now moaning, now sighing, offering melancholy harmony to the hymns of the Knights-Incantor.

The songs, which should have stoked Klytos' courage and focused his warrior's heart, now filled him with a strange sense of disaffected dread. True, he was now reforged, ready once more to rejoin the eternal struggle against Chaos... yet he was nonetheless diminished; thinned, like clouds effaced by the wind.

Klytos had died many times, his very essence torn out of the Mortal Realms and returned to the Chamber of the Broken World, there to be superheated into molten impermanence, smashed by the Six Smiths upon the Anvil of Apotheosis, and finally reformed. Vague recollections of some of those deaths yet haunted him: the searing pain as his skull was crushed beneath the hammer of a beastlord; the taste of blood as he was ridden down by the thundering hooves of charging Gore-Gruntas; the panic and terror that gripped him as he was butchered and dismembered by the accursed blade of a laughing daemon prince. He even suffered a recurring nightmare of slowly succumbing to suppurating pustules and a writhing maggot infestation courtesy of the vile plague sorcerers of Nurgle... though he was not sure if that benighted vision was a true memory or only a dream.

He had once tried to keep count of his many deaths and Reforgings, but that count was now lost, like so many other expendable bits of him – gaping, bleeding spaces in the fabric of his consciousness that should contain something yet did not, like the persistent itch of a long-lost phantom limb, empty cavities in his memory stirring impulses he could barely understand or articulate.

The woman was a ghost in his imagination now. He remembered the wood-brown colour of her skin, the cool depths of her eyes, but he could no longer conjure features to make her face anything more than a blurred mask.

Or the babe. Was it a boy? A girl? He yet recalled how small it was in his seemingly enormous hands, but that image – a trembling newborn – was all he could summon.

Then there was the old man... Klytos no longer remembered a face, or a voice, or any wisdom imparted. All he could remember, with great effort and concentration, was the feeling of bony, arthritic hands in his own. A presence, not a person.

Why? Why could he not simply forget, and be content to do so? He saw the after-effects of Reforging in every member of his conclave: the way Barnavos eternally stared into the middle distance, reciting chains of numbers and formulae; the way Hareggar treated the scouring of his war-plate and the oiling of his sword blade as crucial rituals, demanding almost religious fixation; the way Jennaeus, when he thought no one was listening, recited a constantly transforming list of all the ways he had died, making of his many, painful ends a strange, martial litany.

'The sting of a spear, the bite of a blade,' he would mutter. 'Cleft in twain, unwound, unmade...'

Eagerly, hungrily, he listened to the holy hymns of the God-King, praying that the deep and sonorous harmonies of the Knights-Incantor might banish his doubt and grief entirely. He knew that such merciful amnesia, the salvation of an eternal present, should beckon to him, tempt him... but it only filled him with a sense of overwhelming panic and impending tragedy.

A great shadow fell over him. Klytos raised his eyes to find Liberator-Prime Gracchus looming at his elbow. Klytos shot to his feet. Gracchus laid one gauntleted hand on his shoulder pauldron.

'You fought well today, young Klytos,' the Liberator-Prime said gravely.

Klytos nodded. So far as he could reason out, he had been fighting in this Stormhost for several centuries... and yet, to every Liberator-Prime who had ever commanded, he was always 'Young Klytos'.

'I am proud to serve,' Klytos said, and meant it.

'I am surprised,' the Liberator-Prime said, 'to find you back in our midst so quickly. Sigmar must have great need of you.'

In truth, Klytos had been just as surprised. Reforgings usually took longer than several short hours to complete. He had idly wondered if his rushed reconstitution might account for how disordered his thoughts now were, how rattled and empty he felt.

'Sigmar's will is all,' Klytos said, and he meant that too. Or did he? His own feelings defied his understanding.

The Liberator-Prime studied him for a long, curious moment. 'Something troubles you,' he said. It was not a question.

Klytos felt fear stir in him. He could not tell Liberator-Prime Gracchus the truth. Give voice to his shame? His fear? Impossible!

Luckily, Gracchus spoke again before Klytos was forced to. 'Duty,' he said at last. 'Your Reforging has left you disoriented, and only duty will restore the sense of order your still-adjusting psyche now desires.'

Klytos nodded eagerly. 'Command me,' he said, all but begging. *Anything but sitting here, contemplating it all.*

The Liberator-Prime turned towards the dark landscape stretching beyond the ragged edge of the camp's firelight. He indicated a cluster of low, rolling hills to the north-east. 'Earlier, patrols reported signs of scouts in those hills. Investigate and report. And if you find anything, your first task is to make the Stormhost aware, not to slay those you find single-handed. Am I understood?'

Klytos saluted his commander. 'Understood, Liberator-Prime. I live to serve.'

Eager for a purpose – a mission – his mind still awhirl with self-recrimination, Klytos took up his shield and his warblade and trudged off into the night, as commanded, each long stride leading him farther from the camp. In truth, he was thankful for the lone patrol, dearly hoping that duty and vigilance might somehow assuage the storm raging inside him.

Having cleared the ragged edge of the firelight, he scanned the doleful, moonlit landscape surrounding him. To the north, the bright crimson bonfires of Khorne's warband littered the plain to the black horizon. He knew their withdrawal after the day's bloodshed was only a brief reprieve before another, inevitable clash.

He was closer to the hills than the camp he had left behind when he heard the sound of excited voices, followed by the unmistakable tumult of a battle: barked orders, pounding feet and ringing steel.

'Take them!' he heard. The voice was throaty, inhuman.

Behind the hill directly ahead of him, there came a flash of bright green light.

Klytos broke into a run, aiming to remain both swift and silent. He mounted the low slope before him, trudging up towards the broad hilltop. The voices from the other side were much louder now, the din of battle more frantic.

Klytos reached the hilltop, took shelter behind a ragged line of stunted, wind-wracked old trees, and took in the scene below.

Seven enormous figures encircled a lone swordsman, trading blows with the trapped fighter and making escape impossible. An eighth large figure stood apart, watching the proceedings. A smaller figure, wrapped in a flowing cloak and cowl and bearing a wizard's staff capped by a scintillating green gemstone, haunted the edge of the melee, two bulky adversaries lying dead at his feet.

The big loner and the encircling forces were easy enough to identify, even at this distance. Only a slaughterpriest possessed such magically swollen slabs of muscle, and only Chaos-tainted skullreapers could stand beside such a preternaturally massive servant of the Blood God and not be dwarfed by him. The swordsman – lithe and swift amid those lumbering, oversized bodies – stood his ground against the attackers, but it was clear that his defences were flagging.

The cloaked figure suddenly shouted to the swordsman. 'Malazar, fall back!'

The voice was female.

The swordsman, Malazar, met three attackers who all rushed

him at once. One felt the bite of his steel. The other two parried the deft, deadly blows he rained upon them. Then, in desperation, the swordsman withdrew. He put his body between the cloaked woman and their slowly closing adversaries.

Part of Klytos bade himself burst from hiding and rush to their aid – but there was another impulse, a subtler one. *Wait*, it said. *Watch. Something in this makes me uneasy...*

As Klytos watched, the still-cowled woman drew a knife from beneath her cloak. She said something to her companion, but Klytos could barely hear the words.

The swordsman dropped his sword and raised his chin, exposing his throat. He acted swiftly, obediently, never taking his eyes off the advancing skullreapers.

'Back, you fools!' the slaughterpriest suddenly roared.

Two of the Bloodbound withdrew, as ordered, but the rest, rendered reckless by battle lust, advanced towards the woman, blades ready to rip and tear.

The woman stepped close to her sword-wielding companion, placed her knife at his offered throat, and sliced it open. As blood sheeted, thick and hot, from the gaping wound, she shouted strange, guttural words in a language Klytos did not recognise. With each word, the gemstone on her staff pulsed, its luminescence intensifying in seconds.

A great explosion of light suddenly erupted from the staff, an expanding corona of emerald energy that tore through the five advancing skullreapers, ripping the life right out of them and throwing their hellishly enlarged bodies to the earth. Then, as quickly as it had appeared, the great cloud of energy dissipated. Its thinned, ragged edges never touched the plot of ground to which the last two skullreapers and their slaughterpriest master had retreated.

Klytos could not believe his eyes. The woman had slain her

own companion – her protector! – and used the dark energy of his sacrifice to fuel that lethal, magical discharge. Nor had the swordsman hesitated. She demanded his life: he gave it.

But now, magical energies spent, the woman was helpless. The two remaining skullreapers charged, eager to subdue her.

'Blood for the Blood God,' one snarled in ecstasy.

'Aelven blood for the Lord of Slaughter!' his companion growled.

Aelven?

Klytos had to help her. He burst through the screen of twisted trees, ready to join the fight.

'Two Darklings,' the slaughterpriest below said slowly, 'skulking about alone in the night, between two camped armies? Why?'

Klytos froze. *Darklings*. No wonder he had hesitated when moving to defend her. He knew well the blasphemies and dark sorceries attributed to the Darkling Covens. Clearly, some part of him had sensed that darkness emanating from the sorceress and her companion.

The skullreapers were upon her. She fought bravely, using her staff as a weapon with practised assurance, but her adversaries were too large, too savage. In moments, one wrested her staff from her and tossed it aside. The other locked the aelf woman's arms in his huge, muscular hands.

The slaughterpriest approached, all but swaggering in the moonlight. 'Tell us what you're after,' he demanded, 'and the master just might make your end quick and relatively painless.'

Darkling or no, Klytos thought, *she needs help. Is Chaos not the greater foe?*

Klytos found his voice. 'Unhand her!' he bellowed.

The Bloodbound all turned towards him. Klytos did not move. Being outnumbered, he knew he would maintain his advantage only if he could draw them up the hillside and hold the high ground.

'What is this?' the slaughterpriest snarled.

'Just out for an evening stroll,' Klytos said coldly. 'And look what I find...'

'I suppose,' the slaughterpriest answered, 'you shall now tell me there are more of your infernal kind waiting, just over that rise? A battle chamber, ready to destroy us?'

'No,' Klytos said. 'Just me.'

'Kill him,' the slaughterpriest commanded. His two lumbering subordinates unhanded the sorceress, eager for a bloody duel with what they considered a more worthy adversary, and advanced up the slope. One bore a nasty-looking hellblade, encrusted with dried blood that looked black in the moonlight. The other wielded a large, lethal warhammer. Only when the first of them was nearly upon him, raising that warhammer and sounding a hideous battle cry, did Klytos finally move.

He thrust his shield forward, throwing it edge-on. The leading edge of the heavy sigmarite slab slammed hard into the mutant marauder's face and sent the hideous creature toppling backwards, blood gushing from its crushed and broken nose. As the first skull-reaper fell, Klytos pivoted to meet its sword-wielding companion, that ugly blade rising high for a killing blow. Klytos blocked the blade with a powerful, two-handed stroke, then swept his own warblade in a broad, sideward arc while his adversary's steel yet rang. The slash bit deep into the creature's muscular torso. The skullreaper roared, enraged by the painful, seeping wound, but its shock was only momentary. With a monstrous battle cry, it charged Klytos, hellblade crashing down time and again in ferocious hammer blows, its speed and savagery more than a match for Klytos' skill and strength.

As Klytos danced across the hillside, parrying and dodging his would-be killer's attacks and struggling to land his own, he caught sight of the first skullreaper – the one stunned by his shield attack – now creeping in from the right. Below, at the foot of the hill, the slaughterpriest struggled to bind the belligerent prisoner so that he, too, could safely turn his back on her and join the fight. Klytos was fairly certain he could slay the two Bloodbound that he now faced… but if that slaughterpriest entered the fray before the other two were neutralised, any hope of survival – let alone victory – would evaporate.

The shield-stricken skullreaper suddenly charged, bellowing through a face sticky with coagulating gore. Klytos barely avoided a deadly blow from its monstrous warhammer, then ducked under the Khorne-worshipper's reach and lunged sidewards, throwing all of his armoured bulk against the charging monster.

The gambit worked. The hammer-wielder crashed hard into its sword-swinging comrade and the two hit the hillside in a tangle of limbs, weapons and rusted armour. Before either could rise again, Klytos rushed to meet them. His warblade sliced the air once, twice. The heads of both skullreapers thumped down the hillside.

Klytos turned, expecting to find the slaughterpriest still trudging up the slope towards him – but the demagogue was already upon him, having closed the distance that separated them with inhuman speed. The slaughterpriest bellowed praise to Khorne as he revealed his own weapon of choice: an enormous, broad-bladed battle scythe. The blade flashed in the moonlight, sweeping in a wide, savage arc towards Klytos' head.

Klytos ducked the whistling blade… barely. Half-crouched and unbalanced, Klytos thrust his sword deep into the slaughterpriest's exposed flank. The hellish prophet threw back his head and roared, but pain did not deter him. His movement yanked Klytos' warblade from his grip. Already unbalanced, Klytos was thrown to the ground. As the Stormcast raised his eyes, seeking a means of escape or some weapon close at hand, the slaughterpriest brought his death-dealing scythe down towards Klytos' hunkered form.

No escape. Another death. More pieces of Klytos, soon to be lost.

There came a sudden, blinding, sun-bright flash of emerald light. Klytos shrank from the burst, sure that, in the next instant, he would feel the bite of the slaughterpriest's scythe blade.

No killing blow came. Instead, Klytos heard the sound of sizzling, as of meat in a hot frying pan. The stink of burning flesh assailed him. Then, the night was split by an unholy scream of rage and agony. He opened his eyes.

The slaughterpriest twisted and writhed on the hillside, his enormous, muscular frame smoking as his foul skin blistered and cracked. As Klytos stared, horrified, the slaughterpriest's body seemed to be eaten from the inside out by squirming, devouring worms of pure light. The whole process took seconds. In the span of a breath, the slaughterpriest's scream was cut off, echoing into the void that claimed him as the writhing, devouring glow-worms guttered out like spent embers and disappeared.

Stunned, Klytos turned towards the aelf woman. Her cowl had finally been removed. Her long, dark hair waved placidly in the night winds, the tapered points of her ears now visible. Though she was dishevelled and slightly worse for wear, her stark, frighteningly beautiful face suggested a calm strength – fierce determination and indomitable will in equal measure. Clearly, she was not one to be trifled with.

Klytos stood and snatched his warblade from where it lay among the ashen remains of the slaughterpriest. 'My thanks,' he said, nodding towards her. 'But, I had hoped to do the rescuing, not to be rescued.'

'Such gratitude,' the aelven sorceress said drolly, then lowered her staff and turned round. She moved to the still, prone figure of her swordsman companion – the one slain by her own hand as a blood sacrifice – and knelt beside him.

'Who was he?' Klytos asked. 'A servant? A slave?'

'A friend,' the sorceress said, almost to herself. 'True and faithful. He knew his death could fuel magic sufficient to lay them low. Most of them, anyway.' She laid a single, pale hand upon his still body.

'What were the two of you doing here,' Klytos pressed, 'in sight of a Khornate battle camp?'

The aelf sorceress stood again.

'Don't worry your shiny, empty head over it,' she said. Then, staff in hand, she turned northward and began a confident march.

'Hold on!' Klytos shouted. 'You can't go that way! There are more of them!'

'Your grasp of the obvious is astounding,' she said, not stopping. 'I'll find a way through. I have to.'

'That's folly, and you know it,' Klytos said, following close behind her.

She was not listening. Well ahead of him, she mounted the slope of another hill and trudged upwards towards the ridgeline.

It was at the crest of the hill that Klytos finally caught up with her. She stared down upon the vast, level plain, the Khornate horde's camp blighting the landscape like a festering burn scar. On the soughing winds, Klytos heard the rattle of chains and the crackle of flames, mingled with cruel laughter and mournful lamentations. Beyond the Khornate camp, an eerie blue-green glow marked the place where horizon and sky met.

'What is that?' the aelven sorceress asked, eyes narrowing.

'A procession of nighthaunts,' Klytos said. 'They sometimes follow in the wake of the Blood God's minions here in Shyish, scavenging tortured spirits from the battlefield.'

The sorceress stared, eyes locked on the spectral light. Klytos studied her by the glow of the gibbous moon. Her face was a mask of cold analysis: weighing all options, considering all variables.

'Where is it you're trying to get to?' Klytos asked.

The sorceress turned then and seemed to study him, long and hard. Klytos knew that all she saw was the implacable, unreadable mask of his great sigmarite helm, but there was still a strange, probing quality to her gaze that seemed to penetrate beyond the mask, behind his hazel eyes, into the very locus of his soul and consciousness. Though armoured from head to toe, he suddenly felt naked, exposed.

Instinctively, Klytos took a single step backwards – the only retreat he could remember making since being plucked out of mortality by Holy Sigmar.

'Who are you?' he asked.

'My name,' the aelven sorceress said, 'is Lichis Evermourn. My companion and I were sent by our coven to recover something very precious, lost on the other side of that.' She gestured to the vast Khornate camp. 'I need to reach a citadel back in the foothills. That is what my companion and protector died for.'

'Impossible,' Klytos said. 'Even if you get past the camp itself, the country in its wake will be crawling with the servants of Khorne. And that's to say nothing of the terrors of Shyish itself, both living and dead.'

'Then come with me,' Lichis Evermourn said. 'As you've seen, I have powers of my own, but I could use a strong warrior – a faithful warrior – at my side.'

'No,' Klytos said flatly. 'I cannot abandon my Stormhost – my duty.'

'Your duty is not only to Sigmar,' Lichis said, 'but to Order and Light. Believe me when I say, the artefact I seek is powerful enough to risk anything for its recovery... because if the enemy discovers it, its power will be theirs, and serve their vile ends alone.'

'What is this artefact?' Klytos asked.

'A stone,' Lichis said. 'Pure Shyish realmstone, calcified and bound into the form of a large amethyst. In the simplest terms, it restores all things – rebuilds that which is broken, regenerates that which was lost. It's remained safe and hidden in an out-of-the-way redoubt in the foothills, but its keeper and her initiates were forced to flee before she could recover the stone from its hiding place. She tried to backtrack and retrieve it, but her attempt was… unsuccessful.'

Klytos barely heard any of the words she said after *it restores all things – rebuilds that which is broken, regenerates that which was lost.*

No, he thought. *Impossible. It is heresy. Betrayal!*

'If it is so precious,' he said, 'so powerful, then go to the Stormhost commander and ask for a full conclave–'

'There is no time,' Lichis snapped dismissively. 'Besides, a larger force would be a larger target. Malazar and I had thought to slip through alone, the two of us, but now, I am forced to continue without him. And seeing what lies before me…'

She stared down at the plain.

'I need your help, Klytos,' she finally said, eyes still on the enemy camp below. 'And I will reward you for your aid.'

He had not told her his name, nor anything about himself. It had not been his imagination. She *had* opened him, examined him, and learned of his secret yearning.

Lichis Evermourn turned her large, dark eyes upon him. There was pity in those eyes now, even understanding.

'I know what you desire most of all, Klytos. The realmstone can provide it.'

He thought of the child. The woman. That rough, wizened hand in his own.

I could have them again! he thought. *In my mind, in my heart, part of me–*

'No,' Klytos said, turning from her. 'I cannot. This is a violation of my oaths... of my duty...'

He started to descend the hill.

'It's true what they say, then,' Lichis Evermourn said. 'You Storm-casts are a horde of mindless automatons, slaves without a speck of self-awareness or free will–'

Klytos stopped. Rounded on her. 'I am no slave! I serve because I was chosen!'

She moved closer, her gaze meeting his. 'Then prove it and help me. I know you want to. You'll remember *everything*, Kly-tos. Their names. The life you shared with them. If your existence, for all the ages yet to come, is to consist of endless cycles of death and resurrection in the name of Holy Sigmar, should you not be granted the recollection of who you were and what you lived for?'

Their names. Their faces. The woman's dark skin against his own. Songs he sang to his newborn babe. Lazy afternoons among wildflowers under sunny skies. All that, and more, could be his again, his last memento of all they shared...

'The Reforging,' Klytos said, mind already turning to the future.

'Immaterial,' Lichis said. 'Once I restore what's been lost to you, it cannot be taken away again. I swear it.'

This is folly, he thought. *Only disaster can come of this. To aban-don your Stormhost? To aid this woman? To feed a selfish desire?*

I serve, he reminded himself. *I fight and I have been loyal unto death, a thousand times over. Should I not reclaim this one, small thing?*

Klytos sighed. He had already made his decision, hadn't he?

'Let me recover my shield,' he said, and marched down the hill.

Their way through the hills was slow and treacherous, but they eventually cleared the Khornate camp. Once upon the open plain,

Klytos allowed Lichis to guide them. The only words they shared were pointed, utilitarian: time to rest; time to camp; movement ahead, proceed with caution. The farther they wandered from his Stormhost, the more despondent he became, his hope and guilt at war within him.

It was during their second night on the plain that Lichis made an effort to speak with him.

'You're not much for conversation,' she said.

Klytos raised his eyes. He had been contemplating the crackling flames of the pitiful fire before them. The night was cold and dark, and they had not found food since the day before. Even sufficient kindling was in short supply. He could go a long time without sustenance – any Stormcast could – but the lack of need did not quell the desire.

'I have nothing to say,' Klytos answered.

'That may be the case,' Lichis said, 'but I am hungry and bored. Make the effort, for my sake.'

'For your sake,' Klytos scoffed. 'We have nothing in common.'

'You might be surprised,' Lichis said. 'Do endless Reforgings blunt your curiosity, as well? Your ability to empathise?'

Klytos sighed. 'I shall be damned for this. Cast out. Possibly obliterated.'

'Simply for reclaiming your past?' Lichis asked. 'Restoring your soul? I had no idea Sigmar was so cruel.'

Klytos raised his eyes. 'Sigmar is worthy of all praise, all admiration. He is the paragon of virtue. If he punishes me, I well deserve it.'

The sorceress smiled a little. 'And yet, you came.'

'Do not mock me!' Klytos snapped. 'You cannot understand what this feels like.'

'That's a foolish assumption,' Lichis said. 'Let me assure you, Stormcast, I've forgotten a dozen lifetimes and barely wondered what became of them. I know well what it means to lose pieces of oneself, be it to hungry time or soul-flaying trauma.'

'How do you endure it, then?' Klytos asked.

'I remind myself,' Lichis said, 'that I am not what I remember, or who I was in the past. I am only *what I do* in the present. Actions define me, not memories.'

Klytos nodded. He could appreciate that ethos – he truly could – and yet, he still felt she could not wholly comprehend his predicament.

'The memories you've lost were erased by time itself,' he said, 'and ultimately replaced with new experiences. My mind feels like a haunted castle that's collapsed and been sloppily rebuilt a hundred times over. The rooms and corridors keep shifting, changing, yet always, the ghosts remain...'

Lichis studied him in the firelight, like a wizard closely observing a newly fashioned homunculus.

'No wonder you Stormcasts are all so dour,' she finally said. 'You've lost everything that makes you human.'

'You mock me,' Klytos said.

'I pity you,' Lichis countered. 'There is a difference.'

They spent four days trekking steadily towards the mountains. In the foothills, folded into a dreary vale shrouded in mist and shadows, the citadel they sought loomed, dark and ancient upon a craggy promontory, a cluster of gloomy towers, sharp spires and peaked roofs clustered behind high, sheer curtain walls.

Klytos shuddered inwardly upon first espying the bleak old fortress. It was all the darkest essences of Shyish, extracted and distilled into a single agglomeration of sweating, night-black stone, pallid, half-dead creeper vines and brooding shadows. The front gate – tall, narrow and dark as a mountain crevasse – stood wide open, daring them to enter.

'What was this place?' Klytos asked, peering from cover behind a wall of fallen boulders and rocky scree.

Lichis, secreted beside him, met his wondering gaze with her own.

'My coven holds many such redoubts,' she said, 'in all the Mortal Realms. Places where sensitive objects of power can be hidden and guarded.'

Something moved behind the battlements: a figure visible between the crumbling merlons of the parapet. It paused in the gap and glanced out casually, scanning the grey, rocky landscape beneath the wall. It was a man, apparently human.

'Scavenger?' Klytos wondered aloud.

'Not alone, I'll wager,' Lichis said, then pointed. 'Look there.'

Something moved in the citadel's ward-yard, visible through the tall, open gateway. Another man, carrying in his arms an unwieldy pile of some sort: plundered provisions or stolen treasure, perhaps. Above, the skulker on the rampart turned and shouted something down to his companion. An unintelligible answer was given. The man on the rampart withdrew into a corner tower. The one in the courtyard disappeared from view.

'The way is clear,' Lichis said. 'Let's go.'

They hurried over the bleak, open ground before the citadel and shortly arrived at the yawning gate. There before them stretched a deep, dark alley between high, sweating walls, all shrouded in darkness under the looming bulk of the gatehouse. The lower extremities of not one, but two raised portcullises hovered high in the murk above them like titanic jaws, poised to snap. The passage stank of mildew, mould and stale ash.

As they advanced, Klytos more clearly heard voices from the courtyard. He discerned only two of them.

'A good haul,' one of them said.

'How far back to the crossroads?' the other asked. 'A day? Two?'

'It's west for us,' the first answered. 'Over the mountains.'

The second man cursed such a long, dispiriting journey. Klytos was just about to step into the yard, when Lichis suddenly swept past him. Heedless and impatient, the sorceress strode forwards, staff in hand, wearing a narrow-eyed grimace that suggested she deeply disapproved of finding thieves in this place.

'Lichis,' Klytos hissed. 'What are you doing?'

The two men – busy packing the overstuffed saddlebags on their horses – bickered on for a moment before finally noticing that they were not alone.

Lichis stood in the centre of the courtyard, the ferrule of her staff planted firmly beside her. Klytos hurried out of hiding to join her.

'What's this?' the first man asked. 'Some aelven conjuress and her pet Stormcast?'

'Better than a pair of diseased vultures,' Lichis said, 'picking over the bones of a fresh corpse.'

The gem at the head of Lichis' staff pulsed impatiently.

The second man drew a short sword sheathed at his hip, though he looked far too scared to use it. The first man held out a hand, calming his companion.

'Now see here,' he said to Lichis. 'The place was abandoned–'

'So,' Lichis said, 'you thought to help yourself to its treasures?'

'And its stores,' the second man said. 'We were hungry.'

'Lichis,' Klytos said quietly, 'these two are no threat. Settle this peacefully.'

'We don't want any trouble,' the first man said.

'There will be no trouble,' Lichis said. 'Go now, with only the clothes on your back and you shall not be harmed. None of what you found shall leave with you.'

'Just a minute,' the first man said, impatient.

The second man, trembling, suddenly dropped his sword and tried to bolt for the citadel gate.

Lichis levelled her staff. A fat green fireball shot from the pulsing gem and enveloped the fleeing looter mid-stride.

Klytos lunged for his companion. 'Lichis, no!'

The first man stared, goggle-eyed, at his screaming, writhing comrade, now swathed in livid green flames. The looter turned to Lichis, eyes wide, opening his mouth. Klytos guessed he was about to beg for mercy.

Lichis loosed another fireball. The man burst into flame. His words became agonised screams, echoing in the courtyard in atonal harmony with his still-dying companion. Klytos smelled the sickly-sweet stench of burning flesh. Those flames, despite their wholly unnatural green hue, burned forge-hot. In seconds, both men lay still and silent on the debris-strewn earth of the courtyard.

Klytos grabbed Lichis by one thin arm and whirled her round to face him.

'Murderer!' he growled.

'Think of me as an exterminator,' Lichis said. 'Rousting out and eradicating the vermin.' With that, she shook loose from Klytos' grip and marched across the yard. The laden horses had shied from the flames and retreated. Lichis chose the nearer of the two, drew the knife at her belt – the same knife used to sacrifice her companion, Malazar – and slashed the over-stuffed saddlebags it bore. The contents tumbled out in a clamorous clatter.

Klytos stared, stunned and silent as Lichis began rifling through the trinkets and provisions and small, second-rate treasures freed from the saddlebags. She seemed to be searching for something but finding no sign of it. Disgusted, she closed on the second horse, some distance away. In seconds, its saddlebags were slashed and emptied as well.

Klytos looked to the two flaming corpses now bleeding gouts of thick, black smoke. Thieves? Perhaps. Small men, of mean character? Certainly. But worthy of death? And such hideous, agonising deaths, at that? Hardly.

He might have been with his Stormhost at that very moment, doing what he was forged to do: slaying minions of Chaos, shielding those innocent, frightened refugees as they raced for the coast and the ships waiting to bear them away. He should have been serving a greater good… but instead, here he stood, a party to murder, serving his own selfish ends.

I've proven Lichis wrong in this, at least, Klytos thought mordantly. *I am no slave. I have free will. I can make my own choices.*

And I am starting to believe I made the wrong one.

All at once, Klytos found his Stormcast helm constricting, practically choking him. Irritated, he yanked the helm free and tossed it to the ground. He paced the yard, drinking deeply of the stale air.

He suddenly realised that the sorceress was studying him, her normally unreadable face evincing bewilderment, even a kind of wonder.

'What are you staring at?' Klytos asked.

'Your face,' she said. 'I'm shocked by just how *ordinary* you look.'

'Why did you kill them?' Klytos asked. 'These weren't the servants of the Dark Gods. They were two fools looking for baubles to sell and provisions to see them through a night or two!'

'How do you know who they were?' Lichis shot back, voice cold. 'Or what they were capable of?'

'You read me,' Klytos answered. 'Are you saying you read them? Saw undeniable evidence of the threat they posed?'

'A waste of time,' Lichis said. 'Besides, I had to be sure.'

'Sure of what?' Klytos demanded.

'That they hadn't found it first,' Lichis answered.

Klytos had no reply. His presence here, with this woman, was a blight upon his honour as a Stormcast, a stain upon his soul. Suddenly weary and eager to be away from her, he sighed.

'Where is it, then?' he asked.

Lichis turned and set out towards a gloomy span of wall crowded between a looming keep and a low, squat chapel beside it. Only when Klytos squinted and studied the wall did he realise there was an open doorway set into it.

'Follow me,' Lichis said without looking back.

They descended by way of a narrow stone stairway into a winding catacomb littered with ancient bones and choked with cobwebs bestirred by soft, phantom breezes that slithered up and down the subterranean passage. The only light was the sickly green glow from the gem on Lichis' staff.

'I am starting to believe you tricked me,' Klytos said darkly after a long silence.

Lichis stopped. Turned. She clearly wanted him to see her face – to look into her dark, ageless eyes – as she spoke.

'If I wanted to send you back to Sigmar for yet another Reforging, I could have done so long before now. I brought you with me for a reason, Stormcast. Until your purpose is served, it is my responsibility to protect you, not to endanger you.'

Klytos studied the aelven sorceress. He found her face alternately beautiful and terrible in the garish green light of that jewel on her staff. Her dark eyes appraised him, deconstructed him. All he could do was stand, enduring it like a helpless, scolded child.

'And just what is my purpose?' Klytos asked her.

A strange, sly half-smile bloomed on Lichis' face. 'What you were made for. Come along, now. We're almost there.'

With that, Lichis carried on down the passage. Klytos marched after her.

In moments, they emerged into a large, airy crypt. Its high ceiling was supported by elegant ribbed vaulting crusted with ancient, pale fungi and ragged, long-decaying cobwebs. Tombs for interment were carved into the chamber's widely spaced walls, some of the vaults sealed, others smashed and yawning wide. The centre of the room was dominated by twin rows of enormous sarcophagi, each capped by a massive, carved stone slab. At least one of those princely tombs had been broken into and rifled through, for its slab lay broken beside it and the bones of its former occupant – now cracked and degraded with age – lay strewn about on all sides. Piles of old crates, haphazardly stacked furniture and ancient hogsheads crammed into out-of-the-way corners suggested that those who dwelt in the citadel had, at some point, so thoroughly disregarded the sanctity of this crypt that they used it as surplus storage.

But the most troubling sight were the skeletons, along with two corpses that looked – by comparison, at least – rather fresh. These remains were tossed about in various locations and positions, most still wearing scraps of old cloth or rusted mail. A fallen weapon lay close to each: a sword, a maul, a hand axe. Instinctively, Klytos knew these could not be the scattered bones of the crypt's ancient occupants, for the arrangement of each skeleton suggested that it had decayed where it fell. The two fresher corpses, likewise, evidenced signs of distress. One had probably been there four or five years, for it still had skin, though that skin was now dried and wrinkled like old parchment on the cusp of disintegration.

The other corpse, however, looked entirely too fresh. A day old. Maybe two. There was still moisture on the dead man's bulging, affrighted eyes and signs of bruising under his ashen skin. The man's face was a horror, frozen in wide-eyed terror and gape-mouthed disbelief, as if he had died of fright.

Klytos studied the grim tableau as Lichis moved quickly among the sarcophagi, hastily perusing the carved glyphs upon each in search of some sign of her quarry.

'Here,' she said at last. 'Help me.'

'What happened here?' Klytos demanded. 'These dead scattered about – they are not the ones buried here.'

'You're wasting time,' Lichis snapped. 'Help me!'

Klytos, despite his misgivings, hurried to Lichis' side and laid his weight upon the great, heavy slab that capped the sarcophagus. Inch by inch, the slab slid and groaned, revealing dusty, undisturbed darkness within. Overbalanced, the slab pitched sidewards and tumbled to the floor of the crypt with a thunderous crash.

Lichis hesitated for a moment, then clambered over the lip of the open sarcophagus. Inside, she crouched among the old, rotten shroud and long-undisturbed bones of the tomb's occupant. Careless and businesslike, Lichis hastily shoved the old bones and decayed rags aside to reveal a hidden, round carving beneath.

The carving was a seal of some sort, though Klytos did not recognise the swirling, interlocking symbols upon it. As he watched, Lichis planted the ferrule of her staff upon the seal, then gripped her staff tightly in both hands.

'Listen to me carefully,' she said, 'for this is why I need you. I have to open this seal, and it will take a great deal of time and energy for me to do so. The moment I begin, the crypt's guardian will awaken.'

'The guardian?' Klytos drew his sword. 'You bloody, evil witch! You said nothing of–'

'We both have a part to play in this, Klytos,' Lichis said testily. 'You can't get at the stone without my magic and I can't work my magic unless you fend off and slay the guardian. This is why I need you. This is how you earn your reward.'

Klytos was filled with a righteous, murderous fury. He wanted to yank the Darkling sorceress out of the open sarcophagus and hack her limb from limb. How could he have been such a fool?

Lichis continued. 'The guardian is your shadow, Klytos – a Knight of Shrouds, interred here long ago as penance for his betrayal. Your faith is proof against his wickedness. Let that serve you.'

Then she began her work, murmuring a rapid, tripping canticle in an ancient tongue. The green gem at the head of her staff began to glow. Beneath her, the carven inlays on the seal pulsed, the energies locked within them stirring and intensifying, moment by moment.

Klytos felt a strange prickling at the nape of his neck. The air around him was suddenly cold – unnaturally so. He had also become aware of an eerie glow gathering behind him, casting his own, long shadow on the debris-strewn floor of the crypt. Though encumbered by armour and several layers of cloth, he felt goose pimples rising on his flesh. He even saw his breath, pluming hot from between his gnashed teeth. The very air in the crypt had changed, and something vile now stirred behind him.

It spoke before he ever turned to face it.

'Foolish plunderers!' it boomed in a raspy voice like rusted hinges protesting movement after centuries idle. 'What blasphemy is this?'

Klytos turned, steeling himself for the horror that was about to reveal itself. He had faced a thousand enemies, slain bloodletters, Chaos knights, gargants and orruks. He had stood his ground against charging razorgors, slavering jabberslythes and snapping, venomous chimerae.

But now, it would appear, he faced an enemy unlike any other.

The Knight of Shrouds materialised above another opened sarcophagus and hovered there, seemingly anchored where it floated. The phantom's leering, skeletal face bore some subtle and dreadful potency – a deeper, more malignant darkness in its gaping eye sockets, a mocking, lopsided set to its rictus grin – that made its visage more frightening than anything Klytos had ever seen. Radiating the same, sickly, blue-green light that all the ghostly damned of Shyish were imbued with, the abomination towered over him, its flowing, spectral robes simultaneously real enough to grasp and as immaterial as swirling smoke. Only the enormous, two-handed blade it held in one skeletal fist seemed truly solid.

Klytos tightened his grip on his warblade. *Sigmar*, he prayed, *forgive me*.

'*Stormcast*,' the phantasm said slowly, as if savouring the very word. '*Quake, fear, for I am your ruin!*'

Summoning his courage, Klytos reminded himself why he'd come here. He wanted his past. He wanted the people he'd lost and forgotten restored to him. He wanted to be whole again. If he had to slay this beast to do that... so be it.

'Creature of the grave,' he said slowly, 'I am Stormcast, a Celestial Vindicator, and I have no master but Sigmar Heldenhammer. To claim what I have come for, I will gladly cast you back into the pit you slithered out of!'

The ghostly knight howled – whether in disbelief at Klytos' bravado or delight in the challenge to come, he could not say. Its foul, shrieking voice stirred a maelstrom of cold, spectral winds in the vast crypt.

Then, it attacked.

The world around Klytos became a storm of frigid, biting air, ghastly cackling and shifting pools of ghastly blue-green luminescence. He spun and pivoted, seemingly beset by the Knight of Shrouds on all sides: in front, behind, to the left, to the right. Its enormous sword sliced the foetid air, again and again, as his own shining sigmarite blade rose and fell with almost painful slowness to fend off its attacks. Here, a lucky parry. There, a blocked thrust. A clumsy dance sidewards, narrowly avoiding a death blow. A skating retreat. A scrambling recovery.

Preparing for another attack, Klytos stole a glance at Lichis. She still crouched in the sarcophagus, rooted and unmoving, the gem on her sorcerer's staff pulsing brightly as she recited the alien words of the spell intended to unlock that seal. Every muscle in her body was rigid and tense, her immense concentration and adamantine willpower exhausting to behold.

Then the Knight of Shrouds shrieked and charged again. Klytos barely deflected the monster's first attack, then struck in answer. It was a sloppy but savage blow, his sword blade arcing in a wide horizontal chop. As the bright sigmarite passed through the undead knight's ghostly, insubstantial form, Klytos felt a strange sensation.

Resistance. Solidity. His blade had hit *something*.

Confirming his sudden suspicion, the Knight of Shrouds screamed, whirled and retreated. Its cry was high and maddening, boring deep into Klytos' ears, stabbing at the very centre of his consciousness – but he revelled in it. He had struck the spirit! Hurt it!

The Knight of Shrouds recovered and patiently circled, studying its would-be prey. Its howling shriek subsided to a ragged chuckle, low and ominous. Klytos, glad for the moment's reprieve, began his own slow circle of his aetheric adversary, blade ready.

'*Despair, Stormcast!*' the knight taunted. '*Look upon my face and see your own! I betrayed my vows to earn my place here! What shall become of you, oh faithless fool, when I strike you down? Can your shining God-King draw your soul back to Azyr even here, at the threshold of the Afterdark?*'

Then, as its taunt still rang in Klytos' ears, the nighthaunt exploded forwards, swift and shark-like through the empty air. Its sword rose for another attack. Klytos started to retreat, felt one of the sarcophagi blocking that retreat, and knew there was only one choice: forwards.

Without hesitation, he launched himself and his upraised warblade straight towards the onrushing phantom. He managed to get inside the knight's sword-strike, but this time, Klytos' own blade seemed to touch nothing at all. He rushed through the bone-chilling cold of the creature's swirling, spectral essence – through the creature itself – before finally breaking free again on the far side. Shivering with a combination of terror and rage, he crashed to the crypt floor.

Impossible! he thought. *Too fast! Too strong! How can I fight it?*

'Your faith, Klytos!' Lichis suddenly shouted from where she knelt, still at her magical work. 'Remember why you came here! Why you trusted me!'

Klytos turned, preparing to meet another charge from the Knight of Shrouds – this attack likely to finish him.

The knight whirled to face him. It hovered in the stale air of the burial chamber, empty black eyes radiating cruelty and contempt. Its notched and ancient blade reflected the sickly blue-green light emanating from it.

'Tiring, are you, Stormcast?' the fiend hissed. *'Come now! Throw down your sword! Let me show you the way to true eternal life! It has been so long since I've known a companion here...'*

Klytos felt a fury suddenly rise in him. All at once, he realised that it was not Sigmar he had no faith in – only himself. His shame, his desire to reclaim his past, had convinced him that he was inferior... lesser... unworthy.

But had not Sigmar *chosen him?*

Whomever he mourned, whatever he desired, it was part of him, the very essence of who and what he was. And Sigmar – his master, his god – knew every dark and shadowed corner of his heart. Sigmar knew what Klytos wanted...

...and he had brought Klytos here, now, into this chamber, to prove his mettle.

To test his faith.

The Knight of Shrouds dived through the air towards him, sword drawn back for a vicious, killing blow.

Klytos sprang to his feet, lunged, and met the falling blade with a mighty blow from his own. The swords rang like bells in the crypt's dank air.

Determined, enraged, Klytos struck before the knight had even a moment to recover. His blade thrust forwards, its razor-sharp point seeking the misty, blue-green heart of the 'haunt's diaphanous form.

And there, it seemed to strike something.

The knight's skeletal jaw fell open and it screeched, a deafening sound drenched in pain, fury and disbelief.

Klytos laid both hands on his sword-grip and twisted the blade.

The knight dropped its sword and the ancient blade hit the crypt stones with a loud clatter. At its extremities, the spectral devil was discorporating, its grasping, skeletal fingers already swirling into the aether, their blue-green light extinguished.

'For Sigmar!' Klytos roared.

He withdrew his blade and brought it round in a wide, powerful arc, slashing right through the centre of the floating knight. Again, he felt the blade pass through something solid – something now hewn in twain by his attack. As the blade cut the Knight of Shrouds in two, the creature gave a last, mortified scream, then dissipated into swirling smoke and vanished.

Klytos waited, half expecting the vile guardian to suddenly reappear. But, no… the phantom did not return. He turned towards Lichis. The sorceress yet recited her eldritch incantations, the rich green light from the gemstone capping her staff now blinding, since it was the only light in the chamber. The seal beneath her glowed angrily, as though it might turn to molten rock and swallow her at any moment.

Then, as though some unseen boulder had suddenly fallen upon it, the seal shattered. Simultaneously, its glow was extinguished. Realising her spell was, at last, successful, Lichis lifted her staff and stumbled away from the broken seal. She leaned on the edge of the sarcophagus, gulping air, physically exhausted. As the glow of her gem subsided, her eyes darted about the chamber, searching.

'The guardian?' she asked.

'Destroyed,' Klytos said.

'Well done,' Lichis answered. Her lips curled at the corners in something like a proud smile.

'Where is it?' Klytos asked. 'Let us be done with it.'

Lichis nodded, sighed, and knelt back in the sarcophagus again. She hastily yanked out the shattered pieces of the broken seal and tossed them aside, revealing beneath a shallow depression. In that depression rested a square box of medium size and impressive workmanship. Lichis snatched up the box. Her elegant fingers worked the many cunning latches that held it shut. Inside that box lay Klytos' salvation.

It was a gem, about the size of a closed fist, possessing planar facets, rough edges and occluded depths that made it seem both naturally occurring and wilfully made, as if the earth itself had set out to fashion a work of art. A hypnotic glow emanated from within the gemstone: amethyst light, just like the inherent magical energies that had powered and pummelled Shyish through the ages, as though a small, purple sun burned at the heart of the great jewel.

Lichis displayed the gem in her outstretched hand. 'Do you see?' she asked, evincing something like wonder and piety for the first time in the many days that Klytos had known her.

'Indeed,' Klytos breathed in wonder, then glanced at his companion. She wore a strange expression, as if eager to speak but unsure of the right words. Klytos felt cold rage rising in him. 'Why do you hesitate?'

'That which you ask,' Lichis said, 'you may find that you did not want.'

'*No more games,*' Klytos snarled. 'Do your work now, witch! Fulfil your vow to me!'

'I warned you,' Lichis said, then placed both her hands upon the gem and began a new incantation.

Little by little, the light at the heart of the gem intensified. Klytos instinctively felt that he should look away or cover his eyes, but that light, no matter how bright or blinding it became, all but demanded his hungry gaze. It drew him out of himself. It sang to him. Caressed him.

The light became a void, and Klytos plunged into that void.

The woman, his wife: Nara. His one true love. Beauty and grace incarnate. Her wood-brown skin, so smooth and delicate. Her eyes, green as pale emeralds, deeper than forest pools. He remembered kisses. Lazy afternoons beneath bright summer suns. Seeing dream-beasts in the passing clouds. Lovemaking. The joy that leapt in him when she told him she was with child.

Then, the sights, sounds and smells all changed. He heard the ring of steel on steel mingling with shrill screams. Saw fire and smoke. Smelled burning flesh and the coppery tang of blood. There Nara stood, amid surging, panicked villagers searching for egress from a tightening cordon of bloodthirsty reavers – human and inhuman alike. Klytos was too far away from her. He struggled, feet tugged at by sucking mud, tripping upon hacked corpses, his way barred by fallen, flaming debris.

Nara clutched the baby – Xandia, that was her name! A little girl, swathed in her favourite, hand-stitched blanket. The baby screamed in Nara's arms. Klytos saw one small hand emerge from the folds of the blanket, clutching at her mother's trailing braid.

Gods and daemons of an elder age, he knew what was about to happen!

A reaver suddenly towered over Nara. The barbarian's sword was sharp, his eyes alight with cruelty. Nara screamed. Down came the blade. Nara was silenced, forever.

Xandia still lived, wriggling in her slain mother's arms. The marauder who had cut Nara down bent, snatched up the baby in its bundle and lumbered away, Klytos' only child tucked neatly in his filthy embrace.

It did not happen once. It happened again and again, replayed in Klytos' memory like some foul verse from a catchy tavern song, repeating, repeating, repeating, resisting all attempts to purge it. Klytos tried to close his eyes, to summon memories of love and joy to counter the horror that repeated, time and again, before his unwilling gaze. He tried to recall meeting Nara, courting Nara, holding Nara in his arms on a cold winter's night, watching Nara scream and cry as she brought their daughter into the world.

But those memories were little more than a cloud of swirling gnats – tiny, unreal, ephemeral. They could not banish the horribly *real* sight of Nara dying under that reaver's sword. Of Xandia, borne away to live life as a slave – or worse, as the child of the barbarian that stole her, wholly ignorant that her apparent father had murdered the woman who'd given birth to her. Of Klytos, separated from them by slaughter and ruin, too late to protect them, too weak to pursue and overtake their murderer, to avenge them.

Then the old man returned to him. Phiro, father of Klytos, a simple sort: farmer, village elder, trader in orchard fruits and home-fermented wines. A strong man, a proud man, a good man.

Phiro, ruined by a fall in old age. Phiro, bent and twisted by injury and the indifference of time. Phiro, poisoned by an apothecary's out-of-date stock, rendered speechless and vegetative. Phiro, a twisted, bony marionette lying prone in a bed beside a fire, shivering because he was cold – he was *always* so cold – his cataract-clouded eyes begging his son for a final reprieve.

Phiro's skeletal old hand, thick with calluses, squeezing Klytos' own. The old man had no words left, but Klytos understood well enough. His father wanted the mercy – the dignity – of a quiet end at the hand of someone who loved him. The old man wanted peace, release… and Klytos was not brave enough to give it. He allowed that poor, wizened creature to lie there on his piss-stained bed for weeks, dying in slow, small increments. Klytos knew what the old man wanted – what the old man needed – but he was too selfish, to craven, to bestow it.

No. This could not be. These were not the memories Klytos wanted. These were not what he had fought to reclaim. He wanted love, joy, familiarity, the prosaic; the simple, long-forgotten pleasures of mortal life.

He rifled his memories in search of pleasure – any pleasure – amid the now swirling storm that assailed him. He tore through them and tossed them about in desperation, as a thirsty traveller in the desert might ransack an abandoned camp for a hidden gourd containing the smallest drink of water. Intermittently, he found those delights. Childhood. Innocence. Play. Imagination. Love and romance. Hopes and dreams born of affection and intimacy. He found cherished memories of his father's nurturing love and paternal pride, of laughter and friendship, of adventure and excitement. There was dancing. There were drunken revels.

But these pleasures were all isolated, intermittent, fleeting. Sickly, stunted roses on a malignant, ever-expanding thorn bush. Every petal of memory seemed to hide in its shadows a darker twin, the prick of exposed spines, the scuttle of insects and the stains of lurking rot. Slain friends. Ill relatives. His village wracked by plague. A winter famine that forced a nearby tribe to tear itself to pieces, the strong and cunning feasting upon their friends and neighbours. He even relived the bitter, senseless loss of his mother when he was yet a child; how she died twitching after being kicked in the head by a mule.

All pleasures were tempered by loss and pain. All hope was swallowed, over time, by sudden, foolish calamities or incomprehensible cruelties.

Klytos heard someone screaming. After a time, he realised the cries were his own.

'Deserted,' Eigrim said, surveying the citadel's shadowy inner ward. His four companions spread out, weapons at the ready, searching the sheltered corners of the courtyard, certain that some danger yet awaited them.

A stone's throw from where Eigrim stood, Torgo poked at a strange, charred mass – one of two – with the beak of his axe.

'What'd you find there?' Eigrim asked.

Torgo's face twisted up mordantly. 'Dead men,' he said. 'Charred to a crisp.'

Rinz toed through a pile of trinkets spread haphazardly over the gravel. 'Looks like someone was here,' he said. 'There's some good stuff. Trade-worthy, anyway. And look at this...'

Rinz snatched up a large, shining object lying discarded on the well-trod earth. It was a heavy, turquoise-hued helm of a very distinct and unique design.

'That's a Stormcast helm,' Eigrim said.

'Aye,' Rinz agreed, turning the big, heavy object over in his hands to study it. 'But what's it doing out here?'

Eigrim offered no explanation. He had seen Stormhosts in battle, if only from a distance. Their warriors were demigods. Order, discipline and inhuman devotion were their hallmarks. They did not simply abandon those masked helms of theirs. His eyes skated sideward towards the dead men. Could one of those be the owner of the helm?

Impossible, he reminded himself. *When they die, their god yanks them back to his holy halls. If a Stormcast fell here, not a trace would remain.*

'Stormcast or no,' Torgo insisted, '*someone* was here, and not long ago.'

Eigrim said nothing. He was ready to bolt right back out of that gate without a single bauble in hand. Something strange was afoot.

'We should go,' he said. 'Now.'

Then, a voice boomed into the yard. 'You there!' it shouted. 'Looters! Thieves!'

The men went rigid where they stood. Every weapon rose in readiness.

A huge figure in shining plate armour lurched out of a low, dark doorway across the yard: clearly, the owner of the helm. The Stormcast Eternal's war-plate trailed wisps of cobwebs and shone dully where ancient dust lay caked upon it, as though the holy paladin of Sigmar had just crawled out of a filthy cellar. An enormous broadsword was gripped in one hand but trailed behind the Stormcast, its point cutting a shallow track through the dirt.

His face was ordinary enough – olive skin; a mop of black, curly hair; piercing hazel eyes under heavy brows – but the way he staggered and blinked under the wan light of the cloud-shrouded Shyish sun made Eigrim uneasy. He looked weary and hysterical at once, like a berzerker whose bloodlust had just abandoned him. His eyes bulged, darting about anxiously.

Eigrim knew a madman when he saw one.

'Stay where you are,' the Stormcast commanded, and raised his sword in threat. 'I have need of you. All of you.'

Eigrim held out a hand. 'We're not looking for trouble.'

'Kill me,' the Stormcast said.

Eigrim blinked. 'What's that?'

'Kill me,' the Stormcast said again. 'Kill me, now, or I'll hew down the lot of you. This has to stop. If I die, maybe... *maybe...*'

The others looked to Eigrim. Eigrim looked to them. He had no idea what to do. They were far enough from the stumbling

Stormcast that they could, perhaps, make a break for the gate and simply outrun him–

Without warning, the Stormcast charged Rinz, sword rising.

'Kill me!' he cried.

Rinz dropped the helm and tried to run, but he was too slow. The Stormcast cleaved him in two with a single stroke.

The others all gasped, shouted, cursed. What was happening? This was insane! A mad Stormcast, begging death and threatening it in the same instant?

Torgo charged, roaring as he went. Rinz had been his oldest friend. Eigrim knew that the warrior had every intention of cutting that Stormcast down where he stood. His big, beaked axe rose high for a mighty chop.

The Stormcast lowered his sword and opened his arms, as if for an embrace.

'Torgo, stop!' Eigrim shouted.

Torgo skidded to a halt. His axe still hovered, but he was several yards from where the Stormcast stood, waiting for the death blow. The barbarian looked to his commander. Eigrim shook his head and gave a simple gesture. Torgo, shaking with rage, fell back.

The Stormcast, denied his hoped-for death, looked to Eigrim. 'You cowards! I slew your companion. Kill me!'

Eigrim spoke, addressing his men. 'We need to go. Now.'

The Stormcast strode forwards. 'No! Kill me, I said! Kill me now, where I stand, or I'll slaughter you all!'

'Friend,' Eigrim said. 'We have no quarrel with you.'

'I have quarrel with him,' Torgo snarled.

'I remember it,' the Stormcast said quietly, almost to himself, then began babbling. 'I remember all of it. *All of it!* Kill me and send me back to Sigmar, I beg you! She said Reforging would change nothing but maybe, just maybe...'

'Everybody out!' Eigrim commanded, and began a backward

retreat towards the gate. The men obeyed, all effecting their withdrawals in reverse, keeping their eyes on the mad, raving Stormcast.

'Come back here!' the Stormcast Eternal cried. 'I command you, in the name of Sigmar Heldenhammer, *to kill me where I stand!*'

Eigrim wished he had words. Clearly, this fool was hurting, broken somehow. Stormcasts were, in his experience, creatures barely human. They felt no fear, no hate, no love, no pity – they were simply engines of destruction and wrath, given human form and set against the hordes of Chaos. What could have so bewitched this poor devil to leave him murderous and suicidal in the same instant?

I remember it, he kept saying. What did that even mean?

Eigrim was ready to turn his back, to run for the gate, when the Stormcast's mad ranting dissolved into a fierce battle cry. The great, plated giant charged Torgo. His sword was high. His face was a mask of fury and desperation.

'*Kill me!*' he cried as he ran Torgo through with his shining blade. '*Kill me, I beg you!*'

The others hesitated in the shadow of the gate, staring, confused.

'Go!' Eigrim commanded. 'Run!'

The three of them went pounding out of the bleak old fortress through the long, dark tunnel under the gatehouse. Behind them, they heard the Stormcast cursing them, challenging them, even as he cried to the indifferent sky.

'*Kill me!*' he howled, his voice broken and desperate. '*Kill me, in mercy's name...*'

BLOOD OF THE FLAYER

Richard Strachan

She came to him in the wreckage of another Muspelzharr town, a petty settlement of rough farmland where they tilled the ore and sold it on to the Freeguild furnaces in far Andar. Through the choking smoke she moved, past corpses smeared across the dusty grass. By a tent of skinned hides there was a mound of severed heads, and carved on each was an eight-pointed star. There was lament on the air, the old blade-song of widowed women and old men mourning their sundered sons. They would follow them soon enough.

The warlord stood with his back to her, staring up into the cobalt sky. High up there, like meteors, moved specks of light.

'You waste your prisoners, Lord Huthor,' she said boldly. 'They can last for days in the sweetest agonies, if you know how.'

He was a large and brutal man, she saw, scarred in the face, his skin battered by decades of Chamon's flensing winds. He pointed at the lights.

'Do you know what those are?' he asked.

'Yes, lord,' she said, coming near. 'Duardin sky-craft, trading vessels of those who style themselves "Overlords". They come from the Ashpeaks and make for Barak-Zon, if I am not mistaken.'

'Barak-Zon?'

'Their sky-port.' She bowed. 'As I understand these things.'

'Overlords... I thought so. I've seen them often in the last few days. I thought them an omen, at first...' His voice trailed off, and his hand was white-knuckled on the hilt of his sword.

'I do not know if they are an omen, my lord,' the woman said. 'But if they are then they must be a good one. For I am Dysileesh, and I bring you great tidings.'

'If I could but reach up,' he said softly, 'and pull them down from the aether, I would do so... But you have to marvel at them,' Huthor laughed. 'With sweat and toil, to put a crafted thing into the air and sail it like that through the mineral tides – such courage!' He turned to the man at his side. 'Don't you think, Vhoss?'

Vhoss, a hard and compact warrior, his shaved head flecked with scars, gruffly agreed. 'Aye, Lord Flayer' he said. 'You can't doubt their courage.'

'And for what?' Huthor spat, his mood shifting. 'Coin. *Trade*. Lives ordered by the numbers they scrawl in a ledger.'

Dysileesh, seizing her moment, moved forward. She stroked his forearm. 'And wouldn't you like to tear those lives down, my lord? Wouldn't you like to seize those riches for yourself? Fame you shall have, as well as power. Come,' she said, and into that one word she put all the art of her influence, her intoxicating presence. 'Let us talk. I bring tidings of the Dark Prince, the Lord of Excess... You have drawn the eye of Slaanesh, and power untold is yours if you pledge yourself to him.'

Huthor stared down into those violet eyes, and for the first time he took her in entire – the single dark lock cascading from her crown; the chain that linked the silver hoops in her ear and eyebrow and nose; her sickening smell, more alluring than the stench of battle.

'Sweet tears have you spilled on the altar of Ruin,' she whispered closely, 'but the Dark Gods are jealous, and generous to those who dedicate themselves to their service. Make obeisance to the Prince, and all things shall be yours to savour and command. Does not your eye crave more luxurious sights, your tongue crave finer tastes than cheap fare and peasant women? And does not your lust run deeper than simple murders in the dirt... Seek Slaanesh with me and I will show you the thrill of torments untold, the *ecstasies* to be found in the depths of gluttony and starvation...'

Her tongue, a purple, serpentine thing, flicked madly from her lips, and her eyes blazed with lilac fire.

Others to whom she had made this entreaty would have strained to possess her by now, or would have been lost in greedy dreams of power. But the Flayer only took her arm in his iron grip and pulled her close. His face was a mask, grim and unyielding, scarred by battle. He drew her towards the tent. 'Come then,' he said. 'Let me hear what the Dark Prince has to offer...'

It was on a whim, he told himself later. No more than that. A woman as devastating as any he had ever seen; his soul smouldering with black fire and eager to expand into new experiences; a grasp that exceeded his reach – all these things made him take the Godseeker into his tent. He would walk her path for a while, he told himself. Why not? A gift freely given is seldom scorned. And when he was bored of it, he would kill her and cast her body to the dogs.

With blasphemous orgies and sickening violence, with ecstasies of wine and song, the Raging Tide followed Dysileesh's teachings, scouring the plains of Gazan Zhar in a decadent whirlwind. They raided the caravanserais of the free cities, looting fine silks and precious jewels to decorate their wargear. They made cloaks from the skins of their victims and found the most intense pleasures in the limits of their endurance. A troupe of Hellstriders on their freakish reptilian mounts soon swelled Huthor's ranks, and the warband's savage tribal marks were slowly replaced by sinuous tattoos, kohl-rimmed eyes and mocking smears of perfumed oil. Across the plains they plundered for a while, leaving in their passing a sweet and cloying musk, the wail of grief and torment.

Dysileesh was owned by no man or woman of the warband, and although she stayed most often in Huthor's tent she lavished her attention on Elizha too, one of Huthor's charioteers, riding with her as the warband raided across the plains. Soon she took up with Vhoss, Huthor's most trusted lieutenant, although when she announced that she was pregnant Huthor did not reveal his suspicions. Vhorrun, born on the plunder-path, came screaming into the Mortal Realms like a true son of Chamon. His pale skin gleamed like silver, and the thick spikes of his black hair were dusted with gold. Violet eyes looked from an unforgiving face, but Huthor couldn't say who his father might be. No matter. Like his own father, Huthor thought, he was not made to suffer children. So the warband grew, and the further they went on this path, the deeper Huthor plunged into the worship of Slaanesh, dedicating his pains and his pleasures to the Dark Prince and yet in his pride never straying too far from the road of his own self-made fate.

No god ordered his path, he said. He made his own.

They raided on impulse, moving through the mutable land as plateaus melted and reformed around them, as valleys raised themselves into rough, saw-toothed spines that marked the plains like a godbeast's grave.

After a season they found themselves straying towards the Beryllium Coast, where the pickings were richer. It was there, in a chill dusk, that they first came across the ruins of the Golden Fortress. As the warband marched through a desolate landscape, the sultry plains behind them and the Onoglop Swamps to the north, the walls of the shattered stronghold rose from the sea mists to meet them.

'What is this place?' Huthor asked Dysileesh as he swung down from his horse. The warband dismounted around him. Elizha reared back the mounts of her chariot and coiled her silver whip in her hand. 'I don't like it, lord,' she said. 'The wind smells of sickness and death.'

'That's just the swamps on the breeze,' Dysileesh said. She stepped from the chariot, drawing her silken robes around her and gazing with wonder at the tarnished gold of the fortress walls. They were hazy and indistinct in the mist, like the dream of something vaster than the eye could understand. Weeds and scour-grass choked the pathways that led to the massive iron doors, which listed on their hinges. The fortress, Huthor saw as they drew nearer, had not been built, as such. No mortal hand had cast this place. Rather, the land itself had reared it into being, extruding it from the dark and granular soil like a tooth from a gum.

'In truth, I'm not sure,' Dysileesh admitted to him. 'I have heard rumours, but I have never seen it for myself. A fortress made of purest Chamonite, some say, although we see now that it is not the case. Gold, my lord. The Dark Prince gives, and you shall receive! Gold and splendour beyond your wildest dreams!'

'You cannot imagine,' Huthor said, 'how wild my dreams really are.'

The fortress was silent and empty, its cavernous halls looming around them as they led their steeds through. Rotting tapestries depicted scenes from the Age of Myth – Grungni forging the Nineteen Wonders, the lode-griffon uncoiling above the God-wrought Isles. Of the original inhabitants there was no other sign, and whatever race or nation had secured this impossible bastion had been lost in mists of time as dense as the mists that billowed from the Beryllium Sea.

The warband made camp, and they stayed for years. The Golden Fortress became their keep.

'When I was a boy,' he told her, 'I lived alone with my father. He was a simple man, earning a meagre wage from cutting ironthorn branches in the forest and melting them down for slag – he had no more skill than that. He was a brutal man, who feared Sigmar.'

Huthor leaned over the side of the bed and spat on the ground at the God-King's name. Dysileesh drew languidly near across the sheets. Above them, a polished gold ceiling cast back their reflections, distorted by the metal so that they both looked strangely elongated, like pale snakes basking lazily in a savage sun.

'He beat me every day of my life,' Huthor went on, 'and then one day – whether from drunkenness or poverty or simple indifference – he abandoned me deep in the woods. He hoped I would die and free him of responsibility. He craved order in his life, and children are nothing if not disorder personified... I had no idea how to get home. It was cold, silent. No light came through the canopy. High above me I could hear the crackling of the mantys-birds, hopping through the branches, sharpening their copper beaks.'

'How did you escape?' Dysileesh asked him. She trailed her fingers over his chest, tracing the lines of the torture scars she had given him. The air stank of the young man they'd recently skinned, whose body lay cooling on the chamber's marble floor. Three days he had lasted; it had been exquisite.

'I didn't. I found an ironthorn branch and armed myself, fighting off the mantys-birds whenever they came too near. I hacked my way through the forest for days, on and on. I was starving. I had never been so scared.'

'How old were you?'

'Seven.'

'So young…'

'Old enough. Eventually I came to a path I recognised, and at the end of this path was a crossroads. I stood there. I knew the choice had been laid open to me. One road led back to our hovel in the woods, the other led on towards the outer realm. One road to Order, the other to Chaos.'

'And so, you left that miserable life behind,' she whispered in his ear. 'You left for greater things.'

Huthor laughed, without a trace of humour. His lip curled at the memory.

'Not at first,' he said. He reached for a goblet, brimful of the skinned young man's tears. He drank deep. 'No, first I took the path back home. Armed with my iron branch, I went to say fare-well to my father…'

He had often wondered what would have happened if he had taken the other path instead. What if, at the end of his journey through the woods, he had not stood in front of his blazing home, exulting in the flames while his father's flayed body burned inside?

But he had made his choice. He had taken his first, faltering steps on the road of Ruin, and he had been walking that path with grim rejoicing ever since.

The years passed for Huthor in a blur of excess. Nightly the war-band indulged its most perverted desires, breaking off to launch savage raids into the surrounding territories. Before long, fright-ened towns and settlements along the coast paid them desperate tribute. Warriors flocked to Huthor's silken banner, and every-thing unfolded as Dysileesh had promised. He was carving out an empire, a legacy, but daily the Godseeker pressed him to com-mit himself totally to Slaanesh.

'You still hold back,' she pleaded. 'You have seen what the Dark Prince is capable of, and now surely you must pledge yourself to him?'

'Did your Prince give me this?' Huthor countered. They strode to the fortress' half-melted battlements and he swept out his hand to indicate the wild lands before them. Impaled prisoners writhed and groaned across the frontage of the fortress grounds. From the golden corridors beneath them came screams of pleasure and pain. Behind them churned the mercurial sea, lapping in quicksilver waves at the crumbling shore. 'Or did I take it for myself?'

'Could you have gained this without his favour? You speak blasphemies to claim otherwise, lord.'

'Blasphemies? Then let him strike me down – if he can. He languishes in chains, does he not? Why should I follow a chained god, too weak to free himself? It serves me for now to follow your path, Godseeker, but don't think it is a path I will follow forever. The lord of the Golden Fortress makes his own fate. He worships the hurricane of Chaos, the maelstrom. No god commands me!'

She hissed at him, but Huthor replied only with scornful laughter.

All nearby bowed to the Golden Fortress, but in the north, there was one territory that refused them tribute. In the brooding miasma of the Onoglop Swamps, Rotbringer cults met Huthor's scouting parties with axe and blade. Huthor had dispatched a small force to quell them, but this band of Hellstriders and marauders had been swallowed by the swamp's glistening mists and no word of them ever came back.

Mounting his steed and unsheathing his sword for the first time in what felt like years, Huthor personally led a sally from the fortress into the dark lands. For days they marched north, the sky above them whipped with glittering tendrils of teal and cyan, streaked with the corposant of harvested aether-gold as the Kharadron sky-ships plied their vertiginous trade. Huthor had watched them as he rode, straining to catch a glimpse of those impossible craft, willing each to catch fire and plummet to the ground so he could crack them open with his blade. Something about their sheer distance offended him, but his mind was soon taken off the duardin by the gloomy edgelands of the Onoglop Swamps.

Flies buzzed in the reeds. A smell so rank it almost made him sick came pouring from the stagnant waters. Strange, greasy blooms quivered in the rancid breeze. His warriors, drawn up in their battle lines, looked at each other uneasily.

'Do we enter?' Dysileesh asked. She snorted a pinch of emerald snuff. 'This doesn't feel right, lord.'

'You'd have me turn back?'

'The lord of the Golden Fortress turn back?' Vhoss laughed. 'I shouldn't think so. The Flayer doesn't run from a fight.'

'The Flayer…' Huthor said. 'It's been a while since you called me that.'

'I was there when you earned that name,' Vhoss said. He slapped Huthor's shoulder. 'The day we met.'

He smiled at the memory: those ancient days, two lost boys scavenging on the fringes of a warband's camp. Slaves to darkness, brooding in their armour; tribal marauders, fleet horsemen scouting the steppes for villages to raid.

'You stole that dagger from a chieftain's tent, do you remember?'

'Aye. He sent two of his best men into the hills to track us down.'

Vhoss cackled at the memory. 'And you sent him their skins in return!'

'Not the first men I'd flayed,' Huthor admitted.

'No. Nor the last.'

The Flayer. Now there had been a fate worth fighting for.

Huthor reared his steed and drew his army up in fine array. Slowly, silently, he led them into the pestilent darkness.

'The lord is wounded!' Vhoss screamed, bursting through the iron gates. 'The lord of the Golden Fortress is wounded!'

They brought him on a bier of scented cushions and fine coverlets already soaked with blood. The savage wound in his chest pulsed with the beating of his heart, and as Huthor slipped into darkness he heard the frantic pattering of feet along the gilded halls. Healers rushed to attend him. Retainers, those who had not gone out to the fight, roused themselves from debauchery and ran to prepare boiling water laced with Chamonite to tend his wound. Vhoss lashed out at those who were slow to react, beating them with the pommel of his axe.

'Prepare the lord's bed, at once!'

Huthor felt himself being carried to his chamber. The wound tore at him like a lance, darkening his mind, drawing strange fevers into his blood. He felt someone take his hand, wetting it with eager tears – Dysileesh, delighted at this opportunity to indulge herself in the deepest griefs.

'Elizha…' Huthor groaned. He had seen her chariot tip over and had watched in horror as the Rotbringers tore her to pieces. Mishkhar, his luck run out at last, had thrown himself into them, his lacquered topknot spinning as wildly as his blades, but the weight of numbers had brought him down. Hharag was gone too, shouting his lord's name as the swamp water took him, pulled to his doom by whatever infected creatures lurked in its depths. He had laughed as he died. As Huthor led the retreat, hacking through the press, an axe had swung from the gloom and struck him in the chest.

'Vhorrun…' Huthor tried to say. 'My… son…' He caught a glimpse of the boy staring at him from the shadows, his axes spattered with rancid blood, a murderous look in his eyes. Ten years old, and already a great fighter; he had lived, at least. But then the image was gone, and in its place as they lowered Huthor to his deathbed came a vision of placid decay – a hunched and horned figure in a mouldering cloak, atop a rotting steed. The figure slowly raised an armoured hand and hissed.

Your time has come, Lord Huthor. The Grandfather awaits you.

Light broke through the shuttered windows, painting pale, thick stripes across his bed. Huthor woke, drenched in sweat, his skin clammy and chill. The fortress was silent around him. He reached with a flabby hand for the goblet of water on the table at his side, but he knocked it to the ground.

'Help!' he shouted. Only silence greeted him. The wound in his chest, he saw, had been cleaned and raggedly stitched. It throbbed with a dull, low ache.

Wrapped in a sheet as close as a grave-shroud, Huthor trembled on the golden stairs, supporting himself on the bannister.

'Vhoss?' he shouted. There was no reply. 'Dysileesh!' Scattered goblets and spilled wine littered the ground. At the bottom of the stairs lay a twisted body, its stomach burst open, a foul slurry spattered on the marble floor. The expression on the corpse's face was one of sheer, transported joy.

There was a smell in the air of rotting meat and mouldering fruit. As weak as he had ever felt in his life, Huthor followed the smell into the banqueting hall, the stage where his warband had performed some of its most hideous debauches. He stopped at the door and looked onto a scene of utter devastation.

The long, silver table was piled high with decaying food – haunches of meat that were boiling with maggots, platters of fruit and fine pastries now curdled and stale. Crystal decanters of emerald wine were broken on the floor. Chairs were tipped over, the luxuriant curtains pulled from the high windows. Sprawled on the table, or contorted on the ground, were dozens of Huthor's warriors. All of them clutched brutally distended stomachs, their mouths flecked with the vomit that had choked them. They were all dead.

It was a scene replayed throughout the fortress. The mourning feasts held for their lord, who they assumed had died in his chambers upstairs, had turned, as all Slaaneshi rites must, into a crazed pursuit of excess. They had gorged on food and drink until it killed them.

He found Dysileesh lying in an antechamber off the main hall. Her face was blackened with suffocation; she had forced sweetmeats down her throat until they blocked her windpipe, and in absolute euphoria she had died. He knelt at her side and drew a sheet over her body. The Dark Prince had her at last.

'My lord!' came a voice, echoing across the silent hall. Huthor stood and looked back. Vhorrun gazed at him sullenly from the corridor, and in the subtle light, burnished and enhanced by the golden walls, his skin glowed with faint silver. 'My lord, we thought you were dead.'

'Where is Vhoss?' he croaked. He took a step forward and stumbled, and when he looked up he saw for the briefest moment the pale horseman on his rotting steed, beckoning him forward.

The Grandfather awaits you...

It was as if the voice came from inside him, from his very blood, now thick with poisons.

You called and have been answered, and out there great bounty awaits you, life eternal, free of pain...

Huthor shook his head. When he opened his eyes, Vhorrun was leaning over him.

'Vhoss?'

'My father lives,' the boy said. 'Come, I'll take you to him.'

Not everyone had indulged with such desperation. There were perhaps a hundred warriors left, and although Vhoss had joined the frenzy he had not stepped over that final line. The path of excess was over for them now; they all knew it.

Vhoss, dressed once more in his dracoline-hide jerkin, his silken robes cast aside, was waiting in the main hall. Huthor, still clad in his deathbed sheets, came limping to embrace him. The sickness roiled and brewed inside him, fermenting his blood.

'What now, old friend?' Vhoss asked him. Huthor paused, and the pale horseman rose again before his eyes, mouldering and grey.

'We leave this place,' he said. 'We go back.'

'Back where, lord?'

'To the Onoglop Swamps.'

Vhoss stared at him in horror. 'Huthor, we're in no fit state to fight, we'll be slaughtered!'

'Not to fight, no...' he said in a hoarse and drifting voice. 'Don't you see? We're weak here, vulnerable. We've followed this pampered god for too long. The Grandfather calls us, and he can give us freedom from pain, freedom from weakness and death.' He walked towards the iron doors, beyond which was the long road to the north. 'They're expecting us,' he said.

They marched in a ragged train from the Golden Fortress, making the pilgrim journey to the Onoglop Swamps. Huthor staggered on with the guiding light of Nurgle's bounty fore and centre in his mind. The Harbinger met them at the border and, plodding in the muck on his desiccated horse, led them deep into the sweating chambers of the mire. The Rotbringers stood chortling at its centre, like rotting tree-stumps glazed with filth. They welcomed their new brothers and sisters, eager to share the abundance that brewed and boiled inside them. Huthor, aching for eternal life, seized the offer with both hands.

Here, he thought, *here* was true power: to shrug off blows that would kill lesser men; to grow and fade and grow inside the play of constant disease; to never really die but be born anew, again and again. He laughed, and the days of the Golden Fortress fell far behind him.

Those weeks, or months, or years, or however long it was, were feverish and indistinct. Most of all, Huthor remembered the sickness flowering in him, until his skin swelled and split, the wet, bubbling voice of the disease always muttering in his head. There was jubilation and glee, such joyful certainty that they were on the right path at last. Vhoss watched his skin slowly slough away with equanimity, and cheerfully Vhorrun stroked the tentacles that were sprouting from his side. There were so few of them left from the horde that had launched their sallies from the fortress. Now, trudging from the muck, they raided small villages on the swamp's edge, merrily bludgeoning the inhabitants with their poisoned weapons and watching as the bodies cracked and burst apart with putrefaction. Life roiled and flowed in a perfect, sinuous wave. 'The Bringer of Sickness', they called him, those huddled communities. He was a spirit of the swamplands, a nightmare tale to frighten children to sleep.

Who knew how many more weeks, or months, or years, Huthor and his warband would have stayed in the Onoglop Swamps, reiving and raiding, affably spreading the Grandfather's gifts? Time had no real meaning for them any more; but then, one pallid dusk, Huthor's path took an unexpected turn.

The borders of the swamp bristled with energy. There were flashes of sinister light, and the stagnant waters boiled and steamed. Skimming over the reeds on a gnashing disc came a spindly figure in teal armour, his robes streaming out behind him. His head was crowned with two pale horns, and in the middle of his forehead blinked a golden eye. The staff he held blazed with blue fire, and behind him flew a train of razor-beaked beasts on discs of their own.

'I am Tyx'evor'eth,' he said in a crackling voice. 'Magister of Tzeentch, humble servant of the Great Conspirator, and I have come for you, Lord Huthor. The Master of Fate has turned his eye towards you, and offers majesty and power the likes of which you have never experienced.'

'The Grandfather's gifts are all the majesty I need,' Huthor burbled. 'Come to us instead, trickster, see what gifts Papa Nurgle gives to his faithful.' He waved him away with his rusted blade.

Eight times Tyx'evor'eth came to make his offer in the stagnant edgelands, and each time Huthor sent him on his way. The magister showed him visions of plenty – mountains of gold and jewels, hordes of slaves stretching across the plains, the tribute of a thousand tyrannised cities. He demonstrated terrifying magics, spells and illusions that could be Huthor's for the asking. But Huthor was not moved. He had decay and disease, the pleasing dankness of the swamps, and he feared no blade; what more could he need?

'I follow this path,' Huthor told the magister. 'I see no end to it yet.'

On the ninth occasion he visited, Tyx'evor'eth promised nothing of riches or power. He came alone, his warband of Enlightened left behind at his camp. He didn't dazzle Huthor with magic or try to seduce him with visions of the future.

'All I come to offer this time, my lord,' he said, 'is a single word.'

'And what word is that, trickster?' Huthor laughed. The sound was like the stagnant swamp waters bubbling in the stench.

Tyx'evor'eth bowed low. His disc bobbed under him.

'*Legacy*,' he said. He spread his arms to indicate the swamp around them, and his third eye blinked. 'Is this really where

Huthor the Flayer will end his journey? Or will his name yet be writ large across the blazing plains of Chamon, remembered for ever more? Come with me, lord, and you shall make it so. None shall ever forget you.'

'Aye...' Huthor said slowly; and then the swamp around him suddenly seemed a mean and shabby place, not fit to have held him so long. He looked down at his bloated skin, his rusted blade that he had carried since he was big enough to hold it.

'Fear not, my lord,' the magister said. 'Form is a malleable thing to those with the power to change it...'

And so Tyx'evor'eth wove his magics, unravelling the tendrils of disease from their bodies. Over the years he guided them far on Tzeentch's path, teaching them his arcane knowledge – until the Ashpeaks, and a bitter duel under the sun.

The night before the duel, Huthor sat in his tent, scrying the future. In the prismatic jewel known as the Unclouded Eye, he watched tomorrow's combat. He knew he must cast an absurd image to anyone who saw him: a born killer, bearded and uncouth, clad in soft teal robes and hunched over a crystal no bigger than a rust-apple. In its shifting light he saw the Khorne warband they had clashed with earlier that day advancing onto the lower slopes, saw the enveloping strike by his own army, the pyromantic cascade of unleashed spells. He saw glimpses of his forthcoming fight with the Khorne champion: the clash of blades; the inspired stroke that saw Huthor feign a stumble then come cutting up from right to left with incredible force, the blow shattering the champion's face and sending his helmet spinning into the dirt; the counterstroke sweeping laterally to disembowel him. It was a move honed by years of combat, and he looked forward to performing it the next day – at dawn, early, on a hard-packed apron of land beneath the looming Ashpeaks. Tyx'evor'eth had been incredulous that Huthor was willing to risk the fight, but the Khorne champion had made the challenge and it couldn't go unanswered.

In the old days, he thought, it wouldn't even have been a question.

At that moment, the old days pulled back the flap of his tent and entered – Vhoss, his seamed face twinkling with amusement. Like Huthor he was wearing teal robes, but underneath was the old boiled leather of his dracoline-hide jerkin. He smelled of aether, of sorcery. The magister had been tutoring on the eve of battle, it seemed.

'Single combat?' Vhoss scoffed. 'Are you sure about this?' He pulled up a camp stool and sat down, reaching with easy familiarity into Huthor's store-box for a bottle of zephyr-wine. He unplugged the cork with his teeth, spat it out and drank deep.

'You think I'm not up to it?' Huthor said.

'Did you see that vicious-looking sod? Teeth filed to points, eyes bloodshot with rage – even his muscles had muscles. He's going to chop you in half, lad.'

'We'll see,' Huthor said. When their two forces had first skirmished, the Khorne Champion had marched fearlessly into their camp, throwing his challenge down. He did not fear death, Huthor had thought. He would die fighting, gladly.

He slipped the Unclouded Eye into his robes. He knew his old friend was half-teasing, but even without the prism's reassurance he would have felt confident. He couldn't say why, but he knew – he *knew* – the duel would go his way. His path did not end here. 'It may be a while since I last fought man on man, but I've no doubt I've forgotten more tricks than that scum will ever know.'

'Just make sure you haven't forgotten all of them, that's all I'm saying...'

Vhoss passed him the bottle. After a moment's hesitation Huthor took it. He sipped the zephyr-wine, feeling its slow and airy burn deep in his chest.

'Not too much, night before a fight,' Vhoss said, winking at him. Huthor smiled and passed the bottle back.

'Ah, it's been a long road, has it not?' Vhoss sighed.

'It has indeed.'

'When did it change, eh? What was the first step?'

'Dysileesh,' Huthor said quietly. Vhoss closed his eyes, luxuriating in the memory.

'The Godseeker, of course, of course… I've still got the scars she gave me. And the son.'

'Young Vhorrun's done you proud,' Huthor said.

'He has. He looks at me with those violet eyes sometimes, and I see her in him still. You know, I sometimes think it was a path we should have stayed on. The Prince of Excess was a pleasurable master.'

'He was no master of mine,' Huthor said. 'Just a guide for a while.'

'No,' Vhoss agreed sadly. He put the bottle at his feet and stared at his open hands. He looked at Huthor, his oldest friend. 'But then you never could commit to anything for long, could you?'

The Unclouded Eye, Tyx'evor'eth had called it. The Jewel that Sees, the Prism of Foresight. 'In this,' the magister had told him, 'a scholar of the arts will catch echoes of the future, but echoes are all they are. They are the shape of moments cast back from their origin, but not the moments themselves. Do you understand?'

'I understand,' Huthor had said.

'The skill is in reading those echoes, understanding those shapes, and seeing where the shapes fit into the puzzle of the present. Once a scholar can do that, he will see events before they happen, before they can disarm him. Yes?'

'Yes.'

'Good,' he said, the proud tutor gazing at his pupil. And his three eyes, which missed nothing, blinked one by one.

Vhoss moved quicker than was humanly possible; he had cast an incantation of fleetness, it was clear, but he was no true scholar and the move was betrayed in advance by a faint nimbus of dark energy around his eyes. The blade came up, dripping with poison, but Huthor had already seen it in the Eye. He had woven a protective ward before Vhoss had even entered the tent, and as the blade bent and refracted against the sorcerous energy that surrounded him, Huthor brought up his own stiletto and plunged it into Vhoss' stomach. Through the robes, through the dracoline-hide jerkin, deep into the flesh of the man who had been his lieutenant for decades; his brother in arms, his friend – his fellow slave to darkness on the road to red ruin.

Vhoss gasped with pain, dropping his own knife, his spell breaking apart in a faint smear of discordant colours. As his eyes widened in agony, Huthor saw some aspect of the old friend he had known, before any god had demanded their loyalty; when to worship on the altar of Chaos was to worship the violence of the storm, the unyielding power of the earthquake – everything that could reveal just how fragile the notion of Order really was. He had been right. It had been a long road from there to here.

Vhoss slipped to the floor. His eyes fluttered as his life left him. Before he went, Huthor resisted the urge to ask him why. The answer would have been inexplicable. Since Tyx'evor'eth had been tutoring them, such fatal feuds had become commonplace. Always at the heart of them was some twisted maze of half-understood portent and prediction. Assassinations, denunciations, stabbings and poisonings – it was a daily event. Who could untangle the web of Tzeentch? Who knew which thread led to which outcome, and which outcome disguised further eventualities unguessable to those without the insight to see them? It was futile.

He looked down at his old friend, the body cooling on the

ground, and he was surprised at how little he felt. Only boredom and fatigue, and something very close to shame.

He called for his servants and they took the body away.

'Wake me early,' he told them. He packed the bottle of zephyr-wine in his store-box. 'I have a fight to win, at dawn.'

The Ashpeaks, like new-forged steel still glowing from the furnace, cast their shadows on the dusty plain. Up there, beyond their distant caps, a glinting speck of light cut with patient industry through the cloud, a contrail of disturbed silver unspooling behind it. A sky-craft of the duardin, she had told him once. He remembered Dysileesh standing by his side with her musk of dead flowers and stale incense, the looped rings of oiled silver in her ear, eyebrow and nose, the thrilling stench of her. Her silk robes had hung from her body like sheets of ruby wine.

'Those who style themselves "Overlords",' she had said, and he had gripped the hilt of his sword.

He held that sword high now, ready to administer the killing stroke. It had been a worthy fight. The Khornate Champion writhed in his death agonies, blood frothing on his lips. Through shattered teeth and scraps of gum he laughed, one hand scooping up the ropes of his spilled innards, the other still scrabbling in the dirt for his axe.

'Wait,' he gurgled, spitting blood.

'I send you to the Brass Citadel. Isn't that what you want?'

'What I want means nothing,' the dying Champion scorned. 'It is… what *you* want… that matters now.'

He spewed out a stream of black blood. His face darkened with the approach of death, but the closer it came, the more fiercely blazed his remaining eye.

'What I want?'

'You are the one they call the Flayer, are you not, Lord Huthor?'

'The Flayer?' He lowered his sword. 'I had that name once… an age ago.'

'You have had many titles – Lord of the Golden Fortress, Bringer of Sickness, and now Aspiring Magister of Gazan Zhar… Your name is known,' the Champion said, grimacing. 'Across the Spiral Crux, men speak of you in awe and cower in their hovels. We have seen your face reflected in the blood we spill, heard your name whispered by the dying when we cut them down. Khorne guides us to you, Huthor the Flayer. Three paths have you walked since turning from Chaos Undivided. But I say to you the fourth has yet to feel your tread, and it is a road waist-deep in blood and fire…!'

The wind from the Ashpeaks, gritty and with a scent of stale smoke, brought with it the distant roar of the warrior's warband. The duel of Champions was over, but Huthor had never expected the Khorne fighters to abide by the compact. No matter; already, Tyx'evor'eth's fleet of Enlightened were skimming over the foothills to flank them, while Huthor's warriors formed up in illusory ranks to the front. Vhorrun's force was masked by glamours in the low ground to the east. The battle would be brief, violent, the outcome certain. He had seen it coalescing in the Eye last night, before he had killed Vhoss – the caged green flames interlocking inside the prism, forming a picture of just this moment.

Just this moment – apart from the entreaty of the dying Champion at his feet. He had not seen that at all.

Tyx'evor'eth came gliding swiftly over the rusty ground, stinking of ozone. The magister was eager for the fight.

'Huthor, lord,' he said. 'The moment is near. The arc of Fate bends once more to your bidding. Let us be on our way.' His three eyes blinked in a disjointed relay.

Huthor turned once more to the prostrate warrior. He thought of Vhoss last night, clawing at the knife in his guts, lips twitching to speak a final version of the spells he had never really mastered.

None of them had, if truth be known. The weaving of magics had always left Huthor himself feeling drained and hollow, a brackish taste of metal in his mouth. Long had Tyx'evor'eth extolled the virtues of the Weaver of Fate, tutoring Huthor in sorcery and revealing the scale of power and influence that would open to him if he walked the Path of Change. He had given him the Unclouded Eye, the jewel that reveals the future. He had brought his tzaangors and his Enlightened to swell Huthor's ranks, until what had been a powerful warband had become something more like an army, with territories and thraldoms of its own, as powerful as it had been in the days of the Golden Fortress. But for too long now had he been on this road, dabbling and learning but never fully committing to the lure. Had all the magister's work been for nothing, in the end?

All this trickery, he thought. These treacherous plots and labyrinthine plans that curve in on themselves and lose their purpose in the twists and turns of their interminable execution. And here was this fine warrior dying in the dust, mortally wounded, who had thrown himself at Huthor like a hurricane, Chamon's silver sunlight gleaming on his brass plate. In his snarling face had been a look of purest exultation – it had been the most exhilarating fight of Huthor's life. Such simplicity, such purity of purpose: to kill and be killed, and to treat each outcome as a glorious vindication of his brutal god. A trophy for the throne of skulls, deep in a citadel of brass...

'You see it,' the warrior choked. 'I know you do. Why do you think I sought you out if not to see that look in your eyes? You see the Lord of Skulls fuming in the reek, the piled heads, the screaming of the damned. You felt it when you opened me up and saw the blood spill from my guts.'

'I see it,' Huthor mumbled. 'I... I *feel* it.'

'This path shall be your last, Lord Huthor. It has been seen.

Follow him, follow Khorne, and I swear you will cover the lands in blood! It has been seen! You will cover them in blood!'

'Lord Huthor!' Txy'evor'eth demanded. His disc slavered and moved agitatedly under his hooves. 'Battle draws near! Kill this savage and let us be on our way.'

Black dust rose in heavy plumes beyond the foothills. The Khornate warband was advancing from their camp. Huthor could hear the screaming ululation of their war cry, the clashing of swords and axes.

'I give you the mercy stroke,' he said, raising his pale blade. The Khornate Champion sneered. His feet kicked at the dust. Death was near now, very near.

'No mercy!' he spat. 'Only blood! Blood! And Khorne cares not from whence–'

The Flayer brought down his sword.

'It is done!' Tyx'evor'eth laughed. 'Now quickly, lord, let us be away. The savages move ever closer into our trap!'

To cover the lands in blood…

'The Flayer', they had called him once. He recalled his camp tent back then, pitched like a flag of his conquests, every panel the skinned hide of whichever warlord, chieftain or elder had opposed him. He remembered his raiders, the Raging Tide, breaking like a thunderstorm over the Muspelzharr plains, drenching them in blood and tears. Vhoss at his side… Aye, those had been simpler days indeed.

'When this is done, Tyx'evor'eth,' Huthor said, 'we will be parting ways.'

'…My lord?'

'I have come to the end of the path, magister.' He cleaned his sword against his cloak. His muscles were aching; it had been so long since he had had a proper fight. 'Fate now takes me down a different road.'

'But, Lord Huthor, have I not fulfilled all the promises I made?

Has not the Great Architect twisted the thread of your fate in ways that please you?'

'It pleased me for a while. It pleases me no longer. The thread is broken. I shall make a new one.'

'You return to the Undivided path?'

'No,' Huthor said. 'There is one road yet for me to take.'

He had expected anger, disbelief, but instead the magister cackled on his disc and rose higher into the air. His black eyes frosted with foresight. He pointed his staff and Huthor prepared the equations of an unbinding in his mind, drawing energy from the Chamonian wind, but the sorcerer cast no magics.

'Go now, tempter, or I will cut you down as well!' Huthor said.

'You will indeed cover the lands in blood, Lord Huthor... I see it now. That will be your fate, my lord!' He screeched with laughter as he sped away, blue flame flickering from his staff. 'It is all unfolding as the Architect has planned. You think you walk a path, a road of your own making, but you are mistaken, my lord. It is not a path. It is a maze. A labyrinth!'

The tzaangors and Enlightened would be lost to him now, he realised. Already he felt his own powers diminish, the forms of magic fading inside him. The Khorne warband would be on them in moments and he had lost near half his army.

No matter. He sheathed his sword. He dipped his hands into the dead Champion's guts and anointed himself, marching off to join his warriors as the blood cooled on his forehead. The Khornate army was breasting the rise and clashing their swords and axes. He took the Unclouded Eye from inside his robes and cast it far off into the rusty scrub.

'We will do this the old way!' he roared to the sky, and up there, beyond the peaks, the last glint of the duardin ship went sailing on, far from the sun's bold and grasping light.

* * *

The shrieking of chained beasts tore the air. Huthor felt it in his chest, the low bass rumble of the chimeras' leonine heads, the roar of the manticores lashed to the ground by brass anchors and hard-wrought steel. The frantic hissing of the cockatrices was like a foul rainfall, and the ochre ground was scrabbled with claw marks and spattered with blood. He had lost a hundred men corralling these creatures. He did not care.

Vhorrun approached him, snarling, trembling with the urge to kill.

'We're almost ready, lord,' he said. His voice was harsh and grating, an angry rasp, the consequence of a blade he'd recently taken in his throat. Huthor regarded him coolly, one hand resting on the pommel of his sword in case the boy finally made his move. Young, as taut as rendered steel, he was the most perfect warrior among them. Of all the Raging Tide, save Huthor himself, Vhorrun had embraced Khorne with the most fervour. He despised the trace of Dysileesh in him, sickened that even a shadow of her pampered god could lie on his fate. He so scorned his violet eyes that he had plucked one out, only keeping the other so he could still see for combat. His silver skin was a latticework of angry scars, and he had long since shaved off his gold-dusted hair. He was born to kill, born to die, although it puzzled Huthor that in all the long months since Vhoss' death, Vhorrun had never made a move to avenge his father. Perhaps, the warlord thought, he realises the truth of his sire? When he stares with such hatred at me, does he know he stares at the man who gave him life?

Huthor grinned at the thought. He looked forward to killing the boy.

'Now hear me!' Huthor shouted to his men. From across the burnished steppe, his army began to gather: Blood Warriors in their battered crimson plate; bloodreavers in their hundreds. Kh'ezhar, his slaughterpriest, ritually slashed at his skin with his sacrificial knife. 'Today you will gorge yourselves at the Dark Feast! You will rend flesh and tear skin, and you will feast on duardin! You will prise them from their metal ships and spill blood for the Blood God!'

To the exultant roar of the crowd, which drowned out even the screaming beasts he had gathered to serve them, Huthor raised his blade and pointed it skyward. Up there, where the Kharadron ships flew to Barak-Zon, black clouds gathered. The storm was upon them; the deafening murder-song.

You will cover the lands in blood…

He had certainly done that. Since dedicating himself to Khorne, he had done little else, and now his army dwarfed any he had led as lord of the Golden Fortress. Swathes of land had fallen under his bloody footprint. Thousands had died, and hundreds more scrambled to join his brass banners. The scum of Gazan Zhar had partaken of the Dark Feast and were his to command.

Now, madness quivered behind Huthor's eyes. Rage made his fingers tremble always for his sword, and, if no enemy was to hand, he seized whomever was near and butchered them without a thought. He felt Khorne's smouldering brass throne as a colossal weight on his shoulders; the citadel burning with sulphur was like a liminal presence before his eyes, ever-shifting in his maddened sight. In the wake of the fight at the Ashpeaks, won by the narrowest of margins, Huthor's warband had become the Raging Tide once more. Casting off their Tzeentchian glamours, they had stripped the bodies of the Khorne warriors and clad themselves in their spattered armour. None doubted who had led them to victory that day, who had guided Huthor's frenzied blade. Khorne had willed it. The path was freely taken, and the journey since had been one of uncompromising destruction. The further they went on that road, the more their days as dabblers in the other gods' service faded, like sallow dreams dispatched by the light of day.

The central lands of Gazan Zhar receded, hurtling away from him – an ochre smear of oxide and rust. The Ashpeaks stabbed like fangs into the sky, wreathed in steam and dusted with a sooty snow. They loomed and fell back, and then the immense and mind-bending helix of the Spiral Crux seemed to spread itself out below him. The air was freezing and cut like cold steel, but Huthor the Flayer boiled with rage. The manticore beneath him growled with a sound like the mad alloys of Chamon's sub-realms grinding together, and the carrion reek of the creature enveloped him even as the streaming aether-winds plucked his breath away. He screamed with savage joy, turning in his rawhide saddle to see his warband spread out across the sky – hundreds of them clutching to the feathered crests of swooping cockatrices, or grimly lashed to the snarling fury of the chimeras. It was an impossible fleet, murder on the cutting wind. It was the last thing the Kharadrons would see coming.

Kh'ezhar's unholy invocations had slaved the creatures to their new purpose, but some, unleashed once more into their element, soon turned on their masters. Huthor was amused to see the draconic head of one chimera twist round and snap furiously at the bloodreavers on its back, their mangled bodies slipping off to tumble thousands of feet to the ground. A cockatrice spun round and loosed its riders, darting down to snap at their falling bodies with its vicious beak. In contrast, Huthor's manticore seemed not only to tolerate his presence, but also to welcome it; the creature had purred as he mounted it, and only the slightest pressure on its greasy, blood-flecked mane was needed to guide it in the right direction.

'The Enlightened would have been useful now,' Vhorrun had

said as they'd readied themselves to fly. Huthor hadn't been sure if the boy was mocking him. But it was true, he conceded, gaining the saddle; this would all have been much easier with a Tzeentchian disc underfoot.

As they swooped onwards, breaking through the cloud, Huthor saw a dozen elongated shapes ahead. Draped in a sparkling mist from the harvested aether-gold, the Kharadron ships grew more distinct, their strange nautical hulls suspended from globular metal balloons, some of them like vast armoured behemoths and others no more than agile little escort craft. So far, none of them had seen the bestial fleet in their blindside.

'Overlords'... Their very name was a provocation. Wherever Huthor had cast his gaze in the long years of his conquests, the Overlords had always exceeded his grasp. The lands groaned under him, but the sky was pure. Well – no longer. He would stain it with their blood.

'Dive!' he screamed, and the manticore beneath him roared. Even in the slicing wind he could hear the war cry of his airborne army swooping in for the kill, thrashing their mounts and straining for the fight, axes bared, spears raised.

And then the Kharadron responded.

The first wave of bloodreavers vanished in a puff of red mist. The ragged bodies of their mounts listed and fell, keening in pain and trailing ribbons of blood. Ahead, the hulls of the airships were smeared with smoke, crackling with shot from broadside cannons and carbines. Huthor saw a buzzing flock of tiny figures unlatch from the bigger ships, duardin suspended from their own individual balloons, bearing vicious-looking pikes. They sped towards the lead chimeras and engaged, slashing and stabbing and swarming with incredible agility. More of Huthor's army was torn apart when the smaller ships came through on attack runs that peppered their flanks with shot.

'You didn't say it would be this hard!' Kh'ezhar shouted as he wheeled his cockatrice beside Huthor. He laughed with manic fervour before the upper part of his body exploded in a steaming gout of blood. The cockatrice, mortally wounded, screamed and fell, a feathered rag.

This wasn't going to work. Huthor saw his army picked apart in moments, scoured from the skies by the duardin's incredible firepower. Fully half his men were already dead, eviscerated by gunfire or knocked from their perches by their panicked animals, cast down on the long journey back to the plains of Gazan Zhar. The beasts they had so painstakingly herded together were being destroyed.

And yet, it was not all going the Kharadrons' way. Huthor launched his manticore at one buzzing interceptor and laughed at the pilot's panicked reaction as he tried to haul it around. The beast severed the rigging with one sweep of its claws, the ship's hull dropping like a meteor to the earth. He saw one bloodreaver leap boldly through the air from the back of his chimera with a maddened war cry, twin axes in hand, crashing onto the bridge of another escort craft. He hacked the crew to pieces and twisted its wheel to send it slamming into the hull of a bigger ship with a blinding explosion. The larger Kharadron ship split apart with a scream of rending metal. Trailing long streamers of superheated aether-gold, each part slowly listed and fell like a boat succumbing to the pull of deep waters, the bodies of burning duardin spinning from it like falling stars. Other beasts had gained the Kharadrons' main line and were rampaging across the decks, vomiting flame and ripping the deck crews apart. Huthor knew the attack was doomed, but he had never run from a fight. Death was nothing; blood was all. And Khorne cared not from whence the blood flowed.

He guided his own beast towards the deck of the flagship, a vast ironclad bristling with weaponry. He saw the deck crew prepare themselves to repel boarders, scurrying to the gunwale with their carbines raised. A hail of shot enveloped him, striking the manticore in a dozen places and sparking off his shoulder guard, but the Blood God was looking on his favoured son – not a single shot had wounded him. As Huthor drew his sword he grinned to see the duardin run for cover.

The manticore, expiring at the last, hit the deck like an explosion. In its thrashing death agony, sweeping the deck with its barbed tail, it scattered some of the crew into the open air. Huthor was thrown wildly from its back, crashing into the cupola of the ship's skycannon and knocking the gunner over the edge. Dazed, bleeding from a wound across his forehead, he still laughed to hear the duardin's horrified scream.

A dozen duardin in red armour and dark blue fatigues came charging towards him, but before they could even arm their pistols Huthor was on them. He leapt from the cupola with a frenzied scream and barrelled into the stunted figures, hewing left and right in great scything sweeps, like a crazed artist painting the deck in streams of red. He snatched one duardin up and hurled him overboard, grunting then as a pistol shot smashed into his shoulder with a spray of blood and meat. His left arm lifeless at his side, Huthor threw his blade and skewered the duardin who had shot him, pinning him to the fo'c'sle wall.

The deck was littered with bodies. Eddies and swirls of the metallic wind threaded the rigging, and beyond the sky-ship he could see puffs of black smoke, drifts of red mist, screaming warriors and enraged beasts falling to their deaths. What little of his force had made it to the ships was being systematically exterminated, blown from the decks by the Kharadrons' disciplined crews. As the last few airborne beasts were sniped from the sky, Huthor knew it was over. He heard the tramp of approaching boots and pulled his sword from the hull, preparing himself for death, rejoicing that so many had wetted the throne of the Brass Citadel.

'Let them come,' he spat. He held out his sword. 'The path is ended, and it has been a long, strange road indeed...'

But as the duardin charged up the deck towards him, they were immolated in a blaze of fire. Some, maddened by pain, threw themselves over the edge; others kicked and screamed as the flames consumed them. Huthor turned to see Vhorrun's chimera, bleeding from gunshot wounds, spew fire and launch itself at the remaining crew even as the buzzing gunhaulers banked and strafed it with shot. Vhorrun himself leapt to the deck, his axes drawn, but before Huthor could say a word the young warrior had launched himself at him.

It was like the duel in the sun once more, when the Khornate Champion had fought as if the world were ending. Vhorrun's blows were both wildly savage and icily precise, a flurry of axe strikes followed by feints and parries that were then converted into devastating cross-cuts. He hooked at Huthor's sword and drew his guard away, then blazed in with elbows and knees, hammering the warlord back against the gunwale. Huthor, the wilier fighter, who had fought and killed for more than twice Vhorrun's lifetime, was as hard-pressed as he had ever been. He couldn't gain the advantage, each parry and riposte easily swept aside by the whirlwind of Vhorrun's assault. His left arm was ruined, his sword arm was weakening, and the wound on his forehead was leaking into his eyes. Huthor raised his sword to block a twin-handed strike, but Vhorrun's axes shattered the blade and plunged into the meat of his chest. He screamed, his sight blackening, and as he dropped to his knees Vhorrun felled him with a vicious punch to the face.

Huthor coughed blood and rolled onto his back. 'I've... had that sword longer than you've been alive, boy,' he groaned. With superhuman effort, hooking his arm to the gunwale, he hauled himself up. He'd be damned if he'd die on his back, or on his knees. 'Well, it came at last,' he said. He clutched the wounds in his chest. 'Revenge for your father's death.'

'Vhoss was many things to me,' Vhorrun said, prowling the deck. He held his axes ready. 'But I know he was not my father.'

Huthor laughed, and the pain was a torment. 'How long have you known?'

'I've always known. I've always known it was you.'

'And you'd kill me still? You're blood of the Flayer, boy.'

'And it's the only blood I reject! I have always hated you, Flayer. Your greed for glory has ever poisoned my fate. You sired me on some foul Slaaneshi cultist, forced me to moulder for months in those cursed swamps, and then dragged me into a labyrinth of cowardly magics!'

'You make it sound like you had no choice, no will of your own!'

'No,' Vhorrun snarled. 'Only your will mattered! When we still followed the Trickster, I tried to get Vhoss to kill you. Plans within plans, schemes within schemes in those days, but instead you killed the only man who had ever showed me kindness or respect.'

Huthor gave him a bitter, mocking laugh. 'I brought you to Khorne though, didn't I? You seem to have taken to his service.'

'Yes…' Vhorrun said. 'Fair is fair, I follow the one true god now. And by my own hand must it be done.'

'A family tradition,' Huthor said. 'I killed my own father, you know. All sons must, in the end.'

Ferried by their floating comrades, more Kharadron were boarding the vessel at the prow. Vhorrun's chimera expired in a murderous fusillade, and of the Raging Tide only the two of them were left. All were dead. Huthor stooped for the broken hilt of his sword. He would die fighting, with a weapon in his hand.

'I live still,' Huthor said. He grinned. 'The enemy approaches. Will we die together?'

Vhorrun looked at him then, smiling. His lone eye sparkled with violet.

'Huthor the Flayer,' he said. 'You won't have the honour of dying in battle.'

As the Kharadron troops opened fire, Vhorrun shoved him in the chest, pitching him backwards over the edge of the ship. Huthor saw his son break apart under the crossfire, and then the world was a spiral of light and darkness, of lustre and pitch. The wind pummelled him, the sky-ships sinking into the depths of the coruscating sky even as the ground hurtled up to meet him. He fell faster than he would ever have believed possible, the mad tangle of Chamon's uncoiling landscape speeding towards him with its eager embrace, the wind roaring like the apocalypse in his ears. And as he fell, his mind, darkened by his wounds, fled back to that duel in the sun, the Khornate Champion dying at his feet, his muttered promise. *You will cover the lands in blood…* And then Tyx'evor'eth spinning away on his disc, cackling, gaze frosting with arcane foresight… *That will be your fate, my lord!*

He had seen it. He had seen it all happen. Every step on the path had brought him to this point.

Yes, Huthor thought as the ground came near, and as the promise of his fall came closer to its violent fulfilment. *I will indeed cover these lands in blood…*

But Khorne cares not from whence the blood flows!

ABOUT THE AUTHORS

William King is the author of the Tyrion and Teclis saga and the Macharian Crusade trilogy, as well as the much-loved Gotrek & Felix series and the Space Wolf novels. His short stories have appeared in many magazines and compilations, including *White Dwarf* and *Inferno!*. Bill was born in Stranraer, Scotland, in 1959 and currently lives in Prague.

Robert Rath is a freelance writer from Honolulu who is currently based in Hong Kong. Though mostly known for writing the YouTube series *Extra History*, his credits also include numerous articles and a book for the U.S. State Department. He is the author of the Black Library novel *The Infinite and the Divine*, and the short stories 'The Garden of Mortal Delights' and 'War in the Museum'.

Evan Dicken's first story for Black Library was 'The Path to Glory', and he has since penned several more tales set in the Age of Sigmar, including the novella *The Red Hours*, and short fiction for the anthologies *Gods & Mortals* and *Myths & Revenants*. He has been an avid reader of Black Library novels since he found dog-eared copies of *Trollslayer*, *Xenos* and *First and Only* nestled in the 'Used Fantasy/Sci-fi' rack of his local gaming store. He still considers himself an avid hobbyist, although the unpainted Chaos Warband languishing in his basement would beg to differ. By day, he studies old Japanese maps and crunches data at The Ohio State University.

Jamie Crisalli writes gritty melodrama and bloody combat. Fascinated with skulls, rivets and general gloominess, when she was introduced to the Warhammer universes, it was a natural fit. Her work for Black Library includes the short stories 'Ties of Blood', 'The Serpent's Bargain', and the Age of Sigmar novella *The Measure of Iron*. She has accumulated a frightful amount of monsters, ordnance and tiny soldiery over the years, not to mention books and role-playing games. Currently, she lives with her husband in a land of endless grey drizzle.

Michael R Fletcher is an author and grilled cheese aficionado with several dark and grim science-fiction and fantasy novels to his name, including his first story for Black Library, 'A Tithe of Bone'. He lives in the endless suburban sprawl somewhere north of Toronto.

Graeme Lyon is the author of the Age of Sigmar novella *Code of the Skies* and the audio drama *Sons of Behemat,* as well as the Space Marine Battles novella *Armour of Faith*. He has also written a host of Warhammer 40,000, Warhammer Age of Sigmar and Warhammer short stories including 'The Carnac Campaign: Sky Hunter', 'Kor'sarro Khan: Huntmaster', 'Black Iron', 'The Eighth Victory', 'The Sacrifice' and 'Bride of Khaine'. He hails from East Kilbride in Scotland.

David Guymer's work for Warhammer Age of Sigmar includes the novels *Hamilcar: Champion of the Gods* and *The Court of the Blind King,* the audio dramas *The Beasts of Cartha, Fist of Mork, Fist of Gork, Great Red* and *Only the Faithful.* He is also the author of the Gotrek & Felix novels *Slayer, Kinslayer* and *City of the Damned* and the Gotrek audio dramas *Realmslayer* and *Realmslayer: Blood of the Old World.* For The Horus Heresy he has written the novella *Dreadwing,* and the Primarchs novels *Ferrus Manus: Gorgon of Medusa* and *Lion El'Jonson: Lord of the First.* For Warhammer 40,000 he has written *The Eye of Medusa, The Voice of Mars* and the two Beast Arises novels *Echoes of the Long War* and *The Last Son of Dorn.* He is a freelance writer and occasional scientist based in the East Riding, and was a finalist in the 2014 David Gemmell Awards for his novel *Headtaker.*

Anna Stephens is a UK-based writer of epic, gritty, grimdark fantasy. She is the author of the Godblind trilogy, and 'The Siege of Greenspire' is her first story set in the Age of Sigmar.

Miles A Drake is a professional bartender and aspiring author based in Amsterdam, Holland. His work for Black Library includes the short stories 'The Flesh Tithe' and 'Ghosts of Khaphtar'.

Eric Gregory's fiction has appeared in magazines and anthologies including *Lightspeed, Interzone, Strange Horizons, Nowa Fantastyka*, and others. For Black Library he has written 'The Fourfold Wound' and 'Bossgrot'. He lives and works in Carrboro, North Carolina.

Michael J Hollows is a writer, lecturer and researcher from London. He has written in various genres, but has always loved science fiction and fantasy. He fell in love with the Warhammer 40,000 universe when he was young, and when not writing tries to work out how time might be stretched so that he can paint that ever-increasing pile of models. He researches creative writing, lectures audio and writing, and lives in Liverpool. 'Ashes of Grimnir' is his first story for Black Library.

Dale Lucas is a novelist, screenwriter, civil servant and armchair historian from St. Petersburg, Florida. Once described by a colleague as 'a compulsive researcher who writes fiction to store his research in,' he's the author of numerous works of fantasy, neo-pulp and horror. When not writing or working, he loves travel, great food, and amassing more books than he'll ever be able to read. His first story for Black Library was 'Blessed Oblivion', and he has since penned the novel *Realm-Lords*.

Richard Strachan is a writer and editor who lives with his partner and two children in Edinburgh, UK. Despite his best efforts, both children stubbornly refuse to be interested in tabletop wargaming. His first story for Black Library, 'The Widow Tide', appeared in the Warhammer Horror anthology *Maledictions*, and he has since written 'Blood of the Flayer' and the Warcry Catacombs novel *Blood of the Everchosen*.

YOUR
NEXT READ

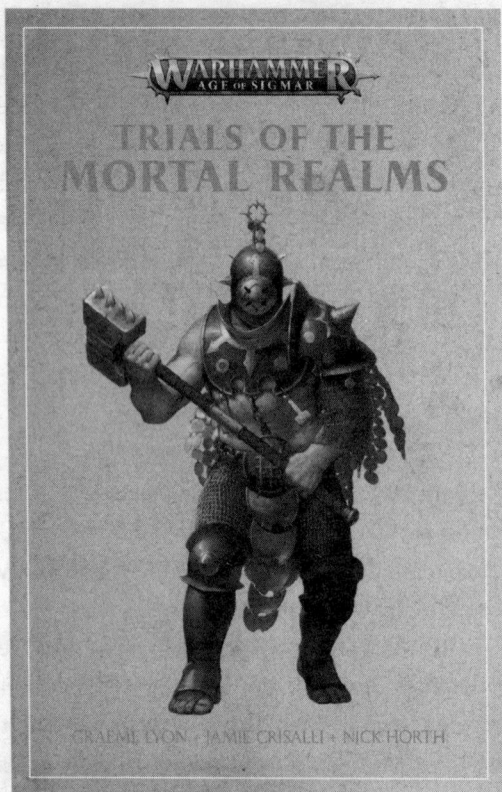

TRIALS OF THE MORTAL REALMS
by various authors

A trio of action-packed novellas take you across the Mortal Realms, from the dangerous skies of Chamon to the nightmare underworlds of Shyish and the war-wracked wastes of the Eightpoints.

An extract from
'The Measure of Iron'
by Jamie Crisalli
featured in the anthology
Trials of the Mortal Realms

Syzek Govus of the Iron Golems stepped into the Realmgate as lightning danced down the metal frame, a murky yellow reflection wobbling in its heart. He closed his eyes instinctively. Cold nothingness washed over his bleached, ashy skin and hissed over his ruddy plate.

For a long moment, he was nowhere at all.

Transformation in permanence, permanence in transformation was how the mantra went. The saying described many of the unknowable mysteries of Chaos, from the madness of the afterlife to the state of the soul. In this way, the Iron Golems also described the space between the realms. Some scholars said it was where the forge-fire burned. Some said it was where the Four Instincts made their home. Some said that there was nothing but void.

Suddenly, heat rolled over him like the breath of a forge. Harsh sunlight pierced through the grille of his helm into his pale eyes and he blinked away tears. It had been years since he had seen a sky. The wet stone was crooked under his bare feet and he stumbled a little.

A ragged scream shocked him out of his disorientation.

Below him, a pack of emaciated men and women cowered, staring up at him with bulging eyes, near-toothless mouths hanging open. When he stepped forwards, they scrambled back like feral animals. Some hid amongst the broken pale ruins that surrounded the gate, others froze, licking their cracked lips.

His mountainous frame encased in heavy plate enamelled in red like old blood, Syzek strode forwards. Sheets of chain mail and brass hammer charms jingled. Cautiously, he drew his heavy warhammer from his back, the spiked head gleaming. The wretches scuttled back, using their hands as much as their feet. He rested his hammer on his broad shoulder.

'So these are the creatures that live in the Bloodwind Spoil,' he muttered, frowning.

Eziel, his drillmaster, appeared at his side with a snort of derision. Like him, she was tall, heavily muscled and armoured in the same ruddy plate. Unlike him, she was at ease under the strange sky, rolling her shoulder as if preparing for some forge-yard feat of strength, not war. The long chain-flail at her hip clinked, more heavy weapon than goad for lesser humans, and a footman's flail dangled on the opposite side. She cocked her head at him.

'You sound disappointed,' she said, amusement trilling through her dry, raspy voice.

'I am,' he said. 'You said that there would be dangers.'

She barked a rasping laugh and the pack moved back further.

'I said that there would be dangers,' she replied, 'but there are also things like these. Most seem to be escapees.' She chuckled again. 'Imagine escaping your drillmaster, rushing through this blessed gate and ending up here.' She pulled the flail-whip from her belt. 'I almost feel bad for them.'

Syzek glanced at her sharply, the quick movement exaggerated by his helm.

'I said almost,' she said with a shrug. 'You know me better than that.'

He shook his head. Most people did not understand Eziel at all. She often spoke in riddles, putting too much trust in her tone to convey meaning. It was only because he had known her since they were children that he understood her strange turns of logic.

Loud rhythmic jangling announced the arrival of his signifer, Somnixes Ozud. In his hand, he carried the war-seal on a heavy iron pole. The broad steel plate bore the spiked portcullis symbol of the Golem's Will; a sheet of small brass discs hung from it and jangled whenever he moved. It was he who announced that war had come to these pathetic wretches. With him came the first supply wagon, pulled by ornery Ghurian pack drevars and loaded with water barrels.

A change rolled over the wretched scavengers. Their backs stiffened, their fingers dug into the sand.

'They have water!'

'Water!'

'They have eating on them!'

'There are only a few!'

The feral crowd charged, hurtling across the sands towards them. More poured out of hiding. Starvelings or not, their numbers might have made up for their relative weakness. No matter how many were there, they could be no match for Syzek's warband, the Golem's Will. They came from the Legion and the Legion was unstoppable.

'Legion, front!' he roared. 'Riot crush!'

Somnixes banged out the order, his thunderous voice carrying like the rumbling of a drum.

With a disgusted grunt, Syzek swung his warhammer off his shoulder, turning the motion into an underhanded stroke. It was a lazy strike, but these weak creatures did not need his full effort.

The first wretch reached him and warhammer met skull. Brains and bone scattered over the sand, the thin body flying back. Another wretch scrambled at Syzek from his left and he backhanded the man to the ground. Without pausing, he staved in the prone man's chest with a single blow, crunching frail bones.

Behind him, his legionaries stepped through the gate, their armour gleaming dully in the light. They numbered twelve, carrying their personal arms, hammers, spiked maces and round shields. It was still strange to him, leading these soldiers. His place had been in the forges as a forge-master, supplying the Legion with its arms. Now he was in the field, leading them as dominar.

Still, war-making was his duty and inheritance as an Iron Golem. It had soaked the air he breathed, the rations he ate, the water he drank. The knowledge simply existed for him. Where so many other decadent civilisations treated their warriors like they had a profession, for Syzek and the Golem's Will, it was simply life. To be otherwise was to be nameless, without citizenship, perhaps less than human.